Adam,
They were hired to
Angie, respectively.
going to protec

In *Adam's Story,*
Caitlin Moran had always hated her "gift"—
until it provided her with the ability to save the man
who'd sworn to protect her. But was it too late?

In *The Gemini Man,*
undercover agent Joel Kramer was hired
to spy on his beautiful neighbor. But was
falling for her part of his job description?

In *Zeke,*
the agent was only feigning interest in
Angie De la Garza to get the scoop
on her drug-dealing uncle. But was the
pretense becoming all too real?

"Annette Broadrick cleverly mixes
powerful characters and emotional depth with
just the right amounts of excitement and romance."
—*Romantic Times*

ANNETTE
BROADRICK

Secret Agent Grooms

Silhouette Books

Published by Silhouette Books
America's Publisher of Contemporary Romance

SILHOUETTE BOOKS

ISBN 0-373-18501-4

by Request

SECRET AGENT GROOMS

Copyright © 2002 by Harlequin Books S.A.

The publisher acknowledges the copyright holder of the individual works as follows:

ADAM'S STORY
Copyright © 1987 by Annette Broadrick

THE GEMINI MAN
Copyright © 1991 by Annette Broadrick

ZEKE
Copyright © 1993 by Annette Broadrick

Visit Silhouette at www.eHarlequin.com

Printed in U.S.A.

CONTENTS

Dear Reader,

I've always been intrigued by the idea of agents who work covert operations. What is life like for them? They have to become two different people in order to catch the bad guys. What sort of personal life can they establish? A secret agent can't stop at five o'clock each day and go home to his real life.

So what does he do?

Each of the stories selected in this volume has a hero who falls in love at the wrong time in his career. He has to deal with his personal feelings all the while he's trying to bring criminals to justice.

Guess I enjoy seeing my heroes suffer a little.

Hope you enjoy these very special men who managed to find a way to deal with their personal as well as their professional lives in a real and meaningful way.

Enjoy!

Annette Broadrick

ADAM'S STORY

This book is dedicated to those people—
and you know who are—who helped me
to understand psychic abilities and how they work....
My grateful appreciation.

One

Adam St. Clair paused for a moment outside his luxury hotel and looked up and down the Monterrey, Mexico, thoroughfare. The February wind off the mountains caused him to raise the collar of his sheepskin-lined denim jacket and to settle his Stetson more firmly on his head.

Hunching his shoulders against the wind, Adam started toward his car.

Tonight was the night. He wasn't sure how he knew, exactly. He'd lost count of the number of leads he'd followed since he'd joined the agency that was trying to stop the flood of drugs crossing the border between Mexico and the United States. Most of them had led nowhere. Some had gotten him into the circle of men who made their living bringing drugs in from South America.

He'd had no trouble with his cover. Playing the part

of a Texas rancher came naturally to him—that's who he was, what he'd always been. Then two years ago he'd become something more—a man determined to do what he could to stop what was happening in his country.

If all went well tonight, he'd have the information necessary to stop one of the major leaders, unless his informant changed his mind.

It was up to Adam to make sure the man didn't change his mind.

He sat in his car for a few minutes, waiting for the heater to warm the chilled interior. According to the directions given to him, he had several hours of hard driving to do, back into the remote area of the mountains.

Adam had removed his hat when he got into the car. Now he ran his hand through his tawny hair, causing the waves to fall into curls across his forehead. His sister, Felicia, had always enjoyed teasing him about his curls. His mouth lifted into a slight smile at the memory. His sister had been able to get away with a great deal. He loved her very much.

Reaching for the ignition Adam forced his thoughts back to the job at hand. He knew that what he was doing was dangerous, had always known that. He felt a twinge of guilt that he'd never told Felicia about this part of his life. But it was better this way. There was no reason for her to be involved, and since she'd been living in Los Angeles for the past several years, he'd had no need to make explanations to anyone about his periodic trips to Mexico.

He glanced at his watch. It was time to go. He hoped this wasn't another one of those fruitless contacts where nobody showed up.

Adam pulled away from his parking space and followed the streets until they connected with the highway that led out of town. Another long evening had begun.

Her eyes flew open, and Caitlin Moran sat up in bed. She looked around her small one-room mountain cabin, trying to decide what had awakened her. Glancing at the windows, she noted that the darkness outside showed no sign of impending dawn.

Caitlin continued to sit there, listening intently. Something was wrong. She slid out of bed, absently pulled on her heavy robe to offset the February chill of the mountains and padded to the window silently.

She could see nothing in the clearing except the heavy frost that tinted the blades of grass silver. Nothing moved. Listening, she could hear the rustling sounds from the surrounding mountainside as the nocturnal birds and animals went about the serious occupation of surviving in the wilderness. She could hear no sound of an intruder.

Then why had she awakened so abruptly? Because of the long hours she put in and the strenuous exercise due to the primitive lifestyle she led, Caitlin never had to worry about falling asleep at night. And morning arrived so quickly each day, bringing with it a myriad of occupations to keep her busy, that she rarely, if ever, woke before dawn.

Disturbed, but unsure why, Caitlin turned away from the window and walked over to the stone fireplace that covered the north wall of the cabin. Coals still glowed brightly through the ashes. She added more wood and watched while hungry tongues of flame suddenly licked the new additions, causing them to smolder, then to glow.

Caitlin stood there for a moment, staring into the flames and warming her hands, filled with unease.

What could be wrong?

She received no answers. Reluctantly turning away from the fire, she crawled back into bed, pulling the blankets around her neck.

Caitlin wasn't alarmed because she was alone. She had lived in her small cabin, high in the mountains near Monterrey, Mexico, for more than five years. Being alone was a way of life for her, one she had chosen.

Staring up at the roof over her head, acknowledging the sturdiness that had sheltered her so well, she tried to calm her mind, letting it drift as it would, willing herself to fall asleep again.

Instead, scenes began to race across the screen of her mind—scenes of violence and destruction. She saw two cars traveling fast over twisting and narrow mountain roads, their blinding headlights bathing the surrounding countryside with an eerie glow.

A shadowed face appeared. At first the features of the face were indistinct, but with practiced concentration Caitlin began to see more of the details as they focused into clear, clean lines. Gray-green eyes with a look of determination and agitation stared back at her, a frown causing the brows to draw together over a well-formed nose. A strong jawline appeared to be clenched, the lines around the tight-lipped mouth making deep grooves in the face.

Caitlin knew she had never seen the man before. She also knew that she would never forget him.

Who was he? She shook her head in frustration.

Although his skin appeared to be deeply tanned, she knew he was not a native of Mexico. Tawny curls fell across his forehead, giving a deceptively boyish look to an otherwise stern countenance.

Who was he? She tried to get more, but nothing came. She sighed, frustrated with her ability to see so much that she didn't want to see, and her inability to pick up more when she tried.

She had lived with her frustration long enough to know there was little she could do to rid her mind of the pictures and messages she received. She had tried. Desperately. Caitlin wanted nothing more than to be the normal young woman who had planned her life so carefully all those years ago.

Being brought up by two people who loved her and each other with a warm, generous love had ill prepared her for the traumatic events that had torn her life apart, leaving her like some sort of freak.

She forced herself to turn over, trying to blank her mind of all thoughts. Instead she began to remember how she had slowly made a place for herself here in the mountains. She couldn't recall how long she had lived here alone before she made friends with the local people.

About once a month she would take the vegetables she had grown and the hand-woven rugs and material down to the small settlement a few miles from her cabin. There she would trade for the supplies she needed.

The people of the village would stare at her reddish-gold hair and blue eyes with suspicion and distrust. Why was she living there? What did she want?

How could she explain to them that she was searching for some answers? She was looking for her sanity, her belief in herself, her ability to function in a world that no longer made any sense to her.

How could she explain what she didn't truly understand herself? All she knew was that by the time she'd finally been released from the hospital, she'd known her life would never be the same again. Her loving parents were gone. The friendships she trusted in and counted on had evaporated, and the man she loved had withdrawn from her in suspicion and distaste.

The stoic natives would probably not be impressed to know that she had run from the world and had chosen their small corner of the universe to find shelter and some measure of peace.

Caitlin had been grateful for the many summers she had spent with her aunt in San Antonio. Languages had come easily to her, and Spanish had a lilting, rollicking cadence that she had enjoyed learning, so that by the time she returned to Seattle each fall, she had continued to increase her vocabulary and her grasp of the language.

Her parents had been amused and had encouraged her to take the language in school, as well. At the time she'd had no thought of adopting Spanish as her own language. Now she couldn't remember the last time she'd spoken English. Probably not since her aunt had passed away.

Caitlin had lost all ties with the woman she'd been before she moved to the mountains. She preferred her life now and rarely thought of the past.

She'd grown used to the villagers and had learned not to expect anyone but the shopkeepers to speak to her. She understood and identified with the villagers' need for privacy. They didn't bother her, and she didn't bother them.

She remembered the day she had been on her way out of the village, leading her burro—who carried a month's worth of supplies for her—when she heard a baby crying. When she paused, she realized there was no baby crying around her, yet she heard the choked whimpering very clearly in her head. Rubbing her forehead with frustration, Caitlin almost groaned aloud.

Since she had moved to the mountains, the pictures and impressions she kept seeing had slowly disappeared, finally leaving her free from their insistent pressure.

Now they were back, and she wasn't sure what to do. The choked crying of the baby indicated that it was sick. The health of the infant was none of her business, but she had a sense that she could help him. Did she dare offer? Would the parents accept her help?

There was only one way to find out.

The sounds of the crying baby seemed to fill her mind once more, and Caitlin made her decision. She began to thread her way through the streets in an effort to locate the infant, walking around dogs and chickens, skirting pigpens, while the sound increasingly grew in her mind.

When she paused in front of a small house, she realized there was no actual sound coming from within. Yet she felt certain the baby was inside. She could see in her mind's eye the baby being held in its mother's arms.

With a great deal of uncertainty and trepidation, Caitlin tapped on the door. After a long moment the door slowly opened, and a young woman with tired, reddened eyes peered out at her. Groping for her best Spanish, Caitlin said, "Your baby is ill?"

"Oh, yes! I fear he is dying!" was the distressed reply.

"May I help?"

"How can you help?" was the agonized response.

Caitlin reached into her cloth bag and pulled out a smaller one. "I have had some experience in healing with these herbs. May I see your child?"

Later Caitlin realized that the only reason the young mother allowed her to come in was because she had already given up hope. When Caitlin stepped into the dimly lit room, she saw the other women, sitting in a circle around the infant, weeping.

The poor infant struggled for every breath. He seemed incapable of crying at this point. Caitlin asked for boiling water, and as soon as it was brought to her, she crushed some leaves into it and quickly made a tent with a blanket lying nearby. She picked up the baby and held him, sitting under the blanket and breathing with him, absorbing the aromatic fumes that enveloped them both.

Then she began to croon to him, rubbing her hands over his body and talking to him in a low voice, explaining there was nothing to fear, that breathing was easy, part of life, that there was nothing to fear from life, that he would enjoy it.

Caitlin continued to request that hot water be added, and she continued to hold the baby upright, forcing his lungs to expel the fluids that were strangling him. And when he began to cough, she helped him rid himself of the life-threatening substance.

Time meant nothing to her as she worked with the

baby. Slowly his breathing eased, and his temperature lowered. His color improved, and after several hours he dropped off into a deep, healing sleep.

When Caitlin stood up to place him in his bed, she realized she was stiff from sitting in one position for so long, holding the baby.

She turned and looked at the mother with a smile. "What is your baby's name?"

"Miguel."

Caitlin gently stroked the infant's back while she spoke to the mother.

"I believe that Miguel will be all right now. When he awakens, make him a liquid from soaking these leaves in boiling water for five minutes. Give him this much," she showed the woman a measurement, "every two hours. By tomorrow he will be ready to eat again."

A clamoring of voices broke out from all the women, and Caitlin was too tired to decipher what they were saying, but it didn't matter. Their actions clearly spelled out that they were elated with her success.

She began to back out of the room, saying over and over, *"De nada, de nada."*

The women followed her into the street, touching her hair lightly, clearly enthralled with what she had done.

Now that the crisis was over, Caitlin discovered that her energy had drained out of her like sand quickly running out of a bag. She had to get home. Smiling and nodding to the women, Caitlin waved her appreciation for their thanks and led her burro away.

The next day Antonio, Miguel's father, appeared at her door, together with his father and two brothers, asking what they could do to pay her for saving the young child's life. She tried to explain they owed her nothing, but they insisted. When they saw how simply she was living there, they told her they would bring her new furniture to replace the small cot she slept on and the crating box she used for a table.

And they had. Over the months each one had shown up at her doorstep with a new offering—a beautifully carved bed, a small round table with four matching chairs, a rocker.

They had brought to her their greatest gifts—their love—and she felt abundantly blessed.

Eventually the surrounding mountainside heard the story of the fair-haired healer who knew mysterious ways to use the plants of the fields and forests to bring strength and peace to a troubled body and soul. She spent many of her days, when she wasn't working in her garden or making hand-spun garments on her loom, traveling from one isolated mountain home to another—visiting, listening, and at times, offering a healing, whether it was of the body, of the mind, or of the spirit.

Caitlin felt truly blessed to have found what she could do with her life. And she was content....

She was almost asleep, lulled by her thoughts of the life she had established here in the mountains, when suddenly, once again, an image of the same face leaped into her mind, a look of dread and horror engulfing its taut expression.

Caitlin involuntarily screamed, "No!"

She shook with the intensity of the feeling that gripped her. The man was in danger, and she needed to help him. But where was he? And where was the danger?

Throwing back the covers, she leaped up and pulled on jeans and a soft woven shirt that tied at the neck. She felt around for the heavy boots she wore when hiking and, finding them, quickly pulled them on over thick socks.

Grabbing her heavy hooded coat and the bag that she always carried, Caitlin threw open the door of the cabin and stepped outside.

The stillness of the night wrapped itself around her in a harmonious serenity that temporarily soothed her. *All is well,* it seemed to say to her.

But she knew better. A man was near death, and she needed to find him. She didn't know where he was or how he had been hurt, but she knew she had to find him.

The crude shelter that protected Arturo, her burro, lay several yards from her front door, and she hastened toward the stall where Arturo slept. She found his bridle and blanket, but instead of attempting to ride, she grabbed his halter and led him away from the warmth of his home, much to his loudly voiced irritation.

"Oh, hush, Arturo," she scolded impatiently. "It won't be long until dawn, anyway. So we're getting an early start on the day. There's no reason to make a scene about it." She scratched behind his ear and he turned his head and looked at her.

She laughed. "All right. So you'll get extra oats tonight; is that a deal? You're already too fat, you know. The exercise will be good for you."

Caitlin hurried down the path, leading the recalcitrant animal and trying to get her bearings.

A desperate sense of urgency pushed her on, but she couldn't pinpoint where it was leading her. She was moving away from the village, even farther away from civilization than her own home, which was isolated. Where was she going? And why?

Wherever it was, she needed to travel quickly, and she continually urged Arturo to hurry, tugging at his halter and promising him all sorts of treats once they returned home.

The path narrowed to no more than a trail where deer and other animals followed the mountain ridge over into the next valley.

Caitlin had never been here before. As far as she knew, no one lived in these parts, particularly not anyone who looked like the man she had seen.

Coming over a ridge, she saw a light moving in the distance. She paused, watching the headlights of two cars.

One vehicle seemed to be chasing the other through the mountain stillness, following twisting, turning roads. She remembered seeing them earlier in her mind. Tired of tugging the lazy burro, she quickly tied him to a young sapling and hurried toward the lights.

She watched with mounting horror while one of the cars began to ram the back of the other car, making the driver lose control. The car in the lead careened back and forth, then grazed a tree, causing the car to roll as though in slow motion, coming to rest at the edge of the steep precipice.

From her position high up on the mountain, Caitlin watched in horror as the scene continued to unfold before her. All the details seemed to have taken place in slow motion, the sound of the squealing brakes and crumpling metal loud in the silence of the night. She broke into a run, then came to an abrupt halt when two men leaped out of the vehicle that had given chase and ran to the other car. She could hear them clearly, their voices carrying in the night.

"Where is he? Is he dead?" one asked in Spanish.

"I don't know. Is he in the car?" The other started toward the car that was leaning drunkenly over the side.

"No. Wait! Here he is. He was thrown out."

She saw a flash, as though from a camera.

"Is he dead?"

"If not, he will be soon enough. Let's get that car over the side. If anyone finds him, they'll think he was just driving too fast and lost control."

Caitlin could hardly believe what she was hearing. These men had done everything they could to cause the other car to wreck. Now they intended to abandon the injured man.

She continued her way down the mountainside, a sense of helplessness overwhelming her. Not only was she outnumbered, she had a hunch those two wouldn't hesitate to kill her if they knew she'd been a witness to what they had done. She watched as the men pushed on the car until it toppled over the side and exploded on impact.

The noise shook the ground, and Caitlin grabbed the limb of a nearby tree to keep her balance.

She heard one of them say "Let's roll him over the side," just as Arturo protested the noise, the night, and being left alone. Caitlin froze, wondering if the men would investigate the sound.

One of them glanced up in her direction.

"What was that?"

"Who knows? There's all kinds of animals living out here."

The other man headed back to the car. "Let's go. Nobody's going to find him here, anyway."

Caitlin saw the first man bend over the motionless form that was spotlighted by the beams of the car. After a moment, he stood up and shrugged. "No matter. He's dead, anyway."

The car turned around and left, returning the way it had come. Caitlin felt paralyzed with shock. In all her experience, she had never witnessed anything so deliberately cruel and callous. Feeling a burning sensation in her chest, she realized she had forgotten to breathe.

Slowly drawing air into her lungs, she once again hurried down the hillside, surprised to notice that she was having no trouble distinguishing where she was going. Unnoticed, the sky had begun to lighten, signaling a new day.

Perhaps for the man who lay so still on the primitive roadway, there would never be a new day. A deep pain seemed to fill Caitlin's chest at the thought.

She was out of breath by the time she scrambled down to the road and dashed along its surface. There had been no movement from the man, and she was very much afraid there was nothing she could do for him.

As soon as she reached his side, she fell to her knees.

His skin was icy, and her heart sank. She felt for a pulse. The pounding of her heart seemed to shake her body with each beat. Her hand was shaking so much she couldn't find any sign of life.

She glanced around, trying to relate where she was with what she had witnessed happening. The man must have either jumped or been thrown from the car.

His clothes were covered with dirt, and his features were all but obscured by blood. She got up from her knees and walked over to the edge of the road, peering over. The fire around the car seemed to have gone out, only the dark smoke curling up beside it evidence that there had been a blaze.

The poor man.

Why had the men been chasing him? Why had they wanted him dead? She wondered if she would ever know the answers.

In the meantime, what should she do? She couldn't leave him lying there while she went for help. It would take her hours. He needed help now, unless it was already too late. She needed to think calmly and rationally about what to do.

Slowly Caitlin walked back over to the man and looked down at him. She couldn't even see what he looked like, but she noted his tawny curls and waves, and winced. She didn't need to see his face to know who he was. He was the man she had seen earlier.

Making up her mind, Caitlin began to climb the mountain once again. She would bring Arturo down and attempt to take the man to the village.

Perhaps it was too late to save him, but he deserved a decent burial.

Decent. The word seemed to ring in her head. He had been a decent man. A kind man. A man who had not deserved to die on some lonely mountain road in the middle of nowhere.

By the time Caitlin reached Arturo, tears cascaded down her cheeks. There were many times when she found life particularly puzzling. Now was one of those times. Why had she seen him so clearly if she

wasn't going to be given the opportunity to save him?
What was the purpose of her being there?

She dried her eyes with the sleeve of her shirt.
Whatever the reason, she was there, and she was going to see that he wasn't abandoned. Turning, she
guided the burro back down the side of the mountain.

After positioning the burro beside the man, Caitlin
discovered that he was much larger than she'd realized. She would have trouble getting him draped
across the small animal without dragging his hands
and feet; that is, if she could even lift him that far.

With infinite care and tenderness, she straightened
the unknown man's legs and turned him so that he
was lying on his back. She knelt and began to wipe
the blood away from his face with one of the clean
towels she always carried. The blood had come from
a gash across his forehead, just beneath his hairline.

There was no expression on his face. He looked as
though he were asleep, peacefully napping in the
early morning light.

She felt a strange resonance inside her, as though
a chord had been pulled. He had a beautiful face—
clean, clearly defined, with high cheekbones and a
strong jawline. His lips, in repose, looked as though
they were made for smiling, and the slight lines
around his mouth seemed to indicate he was a person
who often found life amusing.

She sat and stared at him for a few moments until
she realized she was wasting time. There was no reason to try to put off what had to be done.

Caitlin placed her arms around him, her head resting on his chest where his coat had fallen open, in an
attempt to get him upright.

She froze, her eyes closing in a sudden spasm of excitement. An almost indiscernible rhythm reached her ear, which was pressed so close to his chest.

It was a heartbeat.

Two

Bright sunshine lit the clearing around Caitlin's small home by the time she and Arturo returned. She prayed that she would never experience such a harrowing morning again.

After leading the burro to the roadway, Caitlin had checked to make sure the man didn't have any broken bones. Then she had begun the task of lifting him.

Caitlin wasn't sure where she had found the strength to finally get the man onto Arturo's back. For the first time she fully understood what dead weight meant.

She'd been afraid of damaging the man even more by securing him on the small animal's back, so she had walked beside him, making sure his body didn't slide off.

Other than the thready pulse that she continued to monitor throughout their journey, he showed no signs of life, and she was gravely concerned. She had to keep reminding herself that at least he was alive, though barely. If she could get him back to the cabin, perhaps he had a chance.

Never had a place looked so good to her as her own clearing once they arrived. Caitlin didn't concern herself with the niceties of housekeeping at the moment. She led Arturo inside the cabin, despite his protests, so that she could slide the unconscious man onto the bed. Then she hurriedly returned Arturo to his stall, gave him the promised oats and ran back to the cabin.

The man hadn't moved. His skin felt clammy to the touch, and his gray color gave evidence to his state of shock.

"But you're alive," she whispered. "You're going to make it. Everything is all right. You're going to make it."

Searching in her bag for the small penlight she carried, Caitlin carefully lifted each of the man's eyelids, shining the light into his pupils and watching as they retracted slightly. The movement was sluggish, but at least there was some response, thank God. There was no doubt that he suffered from a concussion, possibly a skull fracture, but his brain was still functioning, at least to some degree.

The gash on his head was deep, and Caitlin knew she would have to stitch it, but not until she could clean and disinfect it.

First things first. She needed to get him out of his coat and boots, and try to make him more comfortable. From her quick check before she'd loaded him onto Arturo, the man had no broken bones, for which she was thankful. His head injury was serious enough.

Forcing herself to stay calm, Caitlin eased his heavy coat off his broad shoulders. The coat had cushioned his fall, probably saving him some cracked ribs. His Levi's had also taken the brunt of his fall. When she slipped his arm out of his coat sleeve, Caitlin flinched at the sight of the shoulder holster nestled securely under his arm.

She wondered how many law-abiding people wore shoulder holsters. *Or get run off the road, for that matter.* She forced herself to unfasten the holster and pulled it away from him. Caitlin knew nothing about guns. On purpose. She stared at the pistol lying in its holster and shivered. Glancing around the room, she didn't know what to do with it.

Was he dangerous? When he came to, would he try to kill her?

No. He was a decent man. Somehow she knew that, even though all other information she sensed seemed to be on the negative side. Whatever he was mixed up in was highly dangerous. She was a witness to that.

With sudden decision she wrapped the gun in a towel and hid it in her suitcase under the storage cabinet. Then she returned to the man lying unconscious on her bed.

After removing his boots, Levi's and shirt, she quickly covered him with blankets, then carefully bathed his face until it was clean. He looked so pale, and he lay there utterly still.

For the first time since she'd returned to the cabin, Caitlin became aware that the fire had gone out and that the room was cold. With the physical exertion she'd been going through all morning, she was almost perspiring, but she knew she had to get this man warm in a hurry. He had been unconscious for several hours, showing no sign of stirring.

Caitlin left him long enough to build another fire. Thank God the coals were still warm. She patiently waited while the kindling caught, then slowly and methodically added small twigs until flames began to dance once more.

Satisfied that the fire could be left on its own, Caitlin straightened slowly, her hand on the small of her back. She absently wondered what the stranger weighed. For a while that morning, her back felt as though she had broken it.

Checking him once again, she hoped that it wasn't her imagination that caused her to think his color was improving. His breathing was so shallow that she had trouble seeing any evidence of life, and she continually checked his pulse to make sure.

Pulling out a few herbs, Caitlin began to add them to some salve she had in a jar, mixing and stirring the concoction until she had the consistency she wanted. Then she returned to the bed and sat beside him.

He looked so peaceful. She traced his brow line, then his nose and jaw. If she were a sculptor, she'd be inspired to reproduce that face. Mentally reminding herself not to daydream, Caitlin began to bathe the man with sudsy warm water and blotted him dry, then covered each of his cuts and abrasions with the concoction she had mixed.

She carefully examined his face and the swelling on his forehead where he'd received a blow. She knew enough about head wounds to know that there was little she could do for him except prevent infection to the open wound. His body would have to heal itself.

After cleaning the gash on his forehead, she carefully stitched it closed, then covered the wound with the mixture of herbs and salve.

She stroked his cheek, where a day's growth of whiskers could be felt, but scarcely seen. His beard was as light as his hair.

"Your body needs time to heal, my friend," she said softly. "You are safe now. No one will harm you. Your body will take care of itself. You will rest and be comfortable. Everything is fine. You are safe."

She continued to sit there beside him, forcing her agitation to leave her and absorbing the calm serenity that always seemed to fill her cabin.

Caitlin couldn't remember the last time she had eaten. However, she knew she'd used up a considerable amount of energy since then. Humming softly, she prepared herself some lunch. She had finished and was washing up her dishes when she heard a soft tap at the door.

Visitors weren't too unusual since the local people thought of her as a healer. In addition, various people brought her food, items for the house and clothing in payment for her services.

She glanced over at the man in her bed. Of course, it was possible someone might be looking for him. She couldn't imagine who would possibly know to search for him here, but she couldn't afford to take any chances, not when she had witnessed an attempted murder.

Caitlin drew the homemade curtain that she had hung on a rod to divide the room in two, effectively concealing him from anyone standing at the doorway. She heard the soft tap again and strode over to the door and opened it.

She laughed. Her visitor wasn't human. "Well, good morning, Chula. Were you looking for me?"

A young deer stood there waiting. When the door opened, she walked inside the cabin with the familiarity of a long-established habit.

"I don't recall inviting you in, you know," Caitlin said with a grin, watching while the deer checked the dish near the fireplace. "Yes, I'm sure you're hungry. You're always hungry. What a panhandler."

Caitlin shook her head, closed the door and went over to the cabinet where she kept the grain. She poured some into the dish and held a small handful in her fist. Slowly opening her hand, she said, "Here you go, greedy."

The deer sniffed at the pan, then immediately moved toward her hand, daintily nibbling from her palm. "I can't believe how spoiled you are."

The spring before, Caitlin had found the deer not too far from the cabin, when it was still a wobbly-legged fawn with large spots and soulful eyes. Its dead mother had lain nearby.

The fawn had been too young and too hungry to know fear, and Caitlin had brought her home and kept her alive on goat's milk until she learned to eat.

Caitlin hadn't intended to make the animal a pet, but she didn't know what else she could have done. Now Chula, as Caitlin called her, had joined the group of animals that seemed to have found their home in and around Caitlin's clearing.

After Chula completed her meal, Caitlin coaxed her back outside. She paused in the doorway, looking up at the sun. What a beautiful day. Caitlin had trouble reconciling the violence she'd witnessed the night before with the peaceful serenity of the mountains and the sunshine.

Several birds swooped down from the trees and landed in a cluster at her feet. She stepped back into the cabin and gathered a double handful of food for them, then tossed it out. She sat down on the stoop and watched, unsurprised that several pecked their way over to her.

Her presence in the clearing had been accepted by the wildlife in ways she'd never fully understood. She'd just accepted it. They seemed unafraid. When she picked up a few sunflower seeds and placed them on her fingers, two of the birds nonchalantly lit on her palm and began to peck energetically.

She started laughing. "That tickles, you little beasts," she said, causing them to fly off, circle, then land back at her feet.

Caitlin went back inside and checked on her patient. He had not moved. However, she could see definite improvement in his breathing. His lungs seemed to be filling more deeply with air, so that his chest moved gently in rhythm.

Carefully tucking the covers around his neck once more, Caitlin decided to work on her loom. She found the steady rhythm of weaving the thread very soothing. Hopefully no one would need her today. She didn't want to leave the man alone, in case he regained consciousness.

Absently pushing the curtain back against the wall, Caitlin picked up what remained of his clothing. The shirt had fared well, since it had been protected by his jacket, and she thought the jeans were salvageable, although badly worn from his landing and rolling on the road. They would at least provide some covering for him once he was on his feet again.

She never allowed herself to think about him except as whole and healthy.

Picking up the jeans, she checked the pockets before placing them in the large kettle of steaming water that she used to wash her own things.

She found small change and a pocket knife in one of the front pockets, but that was all. She remembered the man hovering over his inert body. He must have taken his wallet.

He was a man with no identification. If he never came to, there would be no way to let anyone know what had happened to him.

Who was he?

For the first time since she'd regained consciousness in that Seattle hospital years ago, Caitlin wanted to utilize her unwanted skills: she wanted to solve the mystery of her new patient. Who was he, and why had someone tried to kill him?

She sat by the bed and studied him, letting her thoughts flow freely. Pictures began to form. She saw a woman with long blond hair, emerald-green eyes and a very provocative smile. Caitlin saw her run toward the man and throw her arms around him. They were both laughing.

There was another man, taller than her patient but built along the same lines: broad shoulders, narrow waist and hips, long well-muscled legs. She felt a close tie between the three people, a loving warmth that radiated between them. Caitlin knew with an inner certainty that those two people would be searching for the man who lay motionless beside her.

He was loved, this stranger, and Caitlin felt a moment of poignancy for the three people.

She reached over and lightly stroked his forehead. He felt warmer, as if his body were adjusting to its new environment. She folded one of the blankets away from him and studied his face. His color was definitely improving.

"You're going to be all right, my friend. You are safe now. No one will be able to find you and hurt you here. You are safe. Your body is healing."

And then what? Would he go out and try to get himself killed again? She knew better than to concern herself with future possibilities. Instead Caitlin focused her energies on getting him well.

She began to work at the loom quietly, periodically checking her patient for signs of consciousness.

By dark she felt ready to end her day. After feeding Arturo, her small group of chickens, the goat, and various wildlife that had grown used to coming in at dusk to feed, Caitlin returned to the cabin and lit one of her oil lamps.

She loved the soft glow the light gave to her home. In fact, she loved everything about the small cabin and gave thanks for the wisdom and determination she had needed to give up the life she had known to start over again in this unfamiliar wilderness. The move had been her salvation.

Caitlin glanced down at the man in her bed. Perhaps his salvation had also hinged on her move.

After getting ready for bed, banking the fire and replacing the fire screen, Caitlin came face-to-face with a decision she had unconsciously avoided all day. Where was she going to sleep?

The bed that Antonio had made for her was very

large and would be more than adequate for the two of them. And what choice did she have? Short of curling up in her sleeping bag in front of the fire, she had none.

Leaning over the bed so that she could see his face, Caitlin knew that he would not know where she slept. With calm resolution, she lowered the wick on the lamp, leaving it lit so that she could see him if he should stir. Caitlin crawled into bed beside the stranger, and with a sigh of utter exhaustion, closed her eyes.

Within minutes she was asleep.

Caitlin lost track of time during the next several days. Her routine revolved around the unconscious man in her home. She watched him for signs of consciousness, sitting by the bed and talking to him, touching him, reassuring him in every way she knew that he would regain his strength and be all right.

Secretly she began to wonder. She was afraid to leave him in case he came to and she wasn't there. But she had a sense of danger connected with the village and wanted to check it out. Was it possible his assailants had returned and, not finding his body, realized he was alive? If so, his life could still be in jeopardy.

Caitlin awoke one morning with a feeling of renewed hope and optimism, refreshed and ready to face a new day. Her patient's color was good, and the angry wound showed signs of healing.

"Good morning," she said, as though he could hear her. "How are you feeling?" She stood there and gazed at him, willing his eyes to open and meet hers, but she could see no response in his expression, not even a flicker of an eyelid.

Refusing to become discouraged, she turned away.

Chula entered the cabin as soon as Caitlin opened the door. Caitlin could see why Chula was so eager to be inside. A gray, heavily clouded sky swirled overhead, and she heard the wind whistling around the eaves.

"I suppose you intend to spend your day out of the weather," Caitlin said to Chula after she closed the door. The deer lay in front of the fireplace, her feet neatly tucked beneath her. Caitlin placed food in the bowl and poured some water into a small pan for her.

Quickly dressing in warm woolen pants and a hand-woven shirt, Caitlin made herself some breakfast and put a large pot of stew on the stove. Today she would attempt to feed her patient some broth.

She tried not to think about him as anyone other than a person who needed her help. But Caitlin had never known a man who affected her so strongly, not even Rick.

For almost a year she'd planned to marry Rick Shannon, thinking they had the perfect relationship. But Rick couldn't handle her ability to pick up on his thoughts and emotions after her near-brush with death. Eventually he had found a reason to terminate their engagement.

At the time she had been too immersed in her own grief at losing her parents to care. The very foundation on which her life had been built was gone. What did one more person leaving really mean to her?

Now she recognized that she had never loved Rick. She'd been in love with the idea of being in love. They had enjoyed the same pastimes, but the relationship had been very shallow. Caitlin felt lucky that they had found out before they had made the commitment to a marriage.

So why was she having such a strong reaction to this man? They had no relationship at all.

Are you sure? You saved his life, didn't you?

"That remains to be seen."

He would have died if you hadn't brought him back here.

"But he hasn't regained consciousness."

Give him time. His body needs time to restore itself.

"But when will he be aware of me?"

She received no answer.

Caitlin had never questioned the fact that she had brought him to her cabin. Neither she nor Arturo could have possibly managed to get him down the mountainside and to the settlement. She doubted the man would have survived the trip. He'd needed the warmth and quiet of her place almost as much as she had when she'd first moved there.

Now if he would only regain consciousness.

During the evening, she moved the lamp over closer to the bed and sat beside him. Taking his hand in hers, she said, "Please wake up. You need to eat something. You need to start moving around. Please open your eyes."

She stared at him, willing him to wake up. After several minutes she placed his hand on his chest and patted it. "Will you try for me?"

If she hadn't been studying his face so intently, she might have missed the slight flutter of his eyelashes. But because her hand was still lying on his, there was no way she could mistake the slight twitch of his thumb.

Tears filled her eyes. "Thank you" was all she could manage to say. Surely those weren't reflexes. He had heard her. She knew he had. And she needed to reassure him. "You're going to be all right. I know that now. You're going to be fine!"

Rushing over to the kitchen area, Caitlin began to spoon some broth into a bowl. The time had come to try to feed him. She laughed out loud.

He was going to be all right—she just knew it. He had to be.

Three

Caitlin watched him closely but saw no other signs that he might be regaining consciousness. However, she decided to talk to him as though he were awake and could hear her.

"I have some broth for you. You need the nourishment, and I'm sure you'll find it quite good. It's a recipe I invented since moving here. I throw whatever vegetables are available into the pot and let them cook for several hours. Why don't you try some?"

She sat down beside him with a cup of broth and dipped a spoon into the cup. Placing the half-full spoon on his lip, she gently inserted it between his teeth.

"Please swallow now. You mustn't choke." She set the cup down on the table beside the bed and massaged his neck while tilting the spoon slightly. She held her breath and waited.

Unmistakably she could feel the muscles in his neck as he swallowed. "You're wonderful—did you know that? I'm so proud of you." Quickly grabbing the cup, she dipped the spoon in once more. Caitlin lost track of the time she spent spooning the warm broth into his mouth. She refused to rush him. There was nothing she would rather do than to feed her patient as long as she could get him to take it.

After feeding him, she sponge bathed him and slipped his shirt back on. She needed to make him another one and, since there was no cloth she owned that would cover his broad shoulders, she knew she would have to weave a large skein of material. She would get started on that tomorrow, first thing.

Sometime later Chula stirred, and Caitlin let her outdoors, noting that the weather had not cleared. Since it was almost dark, she decided to feed the animals for the night and get ready for bed herself.

When she fell asleep that night, Caitlin was more and more encouraged with his progress. Although she had seen no further signs of returning consciousness during the past several hours, she was encouraged that he had been able to take some nourishment.

Caitlin slept heavily that night, her body and mind relaxing for the first time since she'd awakened with the sense of impending danger. The danger had been met, and hopefully, overcome.

The cabin grew colder as dawn approached, and in her sleep she drew closer to the warmth of the man beside her.

He kept hearing voices. Who were they, and what did they want? Sometimes they seemed to be whispering, and he strained to understand them.

One voice reoccurred, over and over. A soft, lilting voice that soothed him. Who was it?

"Felicia, is that you?"

No answer.

No, of course it wasn't Felicia. Felicia was in California while he was in—He was—Where? He was so confused. Was he at the ranch?

"Dane? Where are you?"

His body ached as though he'd been trampled by a herd of horses. And his head! Oh, God! He mustn't move his head, not at all. The slightest movement, and he fell back into that black pit of oblivion. Of course, there wasn't any pain there; he had to acknowledge that.

"But he couldn't stay there forever, could he?"

No. There was something he had to do. Right away. He'd worked hard for this meeting.

"Meeting? What meeting?"

Don't tell me you've forgotten the meeting. We were counting on you. Counting on you, counting on you.

The sound of a male voice close to her ear brought Caitlin from a sound sleep to a shocked wakefulness sometime later. What had she just heard?

Caitlin sat up in bed and stared at the man lying beside her. He was shifting restlessly, his head moving from side to side on the pillow. He was muttering something. She leaned closer to hear him.

"You don't understand. I can't move, I can't—" His voice dwindled off into silence for a moment, then came back even stronger. "Let me go, you bastards. Let me go!"

The words were muttered and slurred, but Caitlin could understand them. Whatever was happening in his mind had an urgency about it that he managed to convey in his voice and the tenseness of his body.

"Hello." Caitlin placed her hand on his forehead and smoothed the curls back. "Can you hear me?"

He quietened but didn't respond.

Caitlin got up and poured a small glass of water. Then she returned to the bed. "Would you like a drink?" She sat down beside him and lifted his head slightly by sliding her arm under the pillow. When she placed the glass to his lips, he opened his mouth and took a swallow.

For a moment Caitlin felt like weeping with relief. He wasn't fully conscious, but he was no longer in the seemingly lifeless state that had held him so still for the past several days.

After lowering him carefully, she put the glass down, then went over and built up the fire. Glancing out the window, she saw that dawn had arrived, although the cabin was still in shadows.

Humming to herself, she laid out the clothes she wanted to wear for the day. Then she grabbed her coat and pulled it over her nightclothes, put on her heavy walking boots and went outside to feed the animals and bring in more wood.

Chula followed her back into the cabin. She fed her, then poured some warm water into a bowl and hastily bathed herself before getting dressed. Caitlin stood before the fire, warming herself as she dressed.

Adam thought he was dreaming when he finally managed to focus his eyes. But where would his subconscious have picked up such a scene? He felt as though an oversize sledgehammer was continually tapping on his skull, and he found it difficult to concentrate.

The rustic cabin he seemed to occupy was small and immaculate, the furnishings sparse. Except for the statue of a small deer sitting on a rug in front of the fireplace, there was no ornamentation, unless he counted the woman standing before the large fireplace.

The glow from the fire tinted her skin apricot. She stood with her back to him, wearing a pair of panties that enticingly covered a deliciously curved derriere. Her long reddish-blond hair fell to her waist, the waves and curls beckoning him to run his hands through them.

He watched her as she dressed, unaware of him. Who was she? And what was he doing there?

Adam forced himself to concentrate, trying to ignore the throbbing pain in his head.

His last memory was standing in front of his hotel in Monterrey. Had he gone to a bar and been slipped something in his drink?

He studied the woman in front of him. She didn't look the type. Besides, he'd had something he had to do. What was it? Something important.

The throbbing pain increased when he frowned. He touched his forehead and felt a large welt that was extremely tender. His hand dropped to his jaw where he felt the roughness of a beard.

She turned toward him, reaching for her blouse. She had very delicate features. Her eyes were framed with dark lashes, and their blueness reminded him of a mountain lake.

"Who are you?" he said, his voice husky from disuse.

She grabbed her blouse to her breast in surprise, her expression startled as she stared at him from across the small space. Hastily turning her back to him, she tugged the shirt on over her head and pulled on a pair of jeans.

When she turned around again, her face was composed, but her color was heightened. Walking over to the bed, she sat down beside him and took his hand.

"I'm Caitlin," she said with a smile. "Who are you?"

The room kept receding from him. He blinked his eyes, trying to bring her into sharper focus. "Adam," he finally muttered, his throat dry.

"Adam," she repeated slowly, as though experimenting with the sound. At last she had a name for him. She liked it. Somehow it suited him. "You're going to be fine, Adam. You got a nasty blow to your head, but you'll be fine." She reached up and brushed his hair from his forehead in a familiar gesture, careful not to touch his wound.

He couldn't think. Her touch felt so soothing; it went with the sound of her voice. Her voice was so familiar, the tone as gentle as her touch... Adam drifted off to sleep, his breathing peaceful, his expression serene.

Time didn't seem to have any meaning to him, and he kept fading in and out of consciousness. He would open his eyes to daylight, close them, then reopen them to deep shadows that were only kept from engulfing him by a dim light somewhere nearby.

He was always aware of her presence. What had she said her name was? Caitlin, that was it. Caitlin with the soft voice and soothing hands.

Vaguely he was aware of her instructions to eat.

From some far distant place she urged him to turn so that she could stroke him with a warm, wet cloth, its presence offering a balm to his aching body. He tried to tell her he could bathe himself, but somehow he couldn't find the words. *Takes too much concentration,* he decided.

Caitlin—beautiful angel of mercy and light, who kept the dark shadows away and soothed the pain that seemed to fill his body. How long had he known her? She seemed to be an integral part of his life. Had she always been there?

She smelled so good. Sometimes he would awaken in the darkness, his heart pounding, not knowing where he was, the ghost of a dream still swirling around him. Then her soft scent would reach him from somewhere close by, and he would remember where he was—that Caitlin was there—and he would relax.

Sometimes his dreams were filled with headlights relentlessly shining into his rearview mirror, looming closer and closer. Then he'd hear an explosion and feel as though he were flying through the air. But he never seemed to land.

Other times he dreamed of the ranch...of Felicia...of Dane. He kept trying to tell them he was all right and not to worry, but they never seemed to hear him.

He'd wake up in a cold sweat, trembling with the effort not to cry out with the pain that sometimes bit into his body and pulled him down to the pits of agony.

He became used to her touch, her soft scent, and a rhythmic thumping sound that he associated with her weaving. There were times when he would be aware of the stillness that was night. Once he woke up to find her sleeping curled up by his side. He smiled. Shifting slightly, he moved so that his hand could touch her arm. He found the closeness comforting.

Sometime during those many hours, Caitlin became a part of his thoughts, whether he was conscious or unconscious. Concentrating on her kept the pain from overwhelming him. Her presence kept the fear and confusion he was experiencing at bay.

Caitlin.

At last the day came when Adam could open his eyes and focus without the hazy double vision that had plagued him. He lay there quietly looking around the room that had somehow become familiar to him.

At first he didn't see Caitlin, not until she moved into his line of vision. Her reddish-blond hair hung in a single braid across her shoulder, resting on her breast. He smiled at the tranquil picture she made placing wood on the fire. She had become so much a part of him—an extension of who he was.

When she moved away from the fireplace, he tried to keep her in sight by turning his head. He immediately discovered his mistake when the pain in his head magnified. Adam must have made some sort of noise, because Caitlin glanced up, and when she saw him watching her, she smiled, an enchanting smile that made her eyes sparkle.

"How do you feel?" she asked, walking over to the bed and taking his hand in hers.

"Like my head's been used for batting practice a few too many times," he managed to say. His voice sounded almost rusty. "Where are we?" he asked, his curiosity finally piqued enough to inquire.

"The mountains."

She made her answer sound so simple, as though he should know that. There were no mountains anywhere near the ranch, just rolling hills.

"Are we in Texas?"

She chuckled, shaking her head. "No. Mexico."

Mexico. What the hell was he doing in Mexico?

"What am I doing here?"

"You were in an accident not too far from here and badly injured. Since there's no town nearby, I brought you to my home to help you recover."

He thought about that for a moment but could think of nothing else to ask. He knew he was hurt. He'd never felt so much pain before.

Her hand continued to hold his firmly. Carefully moving his eyes so that the pain wouldn't increase, he studied their clasped hands. His was large and work-roughened, wide, with a callused palm. Hers was dwarfed next to his, her fingers long and slender, and very pale, like the rest of her.

He glanced up and became aware of her expression. She was smiling as though immensely pleased with him. He idly wondered why. He couldn't have been much company lately.

"How long have I been here?" *Forever, surely. Was there ever a time when you and I weren't together?*

"I'm not sure, exactly. I'm afraid I lost track of time...you've been so ill."

Not that it mattered. He was content to lie there looking at her while she held his hand. He could look at her all day, every day, and not grow tired of her face, her very lovely, expressive face.

Caitlin was touched by the tender expression he wore. Touched and slightly alarmed. He mustn't grow attached to her. She felt the inner warning that she was too late—her loving care of him had created a bond between them. After several moments of silence, she realized she needed to distract him.

"Where do you live, Adam?" she asked, unobtrusively releasing his hand and folding hers together on her lap.

Adam had to think about her question for a moment. He felt as though all the moving parts of his brain were buried in gallons of molasses and responded sluggishly whenever he tried to think. He found it much easier to let his mind wander and just to enjoy his sensory perceptions. He missed the touch of her hand.

Frowning slightly, he tried to concentrate on her question. His home. Where was it? "On a ranch…in Texas. Near Mason." His eyes sought hers. "Do you know where that is?"

He watched her as she shook her head. That was all right. He'd show her someday, when he felt better. He would take her back to the ranch, let her meet Dane and his neighbors and friends. Maybe he could convince Felicia to fly home for a visit. He knew the two women would enjoy each other.

"What are you doing here in Mexico, Adam?"

Good question. He frowned once again, trying to force his brain to work. His thoughts continued to swim around inside his head without rhyme or reason.

Car lights shining in the rearview mirror. He'd been going somewhere, meeting someone…. Danger. What he was doing was dangerous.

With a sudden start Adam felt along his side.

"Where's my pistol?"

She nodded toward the corner. "I put it in my suitcase, where it would be safe," she assured him.

The pistol didn't need to be safe. *They* needed to be safe. They would be safer if he had the gun nearby; didn't she understand that? Maybe she didn't.

"How long have I known you?"

Unconsciously Caitlin reached for his hand once more and she began to stroke his knuckles with her other hand. "Just since the accident."

"You don't know why I'm here?"

"Not very clearly, I'm afraid. I've picked up that you were on your way to meet someone, someone important to you, and you never made it."

"What do you mean, you picked up?"

Her grip on his hand tightened, and he watched several expressions move across her face. He wanted to tell her that it didn't matter and that he didn't want to cause her pain.

"I see pictures in my head," she said in a hesitant voice. "That's how I knew about you, that you were nearby, that you would be hurt."

She wasn't making much sense. But then, nothing made much sense to him at the moment.

"You mean my accident."

"Yes, except what happened to you wasn't an accident. You were forced off the road and almost killed."

Bright lights reflected in a rearview mirror, almost blinding him… Yes. He remembered now. He didn't know where they came from. Suddenly they were behind him, coming up fast, and he had no place to go to get out of their way—except down the side of the mountain.

Adam tried to put everything she had told him into

some coherent form. An accident that he could only remember in snatches. An accident that wasn't an accident. She had been there. She... "You saved my life," he said, speaking his thoughts aloud.

Caitlin felt as though she were drowning in the gray-green eyes that gazed up at her. The pain he was still experiencing was apparent. She wanted to hold him to her and comfort him as though he were a child. But this man was no child. Not in any way.

"I'm glad I was able to," she managed to say.

They studied each other in silence for a while, that invisible bond drawing them closer.

Adam's thoughts seemed to drift—away from Caitlin, away from the cabin. He stirred restlessly. "Somehow I have to tell them—"

"I know. There are people who need to know that you're alive," Caitlin responded, understanding his concern. "But they will wait, Adam. First you need to mend."

His eyes drooped shut. "So tired."

Without considering her actions, she leaned down and kissed his cheek. "I know. Go to sleep now. You have plenty of time." Her voice was carefully modulated and very soothing. "Now is the time to rest. You'll feel better soon. The worst is behind you."

Adam smiled at her touch. He loved her soft scent, her warm touch, her tranquil presence nearby. He loved...

The next time he opened his eyes the room was in shadows, with only the glow of the fireplace illuminating the small home. Once again Adam's gaze sought out the woman who seemed to fill all of his thoughts, both waking and dreaming. She sat in a small rocker before the fire, doing handwork.

"Do you live here alone?" he asked, destroying the silence of the room.

Caitlin glanced around and stood up. Coming over to his side, she automatically touched his hand, then his cheek. "Not totally. Chula keeps me company from time to time." She nodded to the deer statue in front of the fireplace.

Adam frowned, wondering if she had been alone too long.

She left his side and went to the kitchen area where she picked up a small bag. Returning to the fireplace, Caitlin reached her hand into the bag and pulled out some oats, placing them in a small bowl he hadn't noticed before.

His eyes widened when the statue unfolded its legs and got up, stepping daintily across the rug to the bowl where it began to eat.

He began to understand how Alice must have felt when she stepped through the looking glass.

Caitlin brought him a bowl of stew and sat down beside him. He started to take the bowl and discovered his arms felt weighted.

"There's no reason for you to exert yourself just yet. Why don't you relax and let me feed you?"

The idea held considerable merit. Adam relaxed against the pillows and obligingly opened his mouth whenever she brought the spoonful of food toward him.

He continued to study her—enjoying the sight of her fair skin, her softly rounded cheek, her small, straight nose, the shape of her finely molded mouth. Although she pretended to ignore his scrutiny, a soft rose coloring washed across her cheeks. Adam was delighted to see her reaction. No matter how she tried, she couldn't pretend that they were strangers. Never that.

When he finished the last spoonful of food, Caitlin stood up. "Why don't you rest now?"

Adam frowned. "All I do is sleep."

"I know," she said sympathetically. "But it's the best thing for you. You're making excellent progress, you know."

His mind returned to the cause of his injuries.

"Did you see what happened to me?"

Caitlin nodded, her expression somber.

"Tell me what you saw. Everything you can remember."

After rinsing out the bowl, she returned to his side. Once again she took his hand, unobtrusively keeping watch over his pulse. He didn't need to get upset. But keeping what happened from him might be just as upsetting. As briefly as possible, Caitlin explained the sequence of events she had witnessed.

When she fell silent, Adam lay there, staring into space. Two men tried to kill him. Why? Were they hoping to keep him from making contact with the possible informer? How had they known about the meeting?

And just as important—how was he going to find them?

"Did you get a look at the men?"

"Not a clear look, no, but I would know them again if I saw them."

He wished he understood how Caitlin had known what was going to happen to him. How could she identify two men she'd only seen in the dark? He couldn't deny that there was something different about her—something that had led her to him. How had she known?

Wearily Adam closed his eyes, trying to crowd out the pain that seemed to engulf him every time he tried to concentrate. Rest. He needed to rest. Adam kept hoping that his patience would be rewarded and the pain would go away.

Adam drifted off to sleep once more.

Caitlin watched him for a long time, grateful to see that he was resting easier. She had added a tea that she had brewed to the food she had given him. Hopefully the tea would help to combat the pain he was experiencing without creating any other problems for him.

With any luck at all, he would sleep through the night. She smiled to herself, wondering what she would do if he woke up sometime and found her by his side? Once he was awake more, she would get the sleeping bag out and sleep in front of the fire. She didn't want to encourage him to think she wanted anything more from him.

Caitlin had been aware of his thoughts earlier. He was attracted to her, just as she was attracted to him. But the attraction would be better if left unacknowledged. His life existed outside of the mountains. She had no desire to ever leave them, not even to be somewhere nearer to Adam.

She already knew that Adam would hold a very special place in her heart. And why not? A person didn't save another person's life every day, she tried to tell herself. But she knew better. Her work with the villagers had already shown her how valuable she had become in the area where she lived.

Adam was different. She just had to keep in mind that there could be nothing between them.

Caitlin lay awake for several hours that night, thinking of the man sleeping so soundly beside her. There was a reason he'd come into her life, a lesson she would learn from the experience. She only hoped the lesson wasn't accompanied with more pain than she could handle.

Adam awoke early, and Caitlin quickly prepared a nourishing meal for him. They talked for a while, with Caitlin choosing light subjects that took little effort on Adam's part. She teased him about his good looks, then found herself embarrassed when he returned her teasing with interest.

She helped him to sit up on the side of the bed for a few moments, then helped him to stretch out once more when he showed definite signs of fatigue. Sleep overcame him once more, and she was free to continue her daily routine.

While waiting for her patient to awaken later in the afternoon, Caitlin decided to make bread. Baking was another soothing task for her. She particularly enjoyed the smell the freshly baked bread gave to her small home. She hummed while she worked, content.

When Adam awakened again, his head was much clearer than it had been. Glancing out the window, he was surprised to see that night had fallen while he had slept. The cabin was filled with shadows except for the firelight and an oil lamp that sat on a table near a hand loom where Caitlin was working. The thump of the shuttles was a familiar sound he'd grown accustomed to.

The small room smelled of fresh bread. For all he

knew, he could be in another century. The surprising thing was that it didn't matter. He felt at peace with the world and all the creatures in it.

If only the ache in his head would let up. The pain was a constant companion. He couldn't seem to remember a time when the steady throbbing hadn't coursed through him.

God! He felt so helpless.

He attempted to turn on his side, causing the throbbing in his head to increase alarmingly, and he groaned.

Caitlin immediately got up and moved to the side of the bed. "I didn't realize you were awake," she said, noting the tension in his face. "I have something ready for you that should help the pain."

He nodded slightly, acknowledging her words. His teeth were clamped together, as though he were afraid that if he tried to speak he would not be able to withhold another groan.

Caitlin poured a cup of the herbal tea she'd prepared and brought it over to him. "It should still be warm," she said, skillfully lifting his head with the pillow and holding the cup to his mouth.

Adam drank the warm liquid, making a face. His gaze sought hers. She was only a few inches away, and he saw tiny gleams of gold deep within the blue of her eyes. He'd never seen a color quite like that before.

"What was that?" he muttered.

She smiled. "You must be feeling better. You're sounding grouchy. The tea is a mixture of herbs that I grow—it should help ease your pain."

"I don't think you need to worry about Lipton trying to steal your formula."

Her chuckle sounded husky and warm. "Probably not."

She put the empty cup down and looked at him for a moment. "We really need to get you up again, if you think you can manage."

She watched as a dull redness filled his cheeks. "I'd prefer getting up to your taking care of me."

Caitlin knew what he meant, but she wasn't sure he could manage on his own. "It's outside, you know."

Without meeting her eyes, he nodded. "I figured as much."

"It's not far, if you'd like me to help you."

"For some reason, the idea of your helping me doesn't improve my self-image at all."

Their gazes finally met, and they both began to laugh at their mutual embarrassment. Adam clutched his head in dismay as the pain accelerated.

"I meant I'd help you walk out there," Caitlin explained, absently stroking his forehead as though to ease the pain. "You're going to be very weak."

Between the two of them, he managed to sit on the side of the bed. For the first time Adam registered the fact that he was only wearing his shirt and briefs. What had he expected, anyway? Hadn't she bathed him and looked after him when he was too helpless to even lift his head?

He glanced up and met her eyes but didn't say anything. She handed him his jeans and watched as he struggled to pull them on. He was mortified by the weakness. Adam had always been healthy and vigorous, and work on the ranch had given him stamina and endurance. Now he could feel himself trembling after no more exertion than sitting up and pulling on a pair of jeans!

She placed a pair of homemade slippers on his feet and helped him to stand.

By the time he was on his feet, he was more than willing to drape his arm around her shoulders for support. "I'm sorry your coat took such a beating," she said, her head braced against his shoulder. "I tried to clean it for you, but I don't think it will ever be the same." She had forgotten what a large man he was until now, when he was on his feet.

"Don't worry about it," he muttered. Beads of perspiration formed on his forehead, and Caitlin felt the effort he made to concentrate as he forced himself to walk to the door, wait for her to open it, then step outside.

Thankfully they didn't have far to go. She helped him open the door, then discreetly walked away and waited until he opened it again. His color was pasty white, and she knew it was only through sheer force of will that he managed to return to the cabin.

Adam stretched out on the bed once more with a sigh, his eyes closed. She pulled the slippers off his feet, glad that she had taken the time to make them for him while he'd been unconscious. Neither one of them would have been able to get his boots on.

She studied him for a moment in silence. He needed to take off his coat as long as he was inside. He'd fallen asleep—exhausted from the exertion— and she knew that without his cooperation, she would have a difficult time.

Nevertheless, she managed to tug the sleeves off, then rolled him slightly so she could pull the coat out from under him. He never stirred.

The herbal mixture would not only ease the pain but once again ensure a good night's sleep.

Caitlin hadn't realized how late it was. She'd become hypnotized by her weaving. She almost had enough material now to make Adam a shirt—tomorrow she would cut it out.

Going through her nightly ritual of checking the animals, banking the fire and dressing for bed, Caitlin realized that she had become used to sleeping with Adam. The cabin would seem so empty when he was gone.

Blowing out the light, she quietly crawled into bed beside him. Touching his face, she was relieved to feel his natural warmth. Thank God his getting up for those few minutes didn't seem to have caused any aftereffects. The next step was getting him on his feet for longer periods of time, so that he could slowly start gaining back his strength.

She had done her job. Adam was definitely on the mend. Soon he would be strong enough to leave.

Caitlin wasn't sure why she found the thought unsettling.

Four

As the days slowly passed, Adam's returning strength became apparent. He stayed up for longer periods of time now than he was in bed. Adam found a quiet pleasure in following Caitlin around as she worked outside, feeding the burro, milking the goat, gathering eggs, as well as feeding half the wildlife in the mountains.

He was surprised to discover the number of people who called on her, either to bring her items in payment for her assistance or to ask for some of her herbal remedies.

At first the local people were shy around him, whispering among themselves whenever they happened to see him watching them. But as the days passed, they seemed to take the presence of the tall, quiet Texan for granted.

He heard one of the women teasing Caitlin about

him one day, referring to him as her sweetheart. Caitlin glanced around to see if Adam had heard the woman, quickly denying any relationship.

He wondered if the tension between them was so obvious to outsiders. Adam couldn't control his reactions to Caitlin. They seemed to have always been there inside of him, waiting to be released. The more he learned about her, the more he delighted in her.

Yet he knew so little about her. He just knew he loved her with a quiet intensity that seemed to grow with every day that passed.

Why was she living alone in the mountains? Whenever they talked, she guided the subject away from herself and asked no questions about him. Didn't she care at all about who he was and why he was in Mexico? As the days passed, Adam found himself filled with questions he couldn't answer.

On one rather warm day Adam sat outside in the sunshine and watched while Caitlin worked in her garden, preparing it for spring planting.

Spring. It certainly felt that way today. He wondered how long he'd been there and why the urgency for him to leave seemed to have disappeared.

He knew that several weeks had gone by. The weather had warmed considerably since he first came to Mexico. No doubt everyone knew he was missing by now. Why had no one come looking for him?

Maybe they had. How could anyone have found him sitting up here on a mountainside? He would have to find a way back to Monterrey. Soon. Very soon. But not today.

Adam glanced up at the sound of Caitlin's laughter. Chula was nudging her with her nose, trying to get her attention. He smiled at the picture she made, playing with the deer. She seemed so content with her life, so innocent in many ways. As though none of life's ills had ever touched her. As though she lived in a magical forest created by Disney and populated with endearing creatures.

She was different from anyone he had ever known. A very special person. What was it she had told him when he'd first regained consciousness? Something about seeing pictures in her mind, knowing when something was going to happen?

What was that called? There was a word for it. Psychic. She was psychic.

Caitlin never talked about it, but then he'd never brought the subject up again. It was as though a barrier appeared between them at the thought of discussing her psychic abilities. Then again, she just might be shy about it. Maybe he'd question her about her strange abilities sometime.

Sometime.

How much longer would he need to stay with her before his body wouldn't betray him with its weakness?

Adam hated the thought of leaving her there on the mountaintop and returning to his world alone. He kept picturing her at the ranch, making pets of all the horses and having Chula trailing along behind her. Adam smiled at the thought.

"Caitlin?"

The sound of his voice seemed to startle her, and she jumped. "Yes?" She walked over to where he sat on a log. He had shaved that morning for the first time, and Caitlin couldn't control her reaction to his handsome good looks. She tried to cover her feelings by saying, "All you need is a sombrero, and you'd be part of the land of *mañana*." He smiled, silently acknowledging his indolent position.

"That's what I wanted to talk to you about. I need to get some exercise. Could we take a short walk, do you think?"

She glanced around the clearing, aware of the warmth and sunshine that was helping to heal him. Looking back at him, she smiled. "Sure. If you think you're up to it."

Adam stood up, stretched, then dropped his arm companionably around her shoulder. "Well, there's no time like the present to find out."

"Where would you like to go?" she asked.

"How about showing me where you found me?"

She shook her head. "I really think that's too far for you to walk. But we can start out in that direction."

Adam soon discovered what she meant. The terrain was rugged, and he could scarcely believe she had been able to bring him back in his unconscious state.

He was more than ready to rest when she suggested they take advantage of an outcrop of rock to sit down. "Don't you ever get lonely living up here?" he asked after they had sat in silence for a while.

"Loneliness is a state of mind. The loneliest time of my life occurred when I lived in a large city."

"Ah—so you didn't suddenly appear here on the planet and choose this place to reside."

She laughed at his whimsy.

"I'm afraid not. Is that what you thought?"

"I've never met anyone like you. I'm not sure what to think."

She grinned impishly at him. "I take it you're not used to people who know what you're thinking."

He stared at her for a moment, then shook his head. "Sorry, I can't buy that one. I'm still trying to get used to the idea you saw what happened to me before it actually occurred."

Caitlin gazed out over the vista of mountains and trees. When she spoke, her voice was soft. "You've been trying to figure a way to ask me to go home with you."

Her quiet words caught him unprepared and he looked at her with a startled expression. Before he could comment, she continued. "The feelings you've been having about me are very natural, Adam, but don't mistake gratitude for something else. What you're feeling will eventually be forgotten once you're back home in familiar surroundings."

"How do you know what I'm thinking and feeling?" he demanded.

"Partly because I was once very ill myself. It's easy to become dependent on those who are caring for you. Your world shrinks to the very basics of existence. Everyone in that world assumes a tremendous importance to your well-being."

"You think that's why I'm attracted to you?" he asked, unconsciously acknowledging his feelings. "It couldn't have anything to do with the fact that I find you very attractive, could it?"

"I know there's a sexual awareness between us. It's very strong."

"But you don't intend to do anything about it, do you?"

"No."

Adam ran his hand through his already rumpled hair. "You refuse to see me as anything other than your patient, is that it?"

"I believe that's the wisest course to follow, yes."

"And you're always so wise," he said in a sarcastic tone.

She laughed. "Now you're feeling like a little boy who was told that candy would spoil his supper."

Adam grinned reluctantly. "I suppose you're right, at least partly. You sound so damned sure of yourself—talking as though feelings can just be brushed aside and forgotten."

"I'm sorry. That isn't what I mean. I just think we both need to recognize that we come from different worlds. It's better not to get too involved."

"What's wrong with my world?"

"Nothing," she replied.

"Then why do you avoid it?"

"I learned that the world you live in is too painful for me."

"In what way?"

"People don't want their thoughts and emotions revealed and understood. They need their masks to face life."

"Only people who have something to hide, perhaps," he offered thoughtfully.

"We all have something to hide."

Adam felt tenderness for Caitlin well up within him at the pensive expression on her face. "What do you hide, Caitlin?" he asked softly.

"Fear," she said after a moment. "Fear of rejection. Fear of being hurt."

"So you stay up here on your mountainside where you're safe."

"Yes."

He stood up and held out his hand. "Let's go home."

They were quiet on the return trip, absorbed in their thoughts.

Adam felt that he had taken the first step in understanding her a little better. He didn't care how she tried to explain his feelings away. He knew they were based on more than gratitude. He just wasn't sure what he was going to do about them.

The next morning, Adam was sitting at the table and had just finished his breakfast when Caitlin came up behind him and began to stretch a tape across his shoulders.

"What are you doing?" he asked, turning around in surprise.

"Getting your measurements. I'm making you a shirt."

Obligingly he stood up and held out his arms with a grin. "I've never had a custom-made shirt before."

"Obviously deprived," she said with an answering smile, writing something down.

"That's better than being depraved," he offered solemnly.

She glanced up at him with a puzzled expression.

He explained. "What if you had discovered once you got me back to your home that I was some sort of monster who would attack you when I recovered?"

"I wasn't worried," she replied. "I had Chula here to protect me."

They both looked over at the deer curled up asleep on the rug in front of the fireplace and grinned at each other.

Adam walked over to the door and looked out. "Think I'll chop some wood. That should help to rebuild some of my strength."

Caitlin watched him leave with something like relief. Each day it was becoming more of a trial to act relaxed and unconcerned when she was around Adam.

She knew as well as he did that what he felt toward her was more than gratitude. The thought of his falling in love with her scared her to death—because she had already faced the truth of her own feelings for him.

She loved Adam.

Who wouldn't? He had a gentleness of spirit that disarmed her, a sense of the ridiculous that kept her entertained, an integrity that shone like a beacon from his eyes. Most men would have resented anyone seeing them as weak and vulnerable as Adam had been at first. Yet he was sure enough of himself to accept his limitations as temporary and not take out any feelings of inadequacy on her.

Caitlin could see his strength slowly grow with each day that passed. Soon he would be well enough to hike down the mountainside. Then he would be gone.

Not once did she consider going with him. She had learned her lesson with Rick. No one could be comfortable living with a person like her.

Adam stayed outside most of the day. The weakness that tired him so quickly seemed to drag on day after day. When he finally went inside, he found the shirt Caitlin had made for him draped over his chair.

She was outside feeding her animals. They hadn't spoken much that day. They didn't seem to need words to communicate. A glance, a shrug, a smile— all seemed to add to the intimacy they had unwittingly established.

Adam sighed.

He was definitely on the mend. His body could attest to that. Just thinking about her created certain body changes that were uncomfortable as well as embarrassing. He had never wanted another woman the way he wanted Caitlin, and yet he had never even kissed her.

Since he'd moved out of her bed—he smiled when he remembered the night that had happened—they had carefully avoided physical contact, as though by unspoken agreement. Perhaps that was why her hands had seemed to scorch his shoulders that morning when she measured him for the shirt he was now holding.

He sat down at the table, thinking about the night when he'd seen her dragging out a well-used sleeping bag.

"What are you doing?" he'd asked, frowning.

She glanced around at him, surprised at his tone. "Going to bed. Why?"

"You don't have to sleep on the floor."

Caitlin registered no expression when she replied. "Yes, I do."

"Since when? You've seemed to rest quite comfortably curled up by my side each night."

He watched as a lovely flow of color spread over her face. "I didn't realize you knew I was there," she murmured.

He walked over to her. "Knowing you were there kept the nightmares away. I thought you knew."

Her gaze didn't quite meet his. "Well, you're not having nightmares any longer."

He took her hand and studied her palm as though preparing to give her a reading. Without looking up, he said, "But I might, if you weren't there."

She pulled her hand away as though it had been burned. "Then you'll have to deal with it. I'm not going to sleep with you."

The smile he gave her was full of mischief. "If you don't want to sleep, I'm sure we can find something to do to while away the hours."

She whirled away from him and knelt on the sleeping bag.

Adam spoke again. "If anyone's going to bed down on the floor, it will be me."

She must have heard the calm determination in his voice because she looked up at him with dismay. "You won't be able to sleep down here. And you need your rest, Adam."

He'd continued to look at her until she'd gotten up and reluctantly walked over to the bed.

Adam stared at the shirt in his hand now as he sat at the table. She had worked all day to make it for him.

Why? Why was she so willing to give her time and energy—not only to him but to anyone who needed her? Yet she was not willing to give her emotions, or herself. What had happened that had caused her to retreat from the world? He didn't know, and he couldn't leave until he had some answers; Caitlin had become too important to him. Adam had begun to face the fact that she had unobtrusively found her way into his heart. He wasn't going to be able to forget her—not now.

Adam had no choice but to try to understand this woman. He couldn't help but wonder if it would do him any good.

Adam lay in front of the fireplace late that night staring into the flickering flames, unable to sleep.

From the corner of the room he heard the quiet rustling of covers and knew Caitlin was no more asleep
than he was.

"Caitlin?"

"Yes."

"Can't you sleep?"

There was a short silence, then a sigh. "Not really.
Can you?"

"No."

"Would you like me to make us something to
drink?"

"Sounds good to me."

He heard her stirring, getting out of bed. He pictured what she was doing by the sounds she made.
He could hear her pour water into a pan, stoke up the
stove, hear the clatter of cups. After a while she appeared beside him, holding out a cup to him.

He sat up, taking the cup, and watched her sit down
in the rocking chair nearby. Caitlin wore her heavy
velour robe with a hood that she had pulled around
her head. The navy blue folds emphasized the red of
her hair and the fairness of her complexion. She gazed
at the fire in quiet contemplation and Adam felt a
calmness seep through him now that he could see her.

"Have you ever been in love, Caitlin?"

If his abrupt question startled her, she didn't show
it. Slowly her gaze moved from the mesmerizing
flames until her eyes met his. With a slight smile she
said, "I thought I was...once."

"Tell me about it."

Perhaps it was the late hour and the fact that they
could only see each other by the light of the fire.
Whatever the reason, Caitlin felt comfortable, even

protected, as though she were functioning in a dream state.

"Rick and I met in high school and dated during our last two years there. We became engaged our sophomore year of college." Her gaze returned to the fire. "We were both only children and spoiled—although neither of us were aware of that, of course. We'd had happy childhoods: things had always happened the way we wanted them to. We saw no reason why we couldn't expect our plans to continue to work out as we envisioned them. We were going to marry after graduation, wait three years to have children—"

She suddenly stopped speaking. Adam waited. Eventually she lifted her hand and made a slight dismissing gesture.

"It didn't work out that way."

After several minutes of silence Adam relaxed on his sleeping bag, his arms folded behind his head. "Did he find someone else?" he asked in a quiet voice.

She shrugged, never taking her eyes off the dancing flames. "The accident ended everything."

"What sort of accident?"

"Mom, Dad and I had been to the King Dome to watch a football game. We were on our way home when we were hit head-on by a speeding car whose driver was attempting to outrun a police car. I happened to be in the back seat. The doctors say that was the only thing that saved me. They say Mom was killed instantly and Dad died a few hours after arriving at the hospital."

"My God!"

"I was in a coma for several weeks. When I began to come out of it I 'saw' the accident happen, as though I was a witness to it. Then I 'watched' Rick when he heard the news of the accident. I saw him visit me in the intensive care unit while I was unconscious and felt his revulsion at the sight of me.''

''Is that when you developed your psychic abilities?''

''I didn't develop them. They were just there after the accident. When I regained consciousness, I knew what the doctors were going to say before they said it. More importantly, I knew what they weren't saying.''

She glanced down at Adam lying on the floor near her feet and for a moment couldn't remember what she had been saying. The light from the fire shed a golden glow over his upper body, lovingly outlining the planes and hollows as he lay there, his cover carelessly pushed to his waist. She couldn't see his eyes but felt their gaze on her.

Her thoughts changed course abruptly, and she wondered why she was telling him about her past. She'd never talked about it with anyone before.

Caitlin shook her head in confusion.

''How did Rick take the change in you?'' Adam asked in a matter-of-fact tone.

''He was appalled when he discovered that I could tell what he was thinking and feeling, particularly when it was a contradiction to what he was saying. He denied it, said I was making up everything as an excuse to break up with him. That's when I knew my relationship with Rick was over, and that at the very best of times, it had been very shallow and one-dimensional.''

Adam found himself thankful that the relationship

had ended, then felt a flash of guilt because he knew how she must have suffered. "What happened then?"

"Eventually I was well enough to go home. Only there was no home for me. Certainly not in the house where I'd spent my entire life with my parents." Caitlin stared into the fire, seemingly lost in her memories. In a low voice she continued, "I couldn't deal with all the changes taking place around me, as well as all the internal confusion I was experiencing at the time."

Slowly turning her gaze until she focused on Adam's face, she searched for the words to try to explain what she had never attempted to express before. "The most difficult part was trying to relate to the people all around me. I could no longer tolerate crowds. Everyone's thoughts and feelings seemed to bombard me and I would go home feeling emotionally bruised and battered."

Adam could see the strain that discussing her past was causing Caitlin. He also sensed that she needed to talk about it—to face it and come to terms with it. He waited patiently for her to continue.

Finally she said, "I didn't understand what had happened to me. I was not only trying to come to terms with my grief, but I was also convinced I was losing my mind."

They sat in silence, and Caitlin realized that she was experiencing a sense of security she hadn't felt since her parents' deaths.

Adam rolled over on his side and propped himself up on one elbow. "I don't believe you were losing your mind. In my line of work our intuitive powers have oftentimes been the only thing that saved us." He absently toyed with the clasp on the zipper of the sleeping bag, flicking it back and forth with his finger. "Obviously your abilities were enhanced in some manner not easily explainable. But that doesn't make them any less real."

For the first time since his arrival, Adam had given her an opening to ask him some questions of her own.

"What is your line of work, Adam?"

He smiled. "I assumed you'd already figured that out."

"I know that you're not what you appear to be. You have a secret life that few people know about. That you're a decent, honest man, but you don't let many people get close to you." She wondered how much she could say without offending him. Hesitating briefly, she added, "There's a wall around you, an emotional wall, that no one would dare try to scale."

Adam's eyes narrowed slightly at her words, but his expression didn't change. "I can see why your friends would be uneasy around you. A person can't have any secrets from you."

She sensed a hint of hostility, which didn't surprise her. She had grown used to that sort of reaction.

"I don't know why you carry a gun," she pointed out with a smile.

He studied her in silence for a few moments. She had responded to his probing questions, despite the pain the answers had caused her. He owed her nothing less than a complete and honest response to her questions.

Adam shifted slightly, aware of the floor's hard surface despite the padding of the rug and sleeping bag.

"Before I can explain that," he finally said, "I need to fill you in a little on my background." He paused for a moment, gathering his thoughts. "The

St. Clair ranch has been in my family for several generations,'' he began slowly. "I was just a kid when my dad died, leaving my mom, sister and I to run the place." His eyes sought hers. "Thank God we had a dependable foreman, or we'd never have made it. Mom died when I was a teenager, and I became responsible for my sister, Felicia."

Now Caitlin had an opportunity to satisfy her curiosity. "Is she tall, blonde, with green eyes?"

Adam looked startled for a brief moment, then grinned. "That's her."

"And she's in love with the man who runs the ranch with you?"

Adam abruptly sat up. "Dane Rineholt?"

"Is he part owner of the ranch?"

Slowly Adam relaxed, staring at Caitlin with something close to dismay. Her abilities were definitely unsettling at times. "Yes," he said, "as a matter of fact he is. He became my partner several years ago. What with low beef prices and a drought, I almost lost the ranch until he came along." In a musing tone he added, "So Felicia's in love with Dane. That explains a lot."

"Didn't you know?" she asked, surprised that he hadn't been aware of something that came to her so clearly.

"I had my suspicions," he admitted. "I'd never seen Felicia react so strongly toward someone the way she did to him. At times I was convinced she hated him. I wonder if he knows how she feels?"

"Yes, I think he does." In her mind, she saw them together. "Is Felicia at the ranch now?"

Adam shook his head. "Not that I know of. As far

as I know, she's in Los Angeles. She works for a
magazine there.''

Caitlin could see Felicia at the ranch and for a moment felt the tremendous grief experienced by the
other woman. Felicia thought Adam was dead. Her
love for her brother was graphically portrayed by the
depth of her suffering. She must have come home
when she heard Adam was missing.

"She loves you very much," she murmured.

"No more than I love her." He stood up, and Caitlin stiffened until she realized he still wore his jeans,
even though he was shirtless and barefoot. Adam
placed more wood on the fire, his movements making
the muscles in his arms and shoulders ripple under
the smooth expanse of his skin.

He's beautiful, Caitlin thought with something like
dismay, *both inside and out. I've never known another man like him.*

When he sat down again, Adam briefly glanced at
Caitlin, then looked away as though uncomfortable.
"You're right, you know," he admitted rather reluctantly. "I don't let very many people get close to me.
Dane and Felicia are the only ones. At one time I had
hopes they'd end up together, but Felicia was all fired
up to have a career of her own. As for Dane—you
never know what he's thinking."

He stretched out on the sleeping bag once more.
"Dane had been at the ranch a few years before I
realized he was involved in something besides ranching. I found out he was working with the authorities
to help stop the drug smuggling across the border. At
the time the whole idea sounded exciting to me, and
I insisted on getting in on it."

"Is that what you're doing down here now?" Cait-

lin forced herself to think about what he was saying
and tried to ignore how much the sight of him affected her.

"Yes. However, after two years I've discovered
there's more drudgery than excitement, and more danger than I anticipated."

She could certainly understand that after what she
had witnessed. "Did those men who tried to kill you
know you were with the drug enforcement people?"

"I don't know. I wish I did. I've been working
undercover, getting involved with a group of smugglers transporting the drugs. In the process other deal-
ers have been pushed out." His gaze met hers. "Any
number of factions could have wanted to get rid of
me without even knowing I'm an agent."

Caitlin shivered. "You're lucky to be alive," she
said, her gaze drawn hypnotically to the blaze once
again.

"Yes. But I wouldn't have made it without you."
He studied her profile, which was partially lit by the
firelight. "You never told me how you got from
Seattle, Washington, to the mountains of Mexico.
What made you move?"

"I used to have an aunt who lived in San Antonio.
When I was younger, I spent part of my summer vacation with her. She loved the mountains, and we always went to Monterrey whenever I visited." She
leaned her head back against the chair and closed her
eyes.

"During the months after the accident when I was
sure I was going crazy, I would remember the mountains and the peace and serenity I'd always felt whenever I was here."

"There are mountains in the States, you know," he said quietly.

"Yes, I know. I lived near the Cascade Range. But these had become familiar friends. I found myself dreaming about them and began to see myself living in a cabin high in the mountains—away from everything and everyone."

"You escaped from the pressure of your new awareness."

"Yes."

"Caitlin, no one can escape life indefinitely."

"I'm not escaping from life. I have my own life here, and I'm content with it."

"Alone?" His intent gaze met hers, and Caitlin discovered she was having difficulty meeting his eyes.

"I enjoy being alone."

"You feel safer being alone, you mean. There's a difference." Adam slowly came to his feet. He reached down and took her hand from her lap, gently pulling her up to stand in front of him.

Cupping his hands around her face, he tilted her head so that she was looking up at him from only a few inches away. "You've left out one very important ingredient in your life, you know."

Her eyes felt locked to his gaze. She could feel his body aligned against hers and could barely prevent the shiver that tingled down her spine. Caitlin seemed to have lost her power of speech, and she unconsciously ran her tongue across her dry lips.

"What's that?" she managed to ask.

"You've allowed no room in your life for love." Adam closed the distance between them, pulling her closer against him while he did what he'd been wanting to do for days…weeks…possibly a lifetime.

Adam kissed her. He touched, tasted and explored the wonders she had to offer, moving with careful ease—touching her upper lip with his tongue, softly nibbling on her bottom lip, pulling it into his mouth and at the same time finding entry for his tongue. He took his time, lazily exploring her with his mouth, his hands, his entire body. She felt so good in his arms, better, if possible, than his dreams and imaginings had led him to believe. He wondered how he had ever been able to live with her this long without touching her. He knew in that moment that he never wanted to spend another day that didn't include her in his arms.

Caitlin felt as though she were in shock. During the past several years no one had touched her. She had forgotten how it felt to have someone's arms around her, hugging her. She hadn't known how it would feel to be pressed so closely to the man who had occupied so much of her time and thoughts during the past few weeks.

His kiss seemed to paralyze her, as though by his touch Adam had taken possession of her soul. No one had ever kissed her in the lazy yet very thorough way he was doing, filling her mind and senses with a yearning to be a part of another person, to accept his possession, give in to his silent insistence that the two of them belonged together.

Was he aware of the growing feelings for him that had become a part of her? Did he know what his touch was doing to her?

Sometime during that kiss Caitlin tentatively began to respond. Her tongue met his in a shy greeting, and she slid her arms timidly around his neck in an effort to get closer to him and to enjoy the wondrous sensations that seemed to be bubbling up from within her and flowing throughout her body like expensive champagne.

When her knees gave way, Adam effortlessly lifted her in his arms and knelt in front of the fireplace, placing her on his sleeping bag. Her hood had long since fallen from her head, and while one arm held her close to him, he slipped the robe from her shoulders.

Stretching out to lie beside her, Adam continued to kiss her—soft kisses on her eyes, her cheeks, her nose—then, as though starved for the taste of her, his mouth sought hers once more.

Her voluminous flannel gown demurely buttoned from the waist to the ruffled neckline at the throat. Because of the tremor in his hand, Adam fumbled with the buttonholes for a moment. When they were opened, he slipped his hand inside her gown and felt the heat of her body against his palm.

Adam wanted her so badly he ached with it. He needed to touch and explore her, to discover everything there was to know about her, to claim her and make her a part of who and what he was, just as he would become a part of her in the same way.

When his hand slid to her breast and encircled it, he felt her body move convulsively.

"It's all right, love," he said in a low, gentle voice. "I want to love you, that's all. Just love you." He leaned down and placed his mouth over the tip of her breast, his tongue playfully nudging the extremely sensitive peak.

Deep-rooted alarms began to jangle within Caitlin. She had always been shy, even with Rick. Despite her engagement, she had never allowed him the freedom Adam was currently enjoying. Caitlin knew that once she gave herself to Adam she would never be the same again. That in the giving of herself to him she would lose a necessary part of her survival abilities—her need to live apart from the world, which included Adam.

She lowered her trembling hands from around his neck so that she could move away from him. Instead, her hands slid to his hair, the soft curls wrapping around her fingers the same way he had managed to wrap himself around her heart.

Adam felt her stiffen, her hands restlessly clutching his head to her breast. Her rapid breathing resulted in a soft panting that he found extremely erotic. Reluctantly he raised his head and looked down into her face.

Slowly she opened her eyes.

He saw her flushed cheeks and kiss-swollen lips. The expression in her eyes was so vulnerable that it almost brought tears to his.

She saw his eyes burning with desire and a deeper emotion that almost frightened her with its intensity. His mouth was slightly moist from repeated contact with hers.

"I love you, Caitlin."

The words were so soft they scarcely made a ripple in the silence around them; their impact was so profound they could have been shouted.

She lay beside him, dazed with the avalanche of feelings that had almost buried her during the past several moments.

"You can't," she finally managed to say.

His mouth turned up with a quirk of amusement. "And who's going to stop me?"

"But you mustn't."

"Why not?"

"It won't work."

"What won't work?" he asked with amused patience.

"You. Me. Us."

"On the contrary, my love. I think you...
me...us...work very well together." He glanced
down at his hand where it rested lovingly cupped
around her breast. One of his legs lay across both of
hers, leaving her in no doubt how much he was affected by her. "There's nothing to be afraid of, you
know," he continued. "Loving someone is very normal and natural. I think you'll find it quite enjoyable,
once you get used to the idea."

Caitlin closed her eyes, unable to face the warm
expression on his face, the loving concern in his eyes.

"I can't, Adam. Don't ask that of me."

"You can't what, little one?"

"Love you." She refused to open her eyes and see
how he accepted her statement. She felt him tense
slightly, then he shifted, moving his hand and leg so
that he was no longer intimately touching her.

"Why not?" he finally asked in the charged silence.

"Surely that's obvious. Our lifestyles are not exactly compatible." She turned her head and opened
her eyes so that she could watch the fire and not see
his face.

"Lifestyles have been altered before, you know,"
he pointed out in a light tone that in no way disguised
the seriousness of his remark.

"Somehow I can't see you spending the rest of
your life here in the mountains with me."

"And is this where you intend to spend the rest of your life, Caitlin? Here in the mountains?"

"Yes."

The word was stark, to the point, and uttered without hesitation.

"I see," Adam finally said in a low voice.

Did he? Could he possibly see and understand the pain she had escaped from? It had taken her years to accept her difference from other people, to realize that she could find no other place where she would be safe from the stigma of being different.

She had tried to fit in, had honestly tried. After missing months of school she had returned to college, only to discover how different the world was when another person's thoughts and desires were known to her and when she learned how seldom a person said what he thought or believed. She discovered how little people respected truth.

Caitlin knew that Adam wanted to make love to her. She didn't need her psychic abilities to gain that information. She even knew that he was sincere in expressing what he felt for her.

For now. Once he returned to his real life, he'd realize how out of place she would be. She didn't belong in his world. She never would.

Adam sat up, leaning his elbows on his bent knees, his head in his hands. His head pounded with the sexual excitement that pumped through his body.

"Your head hurts," Caitlin said, feeling his physical and emotional pain as though it were her own.

"Among other things," he acknowledged wryly.

She got up, slipped her robe back onto her shoulders and went to the stove. The water was still hot. She quickly made him a drink from the herbs that would ease his pain. Bringing it back to him, she silently handed him the cup.

He looked at it in surprise. His mind had been filled with a whirlwind of thoughts, explanations, ideas, arguments. And pain. The pain seemed to wash over all the rest, coloring them, expanding them, overwhelming them.

Without thinking, he took a sip of the hot liquid, belatedly remembering the bitter taste of the drink. Somehow the taste fit his mood, and he quickly drained the contents, then stood up.

"I'll bring in more wood. You'd better try to get some sleep." He didn't look at her. Caitlin could feel his need to get away from her, away from the cloying confines of the cabin. Without saying a word, she walked over, took off her robe and crawled into bed. She watched Adam walk out into the night, his coat collar turned up against the cold. He closed the door quietly behind him.

She hadn't wanted to hurt him. But wasn't it better to face reality now rather than wait until the unsuitability of a relationship between them became as obvious to him as it was to her?

Caitlin curled up on her side, with her back to the door. There was no exact measurement for pain, she decided, drifting off to sleep. It was just there, trapping the unwary with its sudden needle-sharp presence.

Five

Caitlin woke up the next morning to the scent of freshly brewed coffee. Pushing her hair away from her face, she realized she had overslept. Adam had drawn the curtain that shielded the bed from the rest of the room, leaving that corner in shadows.

She must have gone to sleep almost immediately after returning to bed. She never heard Adam come back into the cabin.

As soon as she was dressed, Caitlin slid the curtain back, unsurprised to discover herself alone in the cabin. She was always so aware of Adam that she knew she would have felt his presence had he been there.

Opening the door, she looked around the clearing. It was empty. She felt almost disoriented. This was the first morning since Adam had been at the cabin that she had slept longer than he had. Her morning routine seemed fuzzy in her head, and she wasn't sure what to do first.

Caitlin wandered into the lean-to and found Adam milking the goat.

"You have talents I never suspected," she said with a smile, trying to lighten the atmosphere between them.

He had filled the pail and was setting it aside when she spoke. He glanced up at her, then looked away, but not before she saw the expression in his eyes. Their gray-green depths spoke of love and hurt, passion and pain. He hadn't succeeded in putting the night behind him any better than she had.

"I thought you could use some help this morning," he responded, his tone even. Getting up from the small stool, he leaned over, picked up the pail of milk and handed it to her.

"You didn't have to do that."

"I know. But you needed your rest."

"How long have you been awake?"

"I don't know. Does it matter?" He started back toward the cabin. Without looking at her, he said, "I'm leaving today."

She'd known that from the moment she had opened her eyes. She just hadn't wanted to face it.

"Can you tell me how to get to the village from here?"

"I'll show you."

"That really isn't necessary."

How polite they had become with each other.

"I'm afraid it is. I don't think you would find it otherwise. The path isn't defined. I use several animal trails to get there. You would have to know when to leave one and look for another." She went into the cabin and put the milk away. "I'll get breakfast ready and prepare something to eat along the way."

"How long does it take to get there?"

"About two hours, depending on the pace."

There didn't seem to be much else to say. Caitlin returned his pistol and holster to him. He checked it over, then put it on without comment. They moved carefully around each other, consciously refraining from touching, as though by keeping a proper distance they could maintain the polite fiction they had adopted of being merely acquaintances and nothing more.

Breakfast passed in silence, and within the hour Adam and Caitlin were hiking down the trail toward the village.

She set an easy pace, unobtrusively making certain that he didn't tire, pointing out areas of interest as they went along. He listened without comment, observing everything around them.

By the time they reached the village, Adam knew he'd pushed himself and was disgusted at the signs of weakness. His body had never let him down before, but he knew he was running on nerves and sheer willpower. There was no point in delaying his return to the real world, as he thought of it. And there was a definite danger in staying. He loved Caitlin, and continuing to share the small cabin with her without making love to her was a torture he didn't intend to continue.

They walked through the main street of the village, with Caitlin pointing out the shops, and ended up at a small taverna where they ordered something to drink while Adam talked to the owner.

A few people recognized him from their visits to

see Caitlin, and they surprised him by greeting him with shy smiles. He could see why Caitlin had grown attached to these people.

Right now he had to keep his mind on his priorities. He needed transportation north. Without money or identification, transportation might prove difficult.

His conversation with the owner of the taverna didn't improve his mood any.

"What's wrong?" Caitlin asked when he returned to the table where she waited.

"I hadn't realized how remote we are. There's very little traffic through the village. I'm going to have to stick around and take my chances on getting out of here."

Caitlin could see the lines of strain around his eyes and the dark smudges beneath them that betrayed his lack of sleep from the night before. She felt the dull throb of pain in his head. This was too soon for him to be so active, but she knew she couldn't ask him to stay any longer. For both their sakes, he had to go.

They left the taverna, and Caitlin went to one of the small shops where she bought a few supplies. Conversation had become more and more difficult between them. And why not? There was nothing to add to what had already been said the night before.

Eventually Caitlin faced the fact that there was nothing more for her to do in the village. She glanced around at the empty street, then at Adam. "I really need to start back. It will be dark soon."

"Yes."

Hesitantly she placed her hand on the sleeve of his coat. "Take care of yourself." She watched a small muscle leap in his jaw and knew he was finding their leave-taking as difficult as she was.

"You, too."

They stood there for a moment in silence, then Caitlin said, "Well—goodbye, Adam. God bless."

She turned and walked away from him, forcing herself not to glance over her shoulder.

Caitlin had taken three or four steps when she heard Adam's voice.

"Wait!" She turned around and found him striding toward her. "I'll be damned if I'm going to tell you goodbye in the middle of some godforsaken Mexican settlement with everyone looking on." He took her firmly by the elbow and began to walk beside her. "Since it doesn't look as though I'll be leaving here for a while, I can go partway with you."

Caitlin could feel her heart pounding painfully in her chest. This was much harder than she could handle without breaking down, but she had no choice.

"Are you going to be okay?" he asked when she remained silent.

She nodded without looking at him.

"Aren't you even going to talk to me?"

Looking straight ahead, she said, "What do you want me to say?"

"How about 'I'm going to miss you, Adam'?"

"That goes without saying."

"No, it doesn't. I want to hear it."

She stopped. They were above the settlement now, out of sight of any signs of civilization. The western sun bathed him in a golden glow of gilt. She would never forget the way he looked at that moment, not as long as she lived. She forced herself to meet his gaze, her eyes filling with tears despite her best intentions.

"I'm going to miss you, Adam," she managed to say past the lump that had formed in her throat.

With slow, deliberate movements, he slipped his arms around her, pulling her close to him. "I'm going to miss you, too, darlin'. More important, I'm going to miss my heart, since it's staying here in the mountains with you. I'm not sure how well I'm going to be able to function without it."

Caitlin rested her head against his chest. Her tears finally overflowed and slowly trickled down her cheeks.

"Oh, Adam" was all she could say.

With his forefinger under her chin, Adam tilted her head so that his mouth found hers. His possession seemed perfectly natural to both of them, familiar because she was such a part of him. Adam didn't know how he was going to walk away from her. She had become as necessary to him as the air that filled his lungs and gave him life. He loved her. How could he possibly leave her?

Caitlin felt as though she no longer had a will of her own. As soon as Adam touched her, she became pliant in his arms. Her response to his kiss left no doubt in either one's mind that she shared his feelings.

They stood there in the mountain wilderness, clinging to each other, devastated by the impending loss they faced.

The whine of a bullet and the cracking sound of the discharge came simultaneously, and Adam reacted automatically. He pushed Caitlin toward the ground, shoving her behind a boulder alongside the trail. Another shot was fired, and pieces of the rock ricocheted around them.

"Are you all right?" he whispered, touching Caitlin on the shoulder. Not looking at him, she nodded without speaking.

The sudden unexpected attack left them both stunned. Violence had no business in the peaceful mountains, and yet it had found them.

"I've got to see who this is. Stay here and don't move, okay?" Once again she nodded.

Adam's gun was already in his hand, and he crept farther away from the trail, circling the area where the gunshots had been fired. He kept the brush, boulders and trees between him and his would-be assailant, moving as rapidly as possible on silent feet.

It hadn't occurred to Adam that someone was still out to kill him. How had they traced him to the village? He wondered how long they had been waiting for him to appear. Like some amateur, he'd walked right into their hands without suspecting anything, making no attempt to cover his tracks.

Because of his carelessness he'd managed to involve Caitlin. Damn. He couldn't leave her alone now. The picture had changed. She would have to go with him. Adam silently cursed again. How could he have done this to her?

A cold fury swept over him. He would find out who this was and get to the bottom of the situation.

The woods were silent. The gunman had stopped firing. Adam paused, torn between going after him and getting Caitlin away from there. He couldn't take any chances with her life. Hesitating for only a moment, he made his decision and turned back to where he'd left Caitlin waiting.

She hadn't moved but sat huddled, her head resting on her drawn-up knees. He knelt down beside her.

"I've lost him for the moment," he whispered. "He's probably watching the trail we were on, waiting for us to reappear. There's no telling who he is. He could have been sitting there in the taverna for all I know."

Caitlin raised her head, her face totally without color. Slowly she shook her head. "No, he wasn't. I would have noticed him." She paused, as though gathering her thoughts. "He's the same man who drove the car that forced you off the road."

Adam studied her intently, not liking the look of her eyes. She was going into shock, which wasn't surprising. Not many people were used to being shot at. "Are you sure?"

"Reasonably."

"Damn! I wish I could see him…know who I'm looking for."

He stood, taking her arm and pulling her up, too. She winced and moved away from him. "Look, Adam. I'll go on back to the cabin. Maybe if you return to the village, someone will be able to point him out to you. After all, everyone there would know when there's a stranger in town. I should have thought to ask."

"I wasn't thinking very clearly myself today." All of his thoughts had been on the pain of leaving Caitlin behind. His lack of clear thinking had almost gotten them killed.

She tried to move away from him, but he still held her arm. "I don't want you continuing on that path." He guided her behind the rocks for some distance until he spotted a trail he had seen earlier. "Follow that until you get over the ridge. I'll be along shortly."

"No." She met his gaze squarely.

"What do you mean, no?"

"There's no reason for you to come back to the cabin. You need to stay at the village. I'll be okay."

He stared at her for a moment in silence. She was upset, and he supposed she had every reason to be. Adam saw no point in standing there debating the issue. He would see what he could find, then return to the cabin.

Without commenting on her statement, he leaned over and gently kissed her, then watched as she turned away and began to follow the path. He waited until she had disappeared from view before he started down once more.

He didn't like the shocked state Caitlin was in. Her color was pasty white, her eyes dilated, her breathing labored. He couldn't leave her alone after what she'd gone through today.

But if he could find the gunman first, that would be a relief to both of them.

After thoroughly searching the area, Adam found nothing but some shell casings. Whoever he was, he must have decided to withdraw and wait for another time.

Adam silently thanked him for the warning. He would be better prepared next time.

He started back up the trail toward the cabin and Caitlin. Adam had to know that she was all right. He reached the place where the gunman had fired at them and stepped off the path, intending to follow the same route she had in case he could catch up with her before she reached home.

Glancing down, he caught sight of color, brilliant and damp. He bent closer to examine what looked to be blood. With a gnawing feeling in the pit of his stomach, he touched one of the small drops and confirmed his suspicion.

As he followed the trail of blood that led into the mountains, a helpless anger wrapped itself around him.

She'd been hit. And she hadn't even told him.

Damn her! Why hadn't she said something? He should have known that her shocked condition was more than just being scared. She was too strong for that. He remembered that she'd kept her arms across her chest, her hands tightly gripping her shoulders.

Her shoulder! Of course. He hadn't seen it because he hadn't been looking for it. His mind had been on the gunman. She hadn't made a sound when she was hit. He shook his head. He wasn't sure at the moment what he would do when he found her, hug her or murder her himself!

But first he had to find her.

She had made considerable progress along the trail. He'd almost decided she'd gotten all the way back to the cabin when he saw her. She probably would have made it if she hadn't stopped to rest.

She sat next to a large tree, her body braced against it, her head back and her eyes closed. Her hand still clutched her shoulder, but now the blood had soaked through her heavy hand-woven shirt, covering her fingers and slowly dripping down her arm.

When Adam reached out to touch her, he absently noted that his hand was shaking, which surprised him. An icy calm had seemed to settle over him as soon as he saw her.

"Let me see," he said, his voice gruff.

Her head came up in a convulsive jerk, her eyes

flying open. Her pale skin looked transparent. "What are you doing here?"

He knelt beside her, gently removing her hand from her shoulder and ignoring her question. "Why didn't you tell me you were hurt, dammit," he said through gritted teeth. "How bad is it?"

Wearily she rested her head against the tree once more. "I'm all right, Adam. It's just a flesh wound. By the time I get some medication on it, I'll be fine. There was no reason for you to come back."

"That's a matter of opinion. If I hadn't been worried and decided to check on how you were, you could have been passed out along the trail somewhere."

"No. I just needed to rest a few moments, that's all."

He lifted her shirt away, exposing her shoulder. The bullet had grazed her upper shoulder, leaving a jagged tear in her flesh.

"It's not all that bad," she insisted.

"Bad enough," he replied, getting to his feet. He picked her up and started toward the cabin.

"Adam, don't carry me. You're in no condition to—"

"If you know what's good for you, you won't say another word," he said through clenched jaws. "Not one…more…word."

Caitlin hurt too badly to talk. Every step she'd taken jolted and jarred her until she had almost cried out with the pain. She had seen too many wounds not to understand that hers was not serious. But she couldn't deny that it hurt.

Wearily she leaned her head on Adam's shoulder, too tired to argue. He was there, regardless of what she could say. He was also very angry with her. Caitlin had never seen Adam angry before. She wasn't sure she ever wanted to see him angry again.

That was the last thing she remembered thinking.

By the time Adam reached the clearing, he realized that Caitlin was either asleep or unconscious. Either one was a blessing at the moment. There was barely enough light to find his way across the clearing. He shoved the cabin door open with his foot and felt his way over to the bed.

The room was cold, since they had put out the fire before leaving that morning. Adam lit the lamp, covered Caitlin with a blanket and built a fire that quickly took the chill from the room.

He pumped some water into a bowl and made preparations to clean her wound. Quickly undressing her, he left only her panties on since her bra was in the way of the area where he needed to work. He covered her with a blanket, leaving the wounded area exposed.

"How are you feeling?" he asked in a neutral tone, while he bathed and cleaned the wounded area.

"All right," she whispered.

The weakness in her voice filled him with pain. "Of course you are," he said through gritted teeth. The jagged wound in her delicate skin caused him to curse silently to himself. She didn't deserve this. Caitlin of all people had no use for violence. She was a healer—a gentle, caring person who had no business being mixed up with him and what he was doing.

He poured a cup of water for her and, after gently lifting her head, held the cup to her lips. She drank from the cup, then laid her head back against the pillow with a sigh.

There was no sense letting her know how upset he

was. Brushing her hair away from her brow, he tried to smile, but since he was still concerned over her pallor, his lips barely moved.

"We've reversed our roles, I guess," she said in response to his smile.

"Looks that way."

"Adam, please don't feel you have to stay here with me. I know you need to get back to Monterrey."

"Dammit, Caitlin, don't you understand that things have changed now? Whoever is after me not only knows I'm not dead, but also knows approximately where they can find me and that I'm with you. I can't go off and leave you unprotected."

"They don't want me. Even if they managed to find this cabin—which I doubt very much—once they discovered you were gone, they'd have no further interest in me."

"A nice thought to hold." He got up and added more firewood onto the fire. Without turning around he said, "Do you want something to eat?"

"Not particularly."

"I think I'll heat up some soup. Maybe you'll feel like eating some by the time I have it ready."

He knew he was not hiding his fear and frustration very well, but he couldn't seem to help it. He couldn't remember ever having been quite so scared. The realization that Caitlin was hurt had frightened him even more than the knowledge that his car was being forced off the road.

The relief he'd felt at seeing the flesh wound had been transmitted as anger. Determined to get a grip on his emotions, he found a pan and began to heat the soup.

Caitlin was asleep by the time it was ready, and he decided that rest was the best thing for her.

Adam ate, then paced the floor, trying to decide what to do. Periodically he checked the bandage he'd placed on her shoulder. There was no sign of bleeding. He knew her arm and shoulder would be stiff and sore by morning, but hopefully there would be no infection.

Remembering how effective the drink was for relieving pain, Adam made up some of the tea she had given to him. He almost laughed at the sleepy face she made as she drank it. Served her right. However, the brew worked, and that was the important thing. She would be able to rest more comfortably now.

When he realized there was nothing further he could do, he went outside and fed the animals, including Chula, who had followed him into the lean-to and nosed into his hip pocket, looking for something to eat. Adam returned to the cabin and checked on Caitlin. She hadn't stirred.

Now that the adrenaline had stopped flowing through him, Adam realized how tired he was. After little or no sleep the night before, he'd put in a physically exhausting day, not to mention the wear and tear on his emotions. He was more than ready to get some rest himself.

The bedroll was lying against the wall where he'd left it that morning. He glanced over his shoulder at Caitlin. Would he hear her if she stirred and needed something? He knew she'd never ask him for help; she was so damned independent.

Of course, if he were to sleep on the other half of the bed, she couldn't move without his being aware of it. What a thin excuse to justify something he wanted to do, he reflected. If it was up to him, he would spend every night for the rest of his life in her bed. He wondered if he'd ever convince her that the idea held considerable merit.

Quietly Adam undressed and crawled into bed next to her. He could feel the tight muscles in his body relax, and he sighed with relief. He'd certainly earned the right to a good night's rest.

Caitlin stirred restlessly beside him, and he shifted toward her. Leaning on his elbow, Adam looked down at her. She seemed to be dreaming, muttering something, restlessly shifting her head and arms. He was afraid she was going to jar her shoulder, but he wasn't sure what he could do to help.

Hesitantly he brushed her hair from her forehead. The touch of his hand seemed to soothe her, and she quietened. He moved closer and murmured comfortingly. The slight frown line between her brow disappeared, and she relaxed against him.

Adam drifted off to sleep with his arm draped across her, his hand tangled in her hair.

Caitlin was so thirsty. Her throat hurt whenever she tried to swallow. And her shoulder felt as though a branding iron was being held against it, searing the flesh. She whimpered, the noise bringing her fully awake and aware of her surroundings.

The first thing she noticed was that Adam was beside her in bed, sleeping heavily. The second thing she noticed was that he had an arm and a leg thrown over her, effectively stopping her from moving.

She felt so vulnerable tucked away in his arms, particularly since neither one of them had on much in the way of clothing. She wore a pair of panties, and he'd dispensed with everything but his briefs.

The nights she had slept beside him had been nothing like this. Now they were sleeping like lovers.

Lovers. Wasn't that what they were in every sense—except for the physical expression of that love? In the quiet hours of the night, Caitlin faced the depth of their feelings for each other.

She probably would have fallen for Adam, regardless of the circumstances that brought them together, but caring for him when he was so vulnerable had made an indelible impression on her. She was also aware of his feelings for her. They were equally intense. He hadn't needed to explain them. She knew.

However, not even for the love she felt for him and he felt for her could she leave the retreat that had given her back her sanity. Their love had been given an opportunity to develop and expand in a carefully controlled environment. In the outside world, their love could easily shrivel and disappear through no fault of theirs.

Adam had only been with her in her own surroundings. He didn't know how upset she became around people who seemed to crowd in on her from all directions. And there was no way she could explain her feelings to him so that he would understand.

No one seemed to fully understand the trauma she experienced. She had to deal with it in the best way she knew how. Living in the mountains was her solution.

Perhaps Adam could come back to visit her from time to time. She smiled at the possible positive solution. Just knowing he was a part of her life, however distant, would be a comfort to her.

The throbbing pain in her shoulder drew her atten-

tion away from her thoughts, and she shifted restlessly, trying to ease the discomfort.

Adam woke up immediately.

"Are you all right, darlin'?" he mumbled, his
words slurred with sleep. His hand shifted so that it
lay across her breast. He stiffened and hastily removed his arm and leg from her.

"I'm a little thirsty, that's all," she said in a whisper, her voice nonexistent.

He sat up. "I'll get you some more of that ghastly
brew. It should help the pain, as well as quench your
thirst. In fact, you may never want anything else to
drink after that." He got out of bed and strode over
to the cabinet. While waiting for the water to heat, he
wandered back over to her.

"I hope you don't mind my sharing the bed with
you. I was afraid I wouldn't hear you if you needed
anything."

"I don't mind," she said quietly, although she
didn't look at him.

He went back and made her drink. When she sat
up, she remembered her state of undress. "Would you
mind handing me my robe?" she asked with as much
dignity as she could muster.

"Why? Do you need to get up?"

"No. I don't have any clothes on."

"Oh." He draped a soft woolen shawl over her
shoulders. "There. That should keep the chill off
you."

Since she held the cup in both of her hands, she
had no recourse but to sit quietly while he arranged
the folds of the shawl to suit his purposes, his knuckles continuing to brush provocatively against her bare
breasts.

Her breathing quickened, and Adam knew she was no more immune to what they shared than he was. He crawled back into bed carefully so that she wouldn't spill her drink. Stretching out beside her, he lay there enjoying the intimate view of her profile so close to him.

"Surely you can see that I can't leave you here now," he said in a reasonable tone. "As soon as you're feeling well enough to travel, I'll take you home with me."

His calm determination unsettled her, but she refused to allow him to see her reaction to his statement. "Nothing has changed, Adam. I'm not leaving here."

"The hell it hasn't!" he exclaimed, forgetting his promise to himself to stay calm and quiet. "There's someone out there who tried to kill you!"

"Not me. No one was shooting at me. I just got in the way."

"If you think I find that statement comforting, you're wrong. You can't stay here, Caitlin. That's all there is to it."

"It isn't your choice to make, Adam." Her voice from the shadows sounded very firm and filled with conviction.

But he had to try to get her to see reason. "How are you going to take care of yourself?"

"The same way I always have. My shoulder is going to be a little stiff and sore for a few days, but I'm all right." Her voice was beginning to sound drowsy, and he knew the tea was working its magic on her.

He took the cup and helped her slide back down into the covers. "I love you so damned much," he muttered in frustration.

"You can always come back to visit me, you know."

"You can be certain I'm going to do that! I haven't given up on us. Not by a long shot. But I've got to get back to the States and let everyone know I'm still alive and that someone is trying their best to remedy that situation."

She turned over so that she was facing him. "Be careful, please. You are so special, Adam. I don't want anything to happen to you." She placed her hand along his jawline, feeling the tightness that signaled the control he was keeping over himself.

"Caitlin, love," he said, having to try one more time. "Please come home with me."

"No."

How could he argue with her anymore? No matter what he said, the fact remained that he couldn't force her to do something she refused to do. He'd often thought his sister to be the most stubborn person he'd ever known. Caitlin could give Felicia lessons, heaven forbid.

Her hand slipped from his jaw, and he knew she was asleep.

There was nothing more he could do or say. As much as he wanted to remain in their own little Utopia, Adam knew too much depended on his getting back. Whatever he had accidentally stumbled across in his investigation was too serious for him to lose any more time reporting it.

He knew she would resent his interference, but he intended to contact Antonio's family in the village and have them check on her. Adam had to be sure she was all right and that she didn't suffer because of her own stubbornness.

Pulling Caitlin closer into the circle of his arms, he closed his eyes, enjoying her sweet scent, the warmth of her body, the soft sounds of her breathing. He would have to learn to live without her for a while. He refused to accept that he had to give her up permanently.

Six

Adam's dream seemed to remove him from his present situation, transporting him to a happier time. He was at the ranch, riding in from one of the pastures when he saw Caitlin, waving to him from the bluffs near the river. Her hair was loose, and the wind teased it, causing the curls to dance around her face. He guided his horse away from the homeward trail and allowed his mount to pick its way down the slope, cross the river at the shallow rapids and find the trail that led to the top of the bluffs where Caitlin waited.

In his dream he recognized his relief at seeing her. She'd been gone from his life for so long, but now she was there, waiting for him.

The waiting was over.

Adam slid from the saddle and swooped her up in his arms, twirling her around while his lips covered hers.

Adam's dream dissolved slowly, and he realized that he was holding Caitlin in his arms and kissing her. His breathing sounded harsh in the quiet room. He was holding her as though he never intended to let her go, and when he forced himself to relax his hold on her, he discovered he was shaking.

Caitlin was curled up in his arms with her arms around his waist, her legs entwined with his, her injured shoulder ignored. Her lips were moist and slightly swollen from his kisses, and it was all he could do not to continue.

Her eyelashes slowly fluttered open. "Adam?" she murmured uncertainly.

"Yes?"

"Were you kissing me just now, or was I dreaming?"

"A little of both, I'm afraid. I think we've both been dreaming."

She stretched and sighed, and he realized with a lopsided smile that she was still asleep. Otherwise she would not be so unconcerned with their sleeping position.

And when she pulled his head down toward hers once more, he could no more resist her than he could stop breathing. Her mouth searched for his, and with a sigh of pleasure, she began to kiss him.

He returned her kiss, loving the feel of her in his arms, enjoying the sensations that no other woman had ever been able to create within him.

Adam realized that if they didn't stop now there would be no turning back. He also knew that he could not make love to her tonight and walk away from her tomorrow.

He pulled away slightly, kissing her lightly on her

eyelids, her nose and her cheeks. She smiled. "You probably won't even remember this in the morning, and it's just as well," he whispered. "I know you love me. Your every action fairly shouts your feelings." He traced the slight arch of her eyebrow with his finger. "I'll be back. Even if I have to go through hell first, I'll be back," he vowed, as much to himself as to her. "I'll never be without you in my life, regardless of what it takes to keep you close to me."

When Caitlin woke up, bright sunlight flooded the room. She was alone in the cabin and was reminded of the morning before. Adam was probably outside taking care of the animals for her.

Her shoulder felt much better today. She knew it was healing. She'd slept so well the night before, no doubt partly due to the potent tea Adam had made up for her. The tea was probably responsible for some of her dreams, as well. She smiled at her memories. It was just as well that Adam didn't know what had transpired in some of them.

It took her a while to pull on her clothes and yet Adam still hadn't returned by the time she was dressed. Caitlin decided to go outside looking for him. When she reached the lean-to she discovered that the animals had all been fed but Adam was nowhere around. Puzzled, she returned to the cabin. Only then did she notice that he hadn't made coffee, which was unusual. Caitlin walked over to the counter and for the first time saw his note propped against the coffeepot.

Please forgive me for not waking you to say goodbye. We said that yesterday, and I wasn't sure I could leave you today if I didn't get away now. I have no choice at the moment but to go, but I'll be back as soon as I can. You and I have some unfinished business.

                                    Don't forget me.
                                         Adam

Caitlin stared at the note for a long time, trying not to face the fact that she wasn't going to see him again. Of course he had done what he had to do. There was no reason for him to linger. He knew she was going to be all right.

She kept reading the last line over and over. *Don't forget me.*

How could she possibly forget him? He'd said he would come back, and she believed him. In the meantime, she had her life to live—the life she had chosen.

Caitlin became aware of the ache in her shoulder. She carefully folded Adam's note and placed it in one of her books, returning the book to the shelf.

A part of her life was finished now, but she felt richer because of what she had experienced.

She had learned about love, its pain as well as its beauty. Perhaps one couldn't exist without the other.

Adam's entry into the village was considerably different from the day before. After making sure no one was in sight, he slipped into the taverna by the rear entrance. He waited until the owner was alone, then signaled to him. The man looked at him in surprise.

"Someone shot at me yesterday while I was up in the hills. Did you hear anything?"

The man's eyes widened. "No, *señor*. I heard nothing."

"Have any strangers come into town recently?"

"You, *señor*."

"Besides me."

The man thought for a moment. "No."

"Are you sure? Think about it. Anyone at all."

"Well-l-l-l." The man scratched his head. "Alfredo Cortez, he's lived here a few weeks—I don't know exactly for how long—"

"You mean, since February?"

"Oh, yes. I'd say since then…possibly."

"What is he doing here? Visiting with family, working?"

"I don't know. He comes in here every afternoon—sits around and visits."

"Do you ever hear him ask questions?"

"Like you are?"

"Yes, like I am. Does he ever say why he's here, like maybe because he's looking for someone?"

"Maybe…maybe not. He doesn't bother anybody, you know."

Adam felt the frustration of being the outsider. Obviously this Cortez had managed to mingle with the locals successfully. Adam realized that with his blond coloring and American heritage he was easily identifiable. He didn't dare hang around the village waiting for a ride in the event that Cortez was the man looking for him.

"Thanks for your help. I really appreciate it," Adam said to the owner. He wished he had some money on him. He might have learned more if he could have encouraged the man, but there was no sense in pushing his luck.

Adam slipped out of the taverna without seeing anyone and stood for a few moments in the shelter of the building. He would find Antonio's home and explain about Caitlin's injury. He knew how much the villagers cared for her. She would probably be safer with them than if he stayed to look after her.

Avoiding the main street, Adam eventually found the small house Caitlin had pointed out to him the day before. It didn't take him long to explain, and by the time he left, Adam knew Caitlin would be hovered over by her protective friends. He grinned, thinking of her reaction to their concern. Caitlin probably wouldn't be pleased. She really insisted on being independent.

Hours later Adam was several miles from the village, headed north. He had decided against going into Monterrey. Without any way to identify himself, he was in danger of being picked up as a vagrant, with no chance to prove who he was. During the long walk away from the village he decided to stay as invisible as possible and get to the border. He'd worry about getting across once he got there.

That night he curled up under some brush and tried to sleep. By morning the sky had opened up, and heavy rains fell. For the next several days Adam walked, hitched rides, slept in lean-tos when he could find them, and continued his way north with dogged determination.

Eventually his body rebelled against the abuse he was heaping on himself. He picked up a cough, and his chest hurt. By the time he made it to the border, he was almost too weak to stand.

Adam didn't care. He had made it without getting picked up by the authorities. The next hurdle was to cross into the States.

Getting across the Rio Grande took three days. He

spent most of that time in the border patrol office trying to convince them he was who he said he was.

Adam didn't feel as though he'd slept more than an hour or two at a time since he'd left Caitlin, and he couldn't remember the last time he'd eaten. Eventually he was allowed to get in touch with his superiors in San Antonio who confirmed what he had already suspected: he'd been reported missing, presumed dead.

He was very pleased to inform them that he was still around. His next call was to Dane. He was more than a little surprised when Felicia answered.

"What are you doing at the ranch?" he asked when she answered.

"Adam? Is that you? Is that really you? Where are you?"

He laughed, the relief of knowing the worst of his trek was behind him making him feel light-headed.

He told her, and he asked to speak to Dane, giving him the particulars of where he was and that he needed a ride home.

A couple of Agency men showed up, and he was able to give them as full a report as possible. He discovered that the man he had been gathering evidence on had been arrested and that a successful conclusion to the case seemed to be assured.

No one was sure who was behind the attempts on Adam's life. At this point it was anybody's guess.

By the time Dane and Felicia arrived, Adam's store of energy was gone. He slept all the way back to the ranch and did little more than sleep and eat for almost a week afterward. His body finally demanded some care after the punishment it had received.

Adam discovered that his disappearance had caused

one good thing to happen: Dane and Felicia had gotten married during the time they had spent looking for him. In addition, they were expecting a baby in late fall.

So Caitlin had been right about them.

Caitlin. She was never out of his thoughts. For many days and nights his memories of her were what had kept him going. He thought about the way she looked, the way she felt in his arms, the way she responded to his kisses.

God! He missed her so. He hadn't been teasing when he told her he'd left part of himself there in the mountains. He wouldn't be whole again until he returned.

In the meantime…he bought a car to replace the one that ended up over the side of the mountain and drove to San Antonio. Robert McFarlane, the head of the regional office, had called a private meeting with him.

Robert chose one of the hotels down along the banks of the San Antonio River. It was a beautiful day, and they sat at one of the many outdoor tables to admire the view and soak up the late-spring sun.

Conversation was casual until after the waitress brought their coffee and left.

Adam filled Rob in on everything that had happened since their last meeting. Then he had some questions of his own.

"Was the man I was supposed to meet ever contacted?" Adam asked.

"Yes. Zeke Taylor managed to contact him not long after you disappeared."

"That makes sense. Zeke's the only other agent who knew about the contact. How did it go?"

"The man gave Zeke all the details—place of exchange, names, the whole thing—so we were able to nail Santiago and make it stick. Unfortunately we never got a chance to thank our informant."

"What do you mean?"

"He was killed within hours after Zeke left him."

"By whom?"

"We haven't found out. We may never find out."

They sat for a while in silence, watching people strolling along the River Walk, enjoying the view.

"Does Zeke know I'm back?"

"Sure. The whole Agency knows. You were the one that came back from the grave."

"I bet he's pleased we managed to finalize this one."

"We all are. This has been one hell of a hard case to crack."

"Do you think the informant's death ties in with the attempt on me?"

"Who can say? It would be a help if you knew what your assailant looks like. Then we could start a manhunt."

"I know. I've thought of that more than once, believe me. There is somebody who's seen him. Unfortunately, she—"

"You mean there's a woman who can finger the guy?"

"Well, yes, except that—"

"What are you waiting for? Bring her in. Show her the mug shots, get her to identify him. Why didn't you say something earlier? Your report stated that you had not seen the men in the car or the gunman near the village."

"I know."

"God! This may be the break we're looking for."

"If I can get her to come."

"What do you mean?"

"Well, the witness lives in the mountains of Mexico—"

"Oh, so she doesn't speak English. Well, that's no problem. We're all bilingual around here."

"She's from Seattle, Washington, and speaks English just fine."

"Oh! Well, then, what's the problem?"

"She won't leave the mountains."

"We're not asking her to move! She'd just visit the office, look at the mug shots, see if she recognizes anyone. You're sure she got a clear look at the guy?"

"Yes."

"Good. When can you get her up here?"

"Good question. I was thinking about taking her to the ranch first."

Rob studied the younger man for a moment in silence. "The ranch, huh? Something tells me there's more than Agency business involved here."

"Maybe."

"Is this the woman who found you and nursed you back to health?"

"Yes."

"Could you be mistaking gratitude for something else?"

"What I feel for Caitlin is a hell of a lot stronger than gratitude, Rob. I have no problem understanding the difference."

Rob laughed. "How the mighty are fallen. I never thought I'd see the day that Adam St. Clair joined the lovesick corps."

Adam grinned ruefully. "Go ahead, rub it in. After all, you being the boss means I can't retaliate."

"Tell me another one. My being the boss has never slowed you down in the past."

"True," Adam agreed complacently.

"I want to see the woman here in the office no later than two weeks from now. That's the most time I can allow on this one. We've got to get some answers and tie up the loose ends. After all, it's your neck they're after. We need to know if your cover's been blown before we can use you down there again. Surely she'll want to cooperate to help keep you around."

"I can only hope."

"I have faith in your persuasive powers, St. Clair," Rob said, standing up. The meeting was now over, and Adam had his orders.

Summer weather came early to the mountains. Caitlin welcomed the opportunity to open her door and windows to the warm air. Her flower garden burst forth with riotous colors, as though to help lift her spirits.

The weeks following Adam's departure had been extremely hard for her. She felt bereft. The cabin was no longer her haven. Instead it was a daily reminder of his presence in her life. Everywhere she looked, she saw him—in front of the fireplace, in her bed, at the table, even milking her goat. Caitlin tried to stay busy, too busy to think about a future that didn't include Adam.

She spent more of her time at the village, helping with the newborn babies, visiting with the mothers and listening to the rambling tales of the old ones.

The villagers insisted on teasing her about her handsome *novio*, even though she insisted he was not her sweetheart or fiancé. They thought they knew better. After all, hadn't they seen the way he looked at her, the way he treated her when they had been together at the village? There were no words that could refute what the villagers had seen with their own eyes.

Caitlin accepted their kindly teasing, knowing it would do no good to continue to protest. Once they saw that Adam would not be returning anytime soon, if at all, the villagers would eventually ease up on the subject.

Late one afternoon in May, Caitlin entered the clearing where the little cabin stood. She was weary, not only physically, since she had gotten little sleep the night before, but emotionally, because she had been sitting beside the bed of a woman old in years, but young in heart. A woman whose death left a definite hole in the lives of those who loved her.

And yet Caitlin had seen the peace that stayed with the old woman until the end. Never had death seemed more friendly than at that moment when the woman quietly took her last breath and exhaled with a soft sigh, a tender smile on her lips.

Caitlin knew she was sad for herself, not the woman. She would miss their conversations, their sharing of healing with local herbs, and the old woman's wisdom that had been garnered over the years.

Never had her little clearing looked more peaceful to Caitlin, more inviting. Quietly she led Arturo to his stall and made sure that he was fed and had water before she quickly spread the feed for her chickens and went into the cabin.

The evening rays of the sun followed her through the door, lighting the shadows in the corners of the room and illuminating the figure who stood in front of the fireplace, waiting patiently for her.

"I told you I'd be back," Adam said quietly.

Seeing Adam again after the many weeks without him, together with the emotional strain she'd just undergone, were too much for Caitlin to handle at the moment. She burst into tears.

He was beside her in two long strides. Scooping her into his arms, he walked over to the bed and sat down, holding her close. "What's wrong, my love. Tell me."

His soft words only caused her tears to flow more freely, and she gave herself up to the luxury of Adam's arms and the joy of being comforted. She had not known when to expect him again. He could not have come at a time when she needed him more. Now that he was there, she no longer had to resist the ties they had forged during his stay with her.

"I didn't kid myself that you would be overjoyed to see me," he finally muttered, "but I didn't expect to reduce you to tears."

She slipped her arms around his neck and hugged him, holding him tightly as though afraid he would disappear. When the tears began to diminish, she leaned back slightly so that she could see him more clearly.

The weeks away had obviously done him good. He looked fit—tanned and healthy. She'd never seen him look better.

"Oh, Adam," she finally said. "I didn't know if you would really come."

"You should know me well enough to know I always do what I say.'' He glanced down at her arms, still locked around his shoulders. ''I have the feeling,'' he said with a slight smile, ''that you didn't forget me.'' With a hesitancy that she found endearing, he lowered his head and kissed her softly on her lips. ''Does this mean that you're glad to see me?''

She smiled and nodded.

He rewarded her honesty with another kiss. He took his time letting her know how much he had missed her. Caitlin felt the muscles of his back bunch beneath her hands. She became aware of the strength in his shoulders and arms that held her so fiercely against him. Adam had come back. She recalled the number of nights she'd lain awake, remembering what it had been like to have him lying next to her in bed, and the many nights when her dreams had been full of him. How could she possibly resist him now that he was back with her?

Adam seemed to be trying to memorize her, his hands ceaselessly roaming up and down her back, from her shoulders to her hips, as though reassuring himself that she really did exist and wasn't just a figment of his fevered imagination.

Her response to his kisses encouraged him to continue and he eased back on the bed until they were lying there, side by side, their mouths still clinging, enjoying the taste and touch of each other.

As though they had a mind of their own, his hands slid from her back and lightly traced a line from the hollow in her neck down between her breasts to her waist, then paused. Her quickened breathing seemed to match his own breathlessness.

He needed to get a rein on his emotions, now that he was once again with her. He'd had several weeks to plan what he would say and do once he saw her again, but her tears and the obvious loss of control when she saw him had unnerved him completely. He found himself wanting to comfort her.

She seemed so relaxed with him, as though for the first time she no longer fought her true feelings.

Caitlin began to pop open the snaps on his plaid western shirt so that her hands could find the smooth surface of his broad chest.

Her fingers touching his bare flesh caused him to quiver. Surely she understood what that was doing to him. If she did, she certainly didn't seem to care. She was responding to his kisses as though she wanted nothing more in life than to be there in his arms.

Which was fine with him.

When he found her breasts with his fingertips, he felt her body jump in response, but rather than pull back from him, she merely deepened the kiss. Adam could feel his heart racing. He needed to put a halt to what was happening. Now. Otherwise he would have no control over what happened next.

Her blouse lay open, exposing her breasts, and she leaned closer to him so that they touched his bare chest. He groaned, unable to fight the feelings that were rapidly overtaking him.

"Caitlin, love—"

She paused and looked into his eyes, seeing the love and burning desire, feeling the same emotions stirring deeply within her.

"I love you, Adam," she murmured, her lips pressing against his cheek and ear.

With those words, Adam forgot all about practicing restraint in favor of expressing his love for her in the most physical way possible.

He smoothed her blouse off her shoulders so that her upper body was revealed to him. Her skin glowed with a satiny sheen, her translucent coloring in deepest contrast to her fiery hair which lay in disordered confusion around her head and shoulders.

He traced the scar that followed the line of her shoulder, pleased to see that it had healed well. Then he leaned over and kissed it.

She was so beautiful, even more beautiful than he'd remembered, and he had forgotten nothing about her during their time apart.

He felt her heart fluttering in her chest when his mouth rested on the pink tip of her breast. He felt as though he held a frightened bird in his arms. His tongue lightly flicked over her breast, and he watched her body's response.

Caitlin feverishly explored his shoulders and chest with her fingertips, still in a daze at his presence. His heavy shoulder muscles felt so comforting somehow, and she sighed when his mouth encircled her breast.

Eventually Adam paused long enough to slide off his boots, then he quickly removed the rest of his clothing. He gazed down at her with a possessiveness that seemed to scorch her with its warmth, while at the same time left her feeling shy and uncertain. Without saying a word, he slipped off her pants and shoes, and she felt the cool evening air against her bared skin. She shivered, more from nerves than anything else.

Adam picked her up, pulled back the covers of the bed, and slipped her between them, crawling in beside her.

Had he said anything to her, anything at all, Caitlin might have been able to get a grip on her emotions, but it became obvious that Adam was a man of action, not words. And his actions made it clear how he still felt about her.

Not that he rushed her. On the contrary, he seemed to feel as though they had all the time in the world. If she tensed when he touched Caitlin in a new area, he would pause, then continue to stroke her until she relaxed.

Her body responded to his touch while he gave her slow, intoxicating kisses, reassuring her on the deepest, most fundamental level that he would never hurt her.

By the time he was poised above her, Caitlin watched him with fascinated eyes, her breathing ragged, her skin warm from his touch.

Adam slowly lowered himself to her and wasn't in the least surprised to discover that no one had been there before him. He'd been aware of her innocence on some subconscious level, had known of her purity. He touched her lightly, hoping not to frighten her.

Her eyes widened at the unexpected pressure and the sensation of him, so intimately pressed against her.

"It's all right, my love," he soothed. "Just relax. Everything's just fine."

When he took possession of her body, Caitlin discovered that he was right. Because of his loving concern and his inexhaustible patience, she was ready for him. Once the initial discomfort was past, Caitlin was swept away with the sense of release and freedom of expression.

She had never experienced anything resembling the feelings Adam aroused in her. He was so much an extension of her own being that for the first time in her life she realized what it meant to be one with another person.

He seemed to know what to do to increase the pleasurable feelings that were sweeping over her, and she clung to him as though to a lifeboat so she wouldn't be swept completely away into the sea of sensation rolling over them both.

Caitlin seemed to know instinctively how to respond to him. She met each of his movements with one of her own, delighting in the recognition of what her responsiveness did to him. He seemed to have such control and mastery over them both. Suddenly there was no more caution or patience. He caught fire, causing her to burst into flames, as well.

By the time Caitlin could comprehend what had happened, Adam was drawing slow, deep breaths, his head resting on the pillow next to hers, his body slumped to her side so that his weight was only partially on her. She felt bemused lying in his arms—as though she had spent most of her life there and that it was the most natural place in the world to be.

She studied his face as she'd seen him so often, with his eyes closed, and realized how differently he looked now. His long lashes still hid his expression, but his face was fuller, the scar almost invisible, and his color was very healthy. In fact, he looked flushed, which might be due to the exertion he'd recently undergone.

When his eyes finally opened, she was surprised to see the rueful, contrite expression in them.

"Will you forgive me, love? Because I'm not at all sure I can forgive myself."

She leaned closer and kissed him lightly. "There's nothing to forgive."

"You probably won't believe that I didn't have this all planned."

"I know."

"Are you okay?"

"I'm fine."

He stroked her back. "I came back to convince you that I love you. I wanted you to know that you can trust me." He shook his head ruefully. "I have a funny way of showing it."

"Why do you want me to trust you?"

"Because I have a favor to ask of you."

"Okay. Ask."

Adam eyed her thoughtfully and said, "It isn't going to be easy for you."

"All right," she responded calmly.

"You told me that you saw the man who drove the car the night I was almost killed."

"Yes."

"You said he was also the gunman who shot you."

"Yes."

He paused for a moment, uncertain. "I need you to identify him for me."

She smiled at his serious expression. "I'll do whatever I can to help."

Adam gained enough confidence in her calm acceptance to continue. "What I need you to do is to go to San Antonio with me, look through the tons of pictures we keep on file and see if we have him in our records." Anxiously he watched her face for some reaction.

Caitlin was quiet for several minutes, knowing that whatever decision she made would have an irrevocable impact on her life. Did she have the courage to do what needed to be done?

Adam took her hand and softly kissed the palm. "I know how you feel about leaving here. But I would be with you, love. I want you to come to Texas with me so much. These last few weeks have been hell without you."

I know only too well what it's been like without you, Caitlin silently answered. *I'm not sure I'm strong enough to allow you to leave me a second time.*

"I love you, Caitlin. I want to marry you and take you home to live with me."

Not marriage, Adam, she protested silently. *We can't take that risk.*

"Would you at least give our relationship a chance? I promise to bring you back the minute you want to come."

What could she say? She wanted to find the man who had tried to kill him. Until the man was apprehended, Adam wouldn't be safe. Caitlin couldn't live with the thought that he was still in danger without doing everything in her power to help him.

Then what choice did she have? Adam needed her. Caitlin had faced the truth of their strong ties weeks ago. Today had merely strengthened them, pointing out something important to her.

She needed Adam, too.

His eyes were filled with concern as he watched her. She felt the love and warmth that emanated from him. Caitlin reminded herself that she wouldn't be alone. Adam would be there if she became overwhelmed. After all this time on her own, perhaps she would be better able to cope with what she sensed and felt around her.

"When do you want to leave?" she finally asked.

Adam let out an Indian war cry, the kind that had

echoed over the Texas plains a century ago. He rolled over in bed, holding her tightly against him, until he lay over her, staring down into her flushed face, his own face radiating his delight with her decision.

"We'll leave in the morning, darlin'. I have no intention of moving out of this bed until then."

Caitlin could find nothing to complain about in that statement.

Seven

The gently rolling hills of central Texas were already baking in the sun, although the calendar insisted summer wouldn't arrive for a few more weeks.

Now that they were nearing the ranch, Caitlin could feel herself growing nervous. The drive north had been uneventful. Adam explained that the car was new, and she realized something that she'd given no thought to before—money was no problem in Adam's life.

She refused to dwell on the fact that he wanted to marry her. One step at a time. She had agreed to the visit.

The frustrating part about her abilities was the way her emotions interfered with her reception of messages. Seldom could Caitlin visualize what was happening in her own life or how things would work out. It didn't seem fair, somehow, since she felt more afflicted than blessed with the awareness in the first place.

One thing she knew for certain: Adam had made a definite claim on her. There was no denying his intentions. Since his arrival at the cabin two days ago, he'd rarely let her get more than an arm's length away from him.

Adam had openly revealed the more sensuous side of his nature to Caitlin, surprising her when she remembered the control he had kept on himself during the weeks they had been together. Now that the control had been lifted, Caitlin found herself with a man who couldn't seem to get enough of her.

She understood the feeling. Caitlin had never desired a physical relationship before, never missed or regretted that she and Rick had never made love.

Now, thanks to Adam, she had discovered a means of expressing her emotions in a physical manner, and she reveled in the experience. Adam appeared delighted with her response to his lovemaking and her willingness to share herself with him.

She knew she'd hurt him by not agreeing to marry him. It wasn't from lack of love. If anything, her hesitancy was because she loved him too much to agree to something that might not make him happy. After all, he had seen her only in her own controlled environment. Her agreement to come to Texas with him was in the nature of an experiment.

If she could handle living around people again, then they had a foundation to build a marriage. Adam's passionate lovemaking had gone a long way to convincing her that they belonged together. Perhaps he had known that. She knew she couldn't find it in her heart to regret his possession of her. All she could hope was that their love for each other would be strong enough to ease them through the coming visit.

Her mind kept returning to the night he'd arrived. They hadn't gotten much sleep. Adam had kept reaching for her in the night, as though to make sure she was really there beside him.

"I don't know how I managed not to make love to you before I left," he had said to her the next morning. Caitlin lay limply on top of him, while he stroked her back soothingly. He'd just completed another rather comprehensive lesson in lovemaking.

"I wouldn't have stopped you," she admitted in a shy burst of honesty.

"But you wouldn't have left with me, either. I knew that. I couldn't handle loving you, then leaving."

"Then you must have been confident yesterday that I would agree to go back with you."

"No. If you had refused, I would have stayed here."

She raised her head from his shoulder and stared at him in surprise.

He smiled at the expression on her face. "You are a part of my life, Caitlin. You will always be a part of me. If you find that you can't live in my world, then I intend to live in yours. I will not give you up."

That conversation kept running through her head while Caitlin watched the Texas hill country roll by. For the first time she faced how cowardly her actions had been, by insisting on remaining in the mountains. Adam had put their relationship first. He was determined to work out everything else.

She admired that trait in him. There was so much

about Adam that she admired. She looked over at
him, and his eyes met hers for a brief glance before
returning to the road.

"Tired?"

"A little."

"We should be there in another hour." He took his
hand from the wheel and brushed his knuckles against
her cheek. "You didn't get much sleep last night."

"Neither did you."

"I know. But I'm not complaining."

"What have you told your family about me,
Adam?"

"That you're a very special person and that I love
you very much." His warm tone seemed to ease the
tension within her.

Her relaxed state lasted until they turned off the
highway and followed a winding country road that
Adam mentioned led to the ranch. She straightened
slightly and studied the surrounding area carefully.
This was home to Adam. He wanted her to share it
with him.

When they pulled up into the ranch yard, Caitlin
looked around in dismay at the size of the place.

The two-story house had been built in another era,
when labor and material were cheap. A long porch
wrapped around three sides of the house. There was
also a large barn, a few pens, and several pieces of
machinery sitting around. The ranch looked almost as
large as the small village where she traded for supplies.

As soon as the car stopped, the screen door of the
house flew open, and a young woman came out. Caitlin immediately recognized Felicia. Without a doubt
the woman was beautiful with her long blond hair and

green eyes. What Adam hadn't thought to mention and Caitlin hadn't known was that Felicia was pregnant.

Caitlin felt a sudden sense of identification with Felicia, and she wondered if it was due to the resemblance between the brother and sister. Adam opened the car door and helped Caitlin out. With his arm around her shoulders, he guided her to the house where Felicia waited.

"Caitlin, this is my sister, Felicia." He leaned over and kissed Felicia. "Here she is, sis. I managed to convince her to come for a visit."

Felicia's smile reminded Caitlin even more of Adam, and when Felicia held out her hand, Caitlin found her words echoing her thoughts. "You and Adam look so much alike."

Felicia laughed, a happy sound that warmed Caitlin's heart. Felicia hugged her brother tightly for a moment. "I consider that a compliment, but big brother here seems to think he's been insulted every time anyone mentions the family resemblance."

"I don't, either," Adam retorted. He glanced around and asked, "Is Dane around?"

"He should be back within the hour. Had to run into town for something. We didn't expect to see you this early." She motioned for them to go into the house ahead of her. "Would you like something to drink? How was the trip? Did you run into any bad weather? Dane said—"

"Whoa! Wait a minute!" Adam protested. "One thing at a time, will you? Yes, we'd love to have something to drink, the trip was fine, the weather was great, and what did Dane say?"

The two of them continued their banter as they

moved along the wide hallway. Caitlin peered into
open doors as they went by. She saw a long living
room, dining room, a den and office, then found herself in the kitchen while Adam held out a chair for
her.

Felicia poured each of them a large glass of iced
tea. After placing a sprig of mint in each one and
setting a saucer with sliced lemons on the table, she
sat down at the table and smiled at the two of them.

"I'm so glad you came, Caitlin. Adam was worried
you wouldn't."

Caitlin glanced at Adam. He was leaning back
against his chair, looking relaxed and happy. She'd
never really seen him that way before. She liked the
look on him; he wore it very well.

"I'm glad I came, too," she agreed softly.

"I've put you in my old room. It's got a nice view
of the place. If you aren't too tired later, I'd like to
take you over to see the house Dane and I are building. It's about two miles down the road from here,
overlooking the river." She glanced at Adam and
shook her head. "It would probably never occur to
Adam to reassure you that if you decide to settle here
you aren't going to have to share your home with a
bunch of relatives."

So Adam has told Felicia he wants to marry me,
Caitlin realized. She felt the pressure of knowing that
others were also waiting for her decision. Caitlin cast
around for a way to change the subject, and she remembered the fact that Felicia was pregnant.

Her mind filled with images, and she knew that
Dane and Felicia were delighted. They wanted a family. She smiled at the turbulent relationship the two

had shared for years. Impulsively she leaned toward Felicia and patted her hand.

"I know Dane wants a boy, Felicia," she said with a mischievous grin, "but he's going to love his daughter very much. The boys will come later."

Adam and Felicia stared at her in stunned silence, and Caitlin suddenly realized what she'd said. Why had she spoken the thought out loud? She could see Dane with his tiny black-haired daughter, and the love and laughter they shared like a shimmering light around them. Caitlin had spoken without thinking about the consequences of her words.

Adam was the first one to break the charged silence. "Uhh, Felicia, I did forget to mention one thing about Caitlin. You see, she, uh—"

"You already know I'm going to have a girl?" Felicia said, interrupting Adam as though she hadn't heard him.

Caitlin could feel the tension begin to build behind her eyes. Oh, no. She hadn't been there five minutes, and already she'd managed to create a problem.

She forced herself to meet Felicia's startled gaze. "I seem to have the ability of knowing things like that," she explained with a sigh.

Felicia clapped her hands in delight. "But that's wonderful." She turned to Adam. "Why didn't you tell us sooner, Adam? What an amazing gift. Have you always had it?"

Caitlin gazed at Felicia in surprise. She didn't seem to be shocked or upset. Nor did she seem to question the validity of the statement. She was sincerely interested, and was waiting for Caitlin to respond.

Caitlin soon found that for every question she answered, Felicia had three more for her. It didn't matter. Caitlin felt accepted as she was slowly drawn into the loving circle shared by Adam and Felicia.

Having already talked about her background with Adam, Caitlin discovered it was much easier to discuss it now. Neither one of them treated her as some freak. She began to relax and enjoy herself, even drawing laughs with some of her stories about her curly days in the mountains.

When Dane walked into the room, he found his wife and brother-in-law chatting with a glowing young woman with bright red-gold hair cascading over her shoulders, her face animated and her eyes sparkling. He had no trouble understanding why Adam had fallen head over heels in love. The man had taste, he'd give him that.

Caitlin glanced up and saw the tall, good-looking man leaning against the doorjamb. She smiled. He straightened up and said, "It looks like the St. Clairs are at it again, both talking nonstop." Sauntering over to Felicia, he kissed her, then held out his hand to Adam. "Good to see you managed to get down to Mexico and back this time without any trouble."

Felicia was the first one to respond. "Oh, Dane, I want you to meet Caitlin Moran. Caitlin, this is my lord and master, Dane Rineholt."

Dane pulled a chair out from the table and sat down, leaning back in obvious contentment. "You can't appreciate the irony in that statement yet, Caitlin, but when you get to know her better, you will. Nobody ever tries to dominate Felicia." He glanced at Adam. "No one would dare try, right?"

The men grinned at each other, and Caitlin felt the love that was shared between these three people and had a sudden yearning to be a part of their magic circle. Was it possible?

Adam glanced at his watch. "I hadn't realized how long we've been sitting here talking. I haven't even taken Caitlin upstairs to unpack or rest." He stood up and held out his hand to her. "Let me give you a quick tour of the place, love." He glanced over at the couple still seated. "We'll see you later."

Adam kept her close to his side while he showed Caitlin the main floor of the house, explaining the various additions that had been made to the original structure. Then he took her upstairs and down the hall to her bedroom.

The room was beautifully old-fashioned, with a colorful quilt decorating the four-poster and a braided rug on the floor. Caitlin scarcely had time to see it before Adam pulled her into his arms and began kissing her—deep, soul-searching kisses that caused Caitlin to forget everything but the man who seemed to be a part of her, body and soul. When he finally lifted his mouth from hers, they were both short of breath. "I've been wanting to do that for the past several hours. You've become an addiction to me. The more I have of you, the more I want."

Caitlin felt the same way but didn't want to admit how weak she was. One of them needed to hang on to some perspective. However, she did feel more at ease now that she had actually come into Adam's home and met his family.

The meeting hadn't been as bad as she'd expected. They accepted her and seemed sincerely pleased that she and Adam had found each other. Caitlin began to believe there was a chance that she and Adam could work out their lives so they could be together.

"I know you're tired," he said, rubbing her back with a gentle hand. "Why don't you stretch out for a while and try to get some rest. We'll spend the weekend here and drive into San Antonio on Monday. My boss, Rob McFarlane, is most interested in meeting you."

"Does he know about my psychic abilities?"

"No. I haven't told him because I didn't want you to feel uncomfortable. If you want to tell him, fine. Otherwise, he thinks you saw the driver well enough to identify him. We'll have you go through the pictures and see if you recognize him." He walked over to the window and looked out. "Don't take on more than you are comfortable with, love. Just know I'm here, that I'll always be here, and that I love you."

He turned around and headed for the door.

"I'm not going to kiss you again. If I do, I'll end up on that bed with you, and that's no way to set an example for my sister!" he said with a grin.

Caitlin slipped off her shoes and dress and lay down, pulling a light blanket across her. She had a hunch that Felicia would not be at all shocked to know she and Adam had slept together. But she supposed there was no reason to shatter a brother's illusions about his sister's innocence.

"Dane?" Felicia got up from her chair as soon as Adam and Caitlin left the kitchen and walked around the table to her tall, dark-haired husband. Sinking down into his lap, she curled her arms around his neck. "I've got some news for you that I'm not at all sure you're going to like."

"What's that?"

"You aren't getting a son the first time around."

He looked at her with a puzzled expression on his face. "What are you talking about?"

"I'm going to have a girl."

He laughed. "Who says?"

"Caitlin."

"Caitlin? And how would she know?"

"She just knows. That's what she and Adam have been trying to explain to me since they arrived. Caitlin is different, Dane. She sees things, she knows things, that most other people don't know. She saw you with a black-haired daughter, and she also sees us with sons. I'm afraid she predicts a rather large family."

He grinned. "Is that supposed to scare me or something? Remember, I come from a large family myself."

"I know. It doesn't scare me, either. But having someone around who knows those kinds of things is going to take some getting used to."

"Why? There are many people who have a sense of things to happen. Perhaps Caitlin has a stronger sense of it. Doesn't every family have someone who could always tell when it was going to storm, or knew about a death before it happened, or identified who was calling on the phone before they answered it?"

"Well, maybe, but not like this."

"Maybe not exactly, but it doesn't make her strange or that different. What it makes her is sensitive to other people."

"Have you ever known anyone like Caitlin?"

"When I was in the service, I was stationed with a fella from Arizona, an Indian, who had an uncanny ability of predicting what was going to happen. Managed to save my life a couple of times with his predictions. I got cut off from the rest of my unit once and would have been left if he hadn't known where to look for me.''

''You never told me about that.''

''No. But I definitely believe in man's extra senses. I think we've always had them, but as we've grown more civilized, we've used them less and less until they've grown dormant. I think it's possible for anyone to increase their extrasensory skills with practice and a certain amount of skill in learning to focus their attention.''

''I can't get over the change in Adam since he met Caitlin.''

''In what way?''

''I'm not sure. He's more relaxed somehow, as though he knows what he wants and how he intends to get it. It's as though he's always known that sooner or later he would find her. Adam has always been popular with women, but he never got serious with anybody. And yet as soon as he met Caitlin, he fell like a boulder, immediately and with little warning.''

''I was the same way.''

''Who are you kidding? You played around for years!''

''No. I *waited* around for years. I knew as soon as I first laid eyes on you that I was going to marry you. I just had to wait forever for you to grow up.''

She leaned over and kissed him, a very loving, lingering kiss. When she finally pulled away from him, she noticed that he hadn't opened his eyes. ''It was worth the wait, though, wasn't it?'' she teased.

''You're damned right,'' he agreed, blindly searching for her mouth once more.

* * *

Dinner was a hilarious affair. The four of them found all sorts of subjects to discuss. By unspoken agreement, no one brought up the planned trip to San Antonio or its purpose. Instead Dane and Felicia enjoyed telling Caitlin all about Adam as a boy and later, as a young man. Adam retaliated by describing the relentless war waged between Dane and Felicia before they acknowledged the love that had been between them for years.

By the time Caitlin prepared for bed that night, she knew that she could be very happy living in this house with Adam, with Felicia and Dane nearby.

Her years on the mountain had given her time to come to terms with her heightened awareness, and she no longer felt intimidated by the knowledge that seemed to flow through her at unexpected times.

Now she was going to put that knowledge to use by trying to find who had tried to kill Adam. And why. The why was even more important. Somehow she knew the motive was the key to the whole business.

By the time she fell asleep, Caitlin knew that the following few days would be a turning point in her life. She only hoped she was ready for it.

Eight

Adam's mood was cheerful and teasing during the trip to San Antonio. Caitlin found his lightheartedness contagious. She couldn't remember the last time she'd been so relaxed and happy. Her weekend at the ranch had brought back memories of how she'd felt as a young girl—full of fun and high spirits.

Adam's sudden appearance in her life had been like a bomb bursting—shattering her routine and her views of herself and the world around her. He'd given her the courage to venture out of the safe nest she had created.

"I hope the weekend wasn't too much for you," Adam said, effectively ending the silence. "You haven't said anything since we left home."

"Oh, no. I enjoyed it very much. Dane and Felicia are very special people."

"They enjoyed you, as well."

"I was just thinking…"

"About what?"

"That it might be nice to be married at the ranch."

The car made a sudden swerve before it continued down the highway.

"You pick a hell of a time to accept a marriage proposal, lady. At the moment, I can't do a damn thing about it."

Caitlin looked over at him, her face glowing. "What do you want to do about it?"

Adam gave her a brief glance, then returned his attention to the highway. "I'd much prefer to show you than to tell you." That brief glance raised her temperature considerably.

Admitting that she wanted to marry him seemed to lift a weight off her shoulders. Somehow she had to believe that what they felt for each other was strong enough to weather whatever life presented to them.

They spent the remaining miles discussing dates, making plans for the ceremony and what to do with Caitlin's animals. One of the teenagers in the village had agreed to feed and look after Arturo, Chula, the goat and the chickens while she was gone. Now they would need to make permanent arrangements.

Adam insisted they go shopping and buy her a ring before going to the office. Once in town, they stopped, and he called Rob from a pay phone. Hanging up after a brief conversation, he laughed and caught her in his arms.

"Rob said a few hours wasn't going to make that much difference and if I'd managed to talk you into an engagement, I might as well get the evidence on your finger."

He took her hand and began to lead her through

the large shopping mall. "Let's have lunch first, then we'll get started. I know just what I want for you."

By the time they reached the Agency office, Caitlin felt her thoughts almost whirling. The unaccustomed crowds, as well as Adam's excitement, seemed to put an electrical charge around her. She was relieved to discover that with conscious effort she could block out the snippets of impressions that came through, in the same manner that she ignored bits and pieces of conversation reaching her ear while they moved through the different stores.

Glancing down at the large diamond solitaire, Caitlin could scarcely believe how quickly Adam had gotten organized once she agreed to his proposal. The man striding down the hall beside her was a definite force to be reckoned with.

She found the Agency office a peaceful contrast to the busy mall. The sound of a typewriter in another office—muffled and indistinct—was the only noise that penetrated the quietness of the rooms.

When Adam ushered Caitlin into Robert Mc-Farlane's office and closed the door, even the noise of the typewriter faded away, and Caitlin's frayed nerves felt soothed by the silence.

After the introductions Rob motioned for them to be seated. "I'm very pleased that you agreed to come to San Antonio and help us out, Miss Moran. From what Adam told me on the phone, he's managed to talk you into more than a visit to the Lone Star State."

Caitlin saw Adam shift slightly in his chair and realized with amusement that Adam was embarrassed. She smiled at Rob. "I would like to help in whatever way I can."

"Has Adam explained to you what was happening at the time of his disappearance?"

"No. I never asked."

"He had managed to become friends with Felipe Santiago under the guise of helping to distribute drugs on this side of the river. Santiago was the middleman between the South American contacts and the distribution to the north. After a few successful operations, Santiago had learned to trust Adam."

She looked at the men in dismay. "You mean you were actually bringing the drugs in and distributing them?"

"We brought them in and impounded them. Of course, Santiago wasn't aware of that. Adam had told Santiago he wanted to meet his contact from South America, and Santiago arranged a meeting. That meeting was aborted, although Santiago never knew that, because of a message Adam received just before he left his hotel."

Rob paused for a moment and then continued, "Adam got a call telling him the meeting was a trap, that Santiago was afraid Adam was getting greedy and trying to bypass him. The caller said he could give him the evidence he needed without risk if Adam would agree to meet him somewhere away from Monterrey."

"So that's why Adam was in the mountains?" she offered.

"Yes."

"Only he never kept his appointment."

"No. What we want to know is who knew about the appointment in the mountains. Was it another plot of Santiago's, or is someone else involved? The bottom line here is—does someone know that Adam is an agent, or were they just trying to get rid of competition in the drug trade? I can't send him back over there until I know for certain. That's where you come in.''

"If I can identify the man for you, you'll know why he was trying to kill Adam?''

"That's what we're counting on, yes.''

"And if I can't identify him?''

"We're in no worse shape than we were before. The thing is, we've run out of leads.''

"I see. I appreciate your explaining all of this to me, Mr. McFarlane.''

"If you were merely a witness, I wouldn't have, believe me. But as Adam's future wife I wanted you to understand the importance of the situation. He didn't have the clearance to give you the details. I do.'' He stood up and held out his hand.

"It's been a pleasure to meet you, and I won't hold you up any further. The job ahead of you is long and tedious.''

Caitlin followed Adam down a long hallway to another office. Two desks were pushed together in the center of a small room.

"Zeke Taylor and I share this office whenever we're in town, which isn't very often,'' Adam explained. "Have a seat, and I'll bring in the albums for you to go over. Do you want anything to drink?''

"Not at the moment,'' she replied, sitting down and looking around. "Where's Zeke now?''

"Mexico, as far as I know. He rarely comes out anymore. He's been with the Agency for years and has developed a damned good cover down there. He doesn't want to do anything to jeopardize it.''

He leaned over and kissed her. "I'll be back shortly."

Caitlin closed her eyes and tried to blank out her thoughts, but it was difficult. She saw Adam everywhere: his high spirits in the mall; the beauty of his male body the night he made such exquisite love to her; lying unconscious for those endless days and nights; the look of horror on his face just before his car was hit.

Adam seemed to fill her whole mind. She had never felt anything so powerful before. Yet she knew she had to clear away all of those emotions so that her mind would be free to pick up what she could.

Hours later Caitlin finally had to call a halt to the progression of photographs Adam kept handing her. "I'm sorry, Adam. I can't look at them any longer. This is getting to be more than I can handle at the moment."

Adam took one look at her face and realized he'd been pushing her. She was very pale, and her eyes had a bruised quality about them. "Damn. I wasn't thinking. I'm afraid I get carried away once I start on something like this. You must be exhausted."

"I am, but not because of the number of pictures you've shown me. These people carry such a charge on them I can almost feel their presence when I look at their photograph." She pointed to one. "He's in prison now and filled with hate." She indicated another one. "He's extremely dangerous. Kills for the excitement of it." About a third one, she said, "I don't think he's around any longer. There's a strong possibility he's dead."

Adam stared at her in surprise. "I guess I hadn't given it a thought—how all of this would affect you."

He ran his hand through his hair, not for the first time that afternoon, and sighed. "I can't seem to understand what you do and how you do it, yet I love you completely. I can better see why you're touchy about your abilities. They definitely give a sense of supernatural."

He stood up and held out his hand to her. "Come on. I'll buy you dinner and ply you with wine. That's bound to help you relax. Then I'll take you to a hotel and let you get some rest."

He was as good as his word. By the time they walked into the hotel room, Caitlin felt much more relaxed and more than a little sleepy. The good food and wine had certainly done the trick.

She kicked off her shoes and began to unbutton her blouse while Adam adjusted the thermostat and drapes. When he turned around, he discovered she wore only her panties and a bra. He watched her as she walked into the bathroom and turned on the shower.

He cleared his throat slightly. "I'll stop by in the morning so we can have breakfast together."

Caitlin glanced around in surprise. "You aren't staying with me tonight?"

"I know you're tired and—"

"That doesn't matter. It would be nice to know you're nearby."

He wondered if she had any idea how enticing she looked standing there. "You don't understand, Caitlin. I used up all the willpower I had during the weeks I spent at the cabin with you. I love you too much to be able to spend the night with you without making love to you, especially now."

With deliberate movements she calmly unfastened

her bra and stepped out of her panties. "No one asked you to exercise any willpower, Adam." With a lingering glance over her shoulder, she stepped into the spray of the shower.

Adam needed no further encouragement.

Caitlin looked around in surprise a few minutes later when she heard the shower door slide open. Adam stepped in, wearing only a grin.

"Are you enjoying the convenience of a shower after all those years without one?" he asked with studied nonchalance as he took the soapy washcloth away from her. He began to lightly stroke her arms, her shoulders and, with ever widening circles, her breasts.

Caitlin felt a shiver race through her at his touch. He had such a strong effect on her. When his hands slipped across her stomach and rested at the top of her thighs, she couldn't repress the slight moan of pleasure at his touch.

"Something wrong?"

"Uh-uh," she murmured, unable to find any words.

"Am I disturbing you in some way?"

She looked up at him. "What do you think?"

His hands went around her, pulling her closer until her soap-slickened body pressed against him. He meticulously soaped her back from shoulder to hip, but his touch felt more like a caress than an impersonal bathing.

When Adam finally leaned down and kissed her, her knees gave way, and she would have fallen if he hadn't held her even tighter against him. She twined her arms around his neck and returned his kiss with wholehearted enthusiasm.

Adam felt the difference in her from their first time

together. Her uninhibited response made it clear she felt committed to him and their future. He hadn't thought it possible to love her more than he did, but now his heart threatened to explode with the joy that flooded over him.

She insisted on taking her turn at bathing him and took such an excruciatingly long and loving time to soap his body that he thought he'd lose his mind with all the sensations sweeping through him.

When he'd had all he could take, Adam stepped away from her, turned her toward the water so she could rinse off, then gently pushed her out of the shower. After quickly rinsing off, he immediately followed.

After a couple of careless wipes with a towel, Adam picked her up and strode into the other room. "I've had all the teasing I intend to take from you, young lady," he said in a fierce voice. He dropped her on the bed.

"Who says I was teasing, Mr. St. Clair?"

His breath caught in his throat when he took in the picture she made. The dark blue of the spread was a stark contrast to her bright hair and shining eyes. Her pale skin still glistened from the shower, and with a feeling bordering on reverence, he knelt beside her and began to kiss her—starting with her neck, then her breasts, and slowly downward, pausing to nip her with his teeth and stroke her with his tongue.

His touch set off sparks all around her, and she felt as though her body had caught on fire. "Oh, Adam—"

"Do you love me?" he asked between kisses.

"Oh, yes."

"Do you want me?" He continued to drive her crazy with his mouth.

"Desperately."

"Then show me, sweet Caitlin. Show me what you want—show me how to please you."

With breathless sighs and soft words she let him know what his touch did to her and how much she needed him.

There was nothing gentle about their lovemaking this time. It was an expression of powerful love mingled with need. Neither one of them could get enough of the other during the ensuing hours. Their murmured whispers spoke of their joy with each other, their hope for the future, their unquenchable love.

All of Caitlin's fears and concerns were exorcised during the night. She'd been given a second chance to embrace life. This time she intended to take it.

Something woke her from a sound sleep, and Caitlin sat up in bed, alarmed. She looked around, dazed, trying to figure out where she was. Then she remembered. She was in San Antonio with Adam.

Glancing down at her side, Caitlin smiled. Adam lay on his stomach, his head almost buried under his pillow. The covers lay low on his back, barely covering his hips. He looked so comfortable.

Frowning, she tried to decide what had awakened her. She felt a niggling feeling in the back of her mind—a warning about something.

Getting out of bed carefully, so as not to awaken Adam, she slipped on her robe, then went into the bathroom for a glass of water. When she walked back into the bedroom, she went over to the window and opened the curtains.

The skyline of San Antonio was in front of her. The sky was black and seemed to be filled with stars, and the words to a song she'd sung as a child came back to her—something about the stars at night being big and bright, deep in the heart of Texas.

She stood there and gazed out at the night, feeling a definite unease. Eventually she sat down in the large overstuffed chair by the window and leaned her head back.

Her mind had cleared, her emotions had been nourished and reciprocated by Adam's lovemaking, and she was finally at peace with herself and her world. While she sat there, pictures began to form. She saw the man whose picture she had tried to find today and as thoughts and ideas formed and re-formed, she understood why she hadn't seen him, why he wouldn't be there.

Other people came in and out. Scenes were enacted, and slowly she began to piece the sequence of events together. It was a story of deceit and betrayal, of greed and malice. Pain began to build up within her. Pain for Adam...and for herself.

Now she knew. And in order to protect Adam, she must tell him. Would he accept the truth? Was there any way she could prove to him that it *was* the truth?

He dealt with facts and evidence. She had no facts or evidence. Yet she had no choice. Adam had to know, and she would have to tell him.

Caitlin stared up into the night, trying to blank out her mind once more. She watched as the stars began to fade, as light began to filter across the sky, slowly forcing the night to retreat, accepting another day.

"Caitlin?" Adam had stirred in his sleep and reached for her. When he didn't find her, his eyes flew open, and he saw her sitting across the room. "What's wrong?"

"Nothing, I just couldn't sleep."

"Well, come back to bed, and I'll try to help you relax."

She chuckled at the hopeful tone in his voice. Caitlin got up and came over to the bed. Slipping off her robe, she crawled in beside him.

"I missed you," he said, wrapping his arms around her and pulling her close.

"I'm glad." She kissed him along his jawline until she reached the side of his mouth. Then her mouth lingered on his, her tongue teasing him until he took over the kiss. He took his time, tasting and loving her, teasing and nibbling at her lower lip.

Caitlin closed her mind to everything but Adam. She loved Adam and he loved her. They had this time together, these perfect, precious moments when the world couldn't intrude on them.

She would tell him. But not now. Let the morning sunlight usher in the new day. In the quiet of the early dawn, there would only be love and fulfillment and appreciation of each other.

Nine

Caitlin woke to the smell of coffee, and for a moment she thought she was back in the cabin. Then she remembered.

Rolling over, she opened her eyes and found Adam holding a cup of coffee and sitting on the bed.

"I was wondering if you intended to sleep all morning. I didn't mean to wear you out last night." His grin was full of mischief. Adam St. Clair was so full of life. He was enthusiastic about everything and loyal to those he gave his love and friendship to. It was that loyalty she had to disturb this morning.

Trying to gain some time, she accepted the cup of coffee he offered her and asked, "What time is it?"

"After ten."

She hadn't meant to sleep so long.

"Breakfast is here. I went ahead and ordered."

"Oh." She glanced over at the table, all set up.

Hastily finishing the coffee, she slid out of bed, placing the cup on the bedside table.

"I'll be ready in a few minutes." She went into the bathroom and washed her face, brushed her hair and teeth and reminded herself that she could not be a coward. She would tell him…right after breakfast.

Caitlin dressed and sat down across from Adam whose face shone as though a thousand candles had been lit from within. Conversation was limited while both of them ate. Caitlin didn't realize how expressive her face was until Adam finally set his cup down and looked at her for a long moment. The candles slowly seemed to flicker out, and his face filled with strain.

"Are you going to tell me what's wrong?"

"What do you mean?"

"Something's bothering you. You couldn't sleep last night. You're quiet this morning. Are you sorry about last night? Or is it the engagement? Damn it, don't leave me out of your thoughts. Share them with me."

"I know who is trying to kill you."

Her quiet voice seemed to make the words more intense, and for a moment Adam just stared at her, wondering at her tone and the look of strain on her face.

"You're in considerable danger," she added.

He tried to lighten up the situation a little by joking. "If I didn't get the message the first time, the gunman certainly convinced me of that. So who is he?"

"The gunman isn't important. He's a hired killer. You don't have him in your records because he's never been booked. His territory is Mexico and points south. He's never been to the States."

"Do you know who hired him?"

This was the hard part, and she wasn't sure how to explain. "A friend of yours."

He laughed, a short sound that held no sign of amusement. "Right. A friend."

"I mean it, Adam. He's a man very close to you, and he's betrayed you, not once, but many times."

His stomach clenched as he stared at her. She was obviously upset. He knew she believed what she was saying. "Who?"

She was quiet for a few minutes, her eyes closed. When she began to speak, it was in a clear, detached voice—almost without emotion. "He's tall, but not quite as tall as you. He is American but has dark hair and eyes and can pass as a Latin. He wears a closely trimmed beard...quite a ladies' man." She opened her eyes and looked at him. "You know him very well. You've been with him often. You work together."

Adam stared at her in disbelief. That description fit only one man that he worked with, the one man that it couldn't possibly be. He was stunned. He had counted so much on Caitlin's help. He'd believed in her, trusted her abilities, and now she was coming up with something so totally absurd that he had no choice but to discount everything.

Fighting to keep his voice neutral, he said, "Do you by any chance know his name?"

She was quiet for a moment, shook her head slightly and said, "I'm not sure. I think it starts with a *T*. Maybe Tanner...or Tyler."

Damn, she was good. He'd give her that. He wondered how she managed to get the description so accurately, even down to the name.

"Zeke Taylor?"

"Taylor. Yes. That fits." She looked at him, waiting for his reaction, but he didn't have one. He sat there looking at her with a slight smile on his face without saying a word. He leaned forward and poured himself another cup of coffee, silently holding up the pot to her. She shook her head, and he set it down.

He wasn't taking this as she had expected. She thought he would be more upset. From everything she had seen the two men were very close.

"Zeke Taylor, huh?"

"Yes."

"Well, love, I'm afraid your psychic powers led you astray on this one, but that's all right. Nobody expects you to be a hundred-percent accurate."

"You don't believe me."

"Oh, I don't think you're lying. I'm sure you honestly believe what you're saying is the truth. You're just wrong, that's all."

"Am I?"

She sounded so aloof, not like the warm woman he'd held so close to him the night before. She even looked aloof, her face carefully expressionless. He hadn't meant to hurt her feelings. He knew how sensitive she was to her abilities, and he could understand that. He didn't want her to take personally his refusal to accept what she said.

Adam stood up and walked across the room, then turned around and faced her. He rubbed his neck wearily, trying to find the right words.

"There's no way you could know this, but Zeke and I have been working on this case for as long as I've been with the Agency. He's put in as many hours on this as I have. My God! He trained me, as far as that goes. I never made a move down there that he didn't know about.''

''Yes, that fits. He needed to know what you were uncovering.''

Her cool, unemotional voice infuriated him. Instead of accepting his explanation, she used it to strengthen her own position. He tried to stay calm, reminding himself that she was stubborn. It wouldn't help him if he lost his temper.

All right, he decided. He'd play along with her until he could point out the fallacy of what she was saying. ''Caitlin, why would Zeke Taylor want me killed?''

''Because you found out too much about what was going on down there, more than he thought you would. You got too close to him.''

''That doesn't make sense.''

''You remember the man you were to meet the night you were almost killed? Taylor killed him.''

''That's a lie!'' He strode over to her. ''The facts are that Zeke Taylor met the man after I disappeared and got the information that led to Santiago's arrest. Zeke Taylor was the one who solved the case!''

Caitlin stood and walked over to the window. What was happening was as bad as she had feared. She could agree with Adam that she'd made up what she'd said, and perhaps they could eventually ignore what had just happened. But this was one situation she couldn't run from.

Lifting her chin slightly, Caitlin turned and faced Adam, her gaze meeting his squarely. ''No. Taylor already knew the information he gave about Santiago, Adam. He sacrificed Santiago. Taylor had to decide who was expendable, and he certainly wasn't going to turn himself in.'' She walked back to the table and absently toyed with one of the spoons lying there. ''The man died because he intended to tell you about Taylor's involvement in the operation.'' Restless, she walked to the door, then turned and faced him once more. ''Taylor has kept the smugglers informed of the Agency's movements for years. Periodically he throws someone to the Agency to keep them happy.''

Adam stood there watching her as she wandered back to the window. She explained as she paced. ''Santiago was never that heavily involved with the operation, you see. He was a bored businessman who enjoyed the excitement. Zeke used him to front his own involvement. Zeke's the one who vouched for you so that Santiago accepted you so readily into the operations. Zeke needed you where he could keep an eye on you.''

A noise outside the window distracted Caitlin. She glanced down at the river running along beside the hotel and saw a mariachi band playing in one of the pleasure boats cruising by. The lighthearted music seemed to bring into sharp focus the heavy tension that filled the room.

Adam ignored the music drifting up from the river. Instead of allowing the noise to distract him, he forced himself to concentrate on Caitlin's words. He wouldn't allow his reaction to her words to surface.

Caitlin stepped away from the window and looked at Adam. ''Zeke doesn't know how the man you were supposed to meet found out about him,'' she explained, ''but when you called him that night and told him about the anonymous phone call, he knew he had to do something fast.'' Adam's face remained without expression, and she continued, ''He got to the man first and tried to find out how he got the information, but lost his temper and killed the man before he found out.''

Once again, she looked out the window, wishing she was down there with the relaxed and happy crowd, enjoying the music, anywhere but there in that room, throwing words like missiles at Adam. Yet she knew she had no choice but to tell it all.

Turning to the silent man who was watching her every move with quiet intensity, Caitlin said, ''That's when Zeke realized he was going to have to eliminate you before you dug any deeper and found another source that would lead you to him.'' She walked over to him. ''He underestimated you, Adam. You are much smarter and have a great deal more cunning than he gave you credit for.'' Studying the man she loved, Caitlin could feel the waiting stillness that seemed to be wrapped around him. She wanted so much for him to understand.

''Zeke Taylor has a flourishing business in Mexico, one that he doesn't intend to jeopardize over a little thing like friendship.'' Wishing there was a way to soften what had to be said, she continued, ''He likes you, Adam, but you've become too much of a threat to him. As long as you're alive, he won't feel safe.'' In a musing tone she added, ''He still can't figure out how you survived. He saw a picture taken of you at the scene of the crash and thought you were dead.'' Remembering how Adam looked when she'd found him, she could well understand Zeke's conclusion. ''Later, when he discovered your body was gone, he decided not to take any chances and sent his gunman up in the mountains to look for you.''

Adam felt almost numb with shock. His world

seemed to have broken into small, unrecognizable pieces. His belief in his own perceptions and judgment had just received a shattering blow. He broke out in a cold sweat.

Zeke Taylor? Impossible. Zeke had taught him everything he knew. Took him under his wing when he first started. He and Zeke had become good friends. Zeke wanted him dead?

"I'm sorry, Adam."

He heard Caitlin's voice as though from somewhere far away. He forced himself to focus on her face. Her lovely, adorable, lying face.

She had to be lying. Not intentionally, of course, but the pain wasn't any less. Didn't she know what her farfetched ideas could do to a man? They could reduce him to a babbling idiot. Didn't she understand she couldn't go around making wild accusations against people, without a shred of proof? Where was her evidence? Some vision or other she'd picked up in her head? Caitlin expected him to calmly walk into Rob's office and explain that he knew Zeke was trying to kill him because Caitlin had seen it all in a dream?

Adam could feel the pain and frustration pulling at him. "Why didn't you tell me this at the very beginning, when I regained consciousness? If you're so damned psychic, why did you wait until now? You sat there in the office yesterday afternoon—in Zeke's chair, by the way—looking at all those pictures and not coming up with anything. So what are you trying to do now? Trying to make up for wasting our time? Well, this isn't the way to do it, Caitlin. You don't have to make up something, you don't have to tell a bunch of lies and destroy a friendship out of some misguided need to play God.''

He felt as though he'd run for miles. His chest hurt, and he was having trouble breathing. He wanted to smash his fist into something. Dammit! She didn't understand! She was playing around with something that was too vital to be taken lightly.

Psychic responses should be treated as games and nothing more. Something to amuse your friends and family with. He wanted to calm down and try to talk to her, but he was too upset at the moment, not necessarily at her, but at the situation.

Caitlin stood up. ''I never lied to you, Adam. I'm not lying to you now. I didn't pick up on Zeke Taylor before because I wasn't trying to solve anything. I had no desire to find out who was trying to kill you or why. I was just trying to keep you from dying.''

She walked over to the window and stood there looking out. With her back to him, she said, ''You understand now, don't you? Why I can't live around people? Why I can't have close friends or close ties of any kind? When I'm in the mountains, I can control the flow because there are so few people around.''

When he didn't respond, she continued, her voice husky. ''I know what you're feeling right now, you see. You're feeling betrayed and angry and hurt. And you resent the fact that I understand all of that, as though you have no privacy at all, no place to retreat until you can come to terms with what you're feeling.

''This is why I was so uncertain about marrying you. No one should have to live with someone like me. If it helps any, this is what I was trying to protect you from. I don't feel in the least godlike, I'm afraid. I've never felt more human in my life. You see, I loved you so much I ignored everything I'd so painfully learned over the years and tried to convince myself we could make a relationship work.''

Adam felt overwhelmed with emotions. All he knew was that he needed to get away. Moving toward the door, he said, ''Look, we're both upset right now. I need some time to think. I'm sure you do, too. Why don't you do some sight-seeing, and I'll be back later this afternoon? We can talk then.''

She turned around and saw him standing there, his hand on the door, and knew she was seeing him for the last time. ''I'll be fine, Adam. Go ahead and do what you need to do.''

He nodded and walked out the door, closing it quietly behind him.

Caitlin sank down into the chair and stared out the window. The sky was a pale blue now, filled with bright sunlight. A couple of wispy clouds dotted the blue expanse.

She tried not to think about the pain that seemed to be growing inside of her, minute by minute. She needed to be able to think clearly before the pain took over and she could only feel.

Decisions needed to be made. The truth was, she realized, decisions had already been made. Now they needed to be acted upon. She got up and packed the few things she had taken out of her suitcase the night before.

Glancing down at the ring Adam had given her the day before, she carefully slipped it off her finger. She couldn't leave it lying loose in the room. There was no sense in tempting one of the maids.

She placed it in an envelope furnished by the hotel,

sealed it and put the envelope in Adam's bag. He'd see it when he packed.

Making sure she hadn't left anything that was hers, Caitlin left the room. She tried to think of what she had to do before she could allow herself to feel anything. Go to the airport. Get a plane to Monterrey. Hire a car to take her as far as the village, hike back to her cabin.

Rebuild her old life.

While she waited for the plane at the airport, one thought filtered through the careful blankness of her mind.

I must have needed to experience the loss of our love as strongly as Adam needed to experience the betrayal of a friend. She wondered why life's lessons seemed to come so hard.

Adam walked for several hours without any idea where he was. When he stopped, he realized that he had been following the scenic River Walk, ignoring the other people, his mind wrestling with the shock he'd received that morning.

He knew he'd overreacted. He'd known that at the time. Caitlin hadn't been to blame, and yet he'd accused her of lying, of all kinds of nonsensical things. Even though he didn't understand Caitlin's perceptions, he did know that she was sincere and had only been trying to help.

That was the key, he was sure. Because she wanted to help so much, she had forced some sort of "pick up" that she had misread…misinterpreted…something.

He glanced at his watch and realized it was almost three o'clock. Rob expected them in before now, but he knew Caitlin wouldn't be in the mood to look at any more pictures. Neither was he.

But he needed to go in. Wishing that Dane were there to discuss this with, he headed to the office. When he arrived, Rob's secretary smiled and said, "You're supposed to go on in whenever you show up, I believe were his words."

Adam knew he was going to hear about not coming in until midafternoon the day after he got himself engaged. Schooling his expression not to reveal his thoughts, he tapped at the door and opened it at the same time.

The man seated across from Rob wore a Mexican shirt, faded jeans and Mexican sandals. His wide smile flashed white in contrast to his close-trimmed beard when he saw Adam standing in the doorway. He dropped his feet off the desk where he'd had them propped and stood up. Throwing his arms around Adam, he hugged him and said, "Well, *mi amigo*, Rob tells me congratulations are in order. I can't believe it, you old reprobate. You're finally going to settle down."

"Hello, Zeke, what brings you back to the States?" He asked in a neutral tone.

Adam noticed that Rob and Zeke looked at each other in surprise, then back at him.

"Don't tell me you've already had your first quarrel," Rob asked half seriously.

"Something like that," Adam admitted, pulling up a chair and sitting down. "So what's up?"

When Rob realized Adam wasn't going to explain the mood he was in, he shrugged and said, "Oh, I was just trying to fill Zeke in on things at this end."

"Yeah. I'd heard you managed to get yourself out

of Mexico on your own. That was quite a miracle you pulled off, amigo. Why didn't you contact me and let me know you survived?''

''I wasn't in any shape to contact anyone there for a while.''

''What about later? You didn't contact me when you needed to get out of Mexico.''

''I know. I just headed north.''

''That was crazy, man. You know I would have done everything I could have to help.'' Zeke said with a frown.

''Yeah, I know. I still wasn't thinking very clearly.''

''That's quite a little memento you're carrying,'' Zeke said, motioning to the scar on Adam's forehead.

Adam absently rubbed the scar. ''I've almost forgotten about it. It doesn't bother me much anymore.''

''You were damned lucky. You know that, don't you?''

''I know.''

''Rob tells me the woman who nursed you back to health is your fiancée?''

''That's right.''

''When am I going to meet this lady?''

''You know how it is, Zeke. We haven't been doing much socializing these days.''

Zeke grinned. ''Rob says she's quite good-looking.''

''I think so.''

''I know you. You're afraid I'm going to steal her away from you.''

''Something like that.''

''Seriously, I'd really like to meet her. Rob tells me she saw the man who tried to kill you.''

Adam was finding himself more and more reluctant to continue the conversation. He didn't believe what Caitlin had told him, not for a minute. Zeke's questions and concerns were valid and directly connected with his work. But Adam's emotions had just gone through a wringer, and he wasn't up to much more at the moment.

"Yes, but she wasn't able to identify him from any of our mug shots."

"That's too bad. Is she in our office now? Maybe I'll go on back and introduce myself." Zeke stood up and stretched.

"No, I didn't bring her today. She was tired."

"So you left her sleeping in at the hotel, did you?"

"I think she was going to do some shopping."

"Where are you two staying?"

"At the Hilton."

"Good choice." He turned to Rob. "Well, guess I'll check my desk and see what's been happening. I'll talk to you guys later." He waved and walked out of the room.

Adam looked over at Rob. "Why did Zeke say he was up here? I didn't catch that."

"Oh, said he was checking out some leads. Seemed to be very interested in everything that had happened to you. He says you're one of his most valuable men down there. He was quite upset when he thought we'd lost you."

Damn Caitlin for planting doubts in Adam's mind. There was no reason to suspect Zeke, no reason in the world.

"How well do you know Zeke, Rob?"

"Hell, I don't know. As well as I know you,

maybe. Zeke was here when I transferred in from Washington.''

''When was that?''

''About eight years ago. Why?''

''I just wondered. He's been with the Agency a long time, then, hasn't he?''

''Fifteen years.''

''And he's spent all his time in Mexico?''

''That's right. All but the first two years. Is there some point to all of this?''

''Isn't it unusual that he hasn't been promoted or transferred out?''

''He's turned down numerous promotions. Says he likes field work too much.'' Rob leaned forward. ''What the hell is this all about?''

Adam sighed. He could either bury it right now or go with Caitlin's unsubstantiated report.

''Rob, only two people knew I had a meeting that night—Santiago and Zeke. I didn't make the meeting with Santiago's contact, as you know. Zeke was the only other person who knew I would be going out into the mountains.''

''What are you saying?''

''I'm not sure. All I know is that I would swear I was not followed that night. Whoever came up behind me was waiting on some side road. Someone who knew where I would be going.''

The two men sat across from each other. They both knew what the other was thinking. Their salaries were good but couldn't begin to compare with the kind of money generated by the rapidly expanding drug business.

If Zeke Taylor had succumbed, he wouldn't be the

first agent who had been lured into switching allegiance. He wouldn't be the last.

But if he were straight, how could Adam ever face him again if he pointed the finger at him without any proof whatsoever? He didn't know what to do.

"I'm not telling you you're wrong, Adam," Rob said slowly, rubbing his chin thoughtfully. "But Zeke's the one who pulled this one out of the fire for us. He made the contact you intended to make, got the information and nailed Santiago."

"Yeah, I know. I've spent quite a lot of time thinking about that. However, just for the sake of argument, let's suppose that Zeke *is* involved—up to his eyeballs.... If that's the case, he would already have that information. He wouldn't have needed to get it from someone else.

"Suppose the information I was to get that night was something else entirely. Say...something about Zeke. Isn't it interesting that the informant turned up dead, right after Zeke saw him?"

"You're saying Zeke killed him?"

"I don't know what I'm saying. I'm just thinking out loud."

The men sat there in silence for an extended period of time—men who were trained to do mental gymnastics with any kind of information handed to them. Each of them knew better than to ignore the flimsiest of supposition. Sometimes the most unorthodox information led to the most revealing conclusions.

Eventually Rob sat back in his chair and sighed. He looked tired...almost defeated. There was nothing worse than a traitor in an organization. He'd been around too long not to know that they existed. But he never enjoyed having to face it.

"I could do some investigating if you think it's called for," Rob finally said. "Check on his bank accounts, that sort of thing. He couldn't hide that much extra income, although since he lives down in Mexico, we haven't kept tabs like we could if he were here."

"I don't know what to say, Rob. I really don't. I just have this sick feeling in the pit of my stomach. And I can't help but think about Caitlin's predicament if Zeke had anything to do with what happened to me."

"What do you mean?"

"She can identify the driver. And we have filled Zeke in on everything. If we can find the driver, and he can point the finger at Zeke—"

"That's assuming that the driver is working for Zeke."

"Yeah."

"And that's what you think."

"I don't know what I think."

"Well, dammit, that's what you're saying. Or did you watch too much television last night and dream up this whole scenario?" Rob hated to think where an investigation like this would end, but now that it had surfaced, he couldn't ignore it.

"I just think we need to look at the fact that no one else knew where I was going, that's all. Is that enough to start watching what Zeke is up to? Do we really know what leads he's following up here? Is it possible I'm one of his leads? And that now we've told him about Caitlin, he'll try to find out how much of a threat she is to him?"

Rob picked up the phone and pushed the intercom button. "Would you tell Zeke I'd like to see him?"

Adam glanced up in alarm. Surely he wasn't going to tell him what they were talking about. Not yet. They had no proof. They had nothing. And if Caitlin was right, they'd be giving him all the warning he needed to cover his tracks.

"Oh?" Rob said. "When did he leave?" He frowned at Adam. "I see. No, no problem." He hung up the phone, his frown growing.

"He's gone?"

"Yeah, said he had some things he wanted to do and probably wouldn't be back today."

"Which could be perfectly in line with his job."

"Yeah."

They both sat there for a few moments.

"Where's Caitlin?" Rob finally asked.

"I'm not sure. We had words earlier, and like an idiot I stormed out. I'm not particularly proud of my behavior."

"Don't be too hard on yourself, Adam. You've had a rough few months. We all get a little touchy when somebody's trying to kill us."

"Particularly if it happens to be a friend."

Rob stood up. "Why don't you get back to the hotel and make up with your fiancée? I'd feel a hell of a lot better if you didn't let her out of your sight for a few days, at least until I've had some things checked out." He looked over at the window for a moment, then his gaze returned to Adam. "We need to follow up on this one. I think your concerns are valid, but I hope you're wrong. Something like this is like a cancer in an organization. Once you open it up, you don't know how far it has spread or how fatal the disease." Sitting back down, he waved his hand toward the door.

"Go play besotted fiancé. I've got work to do."

Adam nodded and left the room. He agreed with Rob. He hoped they were wrong about Zeke. But if they weren't…if they weren't? Then Caitlin had given them information that they wouldn't have received from anywhere else. Zeke hadn't made any mistakes, so he thought he was safe.

However, he might feel that both Adam and Caitlin were expendable. Adam found himself walking faster. He needed to get back to the hotel, back to Caitlin.

He had to let her know how much he loved her.

Ten

By the time she heard the announcement that her flight was canceled, Caitlin felt numb, which she considered a blessing. All she wanted to do was to get back to her home and away from the mass of confusion that swirled around her. The announcement put an end to her plans of trying to get back that day.

She couldn't get Adam out of her mind. She still felt his pain and confusion, but she also felt his guilt over his behavior toward her. However, she wasn't ready to face him again. Too many things had been said, too many emotions had been bared. Someday, maybe, she would be able to sit down and discuss with him the fact that they could not have a relationship, but only after she gained some control over her emotions.

When would that be? she wondered. Well, maybe in another five years or so. Could she ever be unemotional where Adam was concerned, particularly if she ever saw him again? Caitlin seriously doubted it.

"Excuse me," she said to the harried airline official behind the counter.

"Yes, ma'am?"

"When is your next flight to Monterrey?"

"Tomorrow afternoon at 3:30."

"You don't have any other flights out today?"

"No, ma'am."

"Does any other airline fly to Monterrey?"

"Not from this airport."

"I see."

"I'm sorry, ma'am. There were problems with the engine of the plane scheduled for this flight, and the plane had to be grounded. We're doing the best we can."

"I'm sure you are," she murmured. "Thank you."

Now what was she to do?

She wished she knew.

Adam felt a distinct sinking sensation in his stomach when he returned to the room and found Caitlin gone. Of course, she could be out shopping, or sightseeing, but somehow he knew better. When he saw that her suitcase was gone, his worst fears were confirmed.

She'd left. And why not, after all the accusations he'd hurled at her? She had more intelligence than to sit around and wait for his next attack.

Adam called the front desk, knowing there was only a slim chance that someone had seen her leave. But he had to try. He had to do something before he faced the fact that Caitlin was gone.

"Can you tell me when my wife left the hotel?"

He wasn't about to get into their marital situation with the desk clerk.

"No, sir, I'm afraid not. I came on at three today. Her key was already here."

Great. She left before three. And she took her luggage, which meant she had no intention of returning. Where would she go?

There was only one place Caitlin would go, her safe retreat from the world. He called the airport.

"What airlines fly to Monterrey?"

When he was given the name of the airline, he called their number, but there was no answer. He glanced at his watch. It was almost seven. What did no answer mean? Had they gone out of business? Gone bankrupt? Or did the pilot answer the phone when the plane was on the ground?

Oh, Caitlin, love, where are you? Do you have any idea how sorry I am for upsetting you? Do you know how much I love you? I've got this damnable temper, but I didn't mean to take it out on you. Please don't run. Please stay here and help me work this out. It's our problem and we need to solve it together.

He paced the floor, trying to decide what to do. Should he go out and walk the streets, go looking for her? And if so, where?

Adam decided to call Rob at home.

"Hello, Sara," he said, when Rob's wife answered. "This is Adam St. Clair. Rob around, by chance?"

He waited impatiently while he heard Sara call Rob to the phone.

"Yes, Adam? Anything new happening?"

"Caitlin's gone."

"What do you mean, gone?"

"I mean that she and her luggage are no longer in the room."

Adam listened patiently while Rob made a few choice comments, none of which were printable.

"My sentiments exactly," Adam added quietly when Rob paused for breath.

"That must have been one hell of a fight you had," Rob finally said. "Where do you think she's gone?"

"Back to her home."

"In Mexico?"

"Yeah."

"Well, that's just great, isn't it? If what we think is true, she's going to be a sitting duck down there."

"Maybe, except no one knows where she lives. That's why I wasn't found earlier."

"So you think maybe she's just as safe there as here?"

"I don't know what to think at this point. All I know is I have royally messed up this relationship, and I don't know where I'm going or what to do."

"Take it easy, old man. If what you suspect is true, your brilliant deductions may have cracked this drug ring wide open."

"They weren't my deductions, Rob. That's what all of this is about."

"What are you talking about?"

"The fight I had with Caitlin. She's psychic, clairvoyant, whatever the hell you call it. She picked up on the man, gave me his motivation, his thoughts and ideas, the whole thing, and I blew up at her."

Stunned silence greeted him for a moment. In a tentative tone, Rob asked, "You mean Caitlin's one of those people who gazes into a crystal ball and tells your future?"

"Not quite that dramatic, but along those lines, yes."

"But you didn't believe her about our man."

"Not at first, no."

"What made you change your mind?"

"I'm not sure. I probably wouldn't have if he hadn't been in the office and I had an opportunity to be with him. Once she planted the idea in my head, it seemed to wipe away all my preconceived ideas of him. I had always seen him through the eyes of friendship. Today I watched him as I would watch any other possible suspect, and I picked up on things I wouldn't have noticed before."

"Such as?"

"Mannerisms, body language, eye contact. That warm, friendly greeting I got looked great, and I probably would never have questioned it, but his eyes were cold, Rob. He was studying me, trying to figure out what I knew, if anything. I could almost feel it."

"Maybe you're psychic, too," Rob said with a chuckle.

"You know as well as I do that our intuitive abilities get overworked in this business."

"I know."

"Well, mine kicked into overdrive during that session, Rob. By the time he left, I wasn't nearly so certain that Caitlin hadn't hit on something."

"You've got a lot to be thankful for in that woman, you know."

"I know. I've just got to find her and convince her that although I'm a complete clod I love her to distraction."

"I just wish we had something concrete to hang on him," Rob pointed out. "I made some phone calls down into the Interior right after you left. I skipped over all our standard means of communication and went to Mexico City. At the moment we don't dare trust any of our usual pipelines. I explained the urgency. We should be hearing something soon.''

"Thanks, Rob. I appreciate your going through all of this.''

"Well, I won't pretend that I don't hope you two are proved wrong.''

"I feel the same way.''

"Call me as soon as you hear something from Caitlin.''

"If...that's the operative word.''

"This is just temporary for you two—any fool could tell that. There's an energy field around the two of you that almost lights up, it's so strong. And I don't have to be able to predict the future to know you'll work this thing out.''

"I appreciate the vote of confidence. I'll talk to you later.''

Adam hung up the phone, feeling somewhat better. Rob was right. There was no way he was going to allow Caitlin to disappear from his life. At the moment his greatest concern was to protect her. If what he suspected was true, bringing her to San Antonio had increased the danger to her considerably.

Sighing, he dropped into the chair in front of the window and gazed out at the night.

Caitlin had lost track of time. She felt as though she'd spent days at the airport, but when she caught a taxi back downtown, she realized she'd been gone for only a few hours.

At least sitting there waiting for a plane that never

took off had given her some time to think. Her thoughts hadn't been particularly pleasant. She'd had to face that she was a coward, something that she had suspected but had oftentimes tried to deny.

She was running away. Just as she had run away before. When was she going to stop running and confront her fears?

She loved Adam. She knew that he loved her. Didn't she have enough faith in them to believe that whatever their problems they could work them out?

Adam's love seemed to surge around her in heavy waves as though he were sending messages to her. By the time she got into the taxi, Caitlin knew that she had to return to the hotel and face Adam.

Perhaps that plane hadn't taken off for a reason. She'd been given another chance to rethink her position. Caitlin didn't believe in coincidences. As much as she dreaded facing him again, she knew that she needed to see Adam.

There were a great many cars and taxis in front of the Hilton, and she suggested the driver of her taxi let her out nearby. After she paid him, she grabbed her bag and started down the street toward the main entrance.

A sense of unease settled over her, and she paused. Something was wrong. Without analyzing her feeling, Caitlin knew that she needed to bypass the lobby area. She went into a boutique that had entrances on both the street and inside the hotel. Watching the hallway, she left the boutique and quietly went toward the lobby.

What was wrong?

The lobby, like the parking area, was filled with a

milling group of people, conventioneers from the look of it. She felt no threat from any of them.

Then her mind's eye clearly focused on a man who was across the lobby, talking to a bellhop—a man with dark hair and eyes and a closely-trimmed beard.

Zeke Taylor.

She had no idea what he was doing in San Antonio but knew without a doubt that he was looking for her. Hastily stepping back, she glanced around and spotted the stairway that led upstairs. After climbing to the next floor, Caitlin got on the elevator and rode to the floor where she and Adam had spent the night before.

When she started down the hallway, Caitlin realized that she hadn't stopped for her key. She could only pray that Adam was in the room. Pausing for a moment, she took a deep breath and exhaled, forcing herself to relax. She tapped lightly on the door and waited, forcing herself not to hold her breath.

Adam heard a soft tap on the door, and he sprang from his chair. Few people knew he was there. Zeke was one of them. He had his pistol in his hand when he asked quietly from the other side of the door, "Who is it?"

"Caitlin."

Adam threw open the door, grabbed her and hauled her into his arms. Kicking the door closed behind her, he held her tightly against him, his forgotten gun pressed against her back.

"Oh, God, Caitlin. I've been so worried. Where the hell have you been? I've been about out of my mind!"

Not giving her a chance to answer him, he began to kiss her, then he seemed to remember that he still held his pistol in his hand, and he paused, looking down at her.

"Do you have any idea how much I love you, lady?" he asked, his voice so gruff she could barely understand him.

"I love you, too, Adam. And I don't blame you for your doubts. I'm just so afraid at the moment."

He'd laid the gun down by the bed and gathered her in his arms once again. "Don't be. Everything's going to work out all right. You'll see. Everything's going to be fine."

"Adam?"

"Hmmm?"

"I know how you feel about Zeke and all. I just think you should know he's in San Antonio."

"Yes, I know. I saw him—" He looked down at her again. "How did you know? Did you pick up something—"

"He's downstairs in the lobby."

"Here?"

"Yes."

He immediately dropped his arms from around her and walked away.

"I know he's your friend, and I understand how you feel, but I'm afraid of him."

"Yeah, well, I can understand that."

"Do you think he's coming up here?"

"There's a strong possibility. I told him where we were staying, and he said he'd like to meet you."

She felt a shiver run over her spine.

"Don't worry; I have no intention of letting him see you. Your best protection from him at the moment is that he doesn't know what you look like."

There was a knock at the door, and they stared at

each other. Adam put a finger to his lips, then asked, "Who is it?"

"Zeke."

Adam glanced around, saw Caitlin's bag and picked it up. In three strides he'd placed it in the bathroom, behind the door, motioned for her to get into the shower, then went back to the door and opened it.

"Well, hello, Zeke. I didn't expect to see you. Come on in."

Zeke wore the same clothes he'd had on earlier. He walked in, glanced around the room, then went over by the windows and sat down.

"Where's your fiancée?"

"Good question."

"What do you mean?"

"I guess I must have made her madder than I thought this morning. When I came back, she was gone, bag and baggage."

Zeke laughed. "Some ladies' man you are, St. Clair. Thought I'd trained you better than to let 'em get away from you like that."

Adam shrugged and sat down across from him. "So what are you up to?"

"Oh, nothing much. Thought I'd stop by and take you guys out for a drink, meet your lady love, that sort of thing."

"Guess you're out of luck, then."

"Where do you suppose she went?"

"Who knows? Probably back to the mountains."

"You never did tell me where you were for all that time. Those mountains are pretty vast."

"To be honest, I couldn't tell you, myself."

"Well, the important thing is that you survived."

"Thanks to Caitlin."

"Yes. Thanks to Caitlin." He looked around the room again. "So. How about you and me going for that drink? It beats sitting around a hotel room and feeling sorry for yourself."

"I'm sure it does, but I don't think I'm up to it tonight. I still get tired easily, and after the past couple of days, I'm pretty beat."

Zeke stood up. "Sure, I understand. I guess I'll see you at the office tomorrow."

"When are you going back to Mexico?"

"I'm not sure, exactly. My plans are still up in the air. What about you?"

"I've been thinking about asking for a leave of absence. There's work that needs to be done around the ranch, and Dane's had his hands full."

"You thinking about giving up your work for the Agency?"

"The thought has crossed my mind more than once these past few months."

"It's a tough business."

"I know. I don't know how you've managed to stay with it so long."

"Oh, it gets in your blood after a while. You get so you can't live without the excitement, that extra boost of adrenaline that comes in from time to time."

"Better you than me." Adam walked him to the door. "I'll see you tomorrow."

Zeke gave a casual wave of his hand and walked out. Adam closed the door, put the night latch on and listened at the door until he heard the elevator arrive. Once he heard the clang of the elevator doors closing, he turned around and found Caitlin standing in the doorway to the bathroom.

"You know about him, don't you?" she said softly.

His eyes met hers. "I do now." Adam walked over to her and began to unbutton her blouse.

"What are you doing?"

"Getting ready for bed."

"Adam, we need to talk."

"I know, I find I can talk better horizontal."

"I'm sorry for running out that way —" Her words died away as she felt his lips pressed along her neck.

"I'm sorry for being a complete fool when you were trying to save both of us," he replied, peeling away her blouse and dropping it to the floor.

"Adam—"

He unfastened her skirt and let it fall to the floor, then pushed her remaining undergarments down. Picking her up, he put her on the bed, where the covers had been turned back by room service.

"Adam, I know how you must feel—"

"Good," he muttered, hurriedly stripping out of his clothes, "then I don't have to explain my intentions."

"No, I mean about Zeke and…everything… Oh, Adam."

His mouth had found her breast, and he tenderly touched his tongue to the peak, his hand gently squeezing the other one.

"I love you, Caitlin," he murmured.

Caitlin was having trouble concentrating on his words. His mouth and hands were using a language all their own, one that caused her body to react in ways that she had no control over.

"Oh, Adam, I love you, too."

"Don't give up on me yet, love. Give me some time to get used to all of your talents and abilities, okay?'' His mouth had touched her intimately, and she could no longer think. She could only feel. Oh, what he did to her, this man. How could she have possibly thought she could leave him? He was too much a part of her. He always would be.

By the time he raised himself above her, Caitlin felt reduced to a mass of sensations, knowing that Adam was the only man in all the world who could fulfill her. She silently prayed that she could be all that he wanted and needed in return.

His possession of her was more than physical. It was as though their very spirits were entwined, and they became lost in the mutual sharing.

Whatever happened, they would face it together. Whatever dangers there were, they would share. Each had something to teach the other—about life, about a heightened awareness, about love.

They had a whole lifetime in which to learn.

Adam and Caitlin fell asleep in each other's arms. The traumas of the day had exhausted them both. Even in sleep they clung to each other, as though aware of how close they had come to losing what they had.

The phone rang several times before Adam was awake enough to answer it. ''H'lo?''

''Good news,'' Rob McFarlane said cryptically.

Adam blinked a couple of times, trying to get awake. He reached over and turned on the bedside light and pushed himself up on the pillow.

''That right?''

''My inquiry detonated a powder keg down south. Seems they've been working on something similar, but going through different sources. The evidence has

been mounting up, but they couldn't put a name or
face to it. Until tonight. As soon as I furnished that,
everything clicked and fell into place. We've got him,
Adam. Got him cold.''

"Why can't I feel better about that?''

"He almost succeeded in killing you, Adam.''

Adam glanced at Caitlin lying next to him, asleep.
Her tousled hair fell across her shoulders, and her
hand rested under her cheek. For the first time he
realized she wasn't wearing his ring.

He suddenly remembered that she had wanted to
talk. He hadn't given her much of a chance to make
any explanations.

She'd responded to him, had admitted that she
loved him, but she'd taken off his ring. Why had he
thought that by taking her to bed he had solved the
rift between them?

"Adam? Did you go back to sleep?'' Rob's voice
sounded amused.

"No, I'm not asleep. But I haven't been thinking
very clearly, either.''

"That's understandable. It's close to three-thirty in
the morning. I'm sorry to wake you up, but I thought
you'd want to know.''

"When are you going to make the arrest?''

"In the morning. There's some paperwork to get
done. And I've got to make sure he can't get out on
bail. If he does, we'll never see him again. If he were
to get across the border, he'd be gone.''

"Are you going to need me for anything?''

"No. You've done enough. You deserve some time
off.''

"Thanks. I need it.''

"I expect a wedding invitation, you know.''

"You'll get one," he replied. *If there's going to be a wedding,* he added silently.

Adam reached over and turned off the light after hanging up the phone, but he continued to lie there, propped up on his pillow. He had a lot to think about. And the biggest selling job he'd ever faced waited for him when Caitlin woke up. He wanted to be ready for it.

Eventually he dozed, sleeping fitfully, his dreams jumbled, but Adam was so aware of Caitlin that he knew the moment she woke up the next morning.

He opened his eyes and looked at her. She was on her side, close enough that he could feel the warmth of her body.

"Good morning," he said, trying to read her expression.

She smiled. "Did I hear the phone ring last night, or was I dreaming?"

"It rang. Rob called to say they had the necessary evidence to pick up Zeke."

"Oh." She propped herself up on her elbow and looked at him. "I know how badly you must feel."

There were degrees of feeling badly, he thought wryly. Losing a friend was tough. Losing your love was a hell of a lot tougher.

She was so endearing. He wished he knew what she was thinking at that moment. He almost envied her the ability to look into another person's head.

"Looks like the case is wrapped up," he offered. "So there's no reason to stay here."

She sat up and stretched. "I know that's a load off your mind, even though it didn't end as you would have hoped. Now you can put all of the past few months behind you and get on with your life." Turning around and looking at him, still stretched out beside her, she asked, "Did you mean what you said to Zeke last night? About getting out of the business?"

"I've given it some thought. Why?"

"I just wondered."

"So what do you want to do now?" Why did his heart rate seem to pick up just because he'd finally put the key question to her?

"Go back to the cabin, I suppose."

Well. He had his answer. Funny that he'd thought all of his fears were behind him. What could he say to that? He couldn't hold her captive on the ranch. She was independent, determined—very determined—stubborn, even. Having previously agreed to marry him didn't lock her into anything. That's what engagements were for, after all. They were a trial period, a testing. And he had flunked the test.

"Do you want me to drive you back?" He was proud of his voice. He sounded carefully neutral, as though his insides weren't churning.

Caitlin paused from sliding out of bed and looked at him, really looked at him. The lighthearted, teasing man she had just begun to know was gone. In his place was the quiet stranger she had nursed back to health.

What was wrong? And why did he ask such a question?

"Don't you want to take me back?"

His eyes looked wintry as they met her puzzled gaze. "Shall I be polite or honest?"

"Okay, so you don't want to make another trip down there. I can understand that." Caitlin stood up and pulled on her robe. "I can fly down there from here, I suppose. But how do you suggest I get every-thing moved from down there to the ranch?''

Her words seemed to shoot a charge of energy through him, and he sat up straight. "The ranch? You're moving to the ranch?"

Caitlin looked at him, worried about his mental condition. She knew he'd been under a tremendous strain for some time. Maybe this latest news had been too much for him. She walked around to his side of the bed and sat down. Taking his hand, she lovingly stroked it between her fingers, lifting it so that she could kiss his knuckles.

"Adam. Most new marriages are begun under a considerable strain. I'm sure ours won't be an excep-tion." She held his palm against her cheek, loving the feel of its work-roughened surface. "I think it only fair that we make the transition between our single and married states as painless as possible. We really need to be together to make it work."

He slid his hand behind her neck and pulled her mouth over to his. When they were only inches apart, Adam muttered between clenched teeth, "Is that your humorous way of trying to tell me that you intend to marry me, after all?"

She blinked her eyes. "What do you mean, after all?"

His mouth clamped tightly to hers in a hard, pos-sessive kiss that left no doubt in her mind that he was perturbed about something. However, it also made it quite clear that he wanted her very badly. By the time he eased the pressure, Caitlin had totally forgotten what they'd been talking about.

Adam hadn't. "Where is your ring?"

She opened her eyes, surprised at his steely tone of voice.

"My ring? Oh! I forgot." Scrambling off the bed, Caitlin hurried over to Adam's suitcase and delved into it. Picking up the envelope she'd left there, she ripped it open and took the ring out. Very carefully she slipped it on her finger and returned to the bed. "There." She smiled at him, a very warm, loving smile.

"Why did you take it off?"

"You know why. I thought our argument proved how unsuited we were and that it proved how right I'd been all along not to get involved with anyone."

He glanced down at the diamond glittering on her hand.

"And now?"

"Now I know that you'll hate it when I know what you're thinking, but it's okay, because we both know the only thing that really matters is that we love each other. That's what counts."

He pulled her down on top of him. "You are a very wise lady, Caitlin Moran. I think you must be a witch."

She chuckled. "That's what the villagers used to call me. Of course they know better now."

"Oh, do they?"

"I'm really very ordinary."

"Um-hm." He began to nibble on her ear. "Caitlin?"

"Yes, love."

"Would you please check your crystal ball and see if there's any reason we have to hurry down to Mexico today?"

"I can't think of any. Can you?"

"No, I can't. I was thinking that maybe we'd want to spend some time today planning our honeymoon."

"You mean this isn't it?"

He rolled over, pulling her down beside him, and began to untie her robe. "No, ma'am. This has been just a preview."

Caitlin ran her hands along his back and shoulders and smiled. "Then I can hardly wait for the main event."

*   *   *   *   *

THE GEMINI MAN

For Jon, another Gemini.

Prologue

"*The Gemini man is not a discerning woman's first choice for a mate if she is looking for a stable home-life and steady companion, although his charm and mental agility may cause her to forget all of her dreams if he is determined to sweep her off her feet. However, a wise woman must use caution and look past his seemingly ageless and invariably attractive countenance to what truly motivates a Gemini man: change.*

For, you see, the Gemini man truly thrives on challenges; boredom swiftly sets in when he finds himself confined to a routine of any kind. His ruling planet is Mercury, the planet that controls communications of all kinds, and his mercurial temperament is readily apparent to all who attempt to draw close to him. Attempt is the operative term because our Gemini man does not want anyone to know who he truly is.

In fact, he isn't all that certain, himself. It is no co-incidence that the astrological sign for Gemini is the Twins. You see, our exhilarating charmer has a dual personality in many respects. He changes his style of dress, his work, his residence, and, yes, my dear, even his love interest, with alarming ease and regularity. He looks for excitement and constant challenge and is determined to disguise his true feelings and desires from those around him.

However, his high energy, his focused interest and charming friendliness sometimes encourages a cou-rageous soul to abandon her caution in an effort to draw closer and attempt to better understand our quicksilver, chameleonlike friend. We may curse him all the while we pursue him, knowing that his mental agility will never allow him to be caught—unless he wants to be, of course. And that, dear friends, is the hope that keeps those who love a Gemini man in de-termined pursuit. If he chooses to share his life with you, make sure that you don't allow yourself to be-come entrapped in dull routine and drudgery. Become a part of his life if you insist, but only at the risk of your need for stability at home.''

Joel Kramer stared blindly at the pages spread be-fore him, feeling conspicuous and exposed, even though he was alone in his small apartment. The as-trological profile had fallen from one of the Sunday supplements of the paper, carefully categorizing both sexes of each of the twelve astrological signs. Be-cause he'd had nothing better to do, he had decided to read what had been written, even though he didn't believe in that sort of thing.

The precision with which he had been portrayed

had more than surprised him. He'd had a shock that made him wince. He didn't like the flippant summary of his personality or the comments regarding his basic characteristics. Joel didn't like the idea that he could be so accurately described. He had a real aversion toward anyone knowing him quite so well. Exactly what the article had said.

Damn! He tossed the offending paper aside and stood, ramming his hands into his pants pockets. He began to pace.

Max had promised to get back to him. Max knew him as well as, if not better than, any other person in the world. He knew that Joel detested inactivity. Once again he winced, remembering the article. Yes, Joel avoided any sort of occupation that was filled with monotonous routine.

He walked to the window and looked down at the river that wound through the wintry Virginia landscape below. It looked cold and forbidding, accurately reflecting what he was feeling at the moment.

At times like this, Joel questioned the wisdom of replacing his father on the agency's payroll. He'd grown up with a parent who had rarely been at home and he'd learned to resent the occupation that had robbed him of a father. But it had taken only one assignment to hook Joel. He'd quickly become addicted to the danger, the uncertainty, the variety of what the agency called on him to do. His first assignment had been twelve years ago. The irony of agreeing to step in and fulfill his father's last assignment had never left him.

Max encouraged Joel's talent for doing the unexpected, for ferreting out information that no one else seemed to find. And yet, for all that, Joel didn't know which branch of the intelligence service he worked for. All he knew was that Max was his only contact with the government.

Joel was good at what he did. He took a certain amount of pride in that knowledge.

Exactly what did he do? Once again he frowned at the offending page that lay scattered in front of his easy chair. Yes. He lead a double life. He was in fact two people—as much as was physically possible for one person without being labeled schizophrenic. His neighbors thought of him as a quiet man who lived alone, who was gone for long periods of time. The landlord had no complaints, either about Joel or from him. He paid his rent on time. He left others alone.

When Max needed him, Joel became whatever Max needed. He gathered information; he watched other people. Like a chameleon, he blended into his surroundings.

Why?

Because he enjoyed the challenge. Because he thrived on outwitting his enemies, staying one step ahead of them in their mental gymnastics.

A mercurial temperament, indeed!

The phone interrupted his frustrated comparisons between his personality and the one described for all the world to see. He felt relief flow through him at the interruption. He knew it was Max before he answered the phone. Who else ever called him? There were no close ties in his life. He didn't need them. He couldn't afford them.

"Yes?"

"You sound a little frustrated, Kramer. Ready to go to work?"

"You know damn well I am."

"I'm afraid the only thing I've got on the books at the moment is a little out of your line. If you don't want to take it, I'll understand."

"At the moment, I'm in no mood to quibble."

"I have a situation that could escalate into a crisis at any time. In order to brief you properly, I need you to meet me. There's someone you'll need to talk with for the necessary background." He gave Joel the name of a hospital and a room number. Joel happened to know that very few people knew of the existence of that particular facility. It was used only for the highest security cases.

"I'll be there."

Joel felt the adrenaline pumping in his bloodstream as he hung up the phone. By the time he left his apartment, the astrology profile had been dismissed from his mind.

Joel went through extensive screening at four separate checkpoints before he made it to the floor where he was to meet Max. This was the first time he'd walked into the place. The only other time he'd been there he'd been brought in unconscious. He'd been a terrible patient. The memories of those days when he'd been so helpless, when he had been forced to rely on others to care for him, flooded his mind at the sights, sounds and smells that surrounded him.

He shrugged his shoulders as though he could shift the memories back where they belonged. As he approached the door to the designated room, Max stepped out and nodded in recognition. "Thanks for your promptness," he said, offering his hand in greeting.

Joel grasped the hand and shook it. "No problem. What's going on?" He glanced around.

"We're not sure, but we don't like the feel of this one. I don't believe in coincidences, and this one is a little too convenient." He motioned Joel around the corner to a grouping of chairs. They sat facing each other. Max leaned back in his chair before continuing.

"Dr. Peter Feldman is one of the foremost research scientists in the United States. Although he is on the payroll of a private corporation, the government has followed his research with a good deal of interest. What he's working on has a great deal of bearing on what we're battling on the domestic front at the moment."

Joel forced himself to assume a relaxed position, sitting back in the chair and placing his elbows on the arm rests.

Max went on. "The war against drugs must be won in this country if we are to survive. However, as long as there is a demand, there will be those countries and people who will supply what is wanted." He paused, raising his eyebrows slightly, as though to invite comment. Joel said nothing since many of his overseas assignments had been gathering information that supported Max's statements.

After a moment, Max continued. "What Dr. Feldman has been working on so diligently is a drug that we hope will be a breakthrough in the field of withdrawal from chemical dependency—such as alcohol and drug addiction." He leaned forward. "He's on the trail of what may prove to be an antidote that, when taken, will cause the body to no longer crave the effects of the particular substance that caused the addiction."

Joel abandoned his casual pose. He leaned forward and asked, "Do you mean a drug to be taken in place of more harmfully addictive drugs?"

"Hopefully the body will eventually develop its own immunity to the abused substances. What Dr. Feldman is currently working on is a short-term regimen that not only will detoxify the body, but help it to overcome the cravings of the particular addiction. The end result, hopefully, will be a permanent repugnance to all types of mood-altering drugs."

Joel whistled softly. "Use of such a drug would effectively demolish the drug trade as we know it."

"Exactly."

"You think somebody knows what Dr. Feldman's been working on?"

"Had you asked that a few hours ago, I would have been emphatic in denying the idea. This particular research project has been as closely guarded as the development of the atom bomb."

"So what happened today?"

"Dr. Feldman decided to go into the lab yesterday, even though it was a Saturday, to catch up on some of the paperwork. He was on his way home last night when his car was run off the road as it approached an embankment. God only knows how he managed to get out before the car went over. He suffered a broken leg and several severe cuts and bruises. He'd already been briefed on who to contact if he ever felt suspicious of anything that occurred around him. One of the first cars on the scene had a cellular phone. He had the driver call us, and we immediately got help out to him."

"And brought him here."

"Yes."

"Did he see the car that ran him off the road?"

"No. It was already dark by the time he left for home. He was traveling a wooded stretch of roadway. Whoever hit him had come up on him without lights. The impact was the first he knew something was wrong."

"You want me to investigate this matter?" Joel asked, his mind already reviewing and arranging the information Max had given him.

"No. What I have in mind is not quite so straight-forward. We already have people working on the accident and its causes. What Dr. Feldman is concerned about is his assistant. That's where you come in."

Joel frowned slightly. "He thinks his assistant may be behind this?"

Max shook his head. "Not at all. He thinks his assistant might be the next target, if this is, in fact, related to their research."

"Which we don't know at this point, I take it?"

"Like I said, I've never cared for coincidences."

"So where do I fit in?"

Max stood and motioned to the room he'd come out of earlier. "I want you to meet Dr. Feldman. He'll be able to explain his concerns to you."

The two men entered the hospital room. Joel paused just inside the door, fighting the memories. Damn, but he hated hospitals! Max walked over to the bed, and Joel slowly followed.

The man lying there was hooked up to various monitoring machines. His left leg was in a cast and in traction. There were several bandages on his arms, hands and around his head. One side of his face was swollen and discolored.

"Dr. Feldman," Max said, "I'd like you to meet the man I spoke of earlier, Joel Kramer."

Joel stepped closer. A pair of vivid blue eyes stared up at him from the battered face. There was no denying the intelligence in them. "I'm sorry that our meeting came about as a result of your injuries, Dr. Feldman. Max tells me that you are doing some innovative research."

Joel knew that the man on the bed had to be in a great deal of pain. He recognized the lack of a narcotic glaze in the eyes that watched him so intently. They reflected the man's pain as well as his refusal to accept relief. ":Thank you for coming," Peter said in a weak voice. "Max assures me that you are one of his most competent men."

Joel glanced at his employer. "I'll remind him of that when my raise comes due."

Max characteristically ignored his jibe and spoke directly to the man in the bed. "Dr. Feldman, perhaps you would like to explain to Joel your concern for Dr. Jordan's safety under the present circumstances."

Dr. Feldman nodded his head slightly. "Yes. She was my first concern when I realized that what happened to me might not be an accident. Max insists that we keep what happened to me quiet. Since I had been planning to take a few days off next week, he wants me to call in sick tomorrow and take the vacation early without letting anyone know the truth, even Dr. Jordan."

"You don't agree?"

"Well, I understand the need for secrecy, but I also don't want to take the chance of having something happen to Dr. Jordan." He closed his eyes for a moment. When he opened them again, Joel could see the pain he fought to ignore. "You see, she isn't aware of the specific nature of our research. I've kept her working on highly specialized tasks without giving her the reasons. I didn't want to place her in a situation where she could be taken advantage of." He moved his head wearily on the pillow. "Over the past several hours, I've come to face the fact that my efforts to protect her were pointless. If someone knows what I am working on, they will automatically assume that my assistant is fully aware of the nature of my research. Her lack of knowledge wouldn't protect her from them." He glanced at Max with an apologetic look. "Even if I tried to warn her, I'm not at all certain that she would believe me. You see, my assistant believes that I have an overactive imagination, which she points out comes from my consuming interest in reading adventure novels." He smiled at the men standing beside his bed. "I must admit that I'm somewhat addicted to them. I read before bedtime as a way to relax in order to sleep. If I explained what happened, she would probably insist that my accident has nothing to do with our research." He moved restlessly in the bed. "And, of course, I can't prove that it has." He focused his gaze on Joel. "But I don't want to take even the slightest chance where she's concerned."

"I see," Joel replied. "I can understand your concern." He glanced at Max. "Don't you trust her to know what is going on?"

"It's not a matter of trust. I want everything to go along as it has without causing possible suspicion in case someone is watching the lab. However, we have already tightened the security, so there is no possibility that anyone could reach her at work."

Joel looked at Max. "Are you suggesting that I need to set up some sort of protective surveillance for Dr. Jordan?"

"Exactly. However, because we don't want to needlessly alarm her, I want you to go in under wraps."

"Protective custody isn't exactly my line of work," Joel pointed out mildly.

"I know," Max agreed. "We can always get someone else to handle this, if you'd like. But since you've been keeping my phone ringing demanding that I give you something to do, I thought you might be willing to take this one."

Joel sighed. As usual, Max knew his people very well. Of course, Joel wasn't going to turn a job down, even if it meant glorified baby-sitting...with a baby who wasn't supposed to know what he was doing!

Max looked at Joel as though waiting for him to deny his comments, but, of course, Joel couldn't. When it became obvious to Max that Joel had nothing further to say, he nodded and said, "The problem as I see it is that Dr. Jordan may or may not be in danger. At this point, we have to assume that she is. Nevertheless, I see no reason to alarm her at this point." He glanced at Joel. "Which is why we prefer that you make yourself a part of her life without her knowing why."

Joel lifted one eyebrow. "In other words, lie to the woman."

"There's no reason to lie. She just doesn't need to know the truth. It so happens that the couple who live directly across from her apartment in Alexandria received a sudden windfall. They are currently closing on the purchase of a condominium near their daughter's home in Florida, which means that their apartment has recently become available."

A fortuitous windfall, indeed, Joel thought cynically.

Max continued. "The apartment is quite nice, and we feel certain that you will be comfortable staying there while you pursue a neighborly acquaintance with Dr. Jordan."

Joel almost groaned aloud. This was not the kind of work he was used to. It wasn't the kind of work he was trained to do. But it was better than sitting at home staring at the four walls. Barely.

"When do I move in?"

Max allowed his features to register surprise. "You mean you'll do it?"

As if there had ever been a doubt in Max's mind! Joel went along with the charade. "Why not? I'm tired of kicking my heels waiting for something to do."

"Your enthusiasm overwhelms me," Max commented.

"I want to make it clear," Dr. Feldman said, "that I don't want Dr. Jordan to feel that she is being spied upon. You see, she is brilliant in the laboratory, her IQ is startling, but she is quite young and inexperienced. I suppose I've become a father figure in her life, in a way. Both of her parents are gone, and she was an only child. I find her modesty refreshing at times, but there are times, such as now, when I recognize that she doesn't realize just how valuable she is to us...or how valuable she would be if the wrong type of people were to get their hands on her."

"Just how young is this woman?" Joel asked.

"Twenty-two."

"Isn't that rather young for the type of work she does?"

"Oh, yes. The woman is truly remarkable. She received her doctorate by the time she was nineteen."

Joel had a mental picture of a studious young woman wearing thick-lensed glasses, a voluminous lab coat and sturdy shoes. She was probably extremely timid, scared of any unexpected sound. And he had to try to befriend her. Great. Just great. He looked at Max. "When do I move in?"

"Tomorrow will be soon enough," Max replied. "Do you know how to type?"

"No. Why?"

"We have to have a reason why you don't leave for work each day. I thought you could tell her that you've taken some time off from your regular job to write a novel."

Joel looked at Max in irritation. "Do I look like a writer to you? Come on, Max. I don't know anything about writing."

Max shrugged. "Doesn't matter. Everyone is convinced that he or she could be a writer if they could find the time to do it. Convince her you're following your dream. Who knows, maybe she can give you some ideas for a story."

Joel shook his head. Sometimes Max's logic eluded him. "You're sure this is the only thing you've got for me to do?"

Max nodded, not bothering to hide his amusement.

"All right, then. Give me the address. I'll go home and pack." Joel glanced down at the man lying on the bed. "In the meantime, you concentrate on getting well. I'll look after your Dr. Jordan."

Dr. Feldman made a slight sound that might have

been a chuckle, then winced. He closed his eyes for a moment before speaking. "Oh, she isn't mine, Mr. Kramer. I'm afraid that Melissa Jordan is totally dedicated to her work. She doesn't seem to have any other interests or hobbies. Her work means everything to her."

"Then she and Joel should get along very well," Max said with a glance at Joel. "He shares a similar trait."

Joel frowned, suddenly remembering the astrology article and what it had said. Like it or not, Joel knew that the article had described him to a T. He didn't like having people know that much about him, including the man he worked for.

He glanced at Max. "I'll be in touch." His first priority was to get out of there. He had a definite allergic reaction to the sight and smell of a hospital.

At least he had something to do, even if it was baby-sitting a success-driven scientist. Max was right. They probably did have a few things in common.

One

Melissa Jordan pulled into the underground parking garage of her high-rise apartment building with a sense of relief. She couldn't remember having experienced such a chaotic day in her entire career. Unfortunately, the blame could be laid at Dr. Feldman's door.

The poor man. As if he didn't have enough to cope with, he ended up coming down with the flu just a few short days before his vacation. She had offered to go to his home and check on him when he'd called that morning, but he'd insisted that he would be all right with a few days of rest. He'd been very apologetic, but, of course, he couldn't help being ill. She sighed. Regardless of the reason, his absence complicated her job. She would just have to do the best she could and wait for his return in a couple of weeks.

Melissa stepped out of her small, bright red sports

car and walked over to the elevator. She shivered,
tugging her coat and hood more closely around her.
She could feel the gusty wind blowing through the
parking area. She glanced around uneasily at the
dimly lit garage. What was wrong with her today?
She'd never been bothered about coming home alone
before. The security of her building was one of the
reasons she had moved to her present apartment. The
iron-grid gate would only open for a specific code that
needed to be punched into the system. Even then,
only one car could get through before the gate closed.

She was just tired, that's all.

After punching the button on the elevator, Melissa
leaned against the concrete wall and stared down at
the toes of her scarlet pumps. Her heavy winter coat
ended at her hips, revealing the skirt of her red
woolen suit. The cold air seemed to encircle her legs.
She shivered again, reminding herself that at least
she'd gotten through the day. By tomorrow, there
would be some type of organization set up until Dr.
Feldman returned.

As soon as the elevator doors opened, she stepped
inside and pushed the button for the fifth floor. She
removed the fur-trimmed hood of her coat from her
head, relieved to be out of the wind, grateful for the
relative warmth of the unheated elevator. The first
thing she intended to do when she reached her apartment was to take a long, soaking bath. Not only
would the hot water warm her chilled body, but it
would also help to remove the tension that had her
muscles in knots.

When the elevator reached her floor, she stepped
out and headed down the hallway, digging for her
keys in her purse.

A slight sound startled her, causing her to raise her head with a jerk.

A man stood in front of the door opposite hers, placing a key in the lock. She'd never seen him before. He glanced around at her, giving her a chance to study him.

He was only a few inches taller than she was with her high heels. Candid silver-gray eyes peered at her from behind rimless glasses. He hadn't gotten that deep tan from around here, she decided. His light brown hair had streaks of blond or silver, she couldn't decide which.

He looked away from her and fumbled with his key. *This must be my new neighbor.* Normally, Melissa wouldn't have dreamed of speaking to a man she didn't know. But if he was going to be her neighbor, that was different. Besides, the startled look he'd given her suggested that he might be shy.

"Have you just moved in?" she asked. The sudden sound of her voice in the quiet hall seemed to startle them both.

He turned his head and glanced at her. "Oh, I, uh—yes. I just moved in this morning."

He had trouble meeting her eyes, and she smiled. *Why, he is shy,* she decided. Impulsively, she held out her hand. "I'm Melissa Jordan, your neighbor. There's just these two apartments on this floor."

The man studied her hand as though unsure what he was supposed to do with it. Tentatively touching it with his fingers, he nodded. "Pleased to meet you."

She could have sworn she saw a blush touch his cheeks. Probably not. His tan would camouflage such a betrayal.

She turned away and put her key into her door.

When it opened, she gave him a little wave. "If I can be of any help to you, don't hesitate to knock. I know how it is, trying to get settled in."

She closed the door, almost amused at the look of stunned disbelief on the man's face. Maybe he wasn't used to friendly neighbors. Well, he could just get used to it, she decided, kicking off her shoes and shrugging out of her coat.

She missed the elderly couple who had suddenly decided to move to Florida to be closer to their daughter. They were the kind of family she'd never had—warm and friendly, popping over to bring her freshly baked bread and cookies, inviting her to share an occasional meal. They had shown her nothing but kindness. If she could, she'd like to repay that kindness by offering a stranger a friendly smile and a warm hello. Maybe this weekend she'd bake him some cookies or something.

Melissa headed for the bedroom, where she intended to get out of her clothes and enjoy a nice, soaking bath.

Joel stood in the hallway, staring at the door marked 5A. *That* was Melissa Jordan? That was the scientist who needed protecting? Was this some kind of joke that Max had decided to play on him?

Melissa Jordan was a far cry from Joel's imagined laboratory assistant. Even in the bulky coat, he'd recognized that her tall, lithe figure would look right at home walking down the runway of a beauty contest. Wide-spaced blue eyes had stared at him from behind thickly fringed black lashes. A slight dimple had flashed in her right cheek when she'd smiled. Her honey-blond hair had been pulled back from her face in a professional coil at her neck and he'd had the unnerving impulse to pull the pins out of it just to see what she would look like with it tumbling around her shoulders.

Joel had a strict policy of never mixing business with personal pleasure. In the past, that philosophy had never come under scrutiny. But how in the world was he supposed to become platonic friends with a woman whose very presence caused his body to instantly respond to her beauty? Even her voice had started an itch somewhere deep inside of him.

He's spent the day familiarizing himself with the location of the building and its surrounding area, checking the security of the building. He'd been given a description of the car owned by Dr. Jordan so that he'd been aware of her arrival. He'd made certain that he was in the hallway when she stepped off the elevator so that he could casually meet her. What had caught him off guard was how differently she looked from the way he'd imagined her. This was no timid laboratory mouse. Melissa Jordan was a real fox.

He could just hear Max laughing if he tried to complain that the woman he was to protect was too good-looking and would be a distraction in his efforts to do his job. No doubt Max would have him back in the hospital…only this time on the psychiatric floor.

The problem was that a job of this nature was way out of his field of expertise. Was Max deliberately giving him assignments that he considered safe? Didn't he trust Joel to take care of himself after that last fiasco?

Only Max knew what he was thinking, and Joel knew beyond any doubt that Max would only tell him what Max decided he needed to know.

Once again, Joel looked at the door opposite his own. At least the first hurdle had been overcome— Dr. Jordan knew that he was her new neighbor. It was now up to him to make the next move.

Melissa sank into the water-filled tub and let out a sigh of pleasure. Heaven, that's what it was. Pure, unadulterated heaven. For a while, she blanked out her thoughts. Instead, she allowed herself to enjoy the sensations that were becoming part of her. She felt the warmth and softness of the water wrapping her in liquid silk; she smelled the provocative scent of the oil; she was soothed by the sound of the gentle swish of water when she moved. Melissa could feel the tension leaving her body as though it were draining out of each pore, until she became a part of the feel, the scent and the sound of the water.

Eventually, her thoughts returned to her new neighbor and her unusual reaction to him. The look he'd given her before dropping his gaze had been one of definite male interest, which had surprised her. She wasn't used to receiving looks of that nature. She considered herself to be a scientist, first and foremost. Any stray thought about her own sexuality was quickly relegated to that part of her brain labeled Nonessential Information.

She frowned slightly. Why was that? she wondered. Her thoughts lazily sought the elusive answer, trained to accept any hypothesis and immediately go into action seeking a satisfactory explanation.

Was it because she was an only child? Surely not. Many people were only children, and they lived normal lives. Ah, that was it. A normal life. When had her life ever been considered normal?

Her parents had been pleasantly immersed in the world of academia when she had unexpectedly made her entrance into the world. No doubt she had been a shock to two dedicated people whose lives were devoted to theory and research.

When had they discovered her unusual intelligence? She had no way of knowing because she had never asked the particulars surrounding her upbringing when they were alive. Now, all she knew was what she could remember.

Her earliest memories were of classrooms where she was the youngest person. Her parents had made certain that she received the education she needed to spark her inquisitive mind. She recalled their pride in her, their encouragement to pursue her studies.

No one had suggested that she needed to learn how to interact with people her own age. She had finished her postgraduate work while still a teenager, too young and too inexperienced to know how to respond to the males with whom she came into contact.

Young, attractive men were alien to her way of life. She could not relate to them.

The problem was, Melissa admitted to herself, she didn't know how to respond to a man when he got that certain gleam of appreciation in his eye when he looked at her. Anyway, it didn't matter. Her new neighbor deserved to be treated with friendly courtesy. She doubted that they would see much of each other. Now that she'd thought about it, he hadn't even told her his name.

I wonder what he does for a living? She wriggled her toes in the water. *I wonder if he's married?* She grinned, amused by her wandering thoughts. What difference did it make? She was beginning to sound like her college roommate, whose entire life had been focused on the male species. Karen would no doubt have already figured a way to see the man again in order to get all her questions answered. There were times when Melissa wished she could be more like Karen—bubbly and outgoing, friendly as a puppy, totally unself-conscious.

When Melissa saw an attractive male, she immediately felt as though she were all elbows and knees, stammering, trying to think of something to say.

She had to face it. Her new neighbor was definitely attractive. Could it be possible that he was as shy as she? Only time would tell, and she had plenty of time.

Feeling better after her prolonged soak in the tub, Melissa reluctantly allowed the cooling water to drain from the tub. She grabbed a thick yellow towel that picked up the color scheme of her bathroom and briskly dried herself. Then she reached for her floor-length bathrobe, slipped it on and zipped it to the collar at her throat.

After vigorously brushing her hair out, Melissa started to the kitchen. Since she enjoyed working in the kitchen, she had long been in the habit of preparing and freezing meals on the weekends to eat when she got home after work during the week. She was trying to decide what she wanted for dinner when the doorbell rang.

She paused in the kitchen doorway, puzzled. Who could that possibly be? The insistent ringing reminded her that the best way to appease her curiosity would be to answer the door. Fighting a certain characteristic reluctance, Melissa walked over to the door and opened it.

Her neighbor stood in the hallway with a slight

smile on his face, his hands in his pockets. "Hi! I'm sorry to bother you so soon, but you did offer to help me if I needed it." He paused, looking at her with appealing diffidence. His eyes stayed focused on hers. "The thing is..." He seemed to be searching for words.

Melissa realized that she was standing there barefoot, still in her robe, no doubt looking flushed from her recent bath. She could feel her color mounting once again.

"The thing is," he repeated hesitantly, "I was wondering if you would be able to tell me where the closest grocery store is located? I hate to get out and start driving without any idea where I'm headed."

"There's a store about three blocks from here," she offered with a slight smile.

"In which direction?"

She pointed without saying anything.

"Okay. Thanks."

She watched uncertainly as he turned away and started down the hallway. He'd almost reached the elevator before she was able to say, "Uh—excuse me?"

He glanced around.

"I, uh, was just about to warm up a casserole that's more than enough for two people. You're welcome to share it with me, if you'd like."

He stared at her as though he couldn't quite believe what he'd heard. "Are you inviting me to join you for dinner?"

Her cheeks felt as though they were on fire. "Only if you want to, of course."

Joel walked slowly toward her. "But you don't know me."

Now she was feeling like a complete fool. "Well, yes, I'm aware of that. However, I know that if you passed the rigid screening done by the management of the building, you're all right."

He stopped in front of her. "You're very trusting, aren't you?"

Suddenly Melissa realized how foolish she was being. "You're right. It was a stupid thing to do."

"No, wait," he said, placing his hand on the door. "Don't get me wrong. I'd really enjoy sharing a home-cooked meal, believe me. You just caught me off guard, that's all."

Melissa didn't know how to respond. He saved her from the necessity of a reply by stepping past her into her apartment.

The impulse to invite him in had shocked her. His acceptance of the invitation completely unnerved her. Slowly, Melissa closed the door, then turned to face him.

"I didn't get a chance to introduce myself, earlier. I'm Joel Kramer. And I think it's very kind of you to invite me to dinner. Thank you." He pushed his glasses up slightly where they rested on the bridge of his nose.

Once again, she noticed an endearing shyness in this man that gave her some much-needed confidence. "I'm glad you decided to accept my offer. I get tired of eating alone," she admitted with a smile.

Trying to hide her nervousness, she motioned him toward the arrangement of sofa and chairs in the living area of her apartment.

He glanced around the room, then looked back at her. "I like the way you have your place arranged. I hope I can manage to get my place into something as livable. The movers set everything in each room without any attempt to arrange the stuff comfortably.'' He stopped talking, but continued to look at her with a quizzical expression on his face. Melissa realized she was still standing by the front door.

"Have a seat,'' she managed to say in a jerky voice, ''and I'll put the casserole on.'' She felt a certain sense of relief as soon as she disappeared into the kitchen. What had she been thinking of, asking him to stay for dinner? Didn't she have any sense at all? She didn't know the man, and she didn't have a clue how to make casual conversation.

Melissa peeked around the doorway. He was studying one of the paintings on her wall.

Melissa took a deep breath. There was no harm in being neighborly, after all, she pointed out to herself. She would feed him and then he would go home. There was no reason to think that he would see her offer as anything but a neighborly gesture.

She hoped.

"Would you like a glass of wine?'' she asked.

He turned abruptly to face her, and she realized that he wasn't as relaxed as he'd first appeared. ''If you're having one.''

She nodded. "I have a nice Rhine, or cabernet sauvignon. Do you have a preference?''

"Not really. Whatever you're having.''

Melissa forced herself to take a deep breath, then slowly exhaled. She placed the casserole in the oven, poured two glasses of wine and returned to the living room.

"Aren't your feet cold?'' he asked, taking one of the glasses.

She nodded. "I just got out of the tub when you

rang. If you'll excuse me for a moment, I'll get dressed.

"Sure." He sat down and watched her go through a door that he assumed led to her bedroom.

Joel sipped the wine, enjoying the fruity flavor and the slight tingle on his tongue. After glancing at the closed bedroom door, he rose quietly and soundlessly moved to the window. With practiced ease, he edged the blind aside enough to look down at the street.

The nondescript car that had followed Melissa home was still there, parked across from the building. He'd spotted the tail shortly after she arrived. He'd reported the license-plate number to Max before he hurried into the hall to greet his new neighbor. Hopefully, he'd have a little more to go on before long.

Was Dr. Jordan aware that she'd been followed? He couldn't tell. Joel moved back to his chair and sat down, deliberately assuming a posture of nonchalance, and waited for her to appear once more. An assignment watching an attractive woman who invited him to join her for a home-cooked meal definitely had its positive side. This assignment certainly beat the last one down in Central America.

The bedroom door opened, and Melissa appeared wearing a royal-blue running suit the color of her eyes.

Joel smiled at her. Now that he was adjusting to being around her, he realized that he'd have to remember to thank Max for the assignment. He didn't think he was going to mind looking after Melissa Jordan at all.

She sat down across from him and nervously sipped her wine. She'd been rehearsing possible conversational gambits while she dressed, but now her mind was a total blank.

"Have you lived here long?" Joel asked after the silence had stretched out for several minutes.

"A little over five years." Melissa took another sip of her wine, hoping it would relax her.

"Are you from Virginia?"

"No. Massachusetts."

Another long silence stretched between them.

"Where do you—"

"Do you work—" They both spoke at once, then stopped.

"What were you—"

"Go ahead and—" Again, they spoke together.

Joel began to laugh, an infectious chuckle that caused a ripple of awareness to flow through Melissa. Once again, she could feel her color changing. She detested her thin skin that so quickly betrayed her emotions.

"What were you going to say?" Joel asked with a grin.

Melissa brushed an errant curl away from her cheek. "Oh. I was just going to ask you where you were from."

Joel always had a cover story for every assignment, but since this particular job was unlike his usual situations, he made the decision to stick to the truth as much as possible.

"I lived on a ranch in Colorado until I went away to college."

"Oh. Your father is a rancher?"

"No. I was raised by my grandparents. My mother died before I was school age. My dad traveled a lot, so he left me with my mother's family."

Although his explanation sounded matter-of-fact, Melissa wondered if he'd been as lonely growing up as she had been. "Were you an only child?"

"Yes." He tasted the wine before asking, "How about you?"

"Yes. My parents were in their late thirties when I was born."

He smiled. "That gives us something in common, at least. Being an only child can be lonely at times, can't it?"

So he *did* understand. Somehow, that made her feel closer to him. "I managed to stay occupied," she admitted.

"Me, too. Since the family owned a working ranch, I spent most of my time out of doors."

Melissa recognized the divergence of their childhoods with his statement. She had spent most of her youth with her nose buried in books.

"What do you do?" she finally asked, wondering if there was any such thing as ranching this far east.

"I'm a writer," he explained in a casual voice. "And you?"

She shrugged. "I work for a pharmaceutical company."

He noticed that she didn't elaborate on what she did there, and he wondered if he should push. Why not? "Doing what?" Ah, that had caught her unaware. He watched as she hesitated, obviously searching for a casual response.

"I, uh, work in the research-and-development lab."

"Oh, all the hush-hush experiments, huh?"

"Nothing so exciting, I'm afraid. Mostly I deal with the mounds of paperwork regarding what doesn't work." Her smile made light of her words.

At least her answer confirmed what Feldman had told them. He began to understand Feldman's concern. There was no denying that she had been followed home. If someone attempted to interrogate her, she would not be in any position to respond.

"What do you write about?" she asked, bringing him back to the present.

This part he had already decided upon, picking a genre that he enjoyed reading whenever he found the time. "I'm working on a Western."

She cocked her head. "And you moved to Virginia?"

Watch it, Kramer. This woman's sharp. "Actually, I've lived on the eastern seaboard since I graduated from college. Any research information I need can be easily picked up at a local library."

"Do you ever visit Colorado?"

"No. The ranch was sold years ago. There's no one there to visit. How about you? Do you ever go to Massachusetts?"

She shook her head. "My family's gone, too."

He leaned forward in his chair. "So we're both alone in the world."

"You make us sound like forsaken orphans."

He grinned. "What I was thinking was that maybe we should adopt each other. Maybe we won't find the world so lonely."

She looked at him uncertainly, wondering if he was teasing her, wishing she understood people better. "I'm not sure I need adopting at this age," she admitted.

"Yeah, I know what you mean. So what if we just become friends?"

"I don't have much time for friendships."

"Neither do I," Joel admitted, wondering if he'd ever really thought about that aspect of his life before. He'd never needed or wanted friends once he finished college. In his business, friendship could get you killed.

"You write at home?"

"Yes."

"No wonder you're lonely. What do you do for fun?"

He thought about all the possible quips he could throw her way, but decided against them. She looked so serious, as though she truly wanted to know. He dredged up memories of what he enjoyed doing when he had a few days to himself. "I love to walk along the beach. I do a little sailing when I can. I feel a real affinity to water."

Her expression grew wistful. "That sounds fun."

"Maybe you'd like to go with me sometime," he responded, his mind busy with the opportunity to get her away from this area for a while, at least until Max checked out possible causes of Dr. Feldman's accident.

"I don't know. At the moment, my boss is on vacation, so things are a little hectic for me."

He finished his wine. "Well, you can think about it and let me know if you can get away. We could always plan something for next weekend."

"Isn't it too cold for sailing?"

"I was thinking more about going to the seashore. Have you ever watched a storm come in over the ocean? It's really awesome."

A sudden buzzing sound startled him and he glanced around.

"Oh, that's the timer. Our dinner's ready." She

leaped up as though relieved to be able to change the subject.

Joel followed her more slowly into the kitchen. She was wary, there was no getting around that. But then, he hadn't expected this job to be easy. He sighed. At least he'd made contact. The next thing was to insinuate himself into her daily life. He didn't consider that task would work much of a hardship on him.

"What can I do to help?" he asked as he joined her, savoring the delicious aroma rising from the steaming casserole she'd set on the cabinet.

Joel had to remind himself that he was being paid for carrying out this assignment!

Two

The first thing Joel did when he returned to his apartment after dinner was to look out the window. The car he had seen earlier was gone. In its place was another nondescript car of an equally neutral color. He reached for his binoculars and waited until the lights of a passing car illuminated the license-plate number of the latest arrival, then he jotted down the number.

The second thing he did, still without putting on a light, was pick up the phone and punch out Max's number on the glowing handset.

"Yes?"

"I have another license number for you to check," he said without identifying himself.

"Let's hear it."

He repeated the numbers. "Have you got anything on the first one?"

"Other than the fact the car's registered to a dummy corporation? No, but we're hoping the lead is going to take us somewhere. We're currently checking out the corporate name for possible use in other areas, as well."

"I don't like it, Max. Nobody is going to spend their days and nights sitting out in this cold just to admire a good-looking blonde."

"Oh she is, is she?"

Joel realized what he'd said and, for a moment, found himself without a reply. Finally he spoke. "As a matter of fact, she's very attractive."

"Hmm. Still want off the case?"

"Very funny."

"Have you made contact with her yet?"

Joel grinned. Without hiding his satisfaction, he replied, "As a matter of fact, she and I had dinner together...at her place."

"Fast work."

"I'll admit I lucked out. I understand why Feldman was concerned about her, though. I don't think she has a clue that something could be wrong or that she was followed. As much as I appreciated the dinner invitation, I think she's much too trusting of people she doesn't know."

Max chuckled. "Why do I get a picture of sending the wolf to look after Little Red Riding Hood?"

"Poor joke, Max. This thing could turn bad real fast."

"We had the earlier car ticketed. We'll get rid of this one the same way."

"They'll just try another method. I'm going to provide taxi service for her from now until this matter is cleared up."

"I'm impressed. How did you manage to convince her that she needed an escort service?"

"Well, actually, I'm just going to be a friendly neighbor offering her a ride in the morning when her car won't start. We'll play it from there…maybe have the car towed to a garage, play around with things like parts on order, shorthanded in the shop, missing invoice ticket, that sort of thing."

"If you think it will work."

"It's the best I can think of on short notice. What I really want to do is to get her out of town. Any chance of that?"

"We're talking to the company officials about closing down for a few weeks until we can sort this affair out."

"Isn't that playing into the hands of whoever is behind this?"

"Maybe. But if they aren't aware we're on to them, we've got a chance to stop them before somebody gets killed. These people mean business. You, of all people, should remember that."

Joel shivered, remembering the condition he'd been in when he'd returned to the States from his last assignment. "Yeah, I know."

"Just stick close to your charge. We'll take care of the rest."

Joel dropped the receiver back into its cradle and headed toward the bedroom. He was pleased with the results of his first encounter with Melissa Jordan. She had bought his story of being a writer. So far, so good. All he needed to do was to make himself available whenever she needed assistance. He'd make sure he was in the parking garage when she left for work tomorrow. After that, he'd count on his luck to get him through the following hours.

Wouldn't you know the morning I oversleep, everything would go wrong, Melissa thought, jerking off the second pair of pantyhose she'd tried on that morning, only to discover a run in them, too.

Impatiently, she grabbed an unopened package and successfully completed dressing. She ignored the growling of her stomach. By skipping breakfast, she would at least be able to put herself back on schedule, traffic permitting.

With her coat and purse in one hand, she hastily locked the front door and sprinted for the elevator. For once, it responded promptly and she began to relax on the way to the basement. Everything was all right now, she decided, pulling on her coat and lifting the hood around her ears.

She waved at one of her neighbors as she stepped out of the elevator and hurried to her car. As soon as she slid into the front seat, she jammed the key into the ignition and turned it.

Nothing happened.

Oh, no! She turned it a couple more times. Nothing. No! She couldn't have car trouble now, of all times. She had to get to work. With Dr. Feldman being gone, she—

"Hi. Having trouble?"

She glanced around and saw Joel standing by the car, looking in. "It looks like it."

"You want me to check on it?"

"Oh, would you, please?" She released the hood, and he obligingly studied the engine, the distributor cap he'd disconnected the night before, the loosened battery cables. Then he walked back around to her.

"I don't know all that much about cars, but it looks like you may have a faulty distributor cap."

She groaned, closing her eyes.

"Could I give you a ride somewhere?"

"Oh, if you wouldn't mind, I'd certainly appreciate it. I really need to get to work."

He opened the car door and held out his hand to her. "No problem. I was on my way to the grocery store to lay in some supplies. Good thing I happened to see you." He led her over to his car, helped her into the passenger seat, then got in on the driver's side.

"You'll have to give me directions," he said, which she quickly did. "If you'd like, I'll see that your car gets to a garage."

"Oh, I hate to put you to so much trouble."

"Hey, that's what friends and neighbors are for."

Melissa couldn't resist his open, friendly smile. What a nice man: uncomplicated, wholesome, straightforward, easy to know. After spending the previous evening with him, she felt as though she'd known him for years. He considered his life boring, but she was impressed with how comfortable he was with himself. He knew what he wanted, and what he wanted was to write. Nothing wrong with that. Melissa found him to be a refreshing change from the ambitious people who made up her contacts in life. Compared to Joel, everyone she knew, herself included, was driven—working long hours, neglecting their health. Just look at Dr. Feldman. She knew he wouldn't be able to enjoy his vacation. He'd probably spend the entire time recuperating from the flu.

No doubt she could learn a great deal from being

around Joel Kramer. When he glanced around at her again, she returned his smile.

"Warm enough?"

"I'm fine. Thank you for the ride. You're a real lifesaver."

"If you'll let me know when you get off work, I'll be here to pick you up."

"That's all right. I can call a cab."

"Why? There's no need to spend the money when I'm available."

"But won't it cut into your writing time?"

He shook his head. "I've probably done all I'm going to do today. I'm a morning person. I've been up for hours, working."

"Oh. Well, if you're sure you don't mind."

"I would consider it a privilege. Then maybe you'll have dinner with me. That's the least I can do for last night."

She eyed him uncertainly. "Dinner?"

"Nothing fancy," he assured her. "I found a restaurant not far from here that serves tasty meals. It will save us both from having to cook tonight."

They pulled up in front of the building she pointed out. When she opened her door, he placed his hand gently on her arm. "Please? Take pity on a newcomer to town, all right?"

His silver-eyed gaze seemed to melt her heart. Whether he wanted to admit it or not, she thought, Joel was lonely. She smiled. "All right. I should be through around six." Melissa slipped out of the car before she could change her mind.

He waved. "See you then," he replied with a nod, and pulled away from the curb.

The cold wind whipped around her legs and she

shivered. She hurried into the sprawling building, her mind already on the tasks that awaited her.

Joel pulled up to the first pay phone he could find and called Max to make arrangements to pick up Melissa's car. Max would see that it got a good tune-up and was effectively unavailable until Joel knew what he was going to do with Melissa Jordan.

If some of the dreams he'd had the night before were any indication, his active imagination had come up with several possibilities.

Melissa spotted Joel's car as soon as she stepped outside the building that evening. He saw her at the same time and climbed out, so that by the time she reached his side, the passenger door stood open, waiting for her. The cold wind kept them from lingering, and she didn't greet him with more than a smile until he sat down beside her in the car.

"What a treat, having a warm car waiting for me at the end of the day."

He grinned. "Hope you're hungry. I got busy and forgot to eat lunch, so I'm starved."

"How's the book going?" she asked.

"Who knows? I just keep putting words on paper and refuse to evaluate them until I get the story down."

She smiled. "That sounds sensible to me. Where are we going to eat?"

He named a restaurant she'd heard of but had never visited. Melissa couldn't believe how happy she felt at the moment, having an attractive male pick her up from work and take her out to dinner. She didn't really understand what was happening to her. Where had her reservations about social activities gone? She didn't know. All she was certain of was the fact that her day had been just as hectic as yesterday, but because she knew that she had plans for the evening, she had breezed through the details, done her work with a crisp clarity and walked out of the lab with a buoyant step and a light heart.

She felt proud of herself. In the past, she'd thought of herself as socially inept, but last night she had proven herself wrong. She had met someone, been friendly with him, and a friendship was forming as a result of her daring to act in a way that was different from her normal response.

"How was your day?" Joel asked.

Melissa glanced around at him. His tone and expression gave every indication that he really wanted to know, despite the banality of the question.

Unfortunately, she couldn't discuss her work with anyone outside of the lab, but it was thoughtful of him to ask. "Like most jobs, everywhere, I guess," she responded with a smile.

"Do you like what you do?"

"Very much."

He reached over and touched her hand that rested in her lap. "I'm glad. I think it's important that a person earn their living in the way they enjoy."

They rode the rest of the way to the restaurant in a companionable silence.

From the time they entered the restaurant until they left, their conversation flowed easily and Melissa's sense of comfort and relaxation continued to grow. She couldn't recall all that was said because they discussed so many things—books, movies, American policies and political attitudes, their favorite foods, hobbies.

What they discovered was that they were alike in many ways, and both were absorbed in their work with little time for outside activities.

By the time they reached their respective apartments, they were chatting as though they'd known each other for years.

"What do you have planned for this evening?" he asked, taking her key from her and opening her door.

"The usual, I guess. Read awhile and go to bed."

"I rented some movies while I was at the store this morning. Want to come over and watch one with me?"

Melissa could feel her heart pick up its tempo. It would be so easy to grow accustomed to having this man around. "Haven't you had enough of me, yet?"

The look he gave her caused the hated heat to fill her cheeks. "I don't believe that could ever happen, Melissa," he said in a barely audible voice.

She studied him in silence for a moment. She'd just been congratulating herself earlier on making new, bold decisions. Now was the time for another one. Could she do it?

"All right. Let me change into something more comfortable and I'll be over in a few minutes."

"Okay. I'll see you soon."

He waited for her to close her door before going inside his own apartment. Good. Having her over here would keep her close for another evening. He glanced around the room, making sure everything had been put away. He stopped off in the small second bedroom to make certain it looked as though a writer had been busy. A small computer sat on the desk, a couple of reference books nearby. The printer had paper fed into the tractor, ready to go.

When he reached his bedroom, he picked up a towel he'd tossed down earlier and threw it into the bathroom. Not that he expected for her to see his bedroom. As much as he would enjoy taking her to bed, he knew better. She was his current assignment, that was all. He could find his pleasure elsewhere.

The sound of a soft tap on the front door drew him back into the living room. He opened the door with a smile, saw the expression on her face and immediately asked, "What's wrong?"

Melissa came into the room. "I wish I knew. I just got a call from the personnel director of the plant. It seems our office building failed some sort of inspection. The explanation doesn't make much sense to me. But, for whatever reason I'm supposed to take the rest of the week off."

Joel grinned. "No kidding. That's great."

Melissa had wandered over to his bookshelves while she talked, and she looked around in surprise at his response. "What's so great about it?"

He shrugged, slipping his hands into his pockets. "Well, now you can have a minivacation."

She smiled at him, as though amused at his obvious misunderstanding of the situation. "I suppose so, but, you see, I don't want a minivacation. I enjoy my job very much. I don't need to do anything else."

He wandered over to her, his hands still in his pockets. "When was the last time you took some time off?"

She thought about that for a moment, then shrugged. "I don't remember. We take the normal holidays off, like most businesses."

"I mean a vacation."

She turned away from him and walked over to the

window. Without looking at him, she said, "I don't really like vacations." She glanced around at him and smiled. "I find them boring, actually." She tilted her chin slightly, as though expecting him to argue the point.

He noticed her tension but couldn't understand its cause. In a careful tone Joel offered, "I suppose that depends on what you enjoy doing to relax."

Melissa turned away from the window in a restless movement. She found the present topic of conversation unsettling, almost irritating, although she didn't know why. "I don't need to relax," she explained. "I enjoy my job. I find it fulfills all my needs. I've never been one to find pleasure in lying around doing nothing."

To stop her restless movements, Joel took her hand and led her over to the sofa in front of the television. Motioning for her to sit down, he sat beside her and turned so that he was facing her. "Who said that a vacation has to be about doing nothing? The whole idea is to do something different. It's a chance to pursue other interests, other hobbies, that sort of thing."

Her gaze returned to the window for a moment, then she shook her head. "This really isn't the time of year for outdoor activities."

"Sure it is, if you enjoy skiing." Personally, he hated the sport; no doubt because he was lousy at it.

"I don't enjoy cold weather."

He grinned. "Me, either." He leaned back and rested his head on the back of the sofa, thinking. "My idea of a perfect winter vacation is to go somewhere warm, preferably a beach somewhere." He closed his eyes. "Just think about it. A chance to soak up some sun, do a little swimming, maybe snorkeling, find a sailboat somewhere.'' He smiled to himself. ''Now that's my idea of living.'' He raised his head and looked at her. ''Haven't you ever wanted just to forget about everything in your life and run away for a few days?''

She looked at him warily. ''No.''

''Haven't you ever done anything on the spur of the moment?''

''Not really, no. I'm more comfortable thinking everything through.''

''You know, Melissa, I think it's time that you create some excitement in your life.''

''Why?''

He stared at her. ''Why? You have to ask me why? By the very fact that you can ask such a question shows me that you are in much worse shape than I first thought.'' He reached over and took her hand, as though comforting her. ''You, my dear neighbor, obviously have been deprived of some of the most delicious moments of life—those little unexpected, unplanned moments, the serendipities that add magic to a person's life.'' He brought her hand up and placed it against his cheek. With a flash of his smile, he said, ''Why don't you run away with me for a few days, Melissa? Live a little…take a chance on life.''

She stared at him with obvious bewilderment. ''Are you serious?''

''Never more serious in my life.''

''You want to just run off somewhere…?'' She eyed him uncertainly. ''Where?''

He shrugged. ''You name it, we'll go.''

She stared at him for several moments in silence and discovered within her a yearning to be the kind of person that could do something so impulsive. But, of course, she couldn't. She didn't even know the man. It was one thing to have dinner with him a couple of times. It was another thing entirely to run away with him.

With surprising reluctance, she shook her head. "I'm sorry. But I can't." She softened her refusal with a smile.

Joel stood and walked over to the VCR. Keeping his back to her, he answered in a casual tone of voice. "What are you in the mood to watch tonight? I can offer you a comedy, drama or an action adventure."

"I thought you had to write your book."

He glanced around at her with a puzzled expression on his face. "Watching a movie isn't going to prevent me from finishing my book."

She grinned. "I meant if you were to go away for a few days."

"Oh!" He shrugged. "I can work anywhere. But you're right. You don't know me. It was a crazy idea."

She shook her head. "I didn't mean to be rude. I'm afraid that I don't know the proper social etiquette surrounding an invitation to share a vacation."

"Neither do I," he admitted. "I've never done it before."

Melissa's eyes widened slightly. "That surprises me."

"Why should it? Do I strike you as the kind of guy who invites every attractive woman he meets to take a trip with him?"

Melissa could hear the irritation in his voice and realized that she was in way over her head. She hadn't meant to be insulting. She just didn't know what to say, how to behave or what to do next. She also found the news that he thought she was attractive more than a little unnerving.

"I didn't mean to offend you," she said after a moment. She watched as he took a long breath and sharply exhaled.

"Forget it. I didn't mean to be so touchy. The thing is, I'm really not trying to come on to you. I just thought it would give us a chance to get to know each other a little better, that's all. Talking about the idea made me realize that I haven't taken any time off this winter, either. I guess one of the reasons I haven't planned anything is because it's not much fun to go somewhere alone." Joel ran his hand through his hair, wanting to change the subject. He looked at the tape in his hand. "So, what sounds good to you?" He read off the names of three movies.

Melissa picked one and he placed the tape in the machine, set it in motion and sat down beside her once again.

Before long, Melissa appeared to be engrossed in the movie. Although he'd never seen it before, Joel found his thoughts drifting, going back to their conversation. For a short while, he'd forgotten the role he'd been playing and had taken her rejection of his offer personally, which was total nonsense. So what had caused him to react like that?

Perhaps it was because he could see the parallels in their lives. He couldn't remember the last time he'd taken a vacation and for the same reasons she had given him. His work was his life, his hobby, his recreation. However, when he heard her expressing a similar point of view, he immediately saw how one-dimensional such an attitude could be. Like him, she refused to consider other attitudes. He'd never looked at his own attitudes from another's perspective before. He wasn't sure he liked them.

He thought of a recent conversation he'd had with Max. His employer had suggested he take a few weeks off. Joel had been furious at the suggestion, demanding that he be given another assignment as soon as possible.

Melissa chuckled, bringing Joel back to the movie. He'd missed whatever she'd found amusing. He needed to pay attention. They might discuss the movie later and he didn't want her to think he'd been bored.

How could he be bored when he was so aware of the woman sitting within arm's reach of him? She'd changed into a pair of faded jeans and a bulky knit sweater. She'd brushed her hair out when she'd changed clothes and had left it hanging loose. One long curl fell across her shoulder and Joel had to resist the impulse to twine the soft mass around his finger. He finally admitted to himself that he'd wanted to run his hands through her hair since the first time he'd seen it down the night before.

This is a job, Kramer. Remember that.

He managed to see the humor in what was happening on the screen when Melissa began to laugh a few minutes later, and he joined in. The sound of their shared laughter sounded companionable, and Joel began to relax a little. Did it really matter if she chose to stay home? He could watch her as effectively here as anywhere. She'd be a lot safer in the apartment building than traveling to and from work. Somehow he'd have to find ways where they could spend large chunks of time together.

After all, what was wrong with making friends with her? He wasn't there spying on her. He was there to look after her. He could become friends with her without compromising his work.

"Could I get you something to drink?" he asked, suddenly remembering his role as host.

She smiled, her eyes filled with amusement at the story unfolding on the screen. "Thank you. I'd like that."

"I have beer, wine and soft drinks."

She named a popular cola drink and he left the room. "Don't you want to stop the movie?" she called after him.

"No need. I'll be right back."

Within a couple of minutes, he returned with two ice-filled glasses, the sparkling cola making soft hissing noises.

He watched her take a drink from the glass, watched the way the moisture beaded on her upper lip, watched as she licked the moisture away with the tip of her tongue. All the while, her attention stayed with the movie.

Joel forced his gaze back to the screen. Damn, but he found her attractive. Sitting this close, he'd noticed a spray of freckles across the bridge of her nose…and the way her bottom lip protruded ever so slightly in an innocently provocative pout. He'd never seen eyelashes as long as hers. He was fascinated by the way they brushed against her cheek when she looked down at her drink.

When she turned her head to look at him, he refused to avert his gaze.

"Is something wrong?" she asked.

He shook his head. "On the contrary. I find you

fascinating.'' He smiled as a fiery blush filled her cheeks. ''I'm sorry. I didn't mean to embarrass you. Surely you must know how attractive you are. The men in your life aren't blind.''

When she just stared at him, he reached over and very gently rubbed his thumb against her cheek. ''Hmm. Your skin feels like a baby's.'' He rested his head against the back of the sofa and watched as the pupils in her eyes seemed to grow. She sat very still.

He leaned slowly toward her, not wanting to frighten her, but wanting very much to touch her again. After slipping his hand from her cheek to the nape of her neck, he massaged the tenseness he felt there, then with a calm deliberation, he placed his lips against hers.

Just before his mouth touched hers, he felt more than heard her soft gasp. But she didn't pull away. Her parted lips invited him to explore, but he could already feel her trembling. Was it possible that she was afraid of him? Or was she afraid of the intimacy of the moment?

He lifted his head slightly and looked into her eyes. ''I won't take advantage of you. Please believe that,'' he whispered. ''You can stop me at any time.''

He watched as her impossibly long lashes drooped across her expressive eyes. Then he closed his eyes, as well. He took his time, touching his lips to hers once again, then against her closed eyelids, against her cheek, her brow, then returning to taste her once more.

She sighed, and with a hesitancy he found endearing, she slipped her arms around his neck, pulling him closer.

He wrapped his other arm around her, holding her

tightly against him. He continued to kiss her—soft, nipping kisses, tantalizing and teasing her with his light touch until she shifted restlessly in his arms.

He knew he needed to let her go, but found the task impossible. Instead, the energy changed between them. There was a new urgency. Their kiss deepened, became more possessive, and Joel lost all sense of what he'd originally intended when he first touched her.

Restlessly he spread his hands along her spine, wanting to draw her even closer to him. She leaned her head back, giving him access to the long slim line of her throat. Dear God, but she was beautiful, and he wanted her with an urgency that shook him.

"Melissa," he whispered, shaken. "I…"

She slowly opened her eyes, looking as dazed as he felt. "Joel?"

"Hmmmm?"

"I don't think this is a very good idea."

Funny how her admitting what he'd just been thinking was not as comforting as he could have wished. He reluctantly released her. "I'm sorry. I shouldn't have—"

"Oh, please don't apologize. You didn't do anything wrong. It's just that…" She paused and rubbed her forehead. "I'm not very good at this sort of thing. And I wouldn't want us to hurt a friendship by moving it along too fast." Her look was beseeching.

Joel stood and moved away from the couch. He needed to get a safe distance between them. "I agree."

The movie ended and the credits rolled. "Well…" Melissa came to her feet. "I guess I'd better go. It's getting late." She looked at Joel, who was standing beside the window looking outside. He turned toward her at the sound of her voice.

"Thanks for coming over." He didn't move closer to her.

"I forgot to ask about my car. Did they say when it would be ready?"

"No. They said they'd call. I gave them my number since I didn't know yours."

"Oh."

They continued to look at each other.

Finally Melissa spoke. "Since I don't have to work tomorrow, maybe we could do something together. That is, if you still want to plan something."

Joel smiled at her. "I'd like that. I'd like that very much."

She returned his smile. "Me, too."

He walked over to where she stood beside the door. "What would you like to do?" Without conscious thought, he rubbed his knuckle lightly against her cheek.

"I don't care."

"I'll think of something."

They stood there, just inches apart, as though neither one wanted to be the first to end their time together. Joel leaned down and kissed her lightly on her lips, then said, "I'll walk you home."

She chuckled. "I'm just across the hall."

"I know." He opened the door and followed her through, then waited while she unlocked her door. "This way, I can tell you good-night," he whispered, taking her into his arms once more and kissing her with all the pent-up emotion that had been gathering within him.

Melissa responded by sliding her arms around his

neck. Having a neighbor like Joel Kramer had certainly turned her life upside down, but she was determined not to allow her shyness to keep her from experiencing all he had to offer.

Three

"When was the last time you explored D.C.?" Joel asked. He and Melissa were approaching the entrance to the Washington Monument.

She shook her head. "I can't remember. I think there was a group of us from school that came down one summer."

Joel pulled her closer by tucking her hand inside his pocket. "Everything looks different in the wintertime, anyway."

"I've always wanted to come when the cherry trees were in bloom, but somehow the time slipped away from me."

"The Potomac Park would be another place to go in the spring for that reason."

Melissa looked around her and sighed. "This was a great idea you had. I'm glad you insisted."

"Otherwise you would be curled up in your apartment reading a book."

"Maybe. Or I might have taken a walk."

"So you're getting your exercise and exploring the country's capital at the same time. You can't beat that."

Within a couple of hours, Joel suggested lunch. Melissa readily agreed. The exercise had stirred her appetite.

They found a cozy tearoom that intrigued Melissa with its delicate decorations. Joel had gamely agreed to try the cuisine.

"What do you think of the soup?" Melissa asked after they were served.

"I like it," Joel replied. "How about the salad?"

"Marvelous. Here," she offered him a bite. "Try it."

Joel obligingly opened his mouth, chewed and swallowed with a smile. "Great house dressing. Here, try the soup."

Melissa leaned on her palm and looked at the man across from her. "You know, I've never known anyone like you."

Joel glanced up from his steaming bowl. "Is that good or bad?"

She smiled. "Good. You're really so much fun to be with. You didn't quibble when I dragged you into this feminine atmosphere for lunch."

He glanced around the room. "I'm not the only male here. Obviously, the food doesn't recognize genders."

"I have a hunch you wouldn't have cared if you'd been the only man here. That's what I'm talking about. You're comfortable wherever you go."

"Aren't you?"

She shook her head. "I've always been dreadfully self-conscious."

"About what?"

She shrugged. "Of being me, I guess. I always felt like a freak."

Joel placed his spoon beside his plate and looked at her with raised eyebrows. "Would you care to explain that remark?"

"As far back as I can remember, I went to classes with students several years older than I was. My parents encouraged me to study and learn, and I wanted to please them. Consequently, I never felt accepted by any of my peers in school. Outside of discussions about homework, we never had anything in common." She took another bite of salad.

"Didn't you make friends with people your own age?"

"No. We lived in an older residential area, so that I was the youngest child on the block. Children my age that I did meet seemed to be uncomfortable around me."

"So you never learned how to play."

"Not really."

"Talk about a lonely childhood. At least I had friends from neighboring ranches to play with. My grandparents were lenient with me, provided I did my share of the chores. I had a great group of friends."

"Do you see any of them now?"

Joel was quiet for several moments. "No. Two of them were killed in Vietnam. I lost touch with the other ones once the ranch sold."

"How sad. The only person that I consider a friend from my younger days was my college roommate.

She lives in New York but stays in touch. Karen's always trying to get me to join her and her family when they go on vacation.''

"She's married?"

"Yes. She's several years older than I am. She married the summer after graduation. I went on for more degrees while she got started with a family." Melissa smiled. "I'm much better at acquiring degrees than I am experiencing life."

Joel leaned back in his chair and observed her with a whimsical smile. "Oh, I don't know about that. You haven't done so badly since I've known you."

"You've made it easy for me. You're very comfortable to be around, you know."

"You're the first person to have noticed that particular aspect of my personality."

Melissa studied his amused expression. With a serious expression of her own, she explained, "I've always considered myself hopeless in social situations. I never know what to say or how to act."

He smiled at her. "Be yourself."

"Like you do..." She paused, thinking about it. "I'd like to be able to do that. Usually, I can never find anything to say. And yet with you, I don't seem to ever stop talking."

"I consider that to be a compliment."

They smiled at each other.

"So, what do you want to do this afternoon?" Joel asked a short while later over coffee.

"Continue playing tourist. I want to see the White House, the Capitol, the Jefferson Memorial, the Lincoln Memorial, the Smithsonian—"

Joel began to laugh. "Whoa, whoa, wait a minute.

We might be able to drive by some of those places, but the Smithsonian would take days to explore.''

Her smile was filled with anticipation. "I've got at least the rest of the week off." Then she remembered. "But you have to write, don't you?"

He nodded. "But if we plan it, I can do both. I try to get three hours a day of writing done. Since I don't need much sleep, I get up early. We could leave around ten or so each day and still see a considerable amount."

"And you'd be willing to do that with me?"

"Of course. We're friends, remember?"

Melissa looked at him, knowing full well that she would always remember. Meeting Joel was an experience she would never forget. She would store each event she shared with him like a souvenir to recall later.

Impulsively, she reached over and placed her hand on top of his. "Thank you."

"For what?"

"For being you."

"I'm glad you picked a warmer day to visit Chesapeake Bay," Melissa said ten days later. She glanced up at the blue sky, then back at the large expanse of water before them.

Joel stood with his hands in his pockets, gazing out into the bay. "I have to confess I've been watching the weather map for the last few days, trying to plan a trip over here that wouldn't be uncomfortable."

She threw her arms out and spun around. "You think of everything, don't you?"

"I try," he responded modestly, then ruined it by rakishly grinning at her. When she stopped turning and looked at him, he grabbed her around the waist and swung her around in a circle, causing her to laugh. When he stopped, he held her close to him.

"You sound like a little girl when you laugh like that."

"I feel like a little girl when you continue to indulge me the way you have these last couple of weeks. At this rate, you're never going to get your book finished."

"Don't worry about my book. I'm certainly not."

"Aren't you writing on some sort of schedule?"

"Not really. I decided to give myself a full year to see what I could do with my writing. I have several months to go."

"What did you do before you began writing?"

"A very boring desk job. One you wouldn't want to spend time hearing about."

"I can't think of anything about you that I would find boring."

"Why, Dr. Jordan, I'm flattered."

She laughed again, the young, free sound of happiness echoing around them. "You have no idea how much I've enjoyed myself. It's as though you had to teach me how to play. I'd never before realized how serious I am about everything." She waved her hand at the scene around them. "I would never have thought to come here at this time of year."

"We managed to beat a great deal of the traffic by getting here a few months early."

"I really need to write Karen and let her know that I finally took her advice. Who knows? I might go with them down to the islands this summer when they go."

"The islands?"

"Yes. She and her husband have a place on one of the smaller islands in the Virgin Islands chain."

He dropped his arm across her shoulder and they headed back toward the car. "Too bad they don't go now, when the weather's so cold here at home."

"I know. But Tony can't ever seem to get away during the winter and Karen won't go without him."

Joel helped Melissa into his car. "Where do you want to go now?"

She glanced at her watch. "Oh, darn. It's too late to pick up my car. They promised it would be ready this afternoon."

"There's no hurry, is there?"

"Hurry! You must be joking. They could have rebuilt the entire car in the time it's taken them to replace the distributor cap and tune it."

"You know how busy auto shops are."

"Well, at least I can get it tomorrow. I'm sure you'll be relieved not to have to drive me everywhere."

"Actually, I thought I'd done a very good job of playing chauffeur. If this book doesn't sell, I'm counting on your good references to find another job."

Melissa loved to watch the light dance in his eyes whenever he teased her. And he teased her a great deal, another thing she loved. She sat beside him and watched as he smoothly shifted gears, his hands resting lightly on the gear shift and the steering wheel.

She felt as though she had known this man forever. Over the past couple of weeks, they had shared so many of their childhood memories with each other. She felt as though she had been there with him as he grew up on the ranch in Colorado. Now when she recalled her solitary childhood, it felt as though he had also been there in the background, encouraging her.

"What are you thinking?" he asked.

She leaned her head against the headrest and smiled. "About you and how fortunate it was for me that you became my neighbor. I'm really glad I met you."

He reached over and touched her hand. "The feeling's mutual."

"I guess what I've noticed is that I like me better when I'm around you. I feel more confident, somehow. I know that you aren't going to laugh at me or make fun of me if I do or say the wrong thing."

"I feel the same way. It was a shock to discover how many degrees you *have* collected. That's pretty intimidating."

"But you weren't...intimidated, I mean. You saw me, the person, and not me, the wunderkind. You have no idea how normal that makes me feel."

He lifted her hand and placed it against his cheek. "I'm glad."

They rode along for several miles in silence before Joel asked, "What would you like to do tomorrow?"

"Surely I'll be able to go into work by then. Dr. Feldman should be returning from his vacation in a few days. I hope he's gotten as much out of his time off as I have mine. I feel like a new person."

According to Max, Feldman *was* working again, but at a laboratory that was known to very few people. Joel had stayed in touch with Max on a daily basis. The investigation into who was behind the attempt against Dr. Feldman and who had been following Melissa was progressing as rapidly as possible.

In the meantime, Joel knew that he was losing his objectivity on this case.

He'd never suspected that someone like Melissa Jordan could exist. Once he'd broken through her initial shyness, he found a delightful, humorous person with a tremendous capacity to enjoy life. Just being around her made him feel years younger.

She'd taught him a great deal about himself. Watching her learn to relax taught him how to do the same. Until he'd thought about needing to contact Max just now, Joel had been able to blot out the true reason they were together.

For the first time in his career, he wished that he could become the person he pretended to be, the person she thought he was. Instinctively, he made certain that they were not followed during their outings, but otherwise, he had allowed himself to become what he pretended to be, a friend who enjoyed her company.

Joel had never known another person in his life with whom he'd shared so much about himself. Instead of finding the idea that she knew so much about him threatening, he found it liberating.

He glanced over and saw that she had fallen asleep. She looked like a child in her jeans, heavy sweater and windbreaker, her hair pulled back into a high-swinging ponytail. She hadn't bothered with makeup. She didn't need to use any with her naturally dark eyebrows and lashes, her brilliant blue eyes and wind-flushed cheeks.

A couple of weeks ago, she had suggested that they not rush their friendship. So he had waited. However, he didn't intend to wait much longer. This woman had caused him to question some of his lifelong patterns. Joel no longer wanted to live a solitary life. He knew that now. It had taken only a few days of being around her for him to realize how much more there was to life than he had ever experienced.

He wanted to experience it all...with Melissa.

"How about a game of Scrabble after dinner?" Melissa asked him the following evening. They were in his apartment, a practice that had grown into a habit for them.

"I wouldn't stand a chance against you," he complained good-naturedly.

"Nonsense! Writers always know more words than anybody."

Joel considered his vocabulary adequate, but nothing unusual. Would she wonder about him if his skills were tested? They had been talking about going to a movie earlier, but decided against it. They hadn't rented any videos, and the television schedule hadn't appealed to them.

So what could they do to occupy themselves for the next few hours?

"Scrabble sounds fine."

"I'll go get my game and be right back." She'd dashed out the door before he could stop her.

Joel began to clear the table. What a darling she was. Watching the change in her over the past few weeks had been a revelation. He'd seen the exuberant young girl emerge from the serious scientist. Once she had gotten used to his sense of humor, she was quick with her own. He found it sad that such a vibrant woman had been hidden away for so long.

If spending this time together had done nothing else, it had helped her to open up to another person.

Selfishly, Joel was glad he'd been the one to have witnessed the transformation.

"Here it is." She'd left his door slightly ajar so that she could get back in.

"How about having our coffee first?"

She disappeared into the kitchen and came out with two mugs filled with coffee. Joel walked over to her, took the mugs and set them on the coffee table in front of the sofa. Then he slipped his arms around her waist.

Her eyes widened. "What are you doing?"

He grinned. "With all those degrees, you still can't tell when a man's going to kiss you?"

Before she could find the words to reply, Joel proceeded to do just that. Melissa had grown accustomed to his affectionate gestures in the weeks she had known him, but this kiss was different somehow— more urgent, more possessive and much more intense.

When he picked her up and moved to the couch, she didn't resist. How could she? All he had to do was to touch her and her bones disintegrated. Somehow, she found herself lying on the couch beside him, responding to his touch.

When he finally paused, his voice shook. "I can't take much more of this, I'm afraid," he said hoarsely.

"Take what? Kissing me?" she managed to ask.

He groaned. "I want to do much more than kiss you."

"All right."

She felt him stiffen as he stared into her eyes. She met his gaze with a serene look. When he didn't say anything she sat up. "But wouldn't we be more comfortable in the bedroom?" She stood and held out her hand.

"Melissa?"

"Hmm?"

"Are you sure you want to do this?"

She nodded, unable to say the words.

Joel came to his feet. He knew he needed to keep a calm head. He was getting too wrapped up in his role-playing. He couldn't take advantage of the situation like this. He would have to tell her that—

A sudden explosion rocked the room.

Four

The blast knocked them to the floor. Joel threw himself across Melissa, holding her close. Sounds of breaking glass and crackling fire filled the air along with the acrid scent of explosives.

Joel raised his head and looked around. Smoke billowed through a gaping hole that had once been the inside wall of his apartment. Long tentacles of flame filled what had been the hallway between their apartments. They could see directly into all that was left of Melissa's living room.

Even though he was dazed by the blast, Joel's training kicked in. Another explosion could occur at any moment. They had to get out of there. Fast.

Joel glanced down at Melissa, only now recognizing that he'd probably knocked the breath out of her when they fell. "Are you okay?"

She had the bewildered expression of a small child

startled out of sleep, as though she didn't know whether to cry or demand an explanation. She blinked. "I think so," she offered in an uncertain voice.

Joel glanced around them. The fire was moving rapidly toward them. If they hadn't already been moving toward the hallway, the blast could have killed them. The couch where they'd been lying less than a minute ago was already on fire. He scrambled to his feet.

"We've got to get out of here. This place could go up any second."

He leaned down and grabbed her wrists, tugging her to her feet. As soon as she gained her balance, he pulled her behind him, running toward the bedroom.

Melissa glanced behind them. The living room was already a curtain of flames. She could no longer see into her apartment.

When she looked forward again, they were in Joel's bedroom. For the first time since the blast, she was aware of the panic beginning to build within her. They were trapped. How could they possibly get out of here?

Joel let go of her hand and sprinted toward his closet. He grabbed a couple of heavy parkas, reached into his bedside table and palmed the pistol hidden there. He turned, concealing the weapon in his hand and held out one of the jackets to her. "Put this on. You're going to need it."

While Melissa was occupied with pulling on the coat, Joel placed the pistol in the waist of his jeans at the small of his back, then shrugged into the other coat and gave the room a final glance. The building's

fire alarm screamed in the still night air. Joel could
hear the distant sound of sirens approaching.

He knew his first duty was to get Melissa out of
there—to keep her safe. With that in mind, he
grabbed her hand once again and headed toward the
window.

"Where are we going? We're five stories up. We
can't just—"

"We don't have a choice. Come on. There's a fire
escape a couple of feet away." He had made certain
there was an escape route in the apartment as soon as
he moved in. He knew all the possible exits.

He shoved the window open and stepped through,
then turned and helped Melissa over the windowsill.
As soon as she was through, he lifted the hood of her
coat and fastened it beneath her chin. She would be
less identifiable in the dark with her bright mass of
blond hair covered.

Joel took time to check out the area below them
before starting their descent. He was counting on the
fact that no one knew Melissa had been with him
tonight. On the off chance she might have survived
the initial blast, whoever had done this would be
watching the windows on the other side of the building.

He hoped.

As soon as they reached the ground, he took her
hand. "We've got to get away from here. The whole
building could go up any time."

He moved into the darker shadows away from the
building. After proceeding cautiously for a few feet,
Joel began to sprint along a tree-lined jogging path
that led into the surrounding park, still holding Melissa's hand.

Thank God she trusted him, he thought after a few minutes. He hadn't had time to explain anything to her. He was also thankful that she was in good physical shape. Every second counted for them at the moment. They needed to disappear—and fast.

Damn. He'd been lulled into a false sense of security these past few weeks. Surveillance had disappeared. Either that or he was getting too old for this job because he hadn't spotted the perpetrators.

So how in the hell had they managed to get inside the building? They must have set off some sort of explosive in the hallway, which was the only thing that had saved him and Melissa. What if the damn thing had gone off when she'd run next door?

It didn't bear thinking about.

So now what were they going to do? He knew he'd have to come up with some fast alternative. Obviously, keeping an unobtrusive eye on his neighbor was no longer a viable option. It was time to jump to Plan B, whatever the hell that was.

The first thing he had to do was to get to a phone and let Max know what had happened, if he hadn't already been alerted.

Joel had gotten to know the surrounding neighborhood well, including the exact locations of the public telephones. The question was, which one would be the safest for them to use?

The convenience store. There were a couple of phones outside the building. He angled off the path without a pause.

Melissa began to fall behind, forcing him to slow his pace. She was panting when she asked, "Where are you going? Why are we running? Shouldn't we have stayed back there to find out what happened?"

Joel heard the short breaths that punctuated every other word. He continued moving away from the lighted area. His adrenaline had kicked in, something he was familiar with. Without looking around at her, he said, "Has it occurred to you that somebody just tried to kill you? Do you want to hang around and give them another chance?"

She stopped dead in her tracks so that Joel was forced to stop and look at her. With his hands on his hips, he drew deep breaths of cold air into his lungs.

"Me?" She stared at him as though convinced he'd lost his mind. "Why would anybody want to kill *me?*" She glanced around them and shivered. "That explosion was an accident! The fire department is going to have some questions. We need to go back. If we aren't there, everyone will think we were killed!"

He shook his head. "Melissa, think about it for a moment. What sort of accident would cause an explosion like that? Someone was making sure that those apartments were destroyed, with us in them. Do you honestly want to go back and take a chance on somebody trying to finish the job?"

Her mind was whirling with confused thoughts. Everything was happening too fast. She couldn't think straight. "I don't understand any of this." She brushed the hood away from her face. "If we'd still been on the couch..." Her voice trailed off.

"I know."

She shuddered, wrapping her arms around her own waist. "I couldn't believe what was happening. It all took place so fast." She looked up at him. "If you hadn't gotten us out of there, we could have died."

"It's amazing how the need for self-preservation can motivate a person, isn't it?" He purposely kept his voice light, but he wrapped his arms around her and held her close. He could still feel her shaking. And why not? His heart was going fast enough to compete with a marathon runner.

He glanced around them. They were still near the jogging path that ran through the park near their apartment building. If someone decided to scout around, they could still be spotted.

"Honey, we need to find a phone. We've got to figure out where we're going to stay." He kissed the end of her nose. "I don't know about you, but I don't want to have to sleep in the park tonight."

She buried her face in his neck and clung to him. "Joel?"

"Hmm."

"Why did you suggest that someone is trying to harm me? I'm nobody important." She raised her head so that she could see his face. "Maybe what happened was meant for you."

"Possibly, but I rather doubt it. None of the editors I know have resorted to bombs to signify their rejection of my work." He took her hand and led her into the trees. "Let's get out of here, okay? I'm not in the mood to run into a mugger out here, either."

"But where can we go?"

At least she began to jog along beside him as he stepped up the pace once again, Joel noticed with a sense of relief. "I thought I'd call a friend to see if he could suggest a place for us to stay." Trying to stave off any arguments, he said, "I don't know about you, but I'd prefer not to go to a hotel, if we can find an alternative."

She didn't say anything and Joel felt a sense of relief that she hadn't argued with him. Now that the immediate danger was past, he could no longer dismiss what had been taking place at the time of the explosion. Another few minutes and they would have been in bed!

For a brief moment, Joel allowed himself to focus on the memory of her pressed against him, his mouth on hers. He could feel her softness, catch the tantalizing scent of her light perfume. Actually, nothing less than an explosion would have stopped him from making love to her tonight.

By the time they reached a well-lighted part of the park, they were both breathing hard. Joel shook his head, disgusted that their flight had come close to winding him. He paused, placing his hand lightly on her upper arm.

"What's wrong?"

Damn, but she was sensitive to his moods. He would have to be careful not to needlessly alarm her. He draped his arm across her shoulders. "Nothing. I just don't see any need to race across the street as though we're being chased by the hounds of hell."

The look she gave him was made up of puzzled amusement. "But you saw nothing wrong with our headlong rush through the park, I take it."

"Hell, no. There's no telling who's lurking in the bushes at this time of night."

Melissa looked back at the way they had come and shivered. In an attempt to lighten the mood, she smiled at him and said, "My hero."

He leaned over so that he could touch his nose to hers. His smile flashed white in his tanned face. "And don't you forget it."

By the time they entered the small store, they

looked like any other couple out for a brisk walk on a cold night.

"Why don't you get us something to drink while I make my call?" He glanced around at the brightly lit store. She would be safe inside while he used the phone. The front wall of the building was made up of glass, which gave him visual access to her.

"What do you want to drink?"

"Surprise me."

Her mischievous smile managed to do just that. He could still see the shock in her face, and yet she was determinedly teasing him in an effort to overcome her fears. Joel had an absurd impulse to hug her to him, to promise her that she would be safe. Instead, he gave her a mock salute and walked back into the cold night air.

He pulled a handful of change out of his pocket, selected a coin and dialed the number. The call was answered on the first ring.

"Yeah. It's me," he said before the other man spoke.

"Joel! Where are you? Is Dr. Jordan all right?"

So Max had already learned of the explosion. "She's with me," he replied, and he gave Max their location. "Looks like we're going to have to look at some alternatives to the original plan."

He could hear the relief in Max's voice. "I'll admit to being shaken when the report came in. What happened?"

"I don't know. We'd finished with dinner and were having coffee when all hell broke loose. Have you heard how bad the damage was?"

"They're still battling the blaze. Authorities on the scene don't see much chance of saving the building."

There was a brief pause before he added in a low voice, "They could have gotten both of you with this one, Kramer."

"Yeah, I know. I think we'd better tell her what's going on, don't you?"

"Not necessarily. Why cause her more alarm?"

"Are you kidding? What's more alarming than having your home blown into tiny particles?"

"What I mean is, there's no reason to let her know she's the target of a possible assassination."

"Come on, Max! She's no dummy. I've got to tell her something. How in the hell am I going to convince her to hide away with me somewhere if I don't tell her the truth?"

Max chuckled. "How about using your charm?"

"Very funny."

"I'm serious. Use that charm of yours and convince her the two of you could enjoy going away together."

"As a matter of fact, we've been enjoying our day trips—to the point where she's mentioned the possibility of a vacation next summer. But we're talking about now."

"Where does she want to go on vacation?"

"I'm not sure. She said something about a friend having a place in the Virgin Islands that she keeps being invited to share."

"Virgin Islands. That might be a good idea. Do you think you could convince her to go now?"

"Without telling her why? No. No, I don't. Look, Max, Melissa is a strong, courageous woman. I don't see any reason to keep her in the dark on this one. Full knowledge might be the extra edge that keeps her alive."

"You don't think you can protect her?"

"I didn't say that."

"Once you get her away from here for a few days, there'll be no reason to tell her. We expect to be in a position to move on this one shortly. Surely you can manage to take care of her that long without discussing what's going on with her."

"And if I can't? Are you willing to take the risk, Max? Because I'm telling you right now, I'm not."

Max didn't answer just then. After a long moment of silence, he finally said, "Don't blow your cover, Kramer. That's an order. If you can tell her anything without explaining who you are, then do it. Otherwise, no."

In all his years at this job, Joel had never come close to stepping out of his assigned role. Max was right. He couldn't afford to do so now. Somehow, he had to continue to be a writer as far as Melissa was concerned.

"If the friend isn't willing to cooperate, do you have any other suggestions for where we could go?"

"The beach house is available."

"Max, it's wintertime, in case you hadn't noticed."

"So? Few people would be hanging around this time of the year. Anyone around would be suspect. I can also put more men on the case without her seeing them."

"We'll go that route if we have to. I'll let you know. But if I have to head for a beach, I'd prefer the Caribbean."

"Yeah, wouldn't we all?"

He glanced up and saw Melissa at the counter paying for two cups of coffee.

"Look, I've gotta go. She'll be here in a moment."

"Good luck. And keep in touch. Who knows, I might have a *real* job for you in a few days. Try not to get too bored."

"I'll try to remember that," Joel drawled before putting the receiver down and turning to the approaching woman.

"Here you are." She handed him one of the containers.

"Thanks."

"You didn't look too happy talking with your friend just now," she offered with a tentative smile. "Is there some problem?"

"Yes and no," Joel prevaricated. "I guess I'm just upset. My friend had picked up the news of the explosion on his police scanner," he improvised. "The whole building has gone up, although the people on the other floors were evacuated without much danger. It's mass confusion there. The best thing we can do is stay away."

Melissa shivered. "We're lucky to be alive."

He glanced around at the darkened street and slowly moved Melissa and himself into the deeper shadows at the side of the building. "Do you remember talking about your friend's place in the Islands?"

His sudden change of subject caused Melissa to look at him in surprise. "Yes, why?"

"I was just thinking about how nice it would be to get away from this cold weather for a few days. I don't suppose she'd be willing to let us use her place since we're temporarily homeless these days."

Homeless. Her mind hadn't fully comprehended all that had happened to her tonight. Her home—all of her possessions—everything was gone. All she had left was what she wore. Not even that, she amended, looking at the coat Joel had loaned her.

"Melissa?"

She hadn't realized that tears were rolling down her cheeks until Joel set his coffee on the ledge by the telephone, cupped her face in his hands and gently brushed the tears away with his thumbs.

"Don't cry, love. Please don't cry. We'll work something out, okay? If you don't want to ask her, we can go somewhere else. My friend has a place on the coast of North Carolina. It's just a summer cottage, but it might be fun to go over there for a couple of days." He leaned down and brushed his lips across her mouth. "We've both been through quite a shock. I think it would do us both good to get away from everything." He held her close to his body. "Let's go somewhere safe and give the police a chance to investigate what happened."

How could she possibly think straight at the moment? She closed her eyes, and he lightly kissed each eyelid, causing them to quiver in reaction to his touch.

"Let me look after you, Melissa. Please."

Joel forgot the role he was supposed to be playing. He forgot everything except the need to stay with this woman and to keep her safe from harm. She intrigued him like no other woman ever had. She was such a mixture of innocence and knowledge, of fierce independence and gentle yielding. He felt as though his heart had paused in its rhythmic beat and the air refused to move in his lungs while he waited for her answer.

"Nothing like this has ever happened to me before," she managed to say in a moment.

"All right. Let's look at your options...at both our

options. We don't have a place to stay. Luckily for you, we still haven't gotten your car, so it wasn't in the garage tonight, but mine was, so at the moment, we're without transportation. We each have friends with summer places. We could go to North Carolina or fly down to Miami and go to the Virgin Islands, if you think your friend wouldn't mind.''

''I don't think she'd mind. She's always told me to feel free to use it whenever I could.''

''Would you mind if I went with you?''

Her gaze met his. ''Is that what you want?''

He nodded. ''Very much.''

Melissa stood in the circle of his arms, trying to come to grips with the unexpected events during the past few hours. Her job came first, of course, but the building was closed for the rest of the week. Her home had been destroyed and she had no place to stay. Joel's suggestion made a lot of sense. He'd made it clear that she wouldn't have to be alone, not if she didn't want to be.

Was it just a few weeks ago when she was stumbling over how to deal with Joel's invitation to spend a vacation together? Hadn't she learned anything during these past few weeks? Hadn't she learned how to break the myriad rules that governed her life? *Live a little,* she reminded herself. *Enjoy the joys of spontaneity. Be outrageous for the first time in your life.*

She gave Joel a tremulous smile. ''I'll call Karen right now.''

Five

Melissa wearily opened her eyes and looked around the Miami airport terminal. At two o'clock in the morning, very few people were there. She located Joel casually leaning against a counter, chatting with an airline employee—a female employee who looked as though she was thoroughly enjoying the attention.

Melissa closed her eyes, wishing she could stretch out for a few moments of rest. Three short hours ago, the idea of flying to an island in the sun had had all the earmarks of an exciting adventure. Now all that could arouse her interest was a place to sleep. Obviously, she was not the stuff that adventurers were made out of.

Karen had been delighted to hear from her, and even more delighted to give her directions to her vacation cottage. Melissa had handed the phone to Joel at that point, which had created a barrage of questions when he'd returned the receiver to Melissa. She knew she'd have a great deal of explaining to do when they returned because Karen had only laughed at Melissa's explanation that she and Joel were friends who happened to need a place to stay for a few days.

Melissa could understand Karen's doubts because she was developing more than a few herself as each hour passed. She hadn't really thought about how much of her time had been taken up with Joel recently and how necessary he'd become to her. Their friendship had grown steadily and naturally. It was only when she heard Karen's astonishment and rapid-fire questions that Melissa realized how out of character her recent behavior had been.

"Melissa?"

Joel's distinctive voice seemed to touch every part of her. She would recognize it anywhere. She opened her eyes and found him crouched beside her knees, a concerned expression on his face.

She smiled at him and absently brushed his hair off his forehead.

"Are you okay?" he asked.

She nodded. "Just tired."

"The first flight out of here won't be for another three hours. If you want, we could check into one of the hotels nearby. We don't have to take an early flight, for that matter."

"It doesn't matter to me. Whatever you want to do."

Joel glanced around the terminal. He felt very exposed there. "I think we both need some sleep. Since this is a vacation, there's no reason to arrive exhausted." He stood and pulled her to her feet. "Let's go get horizontal."

She grinned. "What a romantic offer. How could I possibly refuse!"

He recalled what had occurred immediately prior to the explosion. He'd come so close to making a major mistake. He knew better than to get personally involved, and yet he also knew that he couldn't ignore what was happening between the two of them. *Be a pro*, he reminded himself. He could certainly choose not to allow a physical relationship with Melissa to further complicate matters.

He draped his arm over her shoulders and led her away from the waiting area and toward the exit doors. He nodded to the airline employee when she gave him a wave, but continued walking. "We can hop a shuttle bus to the nearest hotel, check in, get some sleep, then head south tomorrow."

She nodded, too tired to care.

By the time they arrived at the hotel and had been given the key, Melissa looked almost comatose to Joel. She hadn't blinked when he asked for one room with double beds. There was no way he was going to let her out of his sight, not after what had happened, and he was grateful that she hadn't argued.

He found their room and opened the door. She immediately went to one of the beds and sat down. She still carried his parka clutched to her chest. Her hair was tangled and fell in abandoned waves around her face. Her eyes looked swollen from lack of sleep.

"Do you want to take a shower?"

She nodded but didn't move.

"Or would you rather wait until morning?"

She nodded once again.

He shook his head. She'd had a very tough night and had held up very well. He walked over to her and gently removed the coat from her arms, then knelt and untied her sneakers. Reaching around her, he tugged at the covers, lifted her slightly so that he could pull them back, then gently lowered her head onto the pillow. She didn't stir when he lifted her legs and tucked them under the covers.

Joel went into the bathroom and turned on the shower. As soon as he'd stripped out of his clothes, placing his pistol on top of them, he stepped beneath the soothing spray.

Whenever he flew commercially, he contacted the security force of each airline, showed his special ID and checked his pistol with them. It had all been done unobtrusively. He'd explained his purpose for carrying it and had shown his permit.

So far, so good. One more flight, a short boat ride to the small island where they were going, and he would have her safe.

Her friend Karen had sounded as though she wanted to ask a hundred questions, but she had refrained. Instead, her directions had been clear and concise. He grinned. He had a hunch that Melissa would have some explaining to do the next time she and Karen spoke.

He sighed, turning beneath the spray so that the hot water hit his neck and shoulder muscles. The needle-like spray felt as though it were kneading the tense muscles. Joel consciously worked to relax so that he could sleep. He needed to stay alert and he couldn't do that without some much-needed rest. No one had shown any interest in them while they were at the airport, nor had anyone followed them to the hotel. For a few hours, at least, he could relax his guard.

By the time he turned off the water and toweled

himself dry, he was ready to hit the sack. He tied the towel around his waist, gathered up his clothes and quietly entered the bedroom.

Melissa hadn't moved.

He placed the pistol on the floor beside his bed, removed the towel and slipped between the covers. He couldn't remember when a bed had felt so good to him. Within minutes he was asleep.

When Melissa opened her eyes several hours later, she had no idea where she was. A thin strip of light from the window where the drapes did not quite meet was the only illumination in the room.

The only thing she was certain of was that she wasn't at home. Home. Memories began to impinge on her consciousness. Being with Joel…the explosion…running through the night…calling Karen… flying south…sitting in the airport…. But she didn't remember this room.

She raised up on one elbow and looked around. She could barely see the other bed in the shadowed room, could barely make out the outline of someone sleeping there.

Joel. He lay on his stomach, his head burrowed into the pillow, facing away from her. The covers lay draped around his waist. She had never seen him without a shirt before.

If the explosion hadn't occurred when it did, she would have seen much more than his bare chest. She could feel her face flame at the thought. Was the explosion an omen of sorts? It had certainly interrupted what seemed to be inevitable between her and Joel.

She had never felt so close to another person before, not even her parents. It hadn't been their fault that they hadn't been affectionate or demonstrative, and Melissa hadn't missed what she'd never had. However, after being around Joel, she'd discovered the joys of touching—which he seemed to do with ease—and hugging—another thing that seemed to come naturally to him. And his kisses...would she ever get enough of them?

Melissa quietly slid from the bed and tiptoed into the bathroom. She glanced into the mirror and cringed, wondering what she was going to do with her hair.

After quickly removing her clothes, she stepped into the shower. Thank God the hotel furnished complimentary shampoo for people like her, who hadn't brought any. She had escaped with only what she had been wearing.

Joel had suggested that they wait until today to shop for clothes. She was at a loss to know where to start trying to replace what had been lost in the explosion. Even her purse and all her identification was gone. Joel had explained on the flight from D.C. to Miami that everything could be replaced. It would just take time. In the meantime, he would pay for whatever she needed, since his wallet had been in his pocket when the explosion occurred.

For now, she would have to put on her sweater and jeans once again. The thought of wearing what she'd worn yesterday didn't thrill her, but she knew she was lucky to have that, under the circumstances. She was lucky to be alive.

What if she *had* been killed? She would have died without ever having experienced much. It was as though she'd been given a second chance to discover life. This time, she intended to open her eyes to everything around her.

By the time she finished her shower and dressed, Melissa discovered that her stomach was growling. She couldn't remember the last time she'd eaten, but she knew she was going to need something soon.

She opened the door to the bedroom and found Joel sitting on the side of the bed with the sheets draped decorously around him.

"Good morning," she said with a smile.

"You okay?" he asked, studying her intently.

"Of course. Why wouldn't I be?"

"I was worried about you last night. I think we pushed you past your limits."

"Well, you have to admit we had a full day yesterday."

"Agreed."

"Joel, do you by any chance have a comb I could use?"

He grinned at her earnest expression. "Is that all it will take to make you content?"

"Well, a comb and some breakfast would go a long way toward that end."

He leaned over and picked up his pants, searched through them and handed her a small pocket comb.

"Thanks." She disappeared into the bathroom.

As soon as the door closed, he stood and stepped into his pants. He'd had a scare when he awakened and saw her bed empty. For a brief moment, he'd been afraid that somehow, someone had come in and—

But then he'd heard a soft sound in the bathroom and realized where she was. If he didn't watch it, he would become downright paranoid. He'd never been responsible for another person before. It felt much different from just looking after himself. He wondered if that feeling of responsibility was what a parent felt. If so, he wasn't sure he could live with it on a daily basis. His nerves were already on edge, and he and Melissa had only been on the move for about twelve hours.

By the time she came out of the bathroom with her hair combed, but damp, Joel was dressed.

"Let's go get something to eat, do some shopping and grab a plane heading south," he suggested with a grin.

She nodded. "Sounds great."

It was early evening by the time they approached the small cottage that Karen had carefully described. They had already taken a plane and a boat, and were now in a taxi that had enjoyed its prime around the Second World War.

Melissa sat in isolated splendor in the back seat while Joel chatted with the driver, asking about sailboat rentals, scuba diving equipment, the best places to eat and other general information.

What surprised her was that he was carrying on the conversation in Spanish.

"I didn't know they spoke Spanish in the Virgin Islands," she said, not realizing she'd spoken her thoughts until Joel looked around at her.

"It isn't the native language, if that's what you mean," he said. "Carlos is from Puerto Rico."

"Oh. I didn't know you spoke Spanish."

He shrugged. "One of the ranch hands was from Mexico. It's an easy language to pick up. I learned it before I was old enough to consider languages difficult.''

The car slowed and turned onto a path that looked barely wide enough for a vehicle. After following the trail for a few hundred yards, the car pulled into a clearing, and Joel and Melissa saw the house for the first time.

Although small, it looked well built, as though it could withstand the sudden storms that periodically originated in that area.

Joel looked at her. "I believe this is Karen's place.''

She nodded, seeing a small carved wooden sign with the family name on it near the door. ''Yes.'' She couldn't take it all in—the flowering shrubs, the tropical scented air, the lush greenness all around. ''Oh, Joel, this is beautiful.''

He got out of the car and opened the door to help her out, then grabbed the two bags they'd bought that morning to carry their other purchases.

After paying off the driver and arranging for him to pick them up the next day so that they could explore the harbor town, Joel turned toward the house. ''Shall we go in?''

Melissa was almost afraid to move. She felt as though she was under some island magical spell and she didn't want to spoil the sensation. *Don't be silly,* she reminded herself. *Now you understand why Karen has tried to get you to come down here before.*

She climbed the steps to the wide porch that encircled the house. The key was where Karen had told them it would be, and Melissa quickly opened the door, holding it open so that Joel could step through with their bags.

Each room looked out onto the beach. Melissa walked to the sliding doors, unlocked them and stepped outside.

"I've never seen anything like this before."

Joel joined her at the railing. "Now this is my idea of winter weather." He started down the stairs. "Let's go exploring."

The beach was in a small cove that ended at a cluster of rocks. After they clambered to the top, they could see the jungle vegetation had taken over the inlet next to the one they had come from. The foliage grew to within a couple of feet of the water.

Melissa turned and looked back toward the house. The sun was beginning to set, and the scene looked like something from a travel magazine or postcard— the palm trees were silhouetted against a dark blue sky with rays of pink and light blue projected across it. The sand looked as though it had been bleached white.

"I feel as though I'm going to wake up any moment," she whispered. "This can't be real."

"I'm glad you suggested coming down here."

"Oh, me, too."

This was paradise. There was no doubt in Melissa's mind. She watched the lazy waves wash up on the shore, trimming it with lacy foam.

Melissa had always dealt in facts, figures and science; in what could be analyzed, processed and proven. Nothing in her experience had prepared her for the sheer magic of nature in all of her bountiful splendor.

Melissa turned to Joel and found that he was watching her. "I've never seen anything so wonderful," she said softly.

"Neither have I," he replied, his gaze never leaving her face.

She turned away, unable to handle the emotion that washed over her at the look on his face. She began to clamber down the pile of rocks. As soon as she reached the sand, she slipped off her sneakers and walked to the edge of the water. She touched it with her toe. "It's so warm," she marveled, looking around at him.

He stood watching her, his hands in his pockets. "Yes."

"I never realized. I guess I'm used to the water in New England."

He glanced at the sky. "We'd better get back to the house. Darkness comes quickly in the tropics."

Melissa obligingly walked to where he was standing. She held a shoe in each hand. He took one from her so that he could hold her hand, and they walked back to the house in silence.

As soon as they reached the house, they looked through each room. Melissa felt no sense of unease while they chose which bedroom each would use. Then they went into the kitchen to check the supplies.

"We'll pick up fresh food when we go into town tomorrow. But there's enough canned goods here to feed us tonight," Joel pointed out.

Melissa yawned and hastily covered her mouth with her hand.

"It's all that fresh air," Joel pointed out.

"That must be it. It can't be the company."

He looked at her with raised eyebrows. "I certainly hope not, at least not quite so early in our vacation."

"We can't stay long, you know," she said quietly.

"Yes. I know."

"It's going to be difficult trying to make insurance claims, finding a new place to live when we return."

"That's true, but for the next few days, let's enjoy where we are. Let's just live in the moment...forget the past and the future. After all, this is the only time that we have any control over."

She nodded. "Then I intend to enjoy every second." She looked at the cans they had set out on the counter. "As soon as we get this meal put together, I'm going to bed. There's so much to do, I'm not sure what I want to do first."

Joel took her hands and placed them on his chest. "Thank you for inviting me here."

"It wouldn't be the same without you. I'm glad you suggested getting away."

He leaned down and kissed her softly on the lips. "Meeting you has been the most magical experience I've had since I was a child. I'm still not sure you're real."

She slipped her arms around his neck. "I feel exactly the same way." When she kissed him, she allowed all of her emotions full rein. Her Big Adventure had started. She would never again have such a golden opportunity to experience life.

Melissa had every intention of making the most of it.

Six

Bright sunlight streamed through the slats covering Melissa's bedroom windows when she first opened her eyes. The warmth of the room had caused her to kick off her covers the night before. For a few blissful moments, Melissa closed her eyes once again and lay there, content to drift in that delicious time somewhere between dreams and reality.

She was aware of the comfortable bed, the warm air, the soft sounds of the waves nearby and the slight rustle of the breeze through the broad-leaved plants next to the porch. Eventually she could no longer resist peeking once more at the view she'd first discovered when they arrived.

She climbed out of bed and padded barefoot to the window. Bright green foliage and a lush carpet of grass edged the white sand. She could not resist the temptation to go outside. Ignoring the fact that she was wearing only an oversize T-shirt, Melissa pushed open the slatted door beside the window and stepped outside. There was no resisting the compelling pull of the sun, the sand and the sea.

She felt as though she were the only one in this colorful paradise. When she reached the shoreline, she looked up and down the gracefully curving beach but saw no one. Nothing marred the pristine freshness. This must have been how it looked on the day of Creation.

Melissa felt an ache in her chest that seemed to grow and fill her with the pain of unexpressed emotion. She wanted to laugh, to cry, to leap into the air. She wanted to throw her arms in the air and sing praises.

When a curl of a wave brushed lightly across her toes, she looked down and laughed. She threw her arms wide and twirled in a circle, causing the shallow wave to splash against her bare legs. The warm salt water felt like silk, and she waded outward, going up on her toes as the waves lapped around her legs. One audacious wave welled up, striking her at the waist and soaking her nightshirt. She retaliated by diving into its midst. *This must be how a dolphin feels swimming in the water,* she decided when she surfaced, shoving her hair away from her face and allowing it to stream down her back. She felt free to experience the elements.

When she grew breathless and her muscles were in a state of relaxed tiredness, she waded to shore, wringing the water from her hair.

She'd worked up an appetite, one she had every intention of appeasing as soon as possible. With a light step, she retraced her earlier route, let herself into her bedroom and walked into the adjoining bath-room, where she peeled off the sodden nightshirt and climbed into the shower.

Melissa Jordan's day had been jubilantly launched.

Joel stood looking out the sliding glass doors off the living area. Watching Melissa run, jump and frolic in the water had caused a lump to form in his throat. She'd been like a small child who had just discovered how to play in the ocean. And yet...and yet, when she returned to the house, she had been all woman: alluring, tempting and very desirable.

Her wet garment clung to her body, providing little cover. She looked like a water nymph, lightly dancing up the pathway, a part of nature that might disappear before his eyes.

He could feel his heart racing in his chest. What he had just witnessed had affected him to such a de-gree that he felt physically weak.

When had this woman become so important to him? When had being around her become more than a job...had, instead, become a need to last a lifetime? He tried to rationalize his feelings. He understood that the situation was unusual, the circumstances far from normal. None of that mattered.

He loved her. He had loved her probably from the very first—if he had only recognized it. But how could he have identified such an overwhelming emo-tion that he'd never before experienced. His feelings had grown daily until he could no longer ignore or mistake what he was feeling.

He wished to hell he knew what to do about it.

"Good morning! Isn't it a beautiful day?"

He hadn't heard her enter the room. He swung

away from the view and looked at her. She'd changed into a pair of shorts and a summer blouse. Her hair hung in a single braid, her feet were bare.

She looked adorable.

"Did you enjoy your swim?"

For a moment, she looked surprised, then she laughed. "Yes, I did. Very much. You must have thought I'd lost my mind out there."

"Not at all. If anything, I was envying you."

"You should have joined me."

"I don't think that would have been a good idea."

"Why?"

He glanced at his watch. "We might have missed our ride to town. It's almost time."

"Oh! I had no idea it was that late." She turned away. "I'll get my purse. Even without any money, I feel more comfortable carrying it."

A horn honked outside.

"There he is. I'll be right there," she said, and disappeared down the hallway.

They were both in the back seat of the taxi, and on the way to town when Melissa suddenly gasped and said, "Joel!"

"What is it?"

Her hand had flown to her mouth. "Oh, Joel! I just remembered your manuscript. With everything that's happened, I had forgotten all that you've lost, as well. Just think of all that work gone."

He felt a pang of guilt at her obvious concern.

"It isn't the end of the world, I guess. I remember most of my references. I should be able to reconstruct what I've done."

She touched his hand. "It's still a loss that you haven't dwelled on in your efforts to help me. I know how I'd feel if all the work I'd produced over the past months was destroyed.''

He didn't know what to say, so he remained quiet. Damn. He hated the fact that she saw him as some heroic personage suffering in silence. He wished he didn't have to go through with this charade, but could tell her the truth about himself.

Another shock to his system. Never before had he been willing to share who he was with another person. Now, when he'd met the woman who meant the world to him, he couldn't tell her. At least, not right now. Just as soon as Max gave him the all-clear sign, he'd explain to Melissa who he was and what he did for a living.

For now, he'd just have to learn patience.

He turned his hand, catching hers, and slipped his fingers through hers. ''At the moment, all I want to do is to enjoy our tropical island.''

She squeezed his hand. ''Me, too.''

Hours later, Joel wondered if Melissa had any idea of the severe tests she was forcing him to face with regard to his self-control. Didn't she have any idea how irresistible she looked in the bikini she'd finally selected...or the strapless sundress that showed off her soft shoulders and contrasted so attractively with her hair.

The shorts and halter tops she'd chosen revealed her long, shapely legs and tantalizing cleavage.

How was he going to spend any time with Melissa in this romantic paradise without making love to her? And if he did, wouldn't he be taking advantage of the peculiar circumstances that had brought them to-gether?

They were seated at one of the local restaurants, and he kept gazing out over the water, trying to find the strength to leave her alone.

"Joel?"

He removed his gaze from the harbor and focused on her. "Hmm?"

"You're thinking about your manuscript, aren't you?"

"Why do you ask?"

"I just wondered. Every so often, you get a certain expression on your face, as though you're working out some sort of complex problem in your mind. It must be tough knowing how much effort it's going to take to replace what you lost."

He glanced down at the table, hating the thought of making up yet another lie. Instead, he chose to say, "I'm sorry. I know I'm not being very good company at the moment."

She touched his hand that rested on the table. "You don't owe me an apology. I understand what you're feeling."

"Do you?"

She nodded. "No matter how much I try to pretend, I still haven't faced the reality of all that's happened. It's hard to look at the fact that I have nothing left, that when I return, I've got to start all over." They were quiet for several minutes before she spoke again. "I just wish I could make some sense of it all." She cocked her head slightly, meeting his gaze. "Do you have some enemies that might be after you?"

"*Me!* What makes you think that bombing had anything to do with me?"

"Because nothing else makes any sense. If it had

been a random bombing of the entire building, whoever did it wouldn't have placed it on our floor. Since it was placed there, they could have been after only one of us.'' She took another sip of her drink. ''I don't know what you've been doing in the way of research, but could it be possible that you offended someone somewhere? Where were you before you moved to Virginia?''

Joel thought of his last assignment. Was it possible that... No. Of course not. He knew exactly why the bomb had been set. For the same reason that Peter Feldman had been run off the road. The problem was that he couldn't give Melissa that necessary tidbit of information.

Sometimes the agency's need for secrecy became absurd. His job would be so much more simple if he could just explain to her what was going on. There were times when the old need-to-know policy could be a real pain in the posterior.

This was one of them.

''Aren't you going to tell me?''

''Tell you what?''

She dropped her gaze for a moment, wishing that she had never started this conversation. ''Where you were before you moved here.''

He had no choice but to lie. ''Texas. I was doing some research in south Texas.'' Actually, he'd been flown into Brownsville via Mexico when they'd smuggled him out of Central America.

''Can you think of anyone down there who might have been offended by what you were doing?''

He tried not to react to the innocent question, even though it triggered a myriad of memories. Yes, he could think of a few people who hated his guts, all right.

"Not really, no."

She looked disappointed.

"How about you?" he asked in an effort to get her mind off him. "Do you have any enemies?"

Her laughter rang in the room. "I'm afraid not. My life is much too boring to have accumulated anything so exciting."

"What about your work?"

She sobered, obviously considering his question. After a few moments, she shook her head. "I love my work, but it's far from exciting. At least, most of the time."

"You've never told me exactly what you do."

She smiled. "It's classified."

"No kidding. You work for the government?"

"No. It's a private company, but you know how competitive private industry is. Always afraid of industrial spies." She eyed him with mock suspicion. "For all I know, you could be an industrial spy worming your way into my confidence to learn everything I know."

He grinned. "So how am I doing?"

She patted his hand. "I'd look for another line of work if I were you."

"Oh, really?"

She nodded. "You're too open and honest. You're not the type to harbor deep, dark secrets. You're very easy to read, as a matter of fact."

"You don't say. So tell me what I'm thinking at this moment."

She grinned. "I didn't say I could read minds. I just said that you were easy to read."

He slouched back in his chair and stared at her. "Okay. So read me."

She sobered and stared at him for a moment. "All right," she said with a nod. "You don't like working for another person because you don't take orders well. You have a deep-seated desire to be independent, to be free from all restraints and routines. You're easily bored, partly because of your intelligence and strong need to be intellectually stimulated."

Alarms rang inside Joel's head. He sat up abruptly. He felt the same way he'd felt when he read that absurd piece about the Gemini man; he resented the fact that she had been able to describe him so accurately.

"What are you, some kind of witch?" he growled.

"Was I close?"

"Close enough." He took a drink from his neglected glass of rum punch. Setting the glass back down, he responded, "You sound like one of those star gazers."

She laughed, sounding pleased. "I do, don't I?" She reached across the table and took his hand. In a pseudo-solemn tone, she asked, "What is your sun sign, Signore?"

He studied her for a moment before he grinned. "I'll tell mine if you'll tell yours."

"I'm a Libra."

"Hmm...whatever that is." He shrugged. "I'm supposedly a Gemini."

"So you're Joel, the Gemini man," she pointed out with a grin which faded into a look of bemusement. "Do you find me easy to read?"

"Perhaps."

"OK, so read me," she invited with a mischievous smile.

He remembered the information that Feldman had given him about her, then discarded it. Nothing he'd been told described the woman he'd gotten to know over the past few weeks.

"You sure you want me to do this?" he asked.

Her eyes reflected her shyness but she nodded gamely.

He was quiet for a few moments, gazing at her intently. Then in a low voice, he began to speak. "You have a very becoming blush that appears at the most intriguing moments—such as now—that makes me want to know what thoughts are running around in that head of yours." He paused and raised one eyebrow. "Shall I go on?"

Even though her cheeks glowed, she nodded.

"Let's see, then. You're very conscientious in your work, very dedicated. You don't go out very often and seem to enjoy your own company. You have the greatest pair of legs I've seen this side of the Rockettes in Rockefeller Center. You have eyes that haunt my sleep, a smile that melts my heart and a mouth that continues to lure me into indiscretions that could get me into very serious trouble."

Her face matched the color of the setting sun. "Aren't you being a little personal?"

"Weren't you?"

"Not in the same way. I didn't talk about your physical appearance and how it affects me."

He waved his hand. "Feel free," he offered expansively.

She clasped her hands in front of her. With her eyes

GET 2

HOW TO GET YOUR
2 FREE BOOKS AND FREE GIFT!

1. Peel off the MIRA sticker on the front cover. Place it in the space provided at right. This automatically entitles you to receive two free books and an exciting mystery gift.

2. Send back this card and you'll get 2 "The Best of the Best™" novels. These books have a combined cover price of $11.00 or more in the U.S. and $13.00 or more in Canada, but they are yours to keep absolutely FREE!

3. There's no catch. You're under no obligation to buy anything. We charge nothing – ZERO – for your first shipment. And you don't have to make any minimum number of purchases – not even one!

4. We call this line "The Best of the Best" because each month you'll receive the best books by some of today's hottest authors. These authors show up time and time again on all the major bestseller lists and their books sell out as soon as they hit the stores. You'll like the convenience of getting them delivered to your home at our special discount prices . . . and you'll love your *Heart to Heart* subscriber newsletter featuring author news, horoscopes, recipes, book reviews and much more!

5. We hope that after receiving your free books you'll want to remain a subscriber. But the choice is yours – to continue or cancel, anytime at all! So why not take us up on our invitation, with no risk of any kind. You'll be glad you did!

6. And remember...we'll send you a mystery gift ABSOLUTELY FREE just for giving "The Best of the Best" a try.

SPECIAL FREE GIFT!

We'll send you a fabulous surprise gift, absolutely FREE, simply for accepting our no-risk offer!

Visit us online at
www.mirabooks.com

BOOKS FREE!

Hurry!

Return this card promptly to GET 2 FREE BOOKS & A FREE GIFT!

The Best of the Best™

Affix peel-off MIRA sticker here

YES! Please send me the 2 FREE "The Best of the Best" novels and FREE gift for which I qualify. I understand that I am under no obligation to purchase anything further, as explained on the opposite page.

385 MDL C6PQ

(P-BB3-01)
185 MDL C6PP

NAME (PLEASE PRINT CLEARLY)

ADDRESS

APT.# CITY

STATE/PROV. ZIP/POSTAL CODE

▼ DETACH AND MAIL CARD TODAY! ▼

The Best of the Best™ — Here's How it Works:

Accepting your 2 free books and gift places you under no obligation to buy anything. You may keep the books and gift and return the shipping statement marked "cancel." If you do not cancel, about a month later we will send you 4 additional novels and bill you just $4.24 each in the U.S., or $4.74 each in Canada, plus 25¢ shipping & handling per book and applicable taxes if any.* That's the complete price and — compared to cover prices of $5.50 or more each in the U.S. and $6.50 or more each in Canada — it's quite a bargain! You may cancel at any time, but if you choose to continue, every month we'll send you 4 more books, which you may either purchase at the discount price or return to us and cancel your subscription.

*Terms and prices subject to change without notice. Sales tax applicable in N.Y. Canadian residents will be charged applicable provincial taxes and GST.

on her hands, she muttered, "I don't think that's a very good idea."

"Why? Afraid you'll blush? Don't worry about it. I'm used to you changing colors. It's one of your most charming characteristics."

She didn't reply, but Joel was determined not to let her off the hook. While he waited, he signaled the bartender to bring them another round of the island's specialty drink. The alcoholic content made Long Island Tea seem like a bland after-dinner drink by comparison.

They sat in silence and watched the sun set. When the waiter brought their drinks Joel suggested he bring them something from the kitchen, as well.

During their meal, Melissa sighed and finally spoke. "All right. I'm not sure why we're doing this, but here goes." She closed her eyes for a moment, then took a healthy sip from her very potent drink. As though she were afraid that she wouldn't be able to say it unless she got it out quickly, Melissa began to speak in a low, hurried voice.

"You have a way of walking that puts me in mind of a dancer—or maybe a feline...like a jungle cat stalking its prey. You move silently with a conscious intent that I find captivating. When you walk toward me like that, I find that I can't move. I just wait to see what you're going to do." She paused for breath, grabbed her glass and took another large swallow. "You have an air of confidence about you that intrigues and attracts me." She forced herself to meet his gaze. "I find you one of the most attractive men I've ever been around so that I don't know how to hide my reaction to you. I feel like a gawky adolescent with my first crush."

Joel had become instantly aroused from her very first words. He sat there listening to her, reminding himself that he had teased her into disclosing what was obviously a very personal revelation.

She had no sooner finished speaking than he was reaching for his wallet. He threw some bills on the table, stood and held out his hand. "Let's get out of here. Otherwise, I'm going to embarrass both of us."

Seven

Within minutes of leaving the small restaurant, they were by the harbor. The cool breeze helped Joel to gain some control over his reaction to her words.

When had he ever had anyone be so honest with him? She had no artifice or shield to protect herself. He could hurt this woman badly, and that was the last thing he wanted.

He loved her. Like it or not, convenient or not, ethical or not, he was in love with Dr. Melissa Jordan. What in the hell was he going to do?

They reached the end of the boardwalk and took the stairs down to the sand-covered beach. The stars were the only light they had besides the reflected lights from the small town.

"Melissa?"

"Hmm?"

"I need to tell you something."

She stared up at him through the heavy shadows around them.

"All right."

He turned and took her into his arms and held her close, so close that he could feel her heart beating in her chest, could feel the gentle rise and fall of her breasts as she breathed. "Melissa, I lied to you."

She pulled her head away from his shoulder and stared up at him. "What do you mean?"

"Do you remember when we first met?"

She nodded.

"Do you remember when I said that I'd like to be friends?"

Her puzzlement was reflected in the expression on her face. "Yes."

"I want more than that. I guess I've been lying to myself, as well, pretending that you were a friend, someone to spend time with, someone to tease, to have as a companion." He cupped her face in his hands. "But the thing is…" He stared at the light that seemed to glow from within her. "I want everything with you. I know it's too soon. We haven't known each other that long, but think about it for the next few days. I want you in my future." He leaned down and pressed his lips softly against hers. With his lips still brushing across hers, he said, "Don't ever leave me. I'm not sure I could survive a life without you somewhere in it."

His kiss confirmed what he was saying…and more. His kiss expressed what he could find no words to say. He was trembling, but he didn't care. Never had he felt so vulnerable, as though his heart was in her hands, waiting to see what she would do with it.

Melissa wrapped her arms around his waist, holding him tightly, and returned his kiss. He could feel her heart racing…or was that his? Her quickened breathing was no less rushed than his.

Joel discovered that it wasn't always necessary to hear the words in order to understand the meaning. Melissa had answered him. God help them both.

When Melissa finally opened her eyes the next morning, the sun was once again high in the sky. She sighed and slowly stretched, remembering the night before.

Whatever else he was, Joel Kramer was a gentleman. He had known by her response to him last night how she felt about him, but he had not used the knowledge to take advantage of her.

Was she a little disappointed? she wondered with a slight smile on her face. Perhaps, just a little. She found life more confusing than ever before. Living with her head in a book had been much simpler. Somewhere in the printed page, she had always been able to find an answer. Now she didn't know where to look to find an answer to what she felt whenever Joel was nearby. He didn't make her confusion any easier.

She enjoyed him, but she didn't always understand him. There were times when he became introspective, as though he'd withdrawn from her. Perhaps all writers were like that. Maybe he was getting ideas for his novel.

What she needed to do was to relax and enjoy his company without any expectations for the outcome of the relationship. He'd admitted that he was attracted to her. That was a start. After all, they hadn't known each other but a few weeks. Sometimes it was hard for her to remember that.

Now was the time to allow herself to relax and enjoy their growing relationship. What better surroundings could she have chosen than this beautiful tropical paradise?

She rubbed her head where a steady ache seemed to be focused, no doubt caused by the consumption of those powerful drinks they'd sampled last night. Perhaps she wouldn't enjoy herself quite *that* much again.

"Good morning."

Joel stood in the doorway of her room, holding two cups of coffee.

Melissa leaned up on one elbow and pushed her hair from her face. "Good morning. It looks as though I overslept again."

He grinned and advanced into the room. Handing her one of the cups, he said, "Isn't that what vacations are for? No schedules, no appointments." The look in his eyes as he gazed at her made her feel warm. "Besides I haven't been up that long, myself. I don't know about you, but my head felt close to exploding this morning. That rum punch last night was more potent than I gave it credit for."

He sounded relaxed and comfortable being in her bedroom. Melissa fought the impulse to grab the sheet and pull it under her chin. She certainly didn't need to act like somebody's maiden aunt. Not with Joel. Instead, she took a sip from the proffered cup and smiled her pleasure at the delicious taste.

"Did you sleep well?" she asked. She noticed that he didn't meet her eyes before answering.

"Well enough. What would you like to do today?"

She glanced out the window. "Swim and lie out in the sun. We didn't get a chance yesterday, with all our shopping."

He grinned. "I think that can be arranged." He nodded toward the kitchen. "Our driver last night recommended a woman who lives nearby who would be willing to prepare meals for us. I talked with her this morning, and she agreed. She's in the kitchen now, planning some island dishes for us."

"I think coffee is about all I can handle at this moment. Maybe after my shower, I'll be able to face something a little more substantial."

Joel turned and started out of the room, then paused. "I hope you'll thank your friend for me for allowing us to come down here. It's nice to get away from the phone and television and our regular routine."

She smiled. "Thank you for successfully promoting the idea of a vacation. I feel like a new person." Being with Joel had already done that, but she didn't want to tell him that. She'd confessed too much last night. "You managed to make relaxing seem like a skilled art. Maybe that's part of being a writer."

"I suppose."

Joel left before he could say anything more. He'd be glad when he could tell her what he really did. Would it make a difference to her? She had her own career. Would it bother her that he traveled for weeks at a time? Would she be willing to spend time with him whenever he returned home? How could he ask her until he was free to tell her everything?

He'd called Max last night from a pay phone and explained that there was no phone in the cottage. Max had said things were heating up but hadn't gone into any details. It was only a matter of a couple of days and Joel would be able to tell her the truth.

In the meantime, he was going to forget everything but the moment. He'd been given the gift of time and the opportunity to share that time with Melissa. Because their future was too important to take chances with, he was determined not to pursue closer intimacy with her.

He found her innocence endearing, but once he realized how little she had experienced, he made up his mind not to take advantage of their present situation. If the explosion hadn't occurred when it did, would she have given herself to him? Would he have had the strength to refuse such a gift?

He didn't want to be tested again.

In no way did he ever want her to feel that he had taken advantage of her. So he would wait, even if he had to spend more sleepless nights tossing and turning, knowing that she was just in the next room, knowing that she probably wouldn't refuse him.

With fresh resolve, Joel returned to the kitchen and the woman who was preparing various dishes for them to eat at their convenience. She smiled at him.

"Your wife is up now?"

How to answer that one. "Uh, she isn't hungry just now. We'll probably eat later."

The woman smiled and said nothing. What was there in that knowing smile that made him think she was picturing a well-loved wife who was slow to leave the bed shared with her husband the previous night? Joel almost groaned aloud at the thought.

He gazed out at the water, hoping it was cold enough to take care of what he was afraid was going to be a permanent condition.

* * *

Melissa stepped off the porch onto the path that led to the beach. She clutched the beach jacket that she had pulled on to cover the sparse swimsuit she had bought the day before. Whatever had possessed her to think she could wear it anywhere outside of the tiny dressing room in which she had first tried it on? She remembered thinking that the suit would help the new image she hoped to create. However, stripping down to two tiny pieces of material just now had unnerved her more than she thought possible.

She had told Joel to go ahead, that she would be out later. Now she lifted her hand to shade her eyes, looking for him. There he was, swimming out toward the reef that protected the cove from heavier waves. Melissa realized she felt a sense of reprieve that he would not see her as soon as she arrived.

She knew that she would have to get over this ridiculous shyness about being around him. He treated her with patience, understanding and a warmth that made her heart start pounding as soon as he came into view.

The problem was she had never had a relationship with a man before; at least, nothing like this. He seemed to find it natural and normal to spend the day together, kiss her senseless each evening, then bid her a casual good-night at her bedroom door. It had taken her hours to get to sleep the night before. She felt as though all of her motors were running at top speed. She didn't have a clue how to turn them down or shut them off. Somehow, she'd discovered, her switches were controlled by Joel's presence.

With a determined lift of her chin Melissa followed the path to the beach and with a sense of bravado, removed the jacket and tossed it down beside her towel on the sand. She marched toward the water.

She knew she didn't have Joel's experience in hiding his reactions to her. She also knew that he found her attractive. Therefore, she had no reason to cower behind her fears of allowing him to see her so scantily clad. She could deal with it. After all, she was in the midst of an exciting adventure, and she intended to make the most of their time together.

The waves curled around her feet and she smiled. The water felt wonderful—silky and enticing. A sudden sense of euphoria swept over her and she took several running steps and leapt into the next lazy wave approaching the shore.

When she came up for air, she was breathless and laughing. Why hadn't she discovered earlier how much life had to offer outside of the laboratory? She'd had no idea that she could enjoy the feel of the water and sun stroking her body, could savor the scent of the tropical foliage and flowers, could find the delectable taste of the native fruit so pleasurable.

Melissa swam out into the lagoon until the water rippled gently. Then she rolled onto her back and floated, her eyes closed.

She lost track of time, enjoying the soft caress of the warm sunlight on her face. She'd rubbed a sun block that was supposed to be waterproof all over her body before coming outside. She lazily reminded herself to add more once she got out of the water, but for now, she remained content to enjoy the moment.

Something tugged at her heels and she gasped, luckily filling her lungs with air before she went under the water. Panicked, she floundered until strong arms wrapped around her and pulled her to the surface. She and Joel broke through the surface of the water, their faces only a few inches apart.

"You scared me!" she accused, gasping for air.

"I realized that too late to do much about it. I thought you heard me swimming up to you."

Melissa became aware of their respective positions. She had a death grip around his neck. His arms held her tightly against him so that she could feel his lithe, mostly unclothed body pressed firmly against hers. He felt cool to the touch, which surprised her. She felt scalded everywhere her bare flesh touched his.

She loosened her grip around his neck, and he obligingly allowed his hands to slide down her back and fasten at her waist.

"You okay now?" he asked, and she saw the concern in his eyes.

She smiled. "I must have been more than half asleep. Sorry I overreacted."

He continued to hold her, and she became aware of the fact that their legs were intertwined. Her thigh was tucked intimately between his. She jerked away from him.

"What's wrong?"

"Nothing."

"Are you ready to go back?"

She nodded, avoiding his eyes. He swam beside her when she headed for shore. She briefly closed her eyes, wishing she didn't have such a strong reaction to the man. He gave no indication that he even noticed that she was a member of the opposite sex.

By the time they reached the spot where she'd left her towel, Melissa had managed to gain some control over her behavior. Joel picked up a blanket from nearby that he must have brought down earlier and spread it in the shade. As soon as he sat down, he patted the space beside him.

Melissa kneeled down. He stretched out and closed his eyes. "This is a life I could get used to," he murmured with a smile.

She glanced around, wondering if it would be too obvious if she were to put her jacket back on, then decided it would be. After all, she wanted a tan, didn't she? She searched through her bag for her lotion and applied it vigorously to her arms and legs.

"Need some help?"

Startled, she glanced around. Joel was watching her from beneath lowered eyelids. "I can do it."

"You missed some large areas on your back. Lie down and I'll finish for you."

She closed her eyes and handed him the bottle. With careful strokes, he covered her back, then handed the lotion back to her. He hadn't lingered or given her the impression that he was doing more than helping a friend.

After recapping the bottle, she lay down beside him. "Do you have enough room?" he asked lazily.

"Ummhmm."

"Melissa?"

Her eyes flew open of their own accord. There was a change in his tone of voice.

"Yes?"

"Tell me about your childhood."

She relaxed slightly. "What about it?"

"What did you do for fun?"

She closed her eyes once again and thought back to her early days. "Actually, I don't recall having a childhood."

"What do you mean?"

"I think I was a surprise to my parents. I don't think they ever really wanted a family, but, of course, accepted the fact they were going to be parents with their usual attitude of doing whatever was necessary."

"Is that why you were an only child?"

"Oh, yes. They obviously learned from their mistakes."

"And they considered you to be a mistake?"

She thought about that for a moment. "I really don't know. I never heard them say anything like that, exactly. But there was an attitude that I felt all the time I was growing up. A sense of leashed impatience if I didn't respond immediately to any request they made."

"Is that what you meant about not having a childhood? Didn't you ever get a chance to play?"

"I don't remember much of it, if I did. I started reading at an early age and was soon absorbed in the worlds I could find in books. I started to school quite young. I did well in school. It was the one thing I knew I could do that won my parents' approval. I don't suppose I ever thought about playing."

"Did they ever take you to the seashore when you were small?"

"On occasion, but I was never allowed to play in the water or sand." She smiled. "It was too messy, you understand. I learned very quickly that neat was in, messy was definitely out."

"You once mentioned not having friends. Didn't you miss having someone to share things with?"

"Being known as a brain wasn't conducive to making friends, I'm afraid. Nobody seemed to be interested in anything I had to say."

"Except your parents, maybe?"

She smiled. "Of course. We had nightly discourses around the dinner table, discussing what I had read or learned that day."

"How stimulating for you," he drawled.

Melissa laughed. "You have to understand that I really didn't mind it, since this was the only life I knew. Children are resilient and very adaptable. I felt lucky that I had parents who encouraged me and my curiosity."

"But they didn't teach you to play."

"Well, no, that wasn't part of the curriculum."

Several moments went by before Joel asked, "Didn't you say you met Karen in college?"

Melissa smiled again. "Yes. She was my first and closest friend, even though she was older. She probably taught me everything I know about dating men."

Joel rolled over onto his side and propped himself on his elbow. "Oh, really?"

She opened her eyes and saw him only a few inches away. His eyes were dancing, and she smiled at his expression.

"Tell me more," he invited in a soft voice.

She shrugged. "Karen used to come back to the dorm after a date and tell me what had happened— the places they went, some of the moves the guys tried. You know."

He widened his eyes slightly. "I haven't the foggiest. I never finished college."

She swatted at him. "You know what I mean. The kinds of things that all guys try."

He placed his hand on her bare waist. "Ohhh, I understand. You mean moves, like this."

Melissa felt her stomach muscles quiver. "I don't

think she charted each and every one, but I wouldn't be surprised if that was one of them.''

''And did she tell you what to do in case a man carried on in such a reprehensible manner?''

''You're making fun of me.''

''A little,'' he agreed.

''Why?''

''I suppose because I find you such a contradictory person to be around. You're highly intelligent, no doubt very knowledgeable in your field, but every time I get within a few feet of you, you tense up as though you're expecting me to attack you. Is it me that makes you nervous, or all men?''

''You don't make me nervous,'' she said in a softly defiant tone.

He moved his hand so that he cupped her breast. She inhaled sharply. ''I don't? Then why is your heart beating so fast?''

She closed her eyes, trying to think. She had to be nonchalant in order to let him know that she was willing to pursue their relationship in whatever form it took. ''You startled me, that's all.''

''I'm not surprised. There's no telling what nefarious schemes I might be pursuing now that I have you here alone.''

''I sincerely doubt that any scheme you might be dreaming up is either wicked or villainous.''

He leaned closer, so that his mouth was only an inch or so away from hers. ''But you aren't absolutely certain, are you?''

She blinked. ''Not absolutely, no.''

''So you're aware I could take advantage of your trusting nature, aren't you?''

Before she could find an answer, he took the opportunity to respond away from her. His mouth covered hers in a persuasive kiss that caused all of her thinking processes to shut down. She touched his shoulder with her fingertips. The satiny smoothness of his skin coaxed her to explore. She traced the hard muscles bunched there and was intrigued by the contrast of skin and sinew.

Melissa felt as though her heart was going to pound its way right out of her chest. This man had such a strong effect on her that her response to him frightened her. It was that realization that caused her to turn her face away from him.

She could feel his fingers resting lightly against her breast. Their heat seared through the material as though each finger would be permanently imprinted there.

He touched her cheeks and gently turned her head until she was looking at him once more. "You can trust me, Melissa. I want you to know that."

She felt herself slipping into the magic of his gaze.

"I suppose you're used to this sort of thing." She waved her hand toward the surroundings. "I just feel a little out of my depth here."

He closed his eyes for a moment. "Believe me," he said after a moment, "so do I."

"You mean this is unusual for you, too?"

"Very."

She smiled. "I'm glad. You seem to be adjusting to everything that's happened more readily than I am. I've envied your ability to adapt."

Joel felt anything but relaxed at the moment.

She went on. "You're the first man that I've ever spent so much time with on a social basis. I always felt so awkward, never knowing what to say. But with you, it's been different."

"In what way?"

She shrugged. "Oh, I don't know. I guess you've allowed me to be me without feeling self-conscious about my lack of social skills."

"Melissa. There is absolutely nothing lacking in your social skills. You need to let go of that image of yourself. You're warm…and friendly…and very cuddly…and—" He leaned down and kissed her once again. "And I'll always be thankful I found you."

Her gaze returned to him. "You will?"

He nodded.

She touched his cheek. "I feel the same way."

They lay there together on the blanket and looked at each other in silence. Joel knew that he'd never needed his iron control more than he did then. He could see the shy yearning in her eyes and knew that she would not stop him from making love to her. She had no idea how tempted he was to do just that.

Before Melissa could give her actions too much thought, she slid her hand behind his head and pulled him down to her until their lips met. This time, she would not fight the feelings. This time, she was willing to explore the unknown.

Eight

"Is she getting restless to return home?" Max asked.

"She hasn't said. I've kept her busy—taught her how to snorkel, rented a small sailboat as well as a car to explore the island."

Melissa had gone to buy souvenirs for some of the people in her office, and Joel had taken the opportunity to call Max from a pay phone nearby.

"Has she said anything about needing to get back to work?"

"She called and talked to one of the management heads who told her there were still problems to be worked out before the building could be reopened. She plans to call again tomorrow."

"Then it sounds to me as though everything is under control."

"How's Feldman?"

"He's doing well. Working full-time and seems to be excited about his latest experiment."

"Has he asked about Melissa?"

"Only to be certain she was all right. The bombing really upset him."

"It managed to put a few wrinkles in my plans, as well."

"Are you trying to tell me you would prefer to be up here dealing with the ice and sleet? If so, I'm sure we can figure a way to bring her back and put her under surveillance."

"Did I say that? I'm just a little concerned over how long this whole matter is taking. The last time we talked, you said this thing should be over in a couple of days. That was almost a week ago."

"I know that's what I said. But there's no timetable on situations like this. We're doing everything we can."

"One of the local restaurants agreed to take my calls and said they'd get word to me. Let me know the minute this thing is taken care of, will you?"

"You know, Kramer, I'm really getting worried about you. There you are on a tropical island with a beautiful woman, and all you can talk about is finishing the job."

What Joel wanted was the release of the need to stay with his cover. As soon as the matter was dealt with, he intended to explain everything to Melissa.

Then he intended to ask her to marry him.

However, he had no intention of explaining any of this to Max.

"You know how dedicated I am to my work," he drawled, causing Max to laugh.

"The inactivity getting to you?"

"Let's just say I'm ready to forget about my career as a writer."

"Just remember to keep Dr. Jordan happy, okay?"

"I'm doing my very best, boss. Talk to you later."

Joel hung up and turned away from the phone. His frustration level continued to escalate the longer the time they spent together. He didn't want to do anything to betray the growing trust she had in him. He felt as though he held a very delicate flower in his hands that he could easily crush and destroy if he were to mishandle it.

Melissa had taught him so much about himself and his own attitudes of distrust toward people. She believed in the basic goodness of everyone. He had reason to know that a person could get killed believing in people. And yet he didn't want to awaken her to the darker aspects of life. He wanted to continue to protect her from so much.

"Joel?"

He turned around to find Melissa standing there, holding a large bag.

"I take it you decided to buy one of everything in the shop."

She laughed. "Just about. Thank you for loaning me the money."

"No problem."

She glanced at her watch. "If we're going to do any snorkeling today, we'd better get back."

"My thoughts exactly."

They smiled at each other. He caught her hand and led her to the car.

During the drive to the cottage, Melissa asked, "Are you getting restless about not writing?"

"Why do you ask?"

"I heard you pacing in your room last night. Then later, I saw you walking along the beach."

Joel glanced at Melissa, trying to read the expression on her face. "You should have joined me."

"I assumed you wanted to be alone."

Joel wasn't sure how to respond. Most of his nights were restless with very short periods of sleep. Being around Melissa all day, every day, was definitely having its effect on him.

When he didn't respond, she asked, "Why don't we go home?"

Joel slowed and turned into the driveway. As he parked the car, he asked, "Is that what you want?"

"I think that's what *you* want."

His grin was meant to reassure her. "Given the choice of swimming in the Caribbean or sweating over a manuscript in the frozen north, I much prefer the water." He got out of the car and walked around to open her door. "But if you're getting bored—"

"It isn't that."

Melissa wasn't sure what it was that was bothering her, but she knew that Joel wasn't being completely honest with her. He was too restless to be enjoying himself as much as he wanted her to believe.

In the days since they had arrived, he had kept them on such a busy schedule that she fell into bed each night exhausted. She almost longed for the sedate days of the laboratory, even though she had to admit she looked and felt better than she had for some time.

Her skin had turned the color of toast; her hair had lightened considerably, with streaks of platinum mixed in with the darker blond, and the regimen of daily swimming had toned up her muscles considerably.

Considering all their activities, she found it surprising that Joel had the energy for midnight walks...and the other morning she had spotted him on the beach doing push ups! Like everything else, he'd laughed off her questions.

But she could read the signs; he was becoming bored with her.

Unfortunately, the same wasn't true for her. The more she was around him, the more she wanted to be around him. Even worse, she finally recognized the malady that explained all of her symptoms lately. She was in love with Joel Kramer.

He'd admitted that he wanted to be more than friends, but had made no moves to deepen their intimacy. She still cringed when she thought back to the night when she'd offered herself to him. He must have thought her totally brazen. He was probably relieved that he hadn't had to respond, even though she distinctly remembered him heading toward the bedroom with her.

But he hadn't mentioned that scene since. She had wondered if he would once they were alone on the island. He continued to kiss her until she became limp; he continued to caress her until her body came vibratingly alive; and he continued to sleep alone.

Melissa hadn't a clue what all of that meant, other than the obvious: he was driving her out of her mind.

"I'll meet you on the beach in fifteen minutes," he said as soon as they walked inside the house.

Melissa wandered back into the bedroom and put away the items she'd bought that morning. She slipped into her bikini, no longer self-conscious about wearing it around him.

He was waiting for her by the water's edge when she arrived, their gear lying at his feet. Melissa was glad she wore her sunglasses to shield her eyes. She would have been embarrassed if he knew how much she enjoyed looking at him in his bathing trunks. His dark tan had deepened, and his brown hair had lightened in streaks, much like hers. She had to stop herself from reaching out to touch his muscled chest, from smoothing her hand across that broad expanse, from tracing the way the hair grew into a path that led downward across his stomach and abdomen.

She jerked her gaze upward to meet his.

"Ready?"

She nodded, unable to trust her voice at the moment.

Joel knelt and slipped the flippers onto her feet, then handed her the mouthpiece and goggles. "There you go." She gave him a cheerful wave and waded into the water.

Later, Joel realized that he should have known disaster would hit before the day was over. Things kept happening…unusual and unpredictable things. The strap on his mask broke, Melissa kept having trouble with one of her flippers, and he scraped his hand on some coral.

They spent the afternoon exploring the reef and all its myriad inhabitants. He trusted Melissa in the water now, even though he continued to keep a close eye on her. When he saw the snake slide out from between the coral, he tried to warn her, but he was too late. Nor was he close enough to prevent the snake from striking Melissa as she swam too close to its territory. By the time Joel reached her side, she had doubled over and sunk below the surface.

He'd seen the snake's distinctive markings and knew that it was poisonous. Within a few short minutes, the venom would get into her bloodstream and no one would be able to help her.

The time spent in the Central America jungles had trained him well and he knew what he had to do. Pulling her, he swam toward the shore as soon as he got her head out of the water. When he reached land, he stripped off his footgear and, with Melissa held securely in his arms, broke into a run.

Joel jerked the mask off her face to make sure she could breathe. Her face looked white beneath her tan. He was thankful that she had fainted.

He got her inside the house and placed her on her bed, then sprinted to the kitchen where he found a knife. Taking precious seconds to sterilize the blade, he rushed back to where she lay. From what he could see, the snake had struck her on the hip. He jerked down the minuscule bikini bottoms and saw the angry red marks on her upper thigh, near the groin area. Once again, he blessed her unconsciousness as he sliced an X over the wound and began to draw out the poison with his mouth.

Joel worked on her for several minutes, praying that he hadn't lost too much time getting her to the house. When at last he paused, she was shaking from shock and chills.

He made a poultice to place over the wound, then wrapped her in a sheet and covered her with blankets. He lost track of time while he sat beside her, holding her hand and praying.

Eventually, she stirred and opened her eyes. She

seemed to be having trouble focusing. She blinked a couple of times, then whispered, "Joel?"

He tightened the hold he had on her hand. She had been growing increasingly warmer and now felt hot to the touch. "I'm right here. Just relax and try to rest."

"What happened?"

"You got a poisonous bite."

She closed her eyes. "I don't remember anything. I just remember being in the water, then feeling this horrible pain, and..." She shifted restlessly, then opened her eyes and focused on him. "I feel so strange," she whispered.

"You're going to be okay," he said, praying that he spoke the truth. "The poultice is drawing out the poison I didn't get out. But you're going to feel the effects, I'm afraid."

She was having trouble swallowing. After a moment, she whispered, "I'm glad you knew what to do."

I hope to hell it works, he thought. He wiped the moisture that had collected on his brow. "Try to rest, okay?"

"I could have drowned."

"No. That would never have happened. You know I wouldn't allow anything to happen to you."

She was so pale. Her lips were almost white when she smiled and said, "You're always saving me."

"Doesn't matter."

She drifted off to sleep.

The next several hours were hell for Joel as he watched her fight the effects of the snake bite. She alternated between chills and fever, fighting the

covers and resisting his efforts to keep liquids going
down her.

At one point, he stretched out beside her and held
her against him until she quietened.

He must have dozed, because it was the sound of
her voice that awakened him later. He glanced at his
watch. It was after two in the morning.

Once again, she fought the covers, muttering inco-
herently.

"But don't you understand?" she asked in a quer-
ulous voice. "I love him and I don't know what to
do," she complained.

Joel had been reaching for the cloth that he'd been
using to bathe her face when he caught her words.
They slammed into his chest like a fist, taking his
breath. She was in love with someone? Why hadn't
she ever mentioned him? They had spent so many
hours sharing their lives with each other. He'd felt as
though he knew everything of any importance about
her. But she had been hiding something from him. A
knot of pain formed in his throat.

He placed the wet cloth gently against her forehead
and wiped away the dampness there, stricken.

"I don't know what to do," she whimpered. "He
holds me and kisses me, but then walks away. And
he seems so restless…" Her voice faded into mutterings before she said quite clearly, "Maybe he only
wants to be my friend! I don't want to lose him because I wanted more."

Joel realized that she was talking about him and
released the air he'd been unconsciously holding. She
loved him. There was no one else. He felt relief flood-
ing through him like a drug, easing his anxiety, re-

laxing the muscles he'd tensed when she'd started muttering.

He continued to bathe her body in an effort to bring down the fever. She could not seem to lie still. Her limbs kept jerking, and she kept tossing her head. He discovered that she quieted down whenever he talked to her. For hours, he kept a soft litany of words flowing until he was hoarse, but it worked. She appeared more calm and allowed him to stroke her body with the cooling cloth.

She was so beautiful. Her skin felt like satin, and he found himself touching her to reassure himself that she would be all right. She just had to be. He broke out in a cold sweat thinking about what had happened. The snake had struck without warning. He could have lost her in that same quick way.

The early-morning hours seemed filled with his quiet contemplation. Now that he knew how she felt about him, he could no longer accept his decision to wait before claiming her. The job could go on for weeks more.

He loved her and he wanted her. She knew him better than anyone did, including Max. What difference did it make, after all, how he made a living? He pictured them together when he told her the truth. In his vision, she laughed at his fears and reassured him of her love.

So why wait for the nebulous end of this assignment? There really wasn't a problem, was there, once she was well again. Surely God wouldn't allow her to appear in his life only to take her away.

Joel never wanted to experience the fear of losing her again. He'd faced death himself. In fact, he'd been more dead than alive when they'd brought him back from Central America last year. The fear of dying hadn't affected him as strongly as the fear of losing Melissa.

Pale fingers of light entered the room and Joel looked around. Dawn was approaching. He leaned over and turned off the small lamp beside Melissa's bed. In the dim shadows of the room, she lay there, breathing evenly, and he realized that her fever had broken.

Thank God! Tears came to his eyes and he blinked fiercely to prevent them from falling. She was going to be all right.

He eased away from her and went into the other room for fresh sheets. He carefully changed the damp bed linens while she remained in a deep, healing slumber.

Then he walked into his room and sat on the edge of the bed to take off his shoes. Later he never remembered falling across the bed in a sound sleep.

Melissa felt as though she'd been hit over the head repeatedly with a sledgehammer. She groaned, unable to deal quietly with the pulsating ache.

''Here's something for the pain. It should help.''

She opened her eyes at the sound of Joel's deep voice. Bright sunlight found its way through the chinked slats at the window, and she winced, closing her eyes. She felt his arm slide beneath her shoulders, raising her slightly.

''Open your mouth,'' he said, not bothering to hide his amusement at the tone he'd used, as though speaking to a child. She obliged him and he placed a tablet on her tongue, then held a glass to her lips.

The liquid was refreshing to her parched mouth and she took several swallows.

"Thank you," she murmured.

He returned her to the pillow, sliding a second one beneath her. "Do you think you could eat something?"

"I think so." Once again, she opened her eyes, forcing herself to adjust to the long slivers of light. "I'm sorry to be so much trouble."

She'd never seen him look like this. Dark smudges beneath his eyes made him look as though he hadn't slept in several days. Stubble framed his lower face, and his eyes were swollen and rimmed with red. He rubbed his hand across his jaw and made a face. "I'm just glad to see you awake and coherent. I don't mind admitting that you had me worried for a while last night."

She didn't understand why she felt so weak. She started to move and her head began an increased pounding.

Melissa touched her head, rubbing her fingertips across her brow.

"That tablet should help with the pain in a few minutes." He moved away from the bed toward the door.

"Joel?"

He glanced around at her, his eyes wary. "Yes?"

"Thank you."

His smile flashed in his dark face, causing her heart to do crazy things in her chest. "Any time."

It was only after he left the room that Melissa realized she was nude. When had he removed her swim suit? She lifted the sheet and gazed at the poultice placed over the wound. Her face flamed at its location. She certainly didn't have any secrets from the man now!

Despite the pounding in her head, she knew she had to get up. She had to go to the bathroom, and she certainly wasn't going to have him help her! Taking her time, Melissa slid her legs off the bed, then carefully stood up. Her legs felt like overcooked spaghetti. Only through sheer determination did she manage, by holding on to various pieces of furniture, to get to the bathroom. Afterward, she splashed water on her face and looked into the mirror.

Sunken eyes with deep circles around them stared back at her, and her hair tumbled around her shoulders in a mat of tangles. Really glamorous, she decided ruefully.

She managed to return to the bedroom and find a nightgown. She wasn't going anywhere today but bed, and she knew it. As soon as the soft material slid over her body, she felt better, more protected. She was only a few steps from the bed when Joel found her.

"What the hell are you doing!"

He startled her so that she let go of the chair she'd been leaning on. If he hadn't caught her, she would have fallen.

"I had to go to the bathroom," she muttered as soon as he placed her on the bed once more.

"Why didn't you call me?" he demanded.

"I didn't want to bother you."

He shook his head, then turned and picked up the bowl of hot cereal he'd brought into the room with him. He handed it to her. "It's a wonder I didn't spill this when I saw you."

He turned around and walked out of the room without another word, leaving Melissa to feel churlish because she had displeased him when he'd done so much for her.

By the time she finished eating, she could no longer keep her eyes open. She didn't remember Joel coming in later to check on her.

He stood beside the bed, noting that she had found a gown to put on. He'd been so shocked to find her out of bed that he hadn't paid attention at the time to the fact she had managed to dress. He smiled, wishing he could have seen her reaction when she discovered that he had obviously undressed her. It would be interesting to see if she brought up that fact at a later time.

He was pleased to note some color in her cheeks. God, but she'd given him a scare. He never wanted to go through anything like that again.

They were going to have to talk, there was no doubt about that. Considering the way he felt about her, he couldn't let her walk out of his life. All he had to do was convince her that they shouldn't waste this time together.

He couldn't remember when he'd been so nervous. He realized he'd been gruff with her, but he was scared. Scared she wouldn't agree to getting married right away, scared that he would say something to cause her to leave him. Loving someone could be hell, he discovered. Why had he always heard that love was supposed to be wonderful?

If she agreed to marry him, then he could begin to believe the publicity. Right now, he was afraid to believe in much of anything.

They had to talk, but not until she was much better. He didn't want to pressure her. He didn't want to feel as though he had taken advantage of the situation. But the waiting was hard for him. Not knowing could gnaw at a man's guts.

He wouldn't allow himself to think about it. He'd look after her, wait until he felt she was ready to hear what he had to say. In the meantime, he'd continue with the hard physical exercise, the cold showers and the nighttime memories of her beautiful body wearing only the soft lamplight

Nine

Three days passed before Melissa felt well enough to go outside. She sat on the blanket near the water's edge and watched Joel swim toward her.

He'd been wonderful to her these past few days, making sure she was comfortable, looking after her in unobtrusive ways. It certainly wasn't his fault that she'd fallen in love with him. He'd offered her friendship, and like a silly fool, she'd lost her heart.

He came to his feet in the shallows and strode toward her. Would she ever get tired of watching him? she wondered with a pang. He moved with such ease. When he caught her eye, he grinned, the white flash of teeth a deep contrast to his darkly tanned body.

"You're looking like yourself once again," he commented, dropping down beside her on the blanket and grabbing a towel.

"Too bad. I could have auditioned for Methuselah's mother a few days ago with no competition."

He chuckled. "No one looks their best after going through what you just experienced." He tugged her braid. "How long did it take to get the tangles out?"

"Who knows? I seriously considered cutting it off, but I couldn't find anything sharp enough."

"Thank God!" he said. "Your hair is too beautiful to cut."

She shook her head. "This style is hopelessly out of fashion."

"Do you care?"

"It's a little late to care, wouldn't you say? I've never taken the time to follow fashion."

"You know, Melissa, I've been thinking…"

Melissa looked at him in surprise. His tone of voice had changed and his face had sobered from the earlier teasing look. "About what?"

He still held her braid in his hand, and now he studied it with deep regard. "How this island would make a really great place for a honeymoon," he said without glancing up.

She didn't know what to say. Melissa just looked at him, hoping he would explain his remark.

When his gaze finally met hers, her heart suddenly lurched in her chest. She'd never seen that look in his eyes before.

"What are you saying?" she managed to whisper.

"That I want to marry you." The words hung in the air between them, taking on a life of their own.

Melissa continued to stare at him, still not certain that she had heard him correctly. Perhaps she was still in delirium, fighting the ghosts and gremlins produced by her feverish state.

"Did you say...*marry* me?"

He looked away and picked up a handful of sand. Letting it trail through his fingers, he gazed out at the water. "Yeah," he finally muttered hoarsely.

For a moment, she was reminded of the man she'd met all those weeks ago. Dark color filled his cheeks, and she realized once again that Joel could be shy. Not that she'd seen that part of him in some time. He certainly didn't kiss her like a man who was shy. And the way he held and caressed her had certainly shown no tendencies toward shyness.

Now he refused to meet her eyes.

Melissa realized that she had gone into shock at his words. She couldn't feel anything except a tingling numbness. Even in her most creative fantasies, it had never occurred to her that he might love her or want to marry her. She reminded herself that he hadn't said anything about love, but why else would a man propose marriage?

Seen in this suddenly new light, his behavior recently could be perceived in a much different way. He'd been restless, and she had thought he was bored. She'd been restless, as well, but boredom had been the farthest thing from her mind. Frustration had center stage most of the time. Was that his problem?

If so, then he'd been too honorable to take advantage of their present situation. Had they stayed in their own apartments, he would probably have pursued a leisurely affair with her. Because of her strong attraction to him, she would have been more than willing.

But Joel wanted more. Much more.

Was she going to back away from him now that he was offering her the opportunity to spend the rest of her life with the man who had stolen her heart? Of course not! Then why was she trembling so? Why was she so afraid to speak up, to answer him?

Perhaps cowardice was inherited—a genetic flaw.

"Do you mean that we should get married while we're here on the island?"

He picked up more sand and studied it as though he was certain to find treasure there if he searched vigilantly enough.

"I guess it was a really stupid idea. When you decide to marry, you'll want all your friends there, a big wedding, everything—"

"Joel?" She could only see him in profile. "Would you mind looking at me?" With obvious reluctance, he turned his head. She saw the vulnerability in his eyes and felt herself melting with tenderness and love for this wonderfully strong, yet gentle man. "I can't think of anything more wonderful than to marry you…now…while we're here on the island. My friends would understand. Would yours?"

His relief that she agreed to marry him made him weak, and it took him a moment to realize what she'd asked him.

"My friends?" He thought of Max, who would definitely not understand. "It doesn't matter what my friends think." He took her hand. It looked so delicate lying in his. "Are you sure? I don't want to rush you." Which was a lie. That was exactly what he wanted—to rush her into marriage, to rush her into his bed…and to keep her forever in his arms.

Her smiled sparkled like a thousand-watt light. "I think we both must be crazy to even consider doing something so rash." She thought about the life she'd had before Joel moved into the apartment across from hers. How could she have had any idea that she would have changed so drastically in such a short time. From being a shy introvert, she had discovered a whole new world.

From the day she had first seen him, she had made choices totally unlike her usual behavior. She had to trust herself. She had to trust her own instincts.

"Yes."

He stared at her uncertainly. "Yes?"

She nodded.

"You'll marry me?"

She nodded.

"Now?"

She glanced down at their clothing and smiled. "Perhaps we should try for a bit more formality than this, though. What do you think?"

But Joel was no longer thinking. He grabbed her and held her to him, his mouth searching blindly for hers.

She'd agreed, she was willing to marry him, she was going to be his, she—

He broke away from her and stared down at her dazed expression.

"Dear God, but I love you!" He hauled her back into his arms. "Thank you for trusting me. Thank you for believing in me. You won't regret it. I promise. I would never hurt you. Never. I will always take care of you and protect you. Don't ever forget that I love you."

His kiss reaffirmed his words. Melissa felt lighter than air, as though she were floating. Joel loved her. He wanted to marry her. They could deal with the details of their life together later. After all, they had all the time in the world.

When he finally pulled away from her, his gaze was heated. "Let's go find out what we have to do."

It took three days to fill out the forms, pass the necessary tests and be married before a minister. Three very frustrating days. Joel knew better than to go near Melissa. Not even a saint would have that sort of willpower. Those three days were the longest he'd ever spent. The nights were even worse.

But he left her alone. And he waited.

The simple ceremony was held in the chapel of the only church on the island. Joel didn't care where they were married, just as long as it happened. Melissa had told him that she wanted more than a civil ceremony, and he had agreed. He would have agreed to anything.

The sun was close to setting when they returned home. Joel felt very ill at ease now that he'd managed to accomplish his goal. She was his wife now. He was having trouble realizing that his period of self-restraint and self-denial was over.

He hoped.

"Are you hungry?" Melissa asked, peering into the refrigerator. "The woman you hired left several delicious-looking dishes in here."

"Sounds good." He was pleased that he sounded so casual. "I also bought some champagne."

She glanced around at him, her color high. "I've never had champagne."

"There's always a first time."

Neither one wanted to point out the first times that would occur on their wedding night.

She smiled. "All right," she said, then busied herself pulling food from the refrigerator and warming it. Joel checked to see if the champagne was chilled. It was.

They ate out on the deck by candlelight. After Melissa's second glass of champagne, she began to relax.

"No one at work is going to believe this," she said, setting her glass down.

"Believe what?"

She waved her hand. "All of this." She included the sea, the beach, the tropical foliage, the house... and him. "How am I supposed to tell them that in a few short weeks, I met a man and married him, that we spent a large part of our time together on an island." She shook her head. "Dr. Feldman will think I've finally gone over the edge."

"Dr. Feldman?"

"My boss. I'm sure I've mentioned him to you."

"Possibly."

"He should be back from his vacation by now." She leaned her forearm on the table. "We really need to go back home soon, Joel. I have a job that I must return to."

"I thought you told me the office still hadn't reopened."

"Well, I need to at least be there when Dr. Feldman comes back. Surely, he'll do something about getting us back into our lab."

"How do you think he's going to take the idea that you're married?"

"Dr. Feldman? Oh, he won't care. Just as long as I continue to work." She paused as though hit by a sudden thought. "You aren't going to be like some husbands who insist on their wives not working, are you?"

"And if I were?"

"Then you'll have quite a fight on your hands."

He grinned. "Then I'll save my energy for more important things." He almost laughed at the expression on her face. She was so much fun to tease.

They carried the plates and dishes back into the house and quickly washed them. Joel felt that he had waited long enough.

"Melissa?"

"Hmm?" She had her back to him, placing the cleaned plates on the shelf.

"How about another glass of champagne?"

She looked over her shoulder with a grin. "Are you trying to get me drunk?"

"Would it do any good?"

"Do you think you're going to have to coax me to bed?" She turned as she said that and walked over to him.

"Am I?"

She slid her arms around his neck. "I don't think so." Her lips brushed lightly against his, but it was enough to start a blaze from the smoldering emotions that he'd kept forcibly under control. Without another word, he slipped his arms around her, picked her up and headed toward the bedroom. The kiss continued until they both had to pause for air. Then Joel allowed his bride to slide from his arms until she was standing beside the bed.

He forced himself to take his time as he carefully removed each piece of clothing she wore. He'd seen her body before, when she'd been so ill, but now she was vibrantly healthy and he wanted her so much, he ached.

She reached up and began to unbutton his shirt. "You're ahead of me," she managed to say, tugging at his belt. That was the only encouragement he needed to assist her.

The only light in the room came from the moon. There was enough to see each other in the shadows, but not the expressions on each face. Joel sank onto the edge of the bed.

He pulled her so that she was standing between his legs. "I don't want to rush you," he said in a low voice, sliding his hands along her sides. He could feel her body quiver as his fingers trailed across the sides of her breasts, circled around her waist, then caught the top of her panties. He slid them down her legs. When she stepped out of that last article of clothing, he cupped his hands around her curving derriere and pulled her closer, placing a kiss on her navel.

She shivered at his touch.

Tentatively, she placed her hands across his shoulders, then slid them along his neck until she framed his jawline. She sank down on one of his thighs and lightly brushed his lips with hers. "I don't know what's expected of me. I don't want to be a disappointment to you."

He groaned and hugged her to him. "You could never be a disappointment, sweet one, don't you understand that? I've been so afraid I was going to lose you from my life. I wouldn't let myself think about the fact that you'd agree to marry me for fear I would jinx the wedding somehow. I kept expecting someone to burst through the doorway in an attempt to stop us."

She touched his chest. At long last, she could give in to the temptation that had made her fingers itch for weeks. She ran the tips of them through the short curls that matted his chest, luxuriating in the feel of him.

He leaned back slowly until he lay across the bed. "That feels good," he said in a husky voice.

"I'm glad. I've wanted so badly to touch you."

"Then why didn't you?"

"I was afraid you wouldn't like it."

"You must be joking!"

Melissa knew that she was far from stupid. She had a string of degrees to prove differently. She'd studied the human anatomy—the male human anatomy—and was fully cognizant of all the moving parts. So why was she being so shy about seeing the man she loved...her husband, for Pete's sake...totally without adornment?

A silly reaction, but real, nonetheless.

Lying beside him, she determinedly accepted the gift he was offering—the opportunity to explore and get to know him physically. Ignoring shyness, she placed her hands on his stomach. She was gratified to see that his skin rippled at her touch. With a caress that barely skimmed the surface of his skin, she began her exploration.

She discovered the sensitivity of his flat nipples where they nestled in the silky hair. When she brushed lightly across the tip of one of them, it hardened into a tiny nubbin that fascinated her. She leaned down and gently flicked her tongue across the sensitive point.

His body jerked as though he'd been electrocuted. "Good God, woman!"

She lifted her head and smiled at him, then continued her discoveries. Now that he was no longer encumbered with clothing, she could follow the course of chest hair as it narrowed down his body. She fol-

lowed the path with her fingers until she touched him
on the most sensitive part of his body.

Once again he jerked.

"I can't stand much more of this!"

"Of what?" she asked innocently.

With a move so sudden she wasn't prepared for it,
Joel rolled over, pinning her.

"I'll show you," he muttered, stringing a row of
tiny kisses along her collarbone and continuing down
to the peak of her breast. He ignored her squirming
and proceeded to leisurely lave the pink tip with his
tongue, rolling it in his mouth. She gasped when he
pulled on it lightly with his lips, then she hugged him
closer.

Melissa forgot her inexperience; she forgot her shyness; she forgot everything about Joel and what he
was doing to her. He touched sensitive places on her
body that she had never considered before—the bend
of her elbow, the back of her knee, her inner thigh.
He seemed to know exactly where to caress her. She
felt as though her body was a musical instrument being played by a master musician. She knew that if she
listened closely enough, she would be able to hear her
body hum, like the tautened string of a violin.

By the time he paused, kneeling between her legs,
she felt lost in the wonder of what they were sharing.
She also felt blessed to be able to experience this
ultimate sharing with the man she loved.

"I don't want to hurt you," he whispered, leaning
over her, braced by his hands on each side of her face.

"You could never hurt me, Joel. I know that."
With complete confidence in him, she drew him down
as she lifted her body to meet him.

Because of his patience and her trust, their joining

was a small discomfort compared to the pleasure they both received when he claimed her fully as his. He sank deeply into her warmth, knowing that he had come home at last. She was his, and he would never let her go.

Sometime during the night, Joel roused enough to realize that a breeze had sprung up. Melissa curled close to his side. He rubbed his hand across her arm and felt the tiny chills that rippled her skin. Without waking her, he reached down for the covers and carefully tucked the sheet around both of them.

She looked so young, lying there in his arms. There was little more than ten years difference between them in age, but millions of years difference in lifestyles and experience. She had given him back so much that he thought was lost from his life: youth, love, vitality, enthusiasm, joy. It would take him the rest of his life to show her his love and appreciation for all that she was.

It was a task he looked forward to accomplishing.

Ten

The steady pounding finally impinged on Joel's consciousness, at least to the point where he managed to focus on the fact that he was going to have to do something to stop it. He groaned and rolled over in bed.

After forcing his eyes open, he became aware of two things: one...someone was banging on the front door, and two...he was not alone in bed. Only then did he recall the events of the previous day: he and Melissa were married.

The pounding continued its steady cadence. Whoever it was certainly personified the word *persistent*. "Damn it," he muttered to himself. *Doesn't anyone have any respect for a newly wedded couple?*

But then, few people were aware of their new status. Joel tried to muffle a groan as he rolled into a sitting position, swung his legs to the floor and forced himself onto his feet.

His head hurt. Champagne always gave him a headache. So did lack of sleep. He glanced at the sleeping woman beside him and smiled. The constant pounding hadn't disturbed her. After all, she hadn't gotten any more sleep than he had, and how could he possibly sleep for long stretches of time when, even in his sleep, he was aware of her pressed so intimately against him.

He grabbed his jeans and pulled them on, zipping as he walked toward the door. He jerked the door open to growl at whoever had the audacity to make such an ungodly noise, only to recognize the culprit. It was the teenage son of the owner of the restaurant.

"Sorry to bother you. My dad said there was a call for you and that it was very important. You're to call your office right away."

Joel dug into his pocket and pulled out a folded bill. "Thanks," he said, handing the boy the money.

The boy bobbed his head and ran back to his bicycle.

His office. Max's code to call him. Joel ran his hand through his hair, rumpling it further. Damn. He'd been doing a hell of a job blotting out the rest of the world, Max in particular, ever since Melissa had been injured. He hadn't worried about what was happening back in the States because he no longer cared. He could stay here with Melissa from now on, now that their future had been decided.

Unfortunately, the world had its own way of intruding, no matter how hard he concentrated on forgetting all about it.

He turned around and headed for his bedroom. He

needed to get some shoes on, grab a shirt and go find out what Max wanted. Once he was dressed, he peeked into the other bedroom. Melissa hadn't moved. With any luck at all, he'd be back in bed with her before she even knew he'd left.

"Why haven't you called in this week?" were Max's first words. "I have some news."

Joel fumbled for the nearest chair by the pay phone in the small restaurant, drew it closer, and sat down. He knew that tone of voice. He was going to be here for a while.

"I was busy," he said. He signaled a waiter for a cup of coffee, then asked, "What's happened?"

Max ignored his question. "Did it ever occur to you that I might be worried when you didn't contact me on schedule?"

"No," Joel replied truthfully. He knew his boss too well to think that he might possess such human qualities.

"Is Melissa all right?"

Memories of the previous day and evening flitted through Joel's mind. "I think so."

"What do you mean, you *think* so? Don't you know?"

"She's all right, damn it. We just didn't get much sleep last night."

Max absorbed that piece of news in silence for a moment. "Would you like to elaborate on that a little?"

"No, I wouldn't. So, what's your news?"

"We managed to round up the group who were after Feldman and your charge," Max responded without inflection.

"God! There's a relief."

"I thought you'd want to know. Of course, they're denying knowing anything about the wreck or the bombing, but we've got enough evidence on them that it's only going to be a matter of time before they start trying to plea bargain."

"So we can come home now," Joel said slowly, trying to think through what needed to be done next. Now he could tell Melissa everything. There was no longer a need for secrecy. What a relief that was going to be.

"Yes. As a matter of fact, I have another assignment for you."

"I see."

"It's more in your line than what you've been doing, so I think you'll like it. However, I'm keeping you out of Central America for a while. I need you in Southeast Asia."

"Uh, Max. There's been a new development in this case that I haven't bothered discussing with you."

"What's that?"

"Well…" He stopped to clear his throat. "I, uh… That is, we decided that…" He kneaded the muscles in the back of his neck. "Melissa and I were married yesterday."

"You were *what?*"

Joel flinched and jerked the phone away from his ear. Somehow, he'd known that his boss wouldn't take that particular piece of news well. He could hardly blame Max, under the circumstances.

"Are you out of your mind? That's the most unethical stunt I've ever known you to pull, Kramer."

"Do I sound like I'm bragging?"

"So you've blown your cover and gotten married."

"I didn't say that. Since I'm using my own name, there was no problem providing identification."

"Are you telling me she thinks she married a writer?"

"Yes."

"Oh, God."

Joel ran his hand through his hair, so that it was standing in several spikes. "I don't think it's going to make that much of a difference to her. Now that the matter's been resolved, I can tell her the truth."

"Damn it, Kramer. I could fire you for this."

"Somehow, I knew you'd remember to point that out sometime during this conversation. You know, Max, you're allowing yourself to become quite predictable at times."

Max was silent.

"How's Dr. Feldman?" Joel asked after a moment.

"Elated. He's already begging for the return of his assistant."

"We can talk about this when I get back. I'll make the arrangements to return today."

"You do that."

Joel heard the click of the receiver. He slowly replaced the phone on its hook.

The waiter returned with his coffee. Joel thanked him and took the cup out on the deck overlooking the harbor.

So it was over... Their idyllic time together was at an end. How ironic that Max had waited until today to call. Twenty-four hours earlier and Joel could have told Melissa before the ceremony. But then, maybe it was better this way. She might be upset with him at first. After all, they *had* met under false pretenses. But all of that had changed so quickly. Their friendship had grown, creating strong bonds between them.

He finished the coffee and went back inside the restaurant, paid the waiter and drove back to the cottage.

He let himself in quietly and listened, but could not hear her stirring. When he walked down the hallway to the bedroom, he found that Melissa still slept. Her tumbled hair framed her face. The light covering draped across her body, revealing no more than her arms and shoulders, but it didn't matter. Joel had a very good memory and had spent the previous night learning all the contours of that body.

He walked into the bathroom and shut the door. Stripping off his clothes, he turned on the shower and stepped beneath the spray, adjusting the temperature.

Memories of the night before came back to him and he couldn't restrain the smile that appeared on his face.

God, but she was one beautiful lady. She'd been so shy with him at first. But later, she had responded so ardently, without shame and with a trust that humbled him.

He'd never received a more beautiful gift in his life.

By the time Joel stepped out of the shower, he felt ready to face the world. He and Melissa were married. No one, including Max, could do anything about that. He would take her back to Virginia so that she could work with Feldman once again.

If she became upset because he hadn't told her the truth about his occupation he would just remind her that if it hadn't been for this job, they would never have met. Surely she would understand the necessity of what he had done.

When he came out of the bathroom, he went over to the bed and crawled in beside her. She stirred, moving against him. He leaned over and kissed her.

"Melissa?"

"Mmm?"

"Are you awake?"

"Uh-uh."

"Are you ready to go home?"

She opened her eyes. "Today?"

"If you want."

"But I thought we were going to have a honeymoon here?"

"There was a call from the States this morning. They're ready for you to come back to work."

She groaned. "Wouldn't you know it? What timing!"

"That doesn't mean the honeymoon has to be over, does it?"

She smiled sleepily. "I don't suppose so." She ran her hand across his chest. "Mmmmm. You feel so good."

"I was thinking the very same thing about you." He gathered her into his arms and began to kiss her. Max could wait. Feldman could wait. The whole world could wait. Nothing was more important to Joel than the woman he held in his arms.

The next time Joel awoke, it was after one o'clock. He glanced at the bed beside him and realized he was alone. There was a crash in the kitchen and he sat up. Was that what had awakened him?

"Melissa?"

There was another sound, like glass shattering. What was happening? Why didn't she answer him?

He grabbed his pants and slid his feet into sandals. From the sound of things, there was likely to be glass all over the floor.

When he walked into the kitchen, Joel froze. Melissa had broken a glass all right. She'd obviously been surprised by the man who now held her with his arm around her throat, a knife in his other hand.

"So we meet again, amigo," the man said, watching Joel. His heart sank. How in the hell had Benito Ortiz found him here? For that matter, how did the man know his first attempt at killing him hadn't been successful?

In the year since Joel had left Central America, he'd taken Max's advice about this man. Max had promised him that other operatives would get him, and Joel had believed him. Obviously, Max had been wrong. Max didn't like being proved wrong. It made him downright cranky, but no more so than Joel felt at the moment.

"What do you want, Ortiz?"

The man smiled, revealing a gold tooth. "Is that any way to greet a friend?"

"When the so-called friend is holding my wife at knife point, it is."

"*Esposa?*" Ortiz began to laugh. "I had no idea you were married, amigo. She probably wasn't too pleased with your condition after the last time we met."

"She doesn't know about that."

"Oh. Secrets. I like that. She doesn't need to know everything."

"That's always been my philosophy," Joel replied

absently, trying to make eye contact with Melissa in an effort to reassure her. However, her wide-eyed gaze carried too much fear to receive any silent message he tried to send her.

"Let her go, Ortiz."

"But I have come such a long way to find you, amigo. I like having your full attention when we speak."

"What do you want with me?"

"For one thing, I want to know how you managed to survive the blast that destroyed your apartment."

Melissa blinked and stared at Joel.

"My apartment?"

"Apartment 5A, right?"

"Wrong. My apartment was 5B."

"Ah. I see. Then I was misinformed. You were spotted in apartment 5A the night before."

"By whom?"

"Does it matter? Someone was paid to watch you."

"Watch me or my wife?"

Ortiz glanced at the woman he held. "I never knew she existed. Why would I have her watched?"

"You mean you've been tailing me?"

"But of course. How else would I have found you here? You are good, but you are not infallible, my friend."

Joel forced himself to concentrate on the moment. He would think about all of the ramifications of what he'd just heard later.

"Well, now you've found me. What do you want?"

"You have some information I need. I wasn't

aware of who you are until after I tried to kill you last year.''

Joel watched Melissa react to that information.

''What sort of information?''

''Who you report to. How many of you are working in our country. Who in our country is providing help.''

''And, of course, if I give you all that information,'' Joel said, slowly but steadily moving toward Melissa and Ortiz, ''you'll let us both go, right?''

''I have no quarrel with your wife. Only with you, amigo.''

Joel continued to speak softly and soothingly as he edged toward them. ''Well, you don't give me much choice now, do you. There's no reason to include my wife in our discussion, so if you—''

Joel made his move. The knife careened out of Ortiz's hand, and Ortiz released his hold on Melissa, already unconscious from the blow to the side of his head made by Joel's foot. By the time Ortiz hit the floor, Joel had scooped up the knife and grabbed Melissa.

''Are you all right?''

She stared at him as though she'd never seen him before. ''Who are you?'' she whispered hoarsely.

''Your husband, for one thing.'' He let go of her, then stepped over Ortiz's inert body. ''I'll be right back. I've got to find something to keep him immobile until I can get to a phone.''

His mind was racing with all of the information that he had just learned. He had to get some help. He couldn't handle this one alone.

When he came back into the kitchen with a length

of rope, he found Melissa sitting in one of the chairs, staring at Ortiz. She didn't look up.

"I'm sorrier than I can say that this happened, love. I'm going to have to take him to the village so that I can make a phone call. Do you want to come with me?"

She shook her head without looking at him.

He wasted no time tying the unconscious man so that he couldn't move. Then he walked over to Melissa and knelt beside her chair. He took her hands, which she held clenched between her knees, and rubbed them. They were icy. "I've got to go. Are you sure you'll be all right here?"

She nodded.

"I'll get back as soon as possible. Then we can talk." He waited, but when she didn't respond, he turned her chin so that she was facing him. "Okay?"

The look in her eyes startled him. He had seen the fear in their depths when Ortiz had been holding her. The fear was gone. Now she stared at him as though he were a stranger...a not completely acceptable stranger.

It was the shock. Nothing like this had ever happened to her before. Of course, she wouldn't know how to deal with it.

Rising to his feet, Joel said, "Look, I've got to go. But you'll be all right until I can get back. Then I'll explain everything. You'll see."

He found a place with a phone on the outskirts of the village. He knew Ortiz wasn't going anywhere, but he didn't want anyone to see the man if he could avoid it.

After getting permission to use the phone, he quickly made connection with Max. As soon as Max answered, Joel reported what had happened, ending with, "So what do you want me to do with him? At the moment, I've got him tied up in the back seat of the car."

"Let me make some phone calls. I have some contacts in that area who should be able to help us out on this one. Tell me where you'll be."

Thank God he'd studied the island. Joel recalled an abandoned house on a military stretch of road where they could meet without being observed. He gave Max the directions.

As soon as he had finished, Max said, "I'll have someone pick him up shortly. How's Melissa taking all this?"

"Not too well, I'm afraid."

"Not surprising. I want you two out of there as soon as possible. Then I want you to report to me. Maybe we can turn this situation to our advantage."

"I thought you promised me that this guy would be taken care of."

"I thought he was. A positive ID was made on a body."

"Obviously someone was mistaken."

"Joel, these things happen."

"Yeah, I know. It's a rotten business."

"Maybe so. But where would we be without people willing to do what we're doing?"

"At this point, I don't know and I don't care. My wife of all of twelve hours was held at knife point. She could have been killed. As far as I'm concerned, nothing is worth that kind of risk."

"I understand, Kramer. I really do. Come on back and we'll talk about it, okay?"

"Sure. I just don't think that talking is going to

change anything. I can't let anything like this happen again.''

He hung up and went back to the car. Ortiz hadn't moved. If he was conscious, he wasn't giving anything away. Joel didn't care. He almost wished the guy would try something.

It was more than an hour before he returned to the cottage. Melissa was not in any of the rooms. As he searched through the house, he panicked, wondering if Ortiz had been working with a second man. Damn it! Where could she be?

He glanced out the window and spotted her walking along the beach. She was a small, solitary figure in the distance.

His heart twisted in his chest. He loped down to the beach and began to jog to where she was. When he finally got close enough, he called out to her.

''Melissa?''

She stopped walking and turned around, facing him.

He took her by the shoulders. ''It's okay, love. Everything's taken care of. You're safe now. Surely you know I'd never let anything or anyone hurt you. Haven't I always promised you that?''

She looked up at him, her expression calm, her eyes showing nothing but faint curiosity.

''You aren't a writer, are you?''

Whatever he'd expected her to say to him, that wasn't it. He'd planned to give her the explanations about his cover later, after he'd told her about Ortiz and why he was after him. But it didn't really matter. All of it had to be discussed sometime.

He dropped his hold on one of her shoulders and guided her into some shade. Motioning for her to sit down, he sank down beside her. "No. I'm not a writer."

Her next question came at him like a blow to the ribs, effectively knocking the breath from him. "You're a killer, aren't you?"

He stared at her in shock. When he could get his breath, he asked, "Why would you think that?"

"I watched you when you saw that horrible man. You weren't afraid of him at all. I could tell."

He shook his head. "You're wrong. I was petrified when I saw him holding that knife on you."

She gave her head a small negative shake. "No. You knew you could get it away from him."

He thought about that for a moment. "Perhaps," he conceded. "But I wasn't certain that he wouldn't hurt you first."

She met his gaze with a level one of her own. "There was never a doubt in your mind that you had the upper hand. You're a professional and it showed."

Joel didn't know what to say except to reiterate, "I'm no killer."

There was so much to explain that he didn't know where to start. He was searching for the right words when she asked, "Who do you work for?"

That was easy enough to answer. "I work for the government."

"You mean *our* government?" she asked suspiciously.

Joel could feel anger begin to work through his body. He forced himself to take several deep, calming breaths before he answered. "Yes. I work for the United States government."

"How come you moved across the hall from me?"

That question reminded him of what Ortiz had said. "You were right. That bomb was meant for me." He shook his head, still amazed at the turn of events."

"I knew it wasn't meant for me," she pointed out with irritation.

"Melissa. I haven't been cleared to tell you this, but I'm going to anyway." She waited. "Peter Feldman was almost killed in a car accident about a month ago."

She stared at him in shocked disbelief. "Dr. Feldman? How badly was he hurt? Why didn't someone tell me?" Then she looked at Joel suspiciously. "How do you know?"

He tried to answer her questions in order. "Besides bruises and contusions, he fractured his leg. He preferred not to upset you. But he wanted you to be protected. So he contacted my boss."

"Your boss?" she repeated in a careful voice.

"He just wanted you safe."

"You mean, you were hired to watch out for me?" He nodded.

"So all this time when I thought I was making friends with you, you were just doing the job you were hired to do?"

"Of course not! There was a possibility that you needed some protection, but no one was really sure of that. I was between assignments with nothing to do. So I agreed to move in across the hall in case any trouble developed." All the time he was explaining, she watched him politely. He had no idea whether or not she was accepting what he was saying. "Once we met, everything changed. You know what happened. You were there. We spent time together—"

"That was part of your job," she pointed out.

"Partly, yes, it was. But there was so much more happening between us!" He ran his hand through his hair. "Damn! This wasn't the way I wanted to tell you. It wasn't the way you're trying to make it sound and you know it."

"Do I?" She studied him in silence for a few moments. "All right. Perhaps you should tell me how it was."

"The more I was around you, the more I learned about you, the more I enjoyed your company. We became friends. I hadn't realized how lonely my life was until you came into it and filled in all the blank spaces. By the time we came down here—"

"What would you have done if Karen hadn't allowed us to come down here?"

He shrugged. "We could have found a place somewhere safe. But you have to admit this was perfect."

She nodded. "I played right into your hands, didn't I?" She looked away, out toward the water. In a low voice, she said, "I made it so easy for you. Green as grass, too naive to be believed. I actually convinced myself that I had suddenly learned social graces, that I could entertain and please a man, that I could make friends easily and enjoy the bantering that friends share." She looked down at her hands. "And all the time, you were being paid to be my companion." She glanced up. "You're nothing more than a glorified baby-sitter."

"Melissa! It isn't like that. Not at all."

She stood. "But now the game is over, or at least my part is. You said my office is being reopened, so I can go back to work."

He came to his feet and stuck his hands in his pockets. "It's more than that. They caught the two men who were responsible for Dr. Feldman's accident. They didn't want him to finish the research he'd been doing.''

She jerked her head around to look at him. ''No one knows what he's been researching. Not even me.''

''Somebody found out. He was afraid that whoever it was would think that you also knew what he was doing. He was afraid for you, but he didn't want you to be upset.''

She started walking back toward the house. ''And he didn't trust me enough to tell me about it.''

''It wasn't a matter of trust, can't you see that? We just wanted to keep you safe.''

She repeated the word *safe* beneath her breath as though it were an obscenity.

They were almost to the house when she said, ''You didn't need to marry me, you know,'' in a conversational tone. ''I would have made love to you at anytime. All you would have had to do was to let me know that you wanted me.''

He stopped her, his hand on her arm. ''Please stop this, Melissa. Please. Nothing has really changed between us. We are the same two people who spoke their vows together just twenty-four hours ago.''

''Is that what you think, that nothing has changed? How can you possibly look me straight in the eye and say that? *Everything* has changed. Don't you understand? Our relationship was built on lies. You are nothing like the man I thought I married.'' She turned away for a moment and brushed her hand across her eyes. When she turned back, he could still see the sheen of tears.

She gave a small, broken laugh. ''You know, it's

really funny when you think about it. I'd never real-ized how hopelessly naive I am...how gullible. I saw you as shy and a little unsure of yourself with women. I was touched by that shyness, and I found myself reaching out to you, to reassure you.'' She shook her head. ''Isn't that a riot? You're an agent for the gov-ernment, and I thought you were shy? I bet you were laughing your head off about that.''

She spun away and climbed the steps to the house. She walked along the porch to the door of her bed-room.

He followed her. ''Melissa, there isn't a man any-where who doesn't feel a sense of unsureness, a sense of shyness, when he meets a woman who affects him the way you immediately did me. I didn't know what had hit me. Sure, it bothered me that I was assigned to watch out for you once I realized I was falling in love with you. That's why I tried to keep my distance from you as much as possible.'' He threw his arms wide in exasperation. ''Unfortunately, I couldn't keep my damn hands off you. I at least had to be able to hold you, to kiss you, to express the way I feel for you. I think I could have handled that all right if I hadn't learned that you loved me.''

She paled beneath her tan. ''What are you talking about?''

''The night you were bitten by the snake. You were delirious and were talking to someone about me.''

''And I said that I loved you?''

''Yes.''

''So you figured that if I was in love with you, I'd probably marry you.''

''I hoped you would. Yes. The snake bite brought home how devastated I would be if I were to lose you. I didn't want to take any chances. I knew I loved you. When I found out that you felt the same way, I knew we could work out any problems together.''

She shook her head. ''You forgot one small detail.''

''What's that?''

''Our relationship was built on lies. You are nothing like the man I thought I married. You are a liar. Your whole life is a lie. How can you possibly expect me to believe anything you say to me?''

The series of emotional body punches he'd taken were making themselves felt. He had no more explanations. He had no more arguments. When he stood there in silence watching her, she went on.

''Perhaps marrying me appeased your conscience. I don't know. I'll probably never know. All I know is that I want to go home, I want to return to work, and I never want to have anything to do with you again.''

She turned away from him and went into her room, closing the door behind her.

Eleven

A warm tropical breeze wafted over his sensitive body as he lay near the turquoise-blue water. He sighed. The scents of the island were all around him, and he could feel the sun's rays caressing him.

He felt her touch as she brushed her fingertips across his chest. Without opening his eyes, he smiled, pleased that she had decided to join him once again. He caught the delicate scent of her floral perfume and his heart increased its rhythm and became a throbbing drumbeat within him.

She touched his nipple with the tip of her tongue, causing the expected reaction. He slid his hand into her hair and lifted her face to his until their lips met.

She felt so good in his arms, so damned good. He rolled, placing her delectable form beneath him. Their kiss deepened, and their tongues joined in a playful duel. He continued to caress her silken skin...

exploring, loving, delighting in her. She was his, would always be his. He loved her so much. He couldn't imagine life without her, couldn't imagine—

She disappeared, suddenly and without a trace, like an early-morning mist dissipates when touched by the sun. His arms no longer held her. She was gone and there was nothing he could do, nothing he could do, nothing—

Joel jerked awake and pushed himself up on one elbow. The digital clock beside his bed read 4:09.

Damn. It was too early to get up, which meant that he would have to lie there and wait for dawn. Wait and think, because he sure as hell wasn't going back to sleep.

In the three months since he'd last seen Melissa, he'd dreamed about her every damn night. Would those dreams never end?

He'd spent one night with her—one incredible night that continued to haunt him. His subconscious mind had insisted on replaying the events for him like a popular rerun on television. The settings sometimes changed, but the content of the dream remained the same.

He'd tried several remedies to break the pattern, from working until he fell asleep exhausted to a couple of evenings spent with a bottle of bourbon. But nothing helped.

Melissa haunted him, waking or sleeping.

He folded his arms beneath his head and stared up at the shadowy ceiling. His mind slipped into the familiar groove of remembering their last day together.

He'd understood her anger, at least to a degree. He found it hard to believe that she couldn't see, couldn't believe how much he loved her, but he figured that

being as intelligent as she was, she would calm down
if he would give her some time.

He'd gone to his room and packed, told the woman
he'd hired to keep the food that was still in the house,
and when Melissa came out of the bedroom with her
bag, he had placed their luggage in the car. Neither
of them spoke.

They'd gotten a boat ride to one of the larger islands and booked a flight to Miami. Joel attempted
conversation with Melissa during the trip, but she had
either answered his questions with a minimum of
words or did not comment when he spoke.

He'd never seen her like that before, so closed. It
was as though she had withdrawn from her body,
leaving a shell that functioned on autopilot.

When they arrived in Miami, he went to make arrangements for their flight to D.C. Then he returned
to where he'd left her sitting to find she was gone. So
was her bag. She'd left his bag beside the empty
chair.

Joel spent the next two hours looking for her, having her paged, watching every departing plane's line
of passengers as they boarded.

She had just disappeared.

Even after he returned to D.C., he searched for her.
It was more difficult to know where to begin since
she didn't have a home. After spending the necessary
time with Max to hear the details of the case, he went
back to his apartment. There had been no place else
for him to go.

He'd waited until the following morning and called
her office. He'd asked for her, but when the phone
was answered, a male voice spoke.

"Feldman."

"Good morning, Doctor. This is Joel Kramer. I understand you're going to have a complete recovery from your accident. I was pleased to hear the news."

"Joel! Thank God you called. I'd almost decided that you had permanently kidnapped my invaluable assistant. Are you two still on the island?"

The dull pain in Joel's chest, the one that he'd carried with him since her disappearance, increased.

"I'm in Virginia. I'd hoped that Melissa had returned to work. That's why I called—to speak with her."

"You mean you don't know where she is?"

"I'm afraid not."

"But you were supposed to be looking after her!" Joel could still remember the anger in Feldman's voice.

"I did my best. Once she realized that I had been her assigned protector, she became quite upset. She vanished soon after we arrived in Miami."

"I see."

"Look, Doctor, I would really appreciate your taking my phone number and address and giving it to her when she calls or shows up there. We need to talk."

She never called. He waited a week before he gave in to the gnawing desire to hear something and called the lab once again. During that second call, Dr. Feldman explained that he had given Melissa Joel's message when she called in. He'd been concerned because she had called to explain that she would not be returning and asked that her check and any personal items left at her desk be mailed to an address in New York.

Joel eventually had tracked down Karen's phone

number in New York. Another dead end. Karen was polite, but insisted she hadn't talked with Melissa since she'd returned from the island. She asked about their stay, accepted his thanks for their time there and took his phone number and address to give to Melissa as soon as she got in touch with her.

In the three months since then, he'd periodically called both people to see if they had heard from Melissa. Both insisted they had not.

He'd run into a brick wall. He'd lost his wife and didn't know how the hell he was going to find her. He'd finally broken down and asked Max to help. Like it or not, he knew that Max could find out if she was working anywhere in the United States. If she had a job, she would have used her social-security number, she'd have a bank account, she'd be using charge cards.

Max found where she banked. She'd withdrawn all her savings and closed her checking account and had quite effectively disappeared.

How long could she last without working? Surely she'd have to surface somewhere.

Max had promised to keep a watch for her and had insisted on sending Joel on his proposed assignment. He had pointed out that Joel wasn't accomplishing a great deal while he paced up and down his apartment.

Joel had been back in the States a week now. Max had nothing new to report.

How could she just walk away? How could she pretend that their marriage had never happened? Joel had gotten a copy of the recorded marriage license and kept it lying beside his bed as a reminder that he hadn't dreamed the whole scenario.

He didn't even have a picture of her. He had nothing but memories. And dreams.

Sometimes, he had nightmares that Ortiz had somehow managed to escape and had kidnapped her, but Max assured him that Ortiz was locked away in a high-security cell.

Joel finally realized that he could do nothing more. He had to accept the fact that her trust in him had been destroyed. Now all he had to do was to live with that knowledge, to stop replaying all the possible ways he could have handled the situation with the hope of a more positive outcome.

He sat on the side of the bed and rubbed his jaw. He hadn't shaved the day before and his chin felt rough. He grabbed a pair of jogging shorts and drew them on, then went into the kitchen and put on the coffee. While it was brewing, he slipped on his sneakers and went down to the corner for the Sunday paper.

When he returned, the coffee was ready. He poured himself a cup and went into the living room, opening the paper. He hadn't looked at the headlines until now. Now that he saw them, he wondered how they had failed to catch his attention.

BREAKTHROUGH IN CONTROLLING ADDICTIONS ANNOUNCED

Most of the story was on the second page, but it was all there, with extensive quotes from the pharmaceutical company. Dr. Feldman had done it.

There were still months of testing to be done, but the members of the group that had agreed to test the new discovery were enthusiastic with their comments regarding their lack of desire to return to abusive use of addictive substances. The chemical appeared to be working. Only time would tell if the DNA change would be permanent.

Perhaps the company and the government felt that the best protection under the circumstances was a barrage of publicity. The public was being made aware. There would be no chance now to stop the progress Dr. Feldman was making.

Joel turned a few pages before another piece of the paper fell out...the Sunday-supplement magazine. On the front cover were the words, "Can You Tell Your Future by the Stars?"

Joel no longer felt the anger that had swept over him when he'd first read the description of a man born between May 21 and June 20. He'd had time to think about the comments and had come to terms with most of them. Perhaps he did have a dual personality. Perhaps he did prefer change to routine.

But the article had been wrong about willingness to commit himself to a stable relationship. In his case, both aspects of his personality were deeply in love with Dr. Melissa Jordan. He would be willing to give up his double existence, to find a desk job somewhere in order to establish a home with her.

Not that his wishes or desires seemed to matter. He threw down the paper. He'd go get a shower, clean up a little. He rubbed his jaw once more. Might even shave. Then he'd get out of the house for a while. He was sick of his own company, but not ready to go on another assignment. At least he was in the same country with her, or so he assumed. There weren't too many countries she could visit without some kind of identification.

As far as Max could tell, she'd made no applications for a replacement of the documents that were in her purse at the time of the explosion. It was as though she was determined to be a nonperson.

He turned on the shower, then decided to shave first. He was halfway finished when he thought he heard the phone. He opened the bathroom door and listened. Sure enough, the shrill sound rang out clearly. But by the time he reached the phone, it was no longer ringing. He picked it up anyway, but wasn't surprised to hear the dial tone.

Joel punched in the numbers for the only person who would be calling him. As soon as Max answered, Joel asked, "Did you just call me?"

"You already restless?"

"No! My phone was ringing, but by the time I got to it, you'd already hung up."

"It wasn't me, Kramer. I've got better things to do."

Joel thought for a moment, then shrugged. "Probably a wrong number."

"It could be your adoring public."

"Go to hell," Joel grumbled and hung up on the sound of Max's laughter.

He returned to the shower and stepped under the soothing spray. Maybe he'd go out for a late breakfast. He missed having people around. He'd discovered something surprising on this last assignment. Work could be boring, no matter how potentially dangerous. The island vacation had been an eye-opener to him in many ways. He had learned to relax, to enjoy a leisurely schedule.

He'd liked it.

The water had cooled considerably by the time he stepped out of the shower. He'd enjoyed the refreshing feel of it. Even though it was still morning, the day had turned out hot, which was typical for this time of year.

He heard the doorbell while he was still drying the moisture from his dripping body.

"What the hell—"

He strode out of the bathroom, clutching the towel around his waist. If kids were ringing his doorbell, he was going to put a stop to it right now. He jerked the door open, saying, "Now, listen here—" Then forgot what he was going to say.

Melissa stood there before him, looking cool in a sleeveless dress made of a thin material with swirls of color that blended beautifully with her eyes. Sandals with heels put her at eye level with him.

"I'm sorry, I seem to have caught you at a bad time."

"Melissa!" Over the months, he had fantasized all the different ways they would meet again, but in each one, he had envisioned himself as catching her unawares...not the other way around.

His hair was dripping water down his face, but he couldn't use his towel without exposing himself. He motioned her inside. "Hang on a moment and I'll get dressed. I won't be but a second. Uh, have a seat and, uh, help yourself to the coffee."

Joel beat a hasty retreat to the bedroom where he grabbed the first thing he saw to wear, his jogging shorts. As soon as he had them on, he quickly began to towel dry his hair and moved toward the living room once more.

"I can't believe that..." He paused, looking around. She was nowhere in sight. He started toward the front door when he heard the slight clink of china from the kitchen. Joel managed to release the air that he seemed to have been holding in his lungs since he'd first opened the door and found her standing there.

He paused in the kitchen doorway, his hands resting lightly on his hips, and watched her pour coffee into a cup, her back to him. He began to notice things that he'd been too surprised at first to take note of. She was much thinner than she'd been. Her waist looked small enough for him to circle with his hands.

She'd cut her hair. It curled softly around the nape of her neck and around her ears. She'd lost her tan, which was surprising, since the weather had been warm for several weeks now.

"Where have you been?"

He hadn't realized he was going to ask until he heard the words.

She spun around with a gasp. When she saw him standing there, she held her hand to her throat. "You scared me."

"Did it ever occur to you that your disappearing act might have scared me? I had no way of knowing if one of Ortiz's men had grabbed you when my back was turned."

She turned away from Joel and picked up her cup. Without looking at him again, she walked over to the small table and sat down. "I never thought of that," she said, looking down at her coffee. She glanced up. "Did you get in trouble for not protecting me sufficiently?"

He stalked over and dropped into the chair across from her. "What the hell kind of question is that? I've been worried out of my mind about you. I've called everybody I knew who could possibly have heard from you. I've checked every lead I could think of, wondering where you were, how you were surviving—'' He stopped for a moment, then ran his hand through his hair. "I don't understand any of this. Why did you quit your job? Why did you just walk away? Why did you decide to come see me now?"

She toyed with the handle of her cup. "I tried to call first. When there was no answer, I thought you might be out of town, so I decided to come over and put a note in your mailbox. The manager saw me looking at the boxes. I explained that I was looking for you, and he said he thought he'd seen you earlier, coming in with a paper." She tucked a curl behind her ear. "So I decided to come up to see if you'd gotten back."

He leaned back in his chair. "So you found me. I have a hunch it was a little easier for you than what I've been going through."

He watched soft color pinken her face. "Yes. Karen and Dr. Feldman both gave me your messages."

"And you immediately rushed out and called me, right?"

She raised her head and looked at him, her color still high. "I've never seen you like this before—at least, not until that last day when that man was there."

"Oh, yeah. I remember. You were upset because I wasn't the pleasant, shy, introverted writer you'd decided I was."

"That was who you were pretending to be."

"I wasn't pretending anything with you, Melissa. I was always who I am, all except for my occupation, which I was specifically instructed not to tell you.

Everything I told you about my past was true. I hid nothing from you."

"But you are shaped by the job you do, Joel. Everybody is."

"I'm not arguing that. But I'm not a liar. And I'm certainly not a killer, as you so quickly decided." He could no longer sit still. He pushed the chair back, got up and stalked to the window in the living room.

"I know that," she said in a low voice.

"When did you change your mind?" he asked without looking around.

She got up and wandered over to the sofa. When she sat down, she leaned her head wearily against the back. "I don't even remember. I just remember being so confused." She was quiet for several minutes, but he didn't interrupt the silence that was forming around them.

Joel prayed that she wouldn't see the tremor that had taken over his body as soon as he first saw her. It was as though he'd been plugged into an electrical current that was sending a steady charge through him, causing a visible vibration. He'd received many shocks in his life, some nasty ones that other men had been unable to withstand with his composure, but nothing that had ever happened to him had shaken him so much as seeing Melissa so unexpectedly again.

"I was lying in bed a few weeks ago and I finally figured out an analogy of how I felt that last day I was with you."

Her voice was low and a little hoarse, as though she was having trouble getting the words out. Joel slowly turned away from the window and faced her. He didn't speak.

"From the time I met you, my life became magical. The only problem was, I thought it was all real. I got caught up in the magic and the emotions. Because I'd never had a close relationship with a man before, I projected every male role I'd ever conceived onto you. You were the loving, affectionate father I'd never had, the teasing older brother, the flirting boy next door, my first date, my first romance, my first love. You became Sir Lancelot and Sir Galahad all rolled up into one, as well as all the princes in all the fairy tales to me. And because you said you loved me, I became the beautiful princess—with charm and confidence and elegance—all the things I never have been."

He stared at her in amazement at her assessment of herself, but still he didn't say anything.

"I was caught up in all the make believe, and then that horrible man showed up and suddenly, I felt as though the lights were turned on all around me and the curtains were drawn. The play was over and the audience had all gone home. All except for me. I'd gotten so caught up in the story, I hadn't realized that none of it was real. I was still sitting there, waiting for the play to go on and on. But you were no longer willing to play the part. Your lines were through. It was time to return home for a new role."

She had closed her eyes rather than look at him, but that had not prevented the tears from sliding down her cheeks. She looked so vulnerable, and he loved her so much.

Joel sat beside her on the sofa. She opened her eyes and looked at him. "So I blamed you rather than face the fact that all the fantasies and fairy tales had been in my head. Meeting you caused me to realize how much I've missed in my life—fun times with friends, tender times, passionate times. I skipped from child prodigy to adulthood without the learning times that go with being an adolescent. You coaxed the adolescent in me to come out and play.'' The smile she gave him was genuine, even though the tears continued to slip down her cheeks. ''I came here today because I wanted you to know that I'm sorry for blaming you for bringing me out of my beautiful little bubble. You taught me so much about myself, things that I could never have learned on my own.'' She touched his hand ever so gently. ''I came to thank you for everything you did...for taking such good care of me, even when I didn't know that was what you were doing...for being a friend so that I could understand what friendship means...for teaching me about love...for giving me the gifts of understanding, and tolerance, and compassion.''

He turned his hand so that he could clasp hers. ''Melissa?''

''Yes?''

''Why do you think I married you?''

She smiled. ''But you didn't, Joel. I realized that later. You just wanted me to feel better about making love to you. But it really wasn't necessary. I was never so naive as to think a man of your experience would allow himself to be legally tied to someone.''

''A good point and one I'm pleased that you can appreciate. I *am* experienced in the world. No one can force me to do something that I don't want to do.'' He released her hand and stood. ''I'll be back in a moment.''

Joel went into the bedroom and came out holding a folded piece of paper that he handed to her. He watched as she slowly opened it and even more slowly read what it said. He noticed that she recognized her own signature…and his…as well as that of the minister who had married them.

She looked up at him, puzzled and obviously shaken. "But this—this says the original of this document has been recorded—as though this is officially a— That you and I are actually—" She seemed to run out of words.

"So you thought I lied about this, as well," he said, the pain of that knowledge going through him like a sword.

"After I calmed down and really thought about everything that happened, it didn't make any logical sense for you to have taken our relationship to that extreme."

"Well, Dr. Jordan, you overlooked an obvious equation."

She gave him a questioning look.

"There was only one reason why I would marry you. I told you at the time and I did not lie." Joel felt as though a hand suddenly seized him by the throat so that he could not say another word without choking. He swallowed a couple of times and cleared his throat. In a gruff voice, he managed to say, "I love you, Melissa. That was never a fantasy. I'm no knight in shining armor. I'm sure as hell no prince, but I fell in love with you so hard, the crash was probably heard for miles around. I knew that marrying you without telling you why we were together was unethical. I came close to losing my job over it, but at the time, I didn't care. I loved you and I truly believed that you loved me. No matter what else I am, what else I've ever done, I would never say the vows that I repeated to you unless they came from my heart.''

It was only when she brushed her thumb across his cheekbone that he became aware of the moisture there.

''Oh, Joel,'' she whispered. ''What have I done?''

He saw his pain reflected in her face and he knew that she had been suffering these past three months as much as he had. He slid his arms around her and drew her close. ''You've come home, Melissa... where you belong.''

TWELVE

Twelve

Joel discovered that memories paled by comparison to having Melissa there in his arms. She had thrown her arms around his neck and held him so tightly, he could scarcely breathe. He scooped her into his arms and carried her down the hallway to his bedroom.

The bed covers looked as though a battle had been fought with them without a winner. He shoved them aside as he lowered her onto his bed. Her dress was surprisingly easy to remove. Her slip quickly followed. He skimmed her hose and shoes from her as though by magic.

"You've lost weight," he whispered, touching his lips to her breast, her waist, her abdomen.

"So have you."

"Wonder if it could be for the same reason?" He nudged her legs apart so that he could place a trail of kisses along her inner thigh.

"Oh, Joel, I've been so stupid," she said with a quick, sobbing breath.

"You won't get any argument out of me on that one." He leaned forward and first kissed her mouth, traced her lips with his tongue, then nibbled on her bottom lip.

When she opened her mouth to him, all conversation ceased.

Several hours later, the bed covers were on the floor. Joel and Melissa were still intertwined on the bed. He had both arms around her; she had her head on his chest and one of his thighs was sandwiched between both of hers.

"Was that your stomach or mine?" she murmured drowsily.

"Probably both, in perfect harmony."

They continued to lay there, each touching the other from time to time, as though to make sure they were not dreaming.

Finally, he sighed and said, "You never did answer me."

"About what?"

"Where you've been."

"Oh. I'm not that sure. Once I left the airport in Miami, I realized I had no place to go and very little money. I caught a shuttle bus into town, then called my bank to find out how to transfer money. I had a terrible time trying to prove who I was after it was sent."

"I had nightmares of you lost somewhere, cold and hungry, with no money and no way to know how to contact me. I'd wake up in a cold sweat."

"I could have contacted Karen for help if I'd gotten

desperate. I just needed time to think. Once I got my money, I went to the bus station and took the first bus north, then transferred to one going west. I ended up near the Gulf somewhere in Mississippi, found an inexpensive bed-and-breakfast place and spent most of my time walking up and down the beach.''

"Then why are you so pale?''

She touched his chest with her fingers and he shivered. He grabbed them and held them firmly against him. ''No fair. You're trying to distract me.''

"How am I doing?''

''I want to know what happened to that fabulous tan you had, especially if you've been spending your time on the beach.''

She sighed. ''I got sick. I wasn't eating right. I couldn't sleep. I felt as though I was in a nightmare that I couldn't escape.''

''I know the feeling,'' he muttered.

''One morning, I just couldn't force myself out of bed. My landlady came in to check on me later that day and said I was running a high temperature. I was really ill for quite a while.''

''But, of course, you wouldn't call me.''

''I was in no condition to talk with anyone.''

''You could have given the number to your landlady.''

She shook her head. ''I was too ashamed of the way I'd behaved by that time.''

''Has anyone ever pointed out to you just how tough you are on yourself? Cut yourself a little slack, sweetheart. It's all right to be human. And none of us are perfect.'' He ran his hand along her waist, over her hips and down her thigh. ''You come damn close, though.''

"I never told you that I loved you, not in all the time we were together. That's why I was so shocked to learn that you knew."

"Was there a particular reason you didn't want me to know?"

"I didn't want to embarrass you or make you feel obligated to me in some way."

"Are you certain that you actually earned all those degrees, lady? It's hard for me to fathom that some-one with your vast knowledge could be so incredibly unlearned."

"But I am. At least, about love."

He hugged her to him. "I have a confession to make. I haven't been a real scholar on the subject, myself. But it's amazing how quickly a person can learn when he gets involved."

"But it's something that we have to experience to understand, isn't it?"

He kissed the crown of her head, all that he could see at the moment. "I suppose it is," he agreed.

"So, what are we going to do now?"

"Eat?" he asked hopefully.

"I mean about our marriage."

He pulled away so that he could see her face. "If you think you're going to get away from me again, then you're—"

"I just mean, are we going to live here? Or is this a temporary place for you?"

"It's the only home I have, but that doesn't mean we can't look around for something larger, or a house, maybe. Whatever you want."

"I was thinking about contacting Dr. Feldman to-morrow."

"I have a feeling he'd be delighted. We've become

acquainted over the months you've been gone. He's
been quite concerned about you."

"Does he know we're married?"

"I didn't think it was my place to tell him."

"Does Max know?"

"You bet. How do you think I almost got fired?"

"How about your job?"

"What do you mean?"

"Are you going to be watching over damsels in
distress much?"

He grinned. "I don't know. Do you think I have
an aptitude for the job? Should I find me a coat of
shining armor?" He gave a slight grunt when she
poked him in the ribs.

"Your work seems to be very dangerous."

"Not ordinarily, but it does have its moments."

She was quiet for several minutes. "I would rather
have you safe, but I want you to be happy, whatever
you do."

"Then you're in luck, doll. I am extremely happy,
thanks to you. Now that I know where you are, I can
get on with all the plans I wanted to discuss with you
before we were so rudely interrupted by Ortiz."

"What plans?"

He began to kiss her. "I'm sure in a few months,
when you aren't quite as much of a distraction, they'll
come back to me."

"But in the meantime?"

"I'm willing to live our lives one day at a time.
How about you?" His second kiss made her forget
the subject of their conversation.

"Whatever you say, Joel," she murmured, wrapping her arms around him.

Joel leaned over her, content with his new role.
Happy ever after sounded downright exciting to him.

Epilogue

Joel tossed the piece of paper he'd been reading down on the desk and stood up, then stretched. Damn, he must be getting old. After a few hours of sitting, he grew stiff. What he needed was a good workout.

He wandered over to the window of his study and gazed out across the Virginia countryside. They'd been lucky to find a place within commuting distance for Melissa that gave them the acreage and privacy they wanted. The rolling hills beckoned him to saddle one of the horses and take a ride. He glanced at his watch. He might invite some company to join him.

A slight scratching sound at the door caused him to turn his head. "Come in."

A pair of large blue eyes surrounded by a tumbled mop of blond curls peeked around the door. He grinned. "Come on in, Lisa."

A dainty five-year-old tiptoed into the room. "Lucy

said not to bother you," she whispered. She took another few steps. "Am I bothering you, Daddy?"

He walked over to her and scooped her up into his arms. "What do you suppose would happen to you if you were?"

"Lucy would scold me."

"Can't say that I blame her."

Lisa cocked her head. "Well-l-l, I thought if I pretended to be the dog and just scratched at the door, you wouldn't notice me if you were busy."

"I see."

"Mommy says when you're working, you don't hear anything."

"I think your mommy may be right."

Lisa leaned back in his arms and looked at him. "Do you want to go play?"

He thought about that for a moment. "I might. Then again, I was thinking about going for a ride."

"On Blaze?"

"Umm-hmm."

"Me, too?"

"If you'd like."

"Tony, too?"

Joel walked out into the hallway. "If he wants."

Lisa scrambled out of his arms. "Tony! Daddy said we could go riding with him!" she yelled, racing toward the other end of the house.

Joel wandered into the kitchen where Lucy was working. "Any coffee left?"

The middle-aged woman glanced around with a smile. "I always keep coffee ready for you. Melissa would skin me alive if she thought I wasn't anticipating your every need and wish."

He poured himself a cup and leaned against the

counter, watching her. "Lucy, how long have you been with us?"

She looked up, surprised. "A little over eight years now. Don't you remember? I came to work right after Tony was born."

He nodded, smiling. "How could I forget?"

She shook her head. "That was one fella who was determined to stay awake all night and sleep all day. It took all three of us to keep up with him for a while."

Where had the time gone? They'd been married for two years before Tony arrived. By then, they'd found the home they wanted and Joel had discovered a hidden talent within himself that had changed his working habits. He wasn't certain that Max had ever totally forgiven him. He chuckled. The irony of the situation still amused him. After all, Max had only himself to blame since he was the one who had originally suggested the idea.

"Dad!" A tornado in torn jeans and faded shirt came tearing into the kitchen, his eyes glittering with excitement. "Are you going to let me ride Lady?"

"You think you can handle her?"

"Sure I can. Roy's been helping me practice, but he never lets me out of the pasture. Can I really go with you?"

Joel rumpled his son's untidy hair. "You bet!"

"I'll go tell Roy to get the horses ready!" Tony darted out of the room.

Lucy shook her head. "That boy still has more energy than three people combined. I don't know where he gets it."

Joel finished his cup of coffee. "I'd better get my

clothes changed before those two take off without me.''

He climbed the stairs and walked toward the master bedroom. He paused at an open doorway and peered into the nursery. Two-year-old Christopher slept as hard as he played. He lay crossways in his bed, his covers bunched around him.

Joel shook his head and walked on. Sometimes, it was hard for him to remember a time when Melissa, Tony, Lisa and Christopher had not been a part of his life. They had become his entire world.

The same thought occurred to him several hours later as he lay in bed, holding Melissa.

''It's hard for me to remember a time when I didn't have you and the children. I can't imagine how I managed.''

She was curled so that her head was on his shoulder, one leg across his thighs. She ran her hand across the familiar expanse of his chest, never tiring of touching him. ''I know what you mean. I feel the same way.''

''Would we have believed it if someone, announcing that he or she was from the future, had told us the outcome of my moving in across the hall from you?''

''Did you ever think you'd no longer be working for Max?''

''I don't think I ever gave the idea much thought.'' He was quiet for several long minutes. ''But I know I would have argued if I'd been told that someday, I'd be making a living as a writer!''

''And on the *New York Times* bestseller list at that!''

They both laughed, remembering how all of that

had come about. Melissa's accusations that he had lied to her had continued to rankle. After all, all he had lied about was his profession.

For the first eighteen months after their marriage, Joel continued to take assignments and travel, but whenever he could, he started making notes, jotting down ideas, researching whenever possible, and when he was at home, he dug out several of his college textbooks and brushed up on what he had learned years before.

No one was more surprised than Joel when he sold his first manuscript. Then he found an aggressive agent who encouraged him to keep writing the kind of adventure novels that seemed to flow effortlessly from his brain.

Of course, he had to make certain that no accurate intelligence information was used. Not that people would have believed some of the bizarre situations he'd encountered.

"I got a letter from Abe today," he said, suddenly remembering.

"And what does your esteemed agent have to say?"

"I'm being offered an obscene amount of money to produce ten books over the next ten years."

She raised her head. "Joel! That's wonderful. Why didn't you tell me sooner?"

He pulled her head down and gave her a long, leisurely kiss. When he finally raised his head, he murmured, "I forgot. There were too many other exciting things going on."

Melissa recalled her arrival that day. Tony and Lisa were dancing up and down with their news about the ride, Christopher was chattering and showing her the city that he and his daddy had built out of an array of children's construction toys, so proud of himself. Joel had been wearing an identical grin on his face.

She sighed, settling on his shoulder once more. She loved this man to distraction. He'd shown her what love could be, what family life could be. He'd encouraged her to continue her career, convincing her that she could have it all. He'd been right, but only because he'd been willing to be there with the children, to plan his writing schedule around their schedules, to answer their questions, tend to their hurts, encourage their questions, nurture them…and her.

"I love you," she whispered, realizing once again how inadequate those words were to express the tremendous emotion that swept over her whenever she thought of everything that Joel had managed to bring to her life.

He shifted so that he was facing her, which left her in a very vulnerable position. She could feel his arousal pressed against her.

"Care to demonstrate?" he drawled, nibbling on her ear.

"It would be a pleasure, sir," she whispered just as her mouth found his.

It was.

The Gemini Man

It's your fourth date, and you're beginning to think you misunderstood the twinkle you saw in that Gemini man's eyes when he'd first asked you out a few weeks ago. You'd made plans for a Saturday picnic, but it had rained. No matter, your Gemini friend—and you'd already learned about his birth sign and everything else concerning this gregarious gentleman—whisked you off to the Press Club for an informal lunch. You hadn't known he'd moonlighted as a reporter. You thought he was a computer specialist!

Now you've just gotten out of a midnight movie and you've gone to a quaint café. There, you talk about the film until four in the morning. But, hey, isn't this your *fourth* date? This *is* the twentieth century, and he hasn't even gotten to the handholding stage while you're dreaming of happily ever after! Is there something wrong with the man? You sure hope not, but he *is* pretty changeable.

And just when you'd gotten used to him being a reporter and a computer expert, you find out his real dream in life was to sing as a tenor with the Metropolitan Opera. You discovered this goodie when he surprised you with tickets to *Madame Butterfly*.

Afterward, when he *finally* asks you up to his place for a drink, the first thing you see upon entering the house is a grand piano and a set of drums. Why on earth should it surprise you that he can play everything from Chopin to the Rolling Stones?

So what's with this Gemini man, anyway? Deciding on a little investigating, you get out an astrology book and find out that he's ruled by Mercury—the messenger of the Gods AKA the whiz-kid of communication with a finger in every conceivable pie. One book says he's a jack-of-all-trades. He's light, charming and witty. Frequently, he has two careers and needs variety the way the rest of us need air. What does he look for in a woman? Brains. What's his worse fault? He can change his mind on a dime and make perfect sense doing it. It has been known to drive some people crazy.

He is also a silver-tongued wonder. He can be a stunning orator or the kind of glib con man who sells the Brooklyn Bridge to you one day and buys it back at a profit the next. In matters of the heart, these variety-addicted souls have earned a reputation for, shall we say, inconsistency. But if he's mature and you're on your toes, this shouldn't be a problem. Alas, though, he will probably always be a flirt, albeit a charming one.

Gemini's symbol is the twins, and like Pisces, he's

dual-bodied, so it's sometimes difficult to tell which twin is in charge. But if you give this Mercury-ruled man enough room to do his quick changes, and if you can keep up with his facile wit, by the time that fifth date rolls around, he might just do more than talk. Even a Gemini needs a break from all his mental aerobics, and what nicer way to unwind then to cozy up to *you!*

So if you're interested in tripping the light fantastic, you might want to check him out. Look for him in such fields as journalism, travel, education, radio and TV. In short, anything with variety, and preferably something in communications. At first, it may seem that communicating is about all this man *can* do. But given time, he'll find some pretty spectacular ways to communicate his feelings to you. And you will never, ever have a dull moment with this man! After all, Rudolph Valentino and Errol Flynn were Geminis, and they certainly knew how to get across their message!

*   *   *   *   *

Famous Gemini Men

Arthur Conan Doyle
Bob Dylan
Frank Lloyd Wright
Al Jolson
John F. Kennedy

ZEKE

I dedicated my first book, written in 1983,
to Lynn Jordan and Lauraine Snelling,
acknowledging the fact that without their assistance
and encouragement I would never have been able to
finish and polish that first effort of mine.

Now, nine years and thirty-four books later,
Lynn and Lauraine have once again come through
with encouragement, advice and steadfast support
to keep me going when the going gets rough.

Thank you both for always being there for me.
I couldn't have done it without you.

Annette Broadrick

Prologue

Zeke strode down one of the many hallways that formed the maze of offices of his headquarters. Since he'd had little reason to visit the place during the years he'd worked for the agency, he clutched a hand-drawn map in his fist.

He was a field man because that's what he wanted. He enjoyed being on his own, making his own decisions, following up on leads in his own way.

His reports were timely filed with the appropriate individuals and quickly dismissed from his mind. He abhorred paperwork of any kind. He assumed that after he passed on information, it was carefully analyzed and eventually fell onto the proper desk in the prescribed manner.

The fact that he was in the Virginia office at all was proof that the world had changed in a radical way. He was still having difficulty adjusting to some of those changes. Why, the KGB were giving visitors tours through their facilities, for crying out loud! For all he knew, the Langley headquarters had just been purchased by Disney for use as another one of its amusement parks.

So where did that leave him? What was there left for a man of his background and training in covert operations to do?

He rounded a corner, frowned at the map in his hand, checked the numbers and arrows posted along the wall, then proceeded down the next hallway.

Maybe they planned to offer him a position as a tour guide.

When he found the number he was looking for, he tapped on the door before opening it. A woman sat at a desk, working at a computer. She looked up when he came through the doorway, and smiled. "Mr. Daniels?"

"Yep."

"Please go on in. Mr. Carpenter is expecting you."

Zeke nodded, opened the next door and found himself in a comfortable-looking office. Although he had never been there before, he recognized the man behind the desk speaking on the phone. Frank Carpenter had been his superior for more than ten years. Whenever they met person to person, Frank, usually dressed as a tourist, had always come to him in whatever part of the world he happened to be. This was the first time he'd seen his boss in a suit and tie, looking for all the world like a typical businessman.

Frank waved him to one of the chairs and Zeke sat down. He always felt out of place in this type of environment, which was the biggest reason he had turned down the promotions he'd been offered in the past. He had known that a promotion would mean being assigned a desk and an office of his own. He had a sinking feeling that he was about to be offered such a position once again.

He'd rather be a tour guide at a Disney facility.

Frank hung up the phone, stood and walked around the desk with his hand extended. "Good to see you, Zeke. You're looking a hell of a lot better these days than the last time I saw you."

Zeke stood and took the offered hand. "That's not too surprising, considering I'd just had a couple of metal fragments removed from vital parts of my anatomy."

"I was worried about you," Frank admitted. "I felt I needed to be there to be certain you were going to recover fully. Had any residual problems?"

"Except for a knee that gives accurate weather reports, I'm okay."

"Glad to hear it." Frank studied him for a moment before returning to his chair behind the desk. "You didn't have any trouble finding my office, did you?"

Zeke smiled blandly. "I had them draw me a map at the front entrance...and I left a trail of bread crumbs so I would have no difficulty finding my way out of here."

Frank leaned back in his chair, still studying Zeke. "You're really looking fit, I'm glad to see. A little leaner, maybe, but that's probably healthier. The report of your last medical checkup could have been of a man nearly twenty years younger."

Zeke lifted an eyebrow. "You've so little to do these days that you're poring over medical reports to relieve the monotony?"

"Actually, we've been quite busy around here.

There's always a need for intelligence reports from around the world...always something brewing."

"So why the scrutiny into my physical condition? Are you thinking about calling me in on a permanent basis?" Zeke looked around the room, futilely trying to imagine himself working in a similar environment.

"On the contrary, I've received a rather urgent request to lend you to another branch of the government."

Zeke's usually quick tongue betrayed him, causing him to stare at his superior in surprised silence.

"I don't know how well you've been able to keep abreast of the news in this hemisphere during the past few years," Frank began, "but we've got another kind of war on our hands here in the States...a drug war."

Zeke leaned back in his chair, straightened his long legs and crossed his ankles. "I would've had to have been on the moon not to have heard that piece of news. Come to think of it, even there I could probably have picked up some of the satellite transmissions."

"The Drug Enforcement Administration has doubled, almost tripled, its agents along the Texas-Mexico border in an effort to stop the incoming flood of drugs. In beefing up their operations, however, they've managed to develop more problems."

"Such as?"

"They are very much afraid that some of the agents have discovered a sizable second income by looking the other way when a big shipment is due from one of the Mexican cartels...at least that's what some of the department heads in this area are beginning to suspect."

"But they can't prove it."

"No. There are still numerous arrests being made from Brownsville to El Paso and points in between. In charting those arrests, the DEA discovered that most of them were small-time drug runners, some college kids looking for thrills and extra cash, and an occasional expendable member of one of the Colombian cartels. What has them on edge is that despite all their efforts, they've never been able to get anything on Lorenzo De la Garza."

"De la Garza? Who is he?"

"He's a wealthy businessman who lives near Monterrey and owns several factories scattered throughout Mexico. After he gathers the raw product—everything from wool to mineral ore to wood—he turns it into salable merchandise and exports the products made."

"Sounds legitimate to me."

"It's supposed to. About two years ago the agency received an anonymous tip that De la Garza was using his established shipping routes to smuggle drugs. Since they check out every piece of information received, the DEA set up a surveillance on random shipments coming through customs. Although traces of drugs were found on two separate occasions, there wasn't enough evidence to make any arrests.

"The DEA decided to place some agents around De la Garza in an effort to find out more about his operation. Although those agents have been reporting for almost a year now, they insist they can find no evidence to link his organization with drugs. However, his shipments have increased substantially and he continues to expand his business."

"So where do I come in?"

"The DEA is afraid that De la Garza has bought

off their agents. In return, he's being alerted to which shipments will be checked for drugs. The agency came to me with the idea of placing someone inside De la Garza's organization who no one in their group knows to find out who's passing on information. I thought of you.''

"You want me to go undercover on a drug operation?''

"Yes.''

"Pretending to be what, exactly?''

Frank smiled. ''Yourself, with some slight modifications in your work history. We suggest that you present yourself as a mercenary, bored with inaction, and offer your services. De la Garza's been having security problems lately, that much we've learned. He could use a man with your skills to help him. Once you get inside his operation, you'll be able to gain access to his files, find out who's on the take…that sort of thing. In essence you'll be spying on the spies.'' Frank closed the file in front of him. ''The DEA wants verification of what they suspect is happening. They want to nail whoever is giving De la Garza information on their movements along the border. Of course, if you happen to get your hands on enough evidence to get De la Garza at the same time, they won't complain.''

Zeke shook his head. ''They don't ask much, do they?''

Frank shrugged. ''They wanted our best agent, which is why I recommended you. You've gained quite a reputation in the business over the years, you know. Of course, De la Garza will do a check on your background. He's a smart man or he wouldn't be where he is today. What we intend to do is publicize

your exploits to the right people, play up your nickname, that sort of thing. I don't think you'll have a
problem getting hired.''

Zeke eyed his boss with a hint of wariness. "What,
exactly, is my nickname?''

Frank smiled. ''I thought you knew. The opposition
began to call you 'The Intimidator,' a few years ago.
Guess the tag stuck.''

"The Intimidator? Where did that come from?''

Frank shook his head. "Who knows where it
started? The interesting point about it is that everyone
immediately knew who they were referring to—you.''

"You've got to be joking.''

"Nope.''

Zeke tugged on his earlobe. "I don't go around
intimidating people.''

"You think not? Some people think you can read
minds, know when they're lying or hiding something.
They find that particular kind of talent downright intimidating, but we don't need to tell De la Garza how
you got that nickname.''

"So let me get this straight. I'm to walk up to this
guy and offer my services. If and when he hires me,
I'm supposed to figure out which agents he's got on
his payroll and, incidentally, gather enough hard evidence to nail him in U.S. courts. You think he's going to let some stranger learn all his secrets?''

"I don't think he'll have a choice once you're in
there.''

Zeke slowly sat up in his chair and leaned his elbows on his knees. "I don't suppose you have any
ideas about how I can accomplish this assignment, do
you?''

Frank grinned. "A few. I've already requested files

on every one of their field agents so that you can familiarize yourself with their descriptions.'' He nodded to a stack of folders piled on the side of his desk. ''In addition, I've thought of a way to use your background to benefit the role I have in mind for you.''

''I'm listening.''

''We could let it be known that we're terminating you with harsh feelings on both sides. As a soldier of fortune with an extensive background in intelligence work, you might find your talents in high demand in certain circles.''

''That's always good to know,'' Zeke drawled. ''Job security is always reassuring, I suppose.''

Frank thumbed open another file and glanced at its contents. ''Another reason you're a good choice is because you were born in South Texas. You grew up speaking both languages fluently. You know the area. I understand you used to do some camping and fishing in the mountains down in Mexico as a teenager.''

Zeke's jaw tightened. ''Yeah. I had a good friend whose family came from there.''

''Yes. Carlos Santiago...you used to call him Charlie.''

Zeke glanced at the file in front of Frank. ''Pretty extensive study you made there. I suppose you have the name of the girl who stole my virginity noted, as well.''

Frank glanced up from the papers and grinned. ''I could probably make an educated guess.''

Zeke rolled his eyes. ''Never mind. So I was born in the lower part of the Rio Grande Valley. I suppose that would give me something of an advantage.''

''Exactly. It would be logical and perfectly natural for you to return to Harlingen to regroup. De la Garza would be a natural prospect for a man of your talents.''

''If the man is as smart as you say he is, I can't see him offering a job to someone who's worked for the U.S. government most of his adult life.''

''By the time we embellish on your record, add a few shady exploits and plant a few charges, he'll know full well why you left and why you have no particular allegiance to our government. From his point of view you'd be a good man to have around.''

Zeke stood and stretched, looking around the room once more before meeting Frank's inquiring gaze. He nodded, reaching for the stack of files.

''It sure beats tap dancing five times a day at Disney World.''

One

Zeke casually leaned against a wall of the international airport in Mexico City, his hands in his pockets, and watched the trickle of people exiting the customs area.

Ignoring the speculative glances aimed in his direction by some of the women who passed, Zeke kept his gaze and thoughts focused on the passengers who had recently arrived from Madrid, Spain.

Although he had never seen her before, Zeke knew he would recognize Angela De la Garza. During the weeks he had been working for her uncle, Zeke had been in Lorenzo's office many times and had seen several photographs of the woman. He knew what she looked like as an infant in her mother's arms and what she looked like seated on the back of her prized pony when she was eight years old. He had seen her smiling face peering from multiple poses and situations spanning two decades.

Therefore, he would have no trouble recognizing the woman he had come to Mexico City to collect and fly back to Monterrey where she was to visit her uncle. He had no problem fulfilling the assignment. Taking orders from Lorenzo De la Garza was all part of his job, all strictly routine.

According to Lorenzo, Angela had a charming disposition. Too young when her parents died to remember much about them, she grew up considering Lorenzo to be her parent. He now admitted that he may have been too lax with her in an effort to make up for her loss. By the time he had placed her in a private school for her formal education, she had become quite self-willed and independent.

The nuns who taught Angela had reported her on numerous occasions…her lack of behavioral training had shocked them. She was continually being called in to the front office for talking too much in class, for laughing during study hours, and more often than not for failing to turn in completed homework.

Instead of improving when she entered high school, her actions incurred more frequent reprimands. Her hoydenish behavior often ran afoul of the rigid rules of the prim nuns. Lorenzo explained to Zeke that he finally had decided to send her to her mother's family in Spain during her second year in high school to finish her education, in hopes that they would be able to train her in the social graces expected from a properly brought-up young lady.

Lorenzo felt he had made the right decision. His beautiful, bright-eyed niece had matured into a warm, vibrant woman with a great deal of charm. He had made frequent visits to Madrid to see her during those years. She had completed her education and had become an elementary school teacher, much to his surprise and pleasure. Lorenzo enjoyed talking about her whenever he noticed Zeke looking at her photographs.

Consequently Zeke had become inordinately aware of the young girl who stared back at him from all the different poses. The latest one, taken in the spring during Lorenzo's last visit, kept flashing into Zeke's head at night when he closed his eyes to sleep.

The picture was an enlargement of a candid photograph taken out of doors near a waterfall and large outcrop of rock. Green shoots of spring grass framed her as she leaned against one of the boulders. The spring green was reflected by the color of her eyes as she gazed into the lens of the camera. Her hair was a golden riot of waves streaked with shimmering strands of copper and silver. The wind had tossed it into a tousled mass of color that tumbled around her face and shoulders.

She had been laughing into the camera, her face glowing with love for whoever had taken the picture. It was that expression that haunted his dreams at night. During those late-night hours, she was looking at *him* in just that way.

He'd never reacted so strongly to a woman before, much less a photograph. Zeke enjoyed women. He was attracted to those intelligent, self-confident ones who were comfortable with who they were and didn't feel the need for a special man in their lives to feel complete.

In between assignments he generally spent his time with someone whose company he enjoyed. His women friends understood that their relationship created no binding commitments.

For him to be having fantasies about the niece of a man he hoped to bring down was the height of foolishness and he knew it. The fantasies hadn't become a problem until Lorenzo informed him that, despite everything he could say to discourage her, Angela was coming to visit him.

Zeke had known immediately that he had to wipe from his consciousness all of his fantasies now that the woman whose photograph had teased and tantalized him would soon be a part of his daily existence. He would distance himself from her emotionally, intentionally keeping a wall between them, and hope like hell that she would not be staying long.

At least Lorenzo joined him in that final wish, which helped. This was not a safe time to have a member of his family at the De la Garza compound, not after the recent trouble there.

The increasing tension surrounding De la Garza and his business had made Zeke's efforts to get hired by Lorenzo much easier than he or Frank could have planned. Zeke had been hired to beef up the security around the place and to serve as Lorenzo's personal bodyguard. The fact that he had lived in Europe for the past several years with no ties to the area caused Lorenzo to trust him more than he trusted some of the men he already had on his payroll.

Lorenzo knew he had a powerful enemy working hard to destroy him and his many businesses. He just didn't know who. Zeke assumed it was another cartel muscling in on Lorenzo's territory, but if Lorenzo had any suspicions about the identity of his enemy, he wasn't sharing them with anyone.

During the weeks he had worked for Lorenzo, Zeke had learned the layout of the place, met several of Lorenzo's business associates and had identified two undercover drug agents.

What he didn't know was which one was on the take. For that information he would need to get into Lorenzo's personal files in his office.

Lorenzo zealously guarded his office. He never allowed anyone inside when he wasn't there. The room was kept locked. Although locked doors had never been a problem for Zeke, he needed sufficient time to get inside and look through the files without being missed. However, since he rarely left Lorenzo's side, he'd yet to find the opportunity he needed.

Angela De la Garza had become an added nuisance in more than one respect. Not only did she already haunt his dreams, causing more than his fair share of sleepless nights, she would be one more person he had to elude before he could accomplish his assignment.

Zeke shifted his weight and propped his booted foot against the wall, his gaze focused on the incoming arrivals.

As soon as he spotted Angela, Zeke lazily pushed away from the wall and straightened to his full height. She looked smaller than he had expected. He wasn't a particularly large man, but he doubted that the top of her head came to his chin. She was also dressed more sedately than he'd pictured her. She wore a pale green suit and had her hair pulled away from her face in a formal style she had never worn for any of her uncle's photographs. The soft chignon would have been too severe for most women. For Angela, the style framed and emphasized the oval shape of her face and the creamy smoothness of her fair skin.

She bore little resemblance to her father's side of the family. Zeke recognized her resemblance to her mother in the pictures he had seen of her with Angela as a baby.

With a measured tread, Zeke moved toward the woman he had flown to Mexico City to meet, disguising his feelings behind an impassive mask.

Angie felt as though the air terminal were rocking like an ocean liner in a storm, but since no one else seemed to be affected by any unexplained movement she decided her reaction was due to the fatigue of her recent transatlantic flight. She had been unable to do more than nap on the plane during the flight. Now that she had arrived, she hoped that her excitement at seeing her uncle in a few minutes would give her a surge of energy that would carry her through the rest of the afternoon.

She hadn't been home in more than ten years. Despite Tio's repeated suggestions that she wait for a better time to visit, Angela had insisted that she didn't want to wait any longer. Every time she mentioned coming back home, he always had a list of reasons why she should delay her trip.

This time she had ignored him and come anyway. Would he forgive her for being so stubborn? Would he think that she was the same undisciplined person he had sent to Spain all those years ago?

Hopefully she would be able to quickly convince him that it was her love for him and for her home that had made her so insistent. Now that she was an adult he needn't worry so much about her. She could look after herself. She could be a help to him, as well.

Of course she was nervous about their initial meeting. How could she not be? But once he saw her, she knew he would forgive her for ignoring his suggestions about waiting to come visit him. He loved her. She knew that he would forgive her anything.

By the time she cleared customs, Angie had gotten a grip on her feelings. She was ready to face her uncle and—

A tall, broad-shouldered man coming toward her caught her attention, dispelling her reverie. He moved in an indolent stroll that emphasized the superb conditioning of his body. Her gaze was drawn to the subtle movement of his taut thigh muscles rippling beneath the fabric of his snug jeans. There wasn't an ounce of fat on the man.

She idly lifted her gaze to encompass his strong jawline, his unsmiling mouth, and a nose that looked to have been broken more than once. A bolt of shocked awareness struck her when she made eye contact with him. He'd been watching her while she mentally inventoried his physical assets!

Thoroughly embarrassed, Angie averted her gaze so that she was staring past him while she continued along the concourse.

"Miss De la Garza?"

The only thing more embarrassing than to be caught staring at a stranger was to have him speak your name. Angie knew she must be blushing and there wasn't a darned thing she could do about it.

His deep voice had touched a vibrating response from somewhere inside of her. She shivered, confused by her inexplicable reaction to a total stranger.

"Yes?" She paused in front of him, forcing herself to meet his dark-eyed gaze without betraying the swirl of emotions his appearance had provoked.

"My name is Zeke Daniels. I work for Lorenzo De la Garza. He sent me to meet your plane since he couldn't arrange his schedule to come, himself."

She looked around the busy area. "You mean my uncle isn't here?" she asked, suddenly feeling like a lost child who had not been claimed by her parents.

"That's right." He looked past her at the man who pushed a load of luggage on a dolly. "Are all of these yours?"

She stiffened. "Yes." Her gaze met his without flinching. "Do you have a problem with the amount of luggage I chose to bring with me?"

He shrugged. "Not really." He took her elbow. "We can grab a cab to take us over to the private hangar where your uncle's plane is being serviced."

She heard his words with dismay. She had hoped that Tio would agree to spend the night in Mexico City and give her a chance to rest before traveling any farther.

She glanced out one of the windows along the concourse at the dark clouds that had rapidly filled the sky. "But there's a storm moving in. Surely you aren't planning to fly in this weather?"

Zeke dropped her arm and placed his hands on his hips. "Look, lady, I'm just trying to do what I was told, okay? I'm not overjoyed by the prospect of flying through turbulent weather myself, but it wouldn't be the first time, and I doubt it will be the last."

Angie nibbled on her bottom lip and looked around her. She was overwhelmingly tired, so tired she felt as though she could sleep for a month without stirring. She hadn't eaten much on the plane and was hungry. Her uncle's nonappearance had hit her hard. She knew he was not pleased with her, but to send a hired man to pick her up as though she were unwanted freight had pierced all her defenses.

Blindly she turned away from him and started down the concourse alone. Zeke caught up with her in three long strides and took her arm once again. She would have walked into an oncoming couple if he hadn't steered her deftly around them. Angie never noticed.

"Look, I can understand if you're afraid of flying in a small plane in bad weather. I'm sure Lorenzo would understand if we stay over. We'll go to one of the hotels, check in and have an early dinner. How does that sound?"

Another wave of dizziness swept over her and she stumbled. Zeke slid his arm around her waist in alarm. Her fair skin had turned a deathly white.

"Don't faint on me now, Princess," he muttered under his breath. He guided her to one of the entrance doors, pushed it open, and waved at the nearest taxi driver. While the driver and the baggage handler began transferring her luggage to the trunk of the taxi, Zeke eased Angie into the back seat.

She leaned her head against the seat and closed her eyes with a sigh.

As soon as the luggage was stowed, Zeke gave the driver the name of one of the luxury hotels, then crawled in and sat beside Angie.

She opened her eyes. "Sorry for the wobbly knees. I guess I'm just not used to traveling."

Zeke recognized the consequences of crossing several time zones in a short time. "Don't worry about it...happens to everybody. I should have thought about it myself and made plans to stay over. I'll call Lorenzo as soon as we get checked in.''

What had happened to the wall he had intended to place between them? Seeing her so wan and vulnerable had wiped out all of his careful planning. Frowning, he looked away from her and stared at the passing scenery.

The silence that filled the cab for long minutes was interrupted by Angie's asking, "Did you say your name is Zeke?''

He looked around. "That's right.''

She hadn't lifted her head from where it reclined against the seat. Her eyelids were puffy, making her look as though she had just woken up. Her sultry mouth drew his eyes, causing his body to react. Once again he looked away, this time clenching his jaw and reminding his body that *he* was the one in charge here and this woman was definitely off-limits.

His traitorous body ignored his lofty mental reprimands, and he found himself growing uncomfortable in his tight-fitting jeans.

"Are you a native of Mexico?''

He shifted restlessly. Still not looking at her, he replied, "No. I was born in South Texas.''

"Ah. That explains why you speak Spanish like a native.''

When he made no other response, she asked, "Have you worked for my uncle long?''

He shrugged. "A few weeks.''

"Did he hire you as his pilot?''

Since his piloting skills had been part of his résumé, he could only guess at that one. "Among other things,'' he said.

"I'm eager to get back to the hacienda. Even though I've been gone so long, the mountains overlooking Monterrey have always seemed like home to me. I dream about them at times, thinking I'm back there. Then I wake up and discover that I'm still in Spain. I never knew how painful homesickness can be."

"I wouldn't know."

"I don't suppose you have that problem, living so close to where you were born. Do you visit there often?"

"No."

She waited, but he didn't add anything more.

They drew up in front of the hotel at the same time the low-hanging clouds dropped an avalanche of water upon the city. The doorman, prepared, hurried over to the taxi with a large umbrella.

Zeke got out first, then offered his hand to Angela. Her fingers felt small and delicate in his hand. As soon as was reasonably polite, he drew away from her, ostensibly to oversee the transfer of luggage, but more importantly to experience the driving force of the cold rain on his overheated body.

By the time he entered the hotel, Angela was already at the registration desk. When he walked up she turned to him, obviously upset. "They don't have any vacancies. They have two separate conventions booked and all the rooms are spoken for." Even as she spoke, her eyes widened. "Oh, Zeke, you're soaked."

The water had worked its cure, leaving its uncomfortable aftermath of wet clothing. He ruefully plucked at the front of the cotton shirt that was now plastered to his chest, pushed his hair away from his

face and looked at the hotel employee behind the
desk. Reaching into his wallet, he pulled out a large-
denomination bill, palmed it and rested his hand on
the counter. Moving his hand slightly so the amount
of the bill showed between his thumb and his forefinger, he said, "As you can see—" he glanced down
at his clothes with resignation "—we really need a
place to stay for the night. Would you mind checking
again to see if you have *anything* available?"

Zeke wasn't too surprised a few minutes later when
the clerk returned to say he had found a cancellation
he had overlooked.

During their ride up in the elevator, Zeke tried to
think of where he could find a shop to buy some
clothes, since he hadn't brought any along on this trip.
The bellman bringing their luggage held the door for
them, then led them down a long hallway before pausing in front of one of the doors.

When the bellman stepped aside, Zeke followed
Angela into what looked to be a sitting room. Open
double doors revealed a large bedroom.

Zeke turned to the bellman. "I don't think the registration clerk understood that we need two rooms."

The bellman nodded. "Yes, sir. You're fortunate
that this suite has not been claimed. This sofa—" he
pointed "—makes out into a second bed. I'm afraid
it's the best we can do under the circumstances."

"I'll sleep in here if you'd like the bedroom," Angela said quietly.

"Don't be ridiculous. Of course you can have the
bedroom."

"There's another complete bath in here," the bellman said, opening a door off the sitting room. Then

he pushed the cart of luggage into the bedroom and began to unload it.

Zeke turned to Angie, his frustration mounting. "I'm sorry, Miss De la Garza, I—"

"Please, it isn't your fault. And De la Garza is too formal. My friends call me Angie." She smiled at him. "I hope that we will become friends, Zeke."

Feeling trapped by circumstances over which he had no control, Zeke tipped the bellman and watched as he left the room, closing the door quietly behind him.

"You really should get out of those wet clothes, don't you think?" she asked after a moment.

Zeke growled, "Great idea. Hope you have something in one of those suitcases for me to wear because I neglected to bring a change of clothes on this little jaunt."

Angie nodded. "Actually, I do, if you don't mind going a little informal."

"Don't be silly. I couldn't possibly wear anything of yours."

"I was given a terry robe for my birthday, my girlfriend thought 'one size fits all' meant just that. Unfortunately, the robe swallowed me. I brought it, thinking I would give it to Tio. I'm sure it would fit you."

Zeke sneezed. He faced the fact that he didn't have a great many choices at the moment. The rain continued to beat against the windowpane. He sure as hell didn't feel like going shopping while in his wet clothes and the thought of getting dry appealed to him immensely.

Angie went into the bedroom and began to sort through her various bags. Opening one, she made a sound of satisfaction and brought him a forest-green terry-cloth robe. He almost smiled at its size. It would come very close to fitting him, which meant she would be lost in it.

"Thanks," he muttered, taking the robe and going into the bathroom.

He pulled off his boots before peeling off his wet jeans and draped the jeans across the counter to dry. Then he removed his shirt and did the same thing. Even his underwear and socks were damp. After he took off his socks and slid off his shorts, he turned on the shower.

The warm water caressed his chilled skin and he groaned with pleasure. He blanked out his mind to any thought other than the pleasure of that moment. Only when the water began to cool did he readjust it, then he picked up the soap and lazily washed himself.

He wasn't sorry that they weren't flying back today. He hadn't been pleased with the weather forecast when he had landed earlier and turned the plane over to the service department of the privately owned hangar. Perhaps it was just as well Angela had pushed him to delay their departure.

Angela. The familiar smiling photograph flashed into his mind to be slowly superimposed by a newer image, a more sedate, formal image of Angie.

"My friends call me Angie," she had said. "I hope that we will become friends, Zeke."

With another groan he turned off the water and grabbed a towel, vigorously drying himself. Maybe it *was* better that they weren't flying in this weather, maybe she *did* need a good night's rest before seeing Lorenzo again, but damn! why did they have to share the same suite?

He needed some distance from her, at least for a
few hours. The last thing he needed was to be parad-
ing around in a bathrobe while she—

He didn't know what she would be doing, but he
soon found out. When he came out of the bathroom,
she was waiting for him in the sitting room, looking
a little anxious.

"I, uh, hope you don't mind, but I would much
prefer eating up here than having to go to a restaurant.
So I called room service. I ordered their special for
the evening, a seafood dish, for both of us. If you'd
rather have something else—"

"No, I don't care what I have."

"I, uh, also called Tio to tell him about the storm
and that I talked you into staying overnight. He
wanted to speak with you and I explained that you
were in the shower." She stopped and nibbled on her
bottom lip. "Then I had to explain about the lack of
space in the hotel at the moment."

Zeke leaned his shoulder against the doorjamb and
crossed his arms over his chest. "I bet he was delighted to hear about that."

She shook her head. "Not really. He wants you to
call him as soon as you're out of the shower."

"Somehow that doesn't surprise me."

"Our food should be here in another fifteen
minutes or so. I'd like to shower and change before
then."

"Don't let me stop you."

Her worried gaze met his. "I feel as though all of
this—" she waved her hands at the room, at the rain
beating at the windows "—is somehow my fault. Tio
sounded upset and I didn't know what more to say."

"Go get your shower and stop worrying about it.

You have no control over hotel conventions or the weather. Your uncle's just had a lot on his mind lately.''

''Sitting here, waiting for you to come out, I finally realized that my stubbornness has once again gotten me into trouble. I thought he would feel differently about my visit once I got here, but if anything, he sounds almost angry that I've inconvenienced him.''

Zeke straightened and moved over to where she sat on the edge of the couch. He leaned down and took her hand, pulling her up to stand beside him.

''Look, Angie. You're exhausted, that's all. When we get too tired, everything looks gloomy and nothing seems right. Don't let it color your judgment. I'm glad you ordered in.'' He glanced down at his robe. ''I'm certainly not dressed for a restaurant. Go ahead and take your shower. You'll feel better. Then we'll eat and you can get to bed early.''

She turned and walked out of the room and for a moment Zeke felt a strong need to wrap his arms around her and hold her for a long moment.

Instead, he picked up the phone and called his boss.

Two

"**W**hat the hell is going on?"

Zeke jerked the phone receiver away from his ear for a moment before responding to Lorenzo. "I was under the impression that Angie explained the circumstances to you."

"I want to know how you managed to arrange to spend the night in my niece's room, Daniels."

"I'm afraid I had nothing to do with the hotel accommodations. And I won't be spending the night in your niece's room, Lorenzo. There is a bedroom and a sitting room. In case Angie didn't mention it, the sofa in the sitting room makes out into a bed. I'm sure I'll be quite comfortable."

"I don't give a damn about your comfort. What I care about is my niece. What I care about is her reputation. Now why didn't you ignore her when she asked to stay overnight and get the hell back here?"

Once again Zeke stared out the window. The wind and the rain were still very much in evidence. "Look, Lorenzo, the forecast for this afternoon and evening was for heavy thunderstorms, which is the biggest reason I agreed to stay overnight when she suggested it. Angie didn't like the idea of flying in heavy weather. I saw no reason not to accommodate her. I didn't see any emergency about getting her home today under these circumstances. The storm should be gone by morning. The weather bureau is predicting clear skies and sunny weather for tomorrow. There was no need to take unnecessary risks."

"I don't like it."

"You don't like what?"

"Your staying there together."

Zeke sighed. "All right. I'll find another hotel to stay in. Will that make you feel better?"

"Considerably."

"Anything else?"

"Yes. We found an intruder on the grounds today. That new surveillance equipment you suggested paid off. We wouldn't have known he got over the wall, otherwise."

"Glad to be of service. Did you find out what he was doing there?"

"Not yet, but I intend to. When do you expect to get here tomorrow?"

"We should be there by noon. If you like, I'll deal with the man and see what I can find out for you."

"What I want to know is who's behind this rash of break-ins and other problems. I'm sick to death of living under siege against an enemy I can't identify."

"I'm working on that. If you had sent someone else

to pick up your niece, I would still be there working on it.''

"I know, I know. But my other pilot doesn't have your experience. I wanted to know that Angela was safe. I thought you were the man for the job.''

"I'm trying to be, believe me.''

"Okay, okay. Maybe I'm just being jumpy. I wish to hell Angela could have picked another time to come.''

"I'm aware of that. You've voiced your concern on many occasions.''

"Tell her I'm sorry I yelled at her.''

Zeke grinned. "I'm sure that will make her feel much better.''

"I've been under a strain.''

"I'll tell her.''

"No! Don't tell her about the strain. She doesn't need to know anything about what's been going on. Just apologize for me for being in a temper.''

"I'll do that,'' Zeke responded dryly.

"I'll see you tomorrow,'' Lorenzo said, and hung up.

Zeke hung up the phone, shaking his head. Then he dialed housekeeping and asked them to send someone to pick up his clothes. He had to have them dry before he could go looking for another place to stay.

There was a tap on the door and a voice announced, "Room service.'' He tightened the sash of his robe and went over to the door. After viewing the hall through the security opening, Zeke opened the door and waved the hotel employee inside.

The serving cart was set for two people, and the setting included a perfectly formed red rosebud in a cut crystal vase. Zeke signed the charge ticket for the meal, tipped the waiter and closed the door behind him.

Everything was ready, even to a carafe of coffee. Silently thanking Angie for her thoughtfulness, he poured a cup of coffee and sat on the sofa to wait for her.

When she walked through the door and saw him, she blushed. "I hope you don't mind, but I, uh—well, I didn't really want to get dressed again." She glanced down at the silk pajamas and matching robe. "I thought I'd get ready for bed."

Zeke stood, thankful for the concealing folds of his robe. Damn, but she looked adorable standing there with her hair loose around her shoulders. Now she looked like the photograph that haunted his dreams. "You should always wear your hair down like that," he heard himself saying, appalled by his lack of discretion.

Her blush deepened and he could have kicked himself for causing her to be more uncomfortable with their circumstances. He motioned to the table.

"Don't worry about your appearance. Let's eat so that you can get some rest." He pulled out a chair and motioned for her to sit down. There was a knock at the door.

"I'll be right back," he said, striding across the room.

"But who—"

After making sure who was there, he opened the door to a woman who explained she was from housekeeping. He stepped into the bathroom, gathered up his wet clothes, came out and handed them to her with a tip. "Thank you for being so prompt. I'd like to have these back as soon as possible."

She bobbed her head and left.

Zeke returned to the table.

Angie watched him as he sat down and picked up his fork. "I wonder what that woman thought of us in our robes this early in the evening."

Zeke grinned. "Probably thinks we're honeymooners." He almost laughed at her deepened color as she picked up her salad fork, studying it intently, as though fascinated by the pattern.

After a moment, he asked, "Do you really care what she thinks?"

Angie glanced up and became aware of him watching her. "Tio was upset about our sharing a room," she said.

"Yeah. He told me. As soon as my clothes come back I'm going to look for a room in another hotel."

"But there's no need for you to do that!" As though realizing that he might misinterpret her meaning, she explained, "I mean, there's plenty of room here, if you don't mind sleeping on the sofa. Tio is being ridiculous." She took a bite of her salad.

"Is he?"

She picked up her glass and took a sip of water. "Well, of course. There's no reason to think—" She seemed to bog down in that line of reasoning.

"I take it you trust me not to attack you sometime during the night."

"How silly! Why would you do something like that?"

He thought about her comment while he polished off his salad. After retrieving their entrées from the warming oven of the serving cart, he asked, "How old did you say you are?"

Startled, she replied, "I haven't said. Why do you ask?"

"Either you've lived an extremely sheltered life and know absolutely nothing about men," he drawled, "or—" He took a bite of his dinner, chewed it very carefully, swallowed, then continued "—you have absolutely no idea how desirable you are."

She dropped her fork onto her plate and placed her hands in her lap. "You're making fun of me."

That was the last reaction he expected.

"Not at all. Actually, I'm paying you a rather crude compliment. But at least it's sincere." He studied her while he continued to eat. Hesitantly she resumed eating, as well.

"Have you known many men while you were growing up?" Now he really was curious about her.

She shook her head. "Not really, other than relatives, of course. I've always attended private girls' schools. I teach in a coeducational school, and there are a few male teachers, but I don't see them outside of school functions."

"You don't date?"

She shook her head.

"Why not?"

"Because not many have asked me. Those that have I wasn't interested in. Besides, my family frowned on my going out with a man alone."

"You're kidding. Do they still have chaperons?"

"Sometimes. But it isn't that. I have always planned to come back to Mexico. I knew that if I were to get involved with someone living in Spain there was a good chance I would never return home."

"So you've led a very sheltered life and have no idea just how beautiful you are."

Her cheeks lit up like a neon sign.

"Hey, I didn't mean to embarrass you. Really. Think of me as another uncle, one who's too outspoken. Ignore me."

She smiled, but the smile didn't hide her fatigue and he felt like a heel for baiting her.

"If you're through eating, why don't you go to bed?"

"It wouldn't be very polite of me to——"

"Forget polite. You can be as polite to me as you wish tomorrow. I'll wait here for my clothes, then I'll slip out. I'll give you a call in the morning in time to get an early start. How's that sound?"

They both stood, then she held out her hand to him. When he took it, she said, "You've been very kind to me, Zeke. I know I've been a nuisance. Thank you for your patience."

"Hey, the last thing I am is a kind person. You must be more tired than I thought." He rubbed his thumb over the back of her hand, feeling the delicate bones. Without thought, he brought her hand up to his mouth, turned it and placed a kiss in her palm. "Pleasant dreams, Princess," he murmured, releasing her hand.

She stood there staring at him, her eyes wide. This close he could see the different shades of green in their depths. He also saw the dark smudges of fatigue beneath her eyes.

Angie turned and went into the bedroom, closing the double doors behind her. He pushed the serving cart into the hallway, then walked over to the window and looked out. The rain appeared to be lessening, which was a good sign. Hopefully by tomorrow they would have clear skies.

He glanced over at the sofa. He might as well stretch out and get comfortable, maybe take a nap, while he was waiting for his clothes. Then, like an obedient employee, he'd go find himself a room for the night.

Angie crawled into bed, sighing with relief to be able to lie down after countless hours of travel. She snuggled into her pillow, anticipating oblivion for the next few hours.

Instead, her mind raced—playing back the last few hours, leaping ahead to her meeting with Tio, flashing images of Zeke Daniels.

Once again she experienced her disappointment that Tio hadn't met her plane. There was so much she wanted to tell him in person. Now she would have to wait another day before she found out his reaction to her plans. She'd allowed him to believe she was coming to visit when she fully intended to stay. Mexico was her home. She had spent years getting her education so that she could return to Mexico. Her dream was to start a preschool in one of the mountain villages near Tio's place.

She'd been afraid to tell him before because he seemed to discourage any discussion of her returning home. Now that she was here, she intended to show him that she had overcome her impulsive nature and could behave as a responsible adult.

Her mind slowed and her thoughts drifted. An image of Zeke Daniels appeared. She was curious about him, more curious than she'd ever been about a man before. He had an embarrassingly strong effect on her, one she didn't understand. Being around him made her blood race and caused her to stammer in confusion. Never before had she been so aware of a man.

What was it about him that so unnerved her?

He was so self-assured, even in a borrowed bath-robe. He made her aware of her own femininity, of the differences between his strong, muscular strength and her own softness.

He intrigued her. She wanted to get to know him better. Since he worked for Tio, she shouldn't have much difficulty.

She sighed, drifting into sleep, a smile on her face.

Hours later Zeke came awake with a start. The lamp cast a dim glow in the room. He sat up, glancing at his watch. It was after two o'clock in the morning.

He went to the door and checked the hallway. The room service cart was gone, but there was no sign of his clothes. He should have been more specific about when he needed them, but he had thought "as soon as possible" was clear enough.

He had little option other than to stay there. He certainly couldn't go anywhere in a bathrobe. He returned to the sofa and, this time, pulled out the bed and turned back the sheets. After searching for a pillow, he found one in the closet, then, discarding his robe, crawled into bed with a sigh. He turned out the light and closed his eyes, willing himself to sleep once more.

Sometime later a soft tap on the door awakened him. The room lay in the quiet early light of daybreak. Zeke pulled on the robe and went to the door.

"Who is it?"

"Laundry."

He peeked through the door, recognized his freshly laundered clothes on a hanger and opened the door.

"We also have a complimentary toiletry kit in case you needed one," the young man said.

"Thanks." Zeke signed for the delivery, pleased to spot a razor, comb and toothbrush in the small bag.

He headed for the bathroom, ready to get on with the day.

Once dressed, Zeke went over to the bedroom door and rapped. After a lengthy pause during which there was no sound, he eased open the door and peeked inside.

Angie lay sprawled across the bed on her stomach, her face almost obscured by a pillow. One knee was bent, causing the thin pajama material to snugly mold the curve of her bottom. The pajama top had ridden up, exposing a fair amount of her bare back. Her hair lay in a tangle of curls across the pillow, spilling down across her shoulders.

An unexpected jolt of sharp desire shot through him, causing his body to immediately respond to the enticing picture she made.

Zeke stepped back and hastily closed the door. Opening that door had not been one of his better ideas. He should have known she was still asleep. He should have known—never mind. He would call her from downstairs in accordance with the original plan. As far as she knew he had not spent the night there.

He returned the sofa to its original state, folded the bathrobe and left it lying on the arm of one of the chairs. Then he slipped silently out of the room.

Angie knew there was something she needed to do, something that kept tugging at her, but she was too relaxed and comfortable to move. If whoever or what-ever it was would just go away she would continue to drift and to dream…. But the noise continued until she surfaced enough from her deep sleep to recognize the annoying sound was the telephone busily ringing only a few feet from her head.

Groaning, she rolled over and groped for the noisy instrument. ''H'lo?'' she mumbled.

A deep voice growled seductively into her ear. ''C'mon, sleepyhead. It's time to rise and shine. I'll meet you downstairs for breakfast in half an hour.''

The caller hung up before she could manage a reply.

Still more than half-asleep, she fumbled with the receiver until she could replace it on its base. With her eyes still closed, she thought about what she had just heard.

Breakfast. Half hour. Rise and shine.

She forced one eye open and stared at the bedside clock. It lacked a couple of minutes to seven o'clock. How could that be when she had gone to bed only a few minutes ago? She reluctantly sat up and stared around her. The room was unfamiliar and she felt as though she had a severe hangover. Where was she and what had she been doing?

Bits and pieces of the previous day ran across her mind like a silent movie. She remembered a pair of piercing dark eyes staring at her…her disappointment that Tio hadn't been at the airport to meet her…a hauntingly deep voice suggesting—

Suggesting breakfast! Oh, dear. Zeke would be downstairs waiting on her if she didn't hurry. Tossing the covers to the side, she climbed out of bed and hurried to the bathroom.

Her dreams had been a jumble of impressions, but she distinctly remembered seeing those eyes staring at her and feeling the tingling kiss he had placed in her palm.

She would see him in a half hour. Angie realized her heart was racing with a mixture of agitation and anticipation at being in Zeke's company once again.

She saw him as soon as she stepped off the elevators, her eyes drawn inexorably toward his tall, lean figure. She didn't understand what it was about him that drew the eye, but she noticed that she wasn't the only one who noticed the man leaning against one of the pillars in the lobby with his arms folded across his chest.

"Good morning," she said, wishing she didn't sound quite so breathless. "You're looking well rested this morning. Did you have any trouble finding a place to sleep?"

His lopsided grin appeared. "Not at all," he answered in complete honesty. "How about you? Did you sleep all right?" He took her by the elbow and guided her into the coffee shop.

"I must have. I can't believe I slept for almost twelve hours!"

She looked dazzling in the morning sunlight. Zeke was having trouble concentrating on what she was saying. He had known as soon as she stepped off the elevator that he was in a heap of trouble.

Her colorful silk blouse and tailored skirt were probably not considered provocative attire, but they set off the gentle curves that he had dreamed about most of the night. Like it or not, she was a distraction that he was having difficulty overcoming, and his life depended on his not becoming distracted.

As soon as the waiter took their order, Zeke

searched for a neutral topic. "I guess you're looking
forward to getting home today."

"Yes, but I might as well admit that I'm not looking forward to the flight." She sighed. "Small planes
have always frightened me."

He settled back in his chair and said, "Or is it the
pilot you don't trust?"

Her eyes widened. "Oh, no! I'm sure you're very
competent or my uncle would never have hired you."

"Well, I'll try to make the flight as pleasant for
you as possible."

Zeke was thankful when their breakfast arrived and
he didn't have to concern himself with further conversation. They only had a few more hours together.
He could handle that with no problem.

Probably by the time they reached Monterrey he
would be eager to be rid of the woman. Being around
her these extra hours would no doubt wipe out all
those fantasies he'd created, using her image.

He could only hope.

Three

Angie sat beside Zeke in the cockpit of her uncle's plane, listening and watching as he spoke to the control tower through his headset while they waited for their signal to take off.

Now that they were ready to take off the butterflies that had taken up permanent residence in her stomach had multiplied and were busy giving flying instructions to their many young. Was their feverish activity due to her fear of flying in a small plane, her nervousness about facing her uncle, or her awareness of Zeke sitting so closely beside her she could easily rest her hand on his muscled thigh?

Perhaps her butterflies were the result of all three conditions.

Zeke motioned for her to put on the headset lying in front of her. As soon as she had it on, she heard the crackling of static and a disembodied voice giving

them clearance. Zeke taxied the plane to the end of
the runway, saying, "It will be easier to communicate
if you'll keep the headset on." She nodded, wondering what he thought they would be communicating
about.

She thought she had masked her nervousness. Had
he thought she would panic? If so, being tuned in to
control tower conversation was not going to help her
in the slightest.

The noise all around her intensified and the plane
started quivering like a racehorse eager to hear the
opening gun. At an incomprehensible—to Angie—
signal over the headphones, Zeke gave the plane its
head and it leaped forward, moving down the runway
at an ever-increasing speed.

Angie had never ridden in the cockpit of a plane
before. Seeing the ground rush toward her faster and
faster made her catch her breath and forget to breathe.
As the runway quickly shortened, she closed her eyes,
feverishly praying beneath her breath that the plane
would lift off the ground in time.

She wasn't certain how much time passed before
Zeke said, "You can open your eyes now," in a dry
voice.

Reluctantly she forced her eyes open, feeling hu-
miliated by her cowardice. She braced herself for his
open derision but discovered, when she looked his
way, that he was busy comparing the terrain against
an open map in front of him.

"We should have a smooth flight," he went on, as
though continuing a conversation they had been having. "The early morning good weather looks to be
holding. The only bumpy areas are over the mountains, and that can't be helped."

"What do you mean?"

"The air drafts over the mountains are inconsistent at the altitude we're flying. I'll try to give you some warning before we're affected."

She glanced out and down, her eyes widening at the sight. "Why, it's beautiful from here."

"Yes, it is."

"I had no idea. There's a much better view in a smaller plane."

He gave a lopsided smile without looking at her. "That has its good points, as well as its bad."

"I'm sorry for being so frightened. It really isn't scary at all."

"Hey, lady. You don't owe me any apologies. Sometimes I forget what it's like to fly when you're not accustomed to it."

"How long have you been flying?"

"More years than I can remember."

"Do you enjoy it?"

"Never gave the idea much thought. Flying gets me where I need to go faster than any other method I've found."

"How did you learn?"

Zeke realized that she still wasn't over her nervousness. He hadn't planned to give her the story of his life. Then again, maybe he could lull her to sleep with some of the dull details.

"The U.S. government taught me. I was in the air force."

"Oh. When was that?"

"I joined as soon as I graduated from college. Not one of my wiser moves, but it seemed the thing to do at the time."

"Did you stay in the air force long?"

"Six years. Then I found out I could make more money using my skills in civilian life."

"Doing what?"

"I joined an outfit that worked mostly overseas. I spent the next several years learning just how green I was."

She was quiet for a few moments before she asked, "What did your family think about your working so far away?"

"My mother died my senior year at college. My dad remarried and ended up raising his new wife's three children. He didn't have much time to be concerned about me."

"Do you see them very often?"

"No. I doubt I'd recognize any of the children if I were to run into them."

"That's sad."

"What's sad about it?"

"That you aren't close to your family. I've missed having parents and brothers and sisters. Tio has been wonderful to me and I would never hurt his feelings by complaining, but a child alone can become very lonely."

His gaze routinely checked the instrument panel, paused, then swept back to one of the gauges. The oil pressure was dropping. He didn't like the looks of that.

"Tio was so good to me. When I was smaller he used to take me with him on his business trips. We would inspect factories, discuss wool grading, talk to manufacturers. He never made me feel that I was in his way, or that he was sorry he brought me along with him. He—"

"Angie, I don't mean to interrupt, but—"

"What is it? What's wrong?" There was some-thing strange in his voice...carefully neutral, as though...

"I think we're going to have to make a stop before we get to your uncle's place."

She stared out at the landscape. They were over rolling hills that were rapidly becoming a mountain range.

"Where? There's no airport around, is there?"

He reached for the radio and began to give their call letters, asking for assistance.

There was no response.

He muttered something beneath his breath that she felt was just as well she hadn't heard.

She lightly touched his arm and felt the tension there. "What's wrong? Are we out of gasoline?"

"Just as bad. It looks as though we're losing oil...and fast. I'm going to have to put her down. Maybe I'll spot a road. Help me look, would you?"

During the next tense moments, the silence seemed to grow and expand. All Angie could hear was the reassuringly steady sound of the single engine dron-ing away.

"There!" She pointed off to her side of the plane to a brown snakelike path on the side of a mountain. "Do you see it?"

He nodded and banked the plane, decreasing their altitude as he headed in the new direction.

"It's awfully twisty, isn't it?" she breathed.

"Honey, at this point we don't have much choice. Just hang on. I promise I'll get you down in one piece. I never make a promise I can't keep, okay? You're going to be just fine."

For some reason that she didn't understand, her ear-

lier nervousness disappeared. Angie had no way of
knowing whether the stranger beside her could keep
his promise to her, but she discovered that she trusted
him. If there was a way to land safely, this man would
accomplish it.

She watched the hills and heavily wooded area
rushing toward them as they dropped their speed and
altitude. Her eerie calm continued to hold. She
watched as though she were an observer to the action
rather than a participant, as though the outcome of
their forced landing did not truly affect her.

As the land continued to expand in an upwardly
growing movement, she could pick out details—she
saw individual trees instead of a blur of green
color…the road, still winding, seemed to widen and
grow in width and length…boulders took three-
dimensional shape.

Angie felt it was important for her to continue to
face what was happening to them. She didn't want to
close her eyes and wait for whatever was going to
happen to her…to them…when they attempted a
landing.

Zeke knew what he needed for a runway length to
land. He also knew the wing clearance that was man-
datory if they were to survive the next few minutes.
His eyes quickly scanned the area below him, intent
on finding what he needed in the short time he had
left. His choices were limited.

He had been in tight places before, but he'd never
had a plane go out on him before. He was too careful,
going over each one carefully. There had been no
warning on the flight south yesterday. There had been
nothing in the preflight check earlier to point to a
problem with the oil line.

None of that mattered now. What he had to do was to get them down on the ground with as little damage as possible to either the plane or to them.

The plane began to sputter and he knew his options were gone. "Lean down! Put your face on your knees," he shouted without looking at the woman beside him. He didn't have time to make sure she had followed his instructions as he dropped the flaps and pushed the stick forward.

They hit hard...which wasn't surprising considering the rough texture of the road. The plane bucked like an untamed horse after its first taste of a bridle. Grimly Zeke hung on, muttering, not sure if he was praying or cursing.

He saw a tree close to the road and sharply cut the wheel, hoping to miss it. The sudden swerve of the tires caught a rut, causing the plane to tilt slightly.

He continued to fight for control, but it was too late. The tip of the wing came into contact with something, causing the plane to canter and the cockpit to spin.

The last he remembered was cutting off the engine before the screen of trees seemed to rise up in front of him, covering him in darkness.

Angela became aware of how quiet it was after the engine stopped and they had quit moving. Shakily she raised her head and looked around.

They were at a sharp angle, facing a thick line of trees a few feet in front of them. She turned and looked at Zeke, who was slumped over the wheel.

Tentatively she touched his shoulder. "Zeke? Are you all right?"

His lack of response frightened her more than any-

thing that had happened. Didn't they need to get out
of the plane? Wasn't there a fear of fuel leakage and
possible fire whenever a plane crashed?

"Zeke?"

She released her breath when he groaned and attempted to straighten. He let out a hissing sound, then
slowly forced himself upright in the seat. Carefully
he turned his head and looked at her. Blood ran from
a cut on his forehead. Awkwardly he lifted his right
hand and touched the wound on the left side of his
face.

"You okay?" he asked, a muscle in his jaw jump-
ing with tension. He had his teeth clenched.

She nodded. "But you aren't. You're bleeding!"
she said, her voice shaking.

He nodded. "Can you reach the first aid box behind
you? There should be some pads in there."

She fumbled with the straps that had held her so
securely in place, then found the box. Opening it, she
removed some pads and bandages, which she tore free
of their wrappings. She leaned over and held the pad
against his head.

That's when she saw his shoulder. There was something wrong, but she couldn't tell exactly what.
"What's wrong with your shoulder?"

"I think it's dislocated, but I'm not sure. I just
know it hurts like the very devil." He shifted in an
attempt to take the weight off his left arm, which had
been thrown against the side of the plane when they
hit.

Angie had to brace herself to keep from toppling
over on him. After hurriedly tying a strip of gauze
around Zeke's head to keep the pad in place, she un-
did the straps around him and with his help eased him

out of the seat. Because the left wing was crumpled and the door jammed, they had to crawl out of the plane at an upward angle.

Once on the ground, Zeke surveyed the damage. The left wing was finished and the wheel on that side had been broken off. Outside of that, the fuselage and the tail structure appeared intact.

Zeke checked the gas tank, relieved not to find a rupture there. He moved toward Angie, keeping a tight grip on his left arm in an effort to keep the weight from causing the throbbing pain to increase to fiery flames of intense agony. He stopped in front of her while she eyed him uncertainly.

"Will you help me get my shirt off? If we can rig a sling for my arm, I won't need to use my other arm for support."

He fumbled with the buttons until she nudged his hand aside and quickly unfastened the shirt. He held out his good arm. She tugged on the sleeve until he could slip his arm out, then she went up on her toes to slide it off his shoulders. In doing so, she found her nose almost buried in his warm chest.

Angie had never been so close to a shirtless man before. She was intensely aware of the hard planes, as well as the thick mat of curls that covered the broad expanse.

She took a step back, drew an unsteady breath and eased the shirt over his injured shoulder and arm, aware of the hiss of pain that escaped from his clenched teeth.

"I'm sorry," she whispered contritely. Never had Angie felt so inadequate in a situation. Zeke was the one injured and he was having to tell her what to do. She folded the shirt and slipped it around his arm. "If you can lean down toward me, I'll tie it behind your back."

Now that his adrenaline level had dropped a little, Zeke could feel the excruciating pain in his shoulder even more. His head burned where he'd received the cut. He leaned against the wing of the plane and allowed Angie to tie his shirt for him. He hoped the bone in his shoulder wasn't broken. He had enough problems without that at the moment.

"There. That should hold," he heard her say.

Zeke opened his eyes and stared into a pair of worried green ones only inches away. "Thanks."

"I'm sure it hurts quite dreadfully."

He sighed. "Yeah, well, you know how us macho types are…we can't admit to feeling minor pain."

She ignored his attempt at humor. "I've got something for pain in my purse, if you think it will help. I need it every month when I— That is, I'm sure it would help you just as much, if you'd like to try some."

He closed his eyes for a brief moment, considering. When he opened them, he said, "Sounds good to me, even if it shoots my image all to hell."

She found her purse and the small vial inside, then returned to the plane for the thermos that Zeke had filled with water before they left Mexico City. After carefully pouring the clear liquid into the lid, she placed two tablets in his mouth and held the container for him.

She shivered at the touch of his breath on her fingers, feeling foolish at her reaction. Why this man should make her feel so nervous, she wasn't certain. Why he affected her heart and breathing rate whenever she got this close to him was an even bigger mystery.

He took the thermos lid from her quivering fingers and drained the water from it. "Thanks." He looked at the road that turned out of sight only a few yards ahead of them. "At least we made it down in one piece."

"Yes. You did a magnificent job of landing safely."

He started toward the front of the aircraft. "I've got to see what happened to our oil pressure."

"Do you think you should be moving around just yet? Maybe if you rest for a while—"

Zeke cut his eyes around at her from where he stood by the cowl of the engine. "I'll let you know if I need any more help, okay?"

Angie nodded, silenced by his look more than his words. She watched as he lifted the cowl and began to check out the mysterious intricacies of the engine.

Glancing around them, she saw nothing but trees, boulders and the deserted road. "If there were any people nearby they would surely have heard us come down," she said into the silence.

"That's true enough," he replied without looking up from what he was doing. After several more minutes of silence he let out a muffled oath, drawing her attention back to him.

"What's wrong?"

"Someone cut through the oil line."

A tiny wisp of fear wended its way through her stomach. Walking over to where he stood, she paused to clear her throat before asking, "Are you sure?"

He straightened and looked around at her. "I'm sure. Whoever did it had the cut line spliced so that only after the oil got hot would the splice melt away, letting the oil leak out.''

He'd gotten some oil on his hand and on one of his bare shoulders. Her gaze kept returning to his chest. She forced herself to look away, staring at the trees and the sharp incline of the road.

"What are we going to do?"

He looked around the deserted area, as well. "Good question."

"Who would want to cause us engine problems?"

"Another good question. I have a hunch they wanted to cause more than engine problems. We could have easily crashed once the oil was gone and the engine overheated.''

The wisp of fear seemed to grow and wrap around her. She shivered, hugging her elbows. In an attempt to lighten the situation, she asked, "Do you by any chance have an enemy or two you neglected to mention?''

He eyed her warily. "Maybe. Maybe not. Maybe it was someone who didn't want *you* to reach home.''

When he saw the look on her face, he wished he hadn't been so quick to respond to her teasing. However, the facts were obvious. Somebody had decided to get rid of one—or both—of them. Whoever it was had somehow managed to breach the hangar security where he had left the plane the night before. Or maybe it was one of the employees there. Had they been bribed?

Who would want to have him—or Angie—killed?

Was it possible someone had discovered what he was doing in Mexico and had decided to use this opportunity to silence him?

Zeke carefully wiped his fingers on an oil rag,

wincing at the movement of his arm, then walked over to where Angela stood in the middle of the road.

He could feel the beads of perspiration trickle down his back from the heat of the overhead sun. He also knew that once the sun set the air would cool rapidly.

He looked up and down the deserted roadway. "Well, whoever they are, they're going to be powerfully disappointed, aren't they?" He ducked under the wing and stepped up so that he could crawl into the cockpit. He discovered a couple of flying jackets, a towel and more first aid supplies.

He gathered up the flight maps and other items, stuffing them into a small duffel bag, then got out of the plane.

"Did you happen to notice any villages or settlements earlier?" he asked, unfolding one of the maps.

"No."

"Neither did I, although I wasn't concentrating on anything but a landing strip at the time." He studied the topographical map for long, silent minutes. He could see why his request for assistance had gone unanswered. There was very little in the way of civilization along this stretch of the mountains. They were about halfway between Mexico City and Monterrey.

The question now was, what would be the best direction for them to take in order to find help quickly? It was anybody's guess.

He glanced around at the woman standing there watching him. She had regained some color in her face, probably due to the heat. Her hair had come out of its neat coil. Feathery wisps hung around her ears and neck and across her forehead.

She wasn't dressed for wilderness survival, there

was no doubt about that. In her neatly tailored blouse and skirt, she looked totally out of place standing on that dusty and deserted road.

From all indications, they weren't going to get any immediate help from nearby residents. That didn't leave them with very many options. "This road must lead somewhere," he said, wiping a trickle of perspiration from his cheek. He glanced down at the duffel bag at his feet. "I'm going to go look for some help, maybe a ride into the closest town, something." He turned to her. "Do you want to wait with the plane or come with me?"

She looked up and down the road, looked at the plane, then finally met his gaze. "Are you going to leave the plane sitting here blocking the road?"

His head was pounding, the bright sunlight hurt his eyes, and the heat was making him feel nauseous. At the moment he didn't really care what happened to the damned plane.

"Are you afraid we're going to cause a traffic jam?"

She didn't say anything to that, but she felt uncomfortable with the idea of abandoning the plane. However, she liked the idea of staying there alone even less. She glanced down at her clothes, thankful for her low-heeled shoes.

She wasn't sure what she should do. Shouldn't one of them stay with the plane in case they were spotted from the air? But if Zeke was determined to go looking for help, did she dare allow him to go alone?

He could be more seriously injured than he was letting on. What if he barely got out of sight before he passed out? She would be sitting there alone, waiting for help that would never come, while he would be unconscious, a prey to whatever wild animals might live in these mountains.

She shivered at the thought. Why did she have to have such a vivid imagination?

"I'll go with you," she said. "Do you have any idea how long it will take to find someone?"

"In the best of all possible worlds, we'll find a Texaco station around the next bend, but somehow I don't think that's going to happen." He motioned to the plane. "Do you want anything out of your luggage before we go? I can't guarantee that whatever you leave will be here when we return, although I intend to lock it."

She crawled into the plane and opened her bags, staring into them. She was thankful she'd carried a large handbag. At least she could put her smaller necessities in there.

Once she was out of the plane with her clothes, she added them to the items in the duffel bag. Zeke locked the plane and said, "I think we'll head in that direction." He pointed toward the mountains. "Since we didn't see anything as we were flying over, we can only hope there's something up ahead." They started down the road.

Angie didn't give much thought on what was up ahead of them. She was too concerned about Zeke. With his head bandaged and his arm in a sling, he looked like a wounded warrior walking beside her. She tried to keep her concern from him but noticed that he made no effort to move faster than the pace she set.

By the time the sun began to set several hours later, she was hard-pressed not to panic. They hadn't seen a soul, nor had there been any traces of people living nearby.

The side of Zeke's face was swollen and discolored and he was holding his body stiff, as though every jolting step shot through him with agonizing regularity.

They were going to have to find a place to spend the night before the light was gone. She kept glancing at Zeke. He hadn't said anything for more than an hour. She had offered to carry the small duffel bag shortly after they started walking, but he had refused and she hadn't pushed the issue.

Her eyes searched the horizon as she had been doing repeatedly for hours. Only this time she saw a wisp of smoke in the distance.

Four

"Zeke! Look over there!"

The heat and the continued jarring of his shoulder with every step he took had done nothing to improve Zeke's pain these past several hours. He had been forcing himself to keep moving, concentrating on placing first one foot, then the other, in front of him.

Left, right, left, right. Reminded him of the military, always marching somewhere, always—

Angie tugged on his arm, breaking his concentration.

"There's smoke coming from the other side of that hill. Perhaps there's a settlement over there."

Zeke stared in the direction she was pointing, forcing his eyes to focus. After a moment he saw smoke slowly rising above the tops of the trees.

He stopped and absently rubbed his head.

"Is your head bothering you?"

"A little. That and my shoulder. The pain certainly hasn't gone away."

"Do you want to take another one of my pain relievers?"

He was tempted, definitely tempted. Then he looked around them, surprised to see how far the sun had moved along its arc in the sky. Glancing back at the smoke, he said, "Let's check out the smoke. Maybe we can find a phone or a car or something. I'm afraid if I take anything for pain now, I'll fall asleep."

Zeke led the way through the trees, heading directly for the crest of the hill. By the time they reached the top, they were both breathing hard.

They saw a primitive log cabin nestled in a small clearing below them. The smoke was drifting upward from a stone chimney.

"Well, at least we found a place where we can stay," Angie pointed out, trying to find something positive to say. "And we know someone's there." She glanced up at Zeke, worried about his lack of color. "You need to rest. Let's go let them know we're here."

They were lucky to have spotted anyone living in these mountains, Zeke decided, concentrating on taking each step. Those who had chosen to live among the mountains were reclusive by nature and wouldn't appreciate being disturbed by outsiders. He would have to make them understand about the plane... make them understand...what was happening to the light? The sun was going down too quickly. They were running out of light. Thank God, they were almost at the cabin....

Zeke stumbled and, instead of catching himself,

slid to the ground in a boneless heap. Angie grabbed his uninjured arm but couldn't keep him from going down.

"Zeke!"

Angie looked around, wondering what to do. He was too heavy for her to move. Turning toward the cabin, she trotted up to the door and knocked. When no one answered, she knocked again, saying, "Please, can you help us? Our plane went down and the pilot is injured. Please. Won't you help us?"

After agonizing minutes that seemed to stretch into hours, the door slowly swung inward. An elderly woman stood there, looking uneasy.

"Oh, thank you," Angie said as soon as the door opened. "Is there someone who could help me move him inside?" She motioned to where Zeke lay, unconscious. "We've been walking for several hours and he's been in considerable pain." She glanced back at Zeke. "I don't know what to do for him."

The woman stepped out of the cabin with dignified grace. "I'm alone here, but I will see what I can do." She quickly headed toward Zeke. "What are his injuries?"

Angie kept up with the woman's rapid pace. "I think his shoulder is the worst, plus he has a cut on his head."

"How long ago did this happen?"

"Sometime this morning. I don't know how long that's been."

They reached Zeke and knelt beside him. The woman eased the head bandage off and looked at the wound, then lightly touched his shoulder. He moaned without regaining consciousness.

"His shoulder is dislocated. We mustn't leave it

like this. The longer the shoulder is out, the more difficulty he will have.'' She motioned to Angie. ''Come. You must help me.''

Angie had been watching the woman's competent movements with a sense of bewilderment. ''How do you know what to do?'' she asked.

The woman glanced up. ''I was a nurse for many years in a hospital near the coast. I'm too old to work, but I haven't lost the knowledge of what to do.'' She gave Angie instructions on how to hold him down while she worked with the shoulder. ''It is better to do this while he is unconscious, because of the pain, you see.''

Angie braced herself against Zeke, not wanting to see him suffer but understanding the need for what this woman was preparing to do.

The woman made an abrupt move, causing Zeke to jerk and cry out, then his head lolled to the side and the woman nodded, obviously satisfied. ''There. Luckily the shoulder went back into place without much trouble.''

Angie thought her definition of trouble might not be the same as Zeke's.

''We need to get him inside and he's much too heavy for us to carry,'' the woman said. She began to speak to him, rubbing his hands, while Angie watched in amazement.

When Zeke eventually opened his eyes Angie wanted to hug him in relief.

''Zeke? How are you feeling?''

He stared up at her in bewilderment. Then his gaze slowly circled the clearing until it rested on the woman who knelt beside him. She smiled, patting his hand.

"Good evening, Zeke. Do you think you can stand long enough for us to get you inside?"

He blinked. "Who are you?"

"Maria Cerventes. You and your friend found my place while seeking help. I am pleased to offer what I can, but you will need to help. Do you understand?"

He closed his eyes for a moment, then opened them and nodded. The two women helped him to sit up. He groaned, clutching his shoulder.

"Yes, it will be sore for a few days, but the worst is over, I think. We'll clean up that scalp wound once we get you inside. It may need a few stitches."

Zeke looked at Angie. "How did you find someone like her?" he asked.

She grinned. "I can't take credit, you know. She's a trained nurse. We're very fortunate to have found anyone."

Zeke managed to get to his feet, but he was still wobbly. He felt like a fool, allowing this weakness to get the best of him.

With Maria on one side and Angie on the other, he managed to walk to the cabin.

A lamp burned on a small table, lighting up one side of the long room. The fireplace gave a soft glow to the other side. The old woman pointed to a bed in the corner. "Why don't you lie down while I see about—"

Zeke interrupted. "No. I won't take your bed." He glanced around the room. It was well furnished. He pointed to a sofa near the fireplace. "I'll stretch out there for a few moments and rest."

"Whatever you wish." Maria turned away and went over to the sink where she got some water and a clean cloth. "Sit and let me check your head."

Angie felt in the way. She walked over to the fire-place and held out her hands.

Without looking around, Maria said, "I have some stew on the stove. Why don't you help yourself. There's bread on the counter. By the time you have it set out on the table, I should be through with this young man."

Zeke grinned. He hadn't been referred to as "young" in a long time. Age was definitely relative.

"Do you think you can eat?" Maria asked, cleaning his forehead and placing new bandages there.

"It certainly smells good. I guess my appetite hasn't been affected."

"Good. Once you have eaten, I have an herbal tea that will help you to rest by easing the pain you're experiencing."

Zeke and Angie sat at the small table. While they ate Zeke explained to Maria what had happened and how they hoped to find help to get out of the mountains.

Maria listened, nodding occasionally. When he finished, she said, "My son comes to check on me several times a week. I expect him tomorrow or the next day. He has a truck and could take you to a town large enough to be able to call for assistance."

Zeke nodded. "I'd appreciate that very much, if you don't mind having us stay over." He glanced around the cabin.

Maria nodded. "I can make you a bed of sorts with blankets if I can't get you to take mine."

"You've done enough, and I thank you for your generosity."

Maria got up and went over to the stove. She

poured hot water into a cup, added what looked to be dry leaves, stirred it and brought it back to the table.

"Here. This should help your pain."

Zeke took a sip and made a face.

"I know. It isn't very tasty, but it will help you to relax and rest. By morning you will be feeling much better."

By the time Angie and Maria cleared the table, washed and put the dishes away and prepared sleeping pallets on the floor, Zeke was almost asleep. "Whatever you gave me is certainly potent," he managed to say. He tugged off his boots and socks. He looked blearily around the room, then shook his head, unable to concentrate.

Maria guided him to the bed she had made for him. "Don't fight it. Just sleep," she said as he stretched out with a satisfied groan. She smiled at Angie. "He should sleep all right, but if he has any pain during the night, give him the rest of this tea."

"I can't tell you how grateful we are to have found you. Thank you so much for your first aid, your hospitality, your concern."

Maria nodded. "Most of the time I enjoy being here in the mountains near my family, but having company reminds me of how much I enjoy being around other people. This has been good for me as well." She patted Angie's shoulder. "Now, then. You must get some rest, too. We'll be able to visit more tomorrow. Perhaps my son will come. Perhaps not. But we will enjoy our visit while we can."

Maria blew out the lamp, whispered good-night and went to the other end of the cabin. She moved a heavy blanket along a rope, effectively shielding her end of the cabin from them.

Angie went over to the duffel bag. She found her pajamas and pulled them out. Glancing at Zeke, she saw that he was sound asleep. After pouring some of the hot water into a bowl, she bathed herself before going to sleep.

Her bed was no more than an arm's length from Zeke. She felt strange lying there beside him. She barely knew the man, and yet, because of the experiences they had shared, she felt as though she'd known him for a long time.

She thought about her uncle. He must be distraught, wondering what had happened to them. She thought about the cut oil line. What was going on here in Mexico? Did the cut line have anything to do with Tio's reasons for not wanting her to visit?

Why was somone like Zeke working for her uncle? He was different, in a way she couldn't define, from anyone who had worked for her uncle before.

Nothing seemed familiar to her anymore. The life she had dreamed about was all part of the past and had nothing to do with the present that she was experiencing.

She was alone with a man…a very attractive man, one who made her blood sing whenever he touched her. Tio would definitely disapprove. He had already made his disapproval clear while they had been in Mexico City.

What would he think of their sleeping side by side with only an old woman sleeping behind a woolen partition as a chaperon?

She sighed, turning on her side. There was nothing she could do about her uncle's concern. They were lucky to be alive. Perhaps it was their narrow escape that made her feel so restless now, so aware of how close she had come to dying before she had ever experienced what life and love were all about.

Hours later she awoke to the sounds of restless mutterings. She sat up and looked at Zeke. The fire had dwindled to glowing coals, still casting enough light for her to be able to see him.

She placed her hand on his chest and he immediately opened his eyes.

"Zeke?" she whispered. "Are you all right?"

He touched the bandage around his head with the tips of his fingers, then dropped his hand. He glanced around the room, then at her. "I must have been dreaming. What time is it?"

She looked at her watch. "Not quite two. Is your shoulder bothering you?"

He rubbed it and winced. "Yeah. It's definitely protesting." He shoved the blanket aside and got to his feet.

"What are you doing?"

He glanced over his shoulder as he walked away from her. "Answering nature's call," he replied, opening the door.

The air felt cold to his bare skin and he shivered. He took several deep breaths as he followed a path around to the back of the cabin. He needed to clear his head. He needed to forget the scene he'd discovered when he opened his eyes.

Seeing Angie lying so closely beside him, her hand resting on his chest, had brought his fantasies forcibly back to him.

For a brief moment he had allowed himself to forget who she was. In that moment he had enjoyed the sight of her soft beauty, her alluring body, her piquant

personality. He couldn't remember the last time he
had reacted so strongly to a woman.

When he returned to the cabin, Angie handed him
a steaming cup.

"What's this?" Zeke took a sip and made a face.
"How could I forget?" he said to himself. Whatever
it was had eased his pain earlier. He needed to stay
knocked out, at least until morning so that he
wouldn't be quite so aware of the woman nearby. He
upended the cup, draining it, then sat down on his
bed once more.

She sat beside him and they both gazed at the fire.
Zeke couldn't believe how comfortable Angie appeared to be with him under these tantalizing conditions. The scene had a dreamlike quality for him, as
though they had been together for years instead of a
day. The rest of the world faded into nonexistence.

"Your skin looks like satin in the firelight," he
murmured into the long silence that stretched between
them. Tentatively he held out his hand. "I've been
tempted to touch it to see if it was as soft as it looks."

She had been staring into the fire when he spoke.
Now she slowly turned her head, causing her hair to
slide forward over her shoulder. She said nothing
when she saw his hand a few inches away from her
face. Instead, she looked into his eyes and smiled.

Zeke brushed his fingertips across her cheeks. They
grew pinker with his touch but she didn't move away.
Her eyes glowed emerald green in the soft firelight.
He traced the line of her brow, following its shape
until he reached the center of her forehead. He followed the straight line of her nose before pausing at
the slight indentation on her chin. Then he rubbed his
thumb softly across her lips.

As though mesmerized by his sensory exploration, Zeke leaned toward her, longing to taste, as well as to touch. She tilted her face up to his, a tiny sigh escaping from her parted lips. When his mouth touched hers, he felt her lips quiver, but she didn't pull away from him.

He leaned into the kiss, wanting a chance to fully taste and explore. Shyly she pressed back, her sensitive mouth opening for him. Afraid to test his self-restraint by reaching for her, Zeke contented himself with their limited contact with each other. He turned his head slightly to improve the angle of his mouth upon hers and was startled when he felt her hands come to rest upon his chest. Every place her fingers touched him seemed to set a blaze going, shooting flames down through him, causing him to ache with the need to pull her closer so that he could feel her body pressing against him.

Stifling a moan, he brought his hands up and cupped her face as though sipping nectar from her lips. His tongue outlined and explored her mouth until he finally took possession.

She clutched him feverishly, touching his nape, her fingers burrowing through his hair, kneading his scalp like a delicate kitten.

Zeke finally lifted his head, drawing in much-needed air to his oxygen-starved lungs. Her long, thick lashes rested against her flushed cheeks as he stared down at her. The soft material of her pajama top fluttered, betraying her shallow breaths.

Slowly her lashes lifted, revealing the jewellike sparkle of her expressive eyes.

"This is definitely not a good idea, Princess," he whispered. "I've been without a woman for too long to be indulging myself in some heavy necking in front of a fireplace late at night.''

Her mouth was rosy and slightly swollen. His eyes were repeatedly drawn to its shape, invoking memories of how luscious she was, all ripe and inviting.

''You're indulging yourself?'' she repeated in a hesitant voice.

''Without a doubt. I haven't any business kissing my boss's niece, regardless of the situation in which we find ourselves.''

''What's so wrong with it?''

''We're from different worlds, Princess. No one knows that better than I.''

He found the grin she flashed at him adorable and irresistible. ''If I'm not protesting, why should you?''

He eyed her uncertainly. Although her tone was light, she couldn't disguise the unevenness of her breathing or the flush she wore so becomingly on her cheeks. Her kiss had also betrayed her lack of experience, a fact Zeke found endearing.

''I don't want to take advantage of you.'' His voice sounded rough and uneven in his ears.

''You haven't done anything I didn't want you to do,'' she pointed out shyly.

''Well, one of us needs to hang on to some sanity here.''

She nodded solemnly. ''All right. I'll let you be the sane one.'' Because her hands were still behind his back, she had no trouble pulling him closer, fitting against his chest as though she had been designed to be there. Her mouth quickly attached to his once again, this time with more bravery, as she mimicked his earlier moves.

First she allowed her tongue to outline the shape

of his mouth before she nudged his lips apart and touched his tongue with hers.

Zeke wrapped his uninjured arm around her, slipping his hand beneath the hem of her pajama top. He traced each vertebra as they climbed steadily to the base of her neck. Then slowly and with infinite deliberation he circled her rib cage until his hand rested just beneath her breasts.

She could not hide her reaction to this new intimacy, but neither did she pull away from him. Initially he had meant to tease her by exposing his knowledge of her naive assumption that what they were indulging in was a harmless pastime. But when he brushed against the full-bodied warmth of her breast, he forgot about his original intent.

Her breast fit into his palm like a luscious fruit ripe for harvest. When he brushed his thumb against the crest, the tip bloomed into a hard button of temptation. Grimly Zeke fought his reaction and moved his hand to the other breast, evoking a similar response.

He had taken over the kiss, pulling her closer, setting the rhythm that he wanted to experience fully with her. She clung to him, meeting him thrust for thrust with her hot little tongue, teasing him, darting away before returning to taunt him, while her heated breasts pushed against his chest.

He eased the thin fabric from between them until she lay against his bare chest. He lightly rubbed his upper body against her aroused breasts, bringing them close enough for the tips to be stimulated by his slow, swaying movement.

Once again he reluctantly ended the kiss, but instead of apologizing, he pushed the garment aside until his lips could soothe and appease her aroused breasts.

His touch, instead of soothing, seemed to set off an exploding inferno. She whimpered, clutching him to her, and he realized…too late…what he had done.

Angie had never been aroused before. Her innocent little game had backfired on her. Zeke had known better than to continue their love play As much as he wanted to, he had no intention of completing what they had started.

He also knew that he couldn't leave her in such a vulnerable state.

Carefully he lowered her to the blanket, shielding her with his body while he tenderly touched her where he knew the inferno was located. He cupped his hand over the nest of curls at the apex of her thighs, fervently hoping he could bring her to a satisfying conclusion to their reckless and dangerous situation.

Past restraint, she was acting on instinct alone. She lifted her hips, pressing against his hand. Gently he eased his finger into her fully aroused flesh, giving her a chance to grow accustomed to his invasion before he set a rhythm that brought her to a groaning climax within minutes.

When he felt her beginning to peak he covered her mouth with his own, effectively muffling her cry as she surged upward against him, straining… reaching…then finding the release she had been innocently searching for.

He continued to place tiny kisses on her face while he held her firmly against him.

She shook with reaction, her breath coming in soft pants until she began to get her breath once again.

Long minutes passed before she lay quietly. Eventually she raised her eyelids as though they were almost too heavy to lift and peered up at him.

"I never knew…" she began, then seemed lost for words.

"It's okay."

"But I didn't mean…" Once again she seemed at a loss.

"I know you didn't. It really is okay. Why don't you try to get some sleep now, all right?"

"But what about you? You didn't…I mean, you weren't…"

He couldn't hide his amusement while she vainly searched for words.

"It was much safer this way. You were experimenting. I didn't want the experience to destroy your faith in people, men in particular."

She stared up at him quizzically, her eyes full of questions. He sat up, turning away from her. Glancing over his shoulder, he said, "Go to sleep. I'll be back in a few minutes."

"But where are you going?"

"Just outside. Now get some sleep." He edged away from her, then stood and moved silently over to the door. Quietly he opened the door and slipped outside. His last glimpse of Angie was of her pulling the blanket over her shoulders, effectively outlining the sweet curve of her waist, hip and thigh.

He clenched his teeth to stop from groaning out loud.

Zeke knew he had done some stupid things in his lifetime, but his actions over the past hour were by far the most illogical, irrational and potentially disastrous of his career.

The pain he was experiencing in his lower body was only the beginning of what could prove to be a major catastrophe.

He never before had allowed himself to be distracted while on an assignment. It was an easy way to get himself killed.

He stood in the small clearing and stared up at the stars, praying for wisdom and for help. He would need both to successfully conclude this assignment now that he had gotten a sample of the way Angela De la Garza felt in his arms.

Five

The first thing Angie saw when she opened her eyes was Zeke asleep beside her. She raised up on her elbow and looked around.

Pale light filtered through a nearby window. She glanced at her watch and saw that it was after seven. Quietly she got up and went outside.

Sunlight peeked over the trees. It was going to be another clear day. She stretched, then followed the path around the cabin to answer nature's call.

When she returned she paused in front of the cabin, unwilling to face Zeke at the moment. Somehow she had to come to grips with her behavior the night before.

She had thrown herself at him, wanting him to hold her, to kiss her, to make love to her.

He had obliged her. Now she had to be able to look him in the eye without blushing.

She had wanted to experience life, hadn't she? She had been eager to discover what she had been missing. She had picked a man of the world who knew how to please a woman.

Now she knew.

Now she needed to forget.

She was an adult. There was no reason to let him see her embarrassment at her forwardness. In a few days she would be home with her uncle. There was nothing to be gained from having regrets. If she were honest with herself, she would admit to having no regrets whatsoever.

Zeke Daniels had taught her about her own sensuality. She had discovered a new aspect of herself. She would need to come to terms with her new knowledge.

Mentally bracing herself, she entered the cabin once again.

Zeke shifted, rolling over onto his shoulder, which immediately protested his weight. He groaned and opened his eyes. The space next to him was empty.

With a muffled oath he sat up. Where was Angie? The other end of the room lay in shadows. Maria must still be asleep. Zeke tossed his blanket aside and moved to the door. He jerked open the door and came face-to-face with Angie.

Only then did he realize how panicked he'd been by her disappearance. He allowed the door to shut behind him and leaned against the jamb.

"I didn't know what to think when I found you gone," he admitted. He rubbed his hand over his bare chest, only now remembering that he hadn't bothered to look for his shirt.

She nodded toward the path that wound behind the cabin. "I'll certainly appreciate indoor plumbing after this adventure."

He reached out and slid his hand around her nape, massaging the delicate muscles. "Did you sleep all right?" His thoughts asked a different question.

"Yes. And you?" Her eyes were filled with shadows.

He straightened, pulling her against him so that he could wrap his arms around her. After a brief pause she slipped her arms around his waist and hugged him back. They stood there in silence, absorbed with their sensory perceptions.

Finally he spoke, his voice husky. "I know I should apologize for last night. I could make excuses, blame my actions on Maria's tea, or I could be honest and admit that I've spent the last several weeks dreaming about making love to you."

She lifted her head so that she could see his face. "Weeks?" she repeated.

"From the time I first saw your picture sitting on Lorenzo's desk."

"Oh." She rested her head on his chest once more, unable to think of anything else to say.

"I don't want to complicate my life." His statement made a great deal of sense. "However, I think it's too late to avoid it."

When she looked up at him again, he lowered his head until his lips touched hers. Her newly awakened body responded with joy and she went up on tiptoe, leaning against him, her body dissolving into tingling bubbles of pleasure.

What was happening between them was a conscious choice for both of them. Sanity and safety lay in erecting a wall between them, and Zeke knew better than most the consequences of what was happening.

He should have known before he met her at the airport that her coming to visit her uncle at this time would be his downfall...personally and professionally.

A sound from within the cabin caused him to release his tight hold. He felt Angie's knees sag and quickly placed his hands around her waist. "Are you okay?" he murmured, his voice rumbling deep in his chest.

Her smile when she looked up at him was radiant. "If I'm dreaming, please don't wake me up."

"I think Maria is stirring," he said, regret in his voice.

"I'll go see if I can help her with breakfast." Angie disappeared behind the door, while Zeke followed the trail around the cabin.

During the next several hours, Angie worked beside Maria, visiting with her, while Zeke did what he could to help with any repairs he could find around her home. They waited for Maria's son, each with concern for the outcome.

Zeke didn't want to spend another night at the cabin with Angie.

Angie no longer cared if Maria's son ever appeared.

Maria hoped her guests would not be inconvenienced by an additional night in the wilderness.

When she heard the familiar rattle of her son's truck, Maria smiled delightedly. "Ah, Julio is here. I'll go explain your problem."

Zeke and Angie followed her out of the cabin at a

slower pace. The man climbing from the truck embraced his mother and listened as she excitedly talked and gestured to the two of them. He glanced up at them standing on her porch and smiled while he patiently heard her story.

When he joined them on the porch, he held out his hand. "Hello. I'm Julio Cerventes. My mother has been explaining that you need a ride to town."

Zeke took the proffered hand. "Zeke Daniels...and this is Angela De la Garza. How far are we from town?"

Julio tilted his head in thought. "About three hours for one large enough to have phone service."

"I'd be glad to pay you for your trouble."

"I don't need payment, but if you'd like to replace the gasoline necessary to take you, I'd appreciate it."

He turned to his mother and began to question her about her health, whether she needed anything from town, and what he could do for her. She answered his questions and gave him a list for the store. Julio turned back to Zeke. "We need to get started if you want to go today."

Without a word, Angie went into the house and gathered their things, replacing them in the duffel bag. She thanked Maria for her hospitality. Zeke attempted to give Maria money, which she vehemently refused, and within minutes they were in the truck, heading down the mountainside once more.

The road Julio took was not the one they had landed on. When Zeke asked about that road, Julio explained that it connected one side of the mountain range with the other and few of the local inhabitants had reason to travel on it. Zeke realized that they would have been in dire straits if they hadn't found Maria's cabin.

Angie sat between them. In order to give Julio room to work the floor shift, she leaned against Zeke. To accommodate her, he placed his arm behind her on the seat. Before long, he noticed she had fallen asleep.

He wished he could be so relaxed around her. The scent of her floral shampoo tantalized him. He dropped his hand onto her shoulder, just to be able to touch her.

The sun was setting by the time they reached the settlement Julio had mentioned. The place was smaller than Zeke had envisioned, but Julio assured him there was telephone service to the area.

Zeke insisted on buying Julio dinner, filling his gas tank and giving him money to help with his mother's purchases. By the time they waved Julio off, night had fallen.

The only place renting rooms was a cantina on the edge of town. Zeke didn't like the idea of having Angie stay there, but there was little choice. When he asked to speak to the proprietor, the bartender pointed out an overweight man with greasy hair. Zeke took Angie's hand and walked over to the man.

"I understand you rent out rooms here?"

The man looked up from the cards he held in his hand. He glanced at Zeke then his gaze darted to Angie. The smile he gave her caused her to shiver. "Perhaps so. It would depend, of course, on how many you need and for how long." One of his front teeth was missing, which didn't dim his smile at Angie. She took a step closer to Zeke.

"My wife and I would like a room for the night.

We would also like to use a phone if there's one available here.''

At the word *wife* the proprietor's smile disappeared. "We have a room for you. The phone is at the front desk." He pointed to a wide doorway.

"Thanks." Zeke kept his grip on Angie's hand and escorted her into the other room, which served as the entry to the upstairs rooms.

A young man nodded. "You wish a room?"

"Yes."

"We have special two-hour rates, if you like."

"I'm sure you do. However, my *wife* and I will be staying the night. I also need to arrange transportation out of here tomorrow. Would it be possible to use your phone?"

"Certainly. We do not have phones in the room, but you may use this one."

After he paid for their room, he called Lorenzo. The phone rang only once before it was picked up.

"Yes?"

"She's okay, boss. We ran into a little difficulty and I had to put the plane down on the side of a mountain. We just reached civilization."

"Thank God! All I could think about was how much Angela had wanted to come home and how hard I tried to convince her not to come. Is she there? May I speak with her?"

Zeke handed the phone over to Angie without comment. She looked at him in surprise, then placed the phone to her ear.

"Hello, Tio? We're all right. Didn't you believe Zeke when he told you?"

"Angela! Ah, my sweet angel, I have been distraught. I have not slept since I learned your plane was missing. I am so very sorry for yelling at you. I was upset, you see. It has nothing to do with you. I love you, little angel.''

''I love you, too, Tio. Zeke is taking very good care of me.''

''Good, good. I'm glad he's there with you. Let me speak with him, all right?''

''We'll see you soon, Tio. Get a good night's rest, please. Hopefully we'll be home by tomorrow.'' She handed the phone back to Zeke.

Before he could speak, Lorenzo said, ''Tell me where you are. Do you need someone to come get you?''

Zeke described their location and continued, ''It would save considerable time if you could find someone to fly in and pick us up, but I'm not sure about landing strips.''

''Tell me how to find you. I'll send a private helicopter. Was my Angela frightened when the plane went down?''

''She has the courage of ten men, Lorenzo. You should be proud of her.''

''Oh, I am. I am.''

''She's going to need all the courage she can muster to take to the air again. This hasn't been a very positive experience for her.''

''Once I get her home, I'm not going to let her out of my sight!''

''I can understand that reaction.''

''What about my plane. Can it be salvaged?''

''I think so, but you're going to need to send something to have it towed in. One of the wings is gone. We clipped something after we were on the ground.''

''But no one was hurt?''

"No. I just bruised my shoulder a little."

"I'll have someone there to pick you up as soon after daylight tomorrow as possible. Get some rest tonight."

"I intend to. G'bye, Lorenzo."

Zeke put down the phone and turned away from the desk, a room key in his hand. With his hand at the small of her back, he silently guided Angie up the stairs.

She waited until they were inside the small room with a single bed, a wooden table and a chair before she repeated, "Your wife?"

Zeke's shoulder ached and he wasn't looking forward to the night ahead of him. "You're welcome to take your chances in a room alone, but the clientele of a place like this doesn't pay much attention to locked doors, not to mention the proprietor of the place. He was looking at you like a starving dog looks at a juicy steak."

She hugged her elbows and looked around the room.

He almost smiled. "Not much like the hotel room in Mexico City. I don't think we'd have much luck with room service, even if there *was* a phone." He walked over to the window and looked out. The room was probably the most quiet of the group. It faced away from the street. He could see a straggling line of houses listlessly climbing the hill.

When he turned back to face her, Angie sat on the edge of the small wooden chair.

"The one thing you don't have to worry about, Princess, is my taking advantage of this situation. You can have the bed and I'll—"

"No! I'm not a child. There's no reason why we can't share the bed."

"Don't kid yourself. There's an excellent reason. I don't have the energy or the willpower to leave you tonight if things get overheated...and I can't imagine sharing a bed with you and *not* having things get overheated." He walked over to the table where he had set the duffel bag. "I'm going to see if this place has a shower I can use. There's a sink over there if you'd like to wash up. I wouldn't suggest your showering tonight." He opened the door and paused, looking back. "I'm taking the key with me. Don't open the door for anyone, do you understand?"

She nodded and he closed the door.

Angie sat there hugging herself, feeling as though she were going to fly into tiny pieces if she let go of her grip. Never had it occurred to her that they wouldn't find comfortable rooms to spend the night.

Her traitorous body had already acknowledged awareness of their situation. She was aware of every move Zeke made, every breath he took, every word he said. She felt as though she would be able to find him in a crowd if she were blindfolded...by the very essence of who he was.

She had placed her life in his hands just a few days ago. It was only now that she realized she had also placed her heart in his hands, as well.

Zeke Daniels defined the word *tough*. There were no soft edges. A man like Zeke might sample something that attracted his attention, but he would never buy.

She wasn't surprised that he had worked for her uncle only a few weeks. She had a hunch he never stayed anywhere for very long.

She could never have imagined that she would give her heart to such a man because, in her innocence, she had never known such a man existed.

They would return to Monterrey tomorrow, when she would once again be the daughter of the manor and he the hired hand. He didn't seem to have any regrets about their situation. Why should he? Once he turned her over to her uncle, his duties would be finished.

Tonight would be the last night she had with him. She could literally turn her back, ignore him and fall asleep, or she could have one more night with Zeke, a night in which she would collect some unforgettable memories for the time when he would be gone.

After his shower, Zeke went downstairs to the cantina. He intended to give Angie plenty of time to get ready for bed and to fall asleep.

From the moment he realized that the only way he could protect her was to keep her in his room, he knew he was in for a sleepless night. He ordered a drink and watched a card game at the next table. When one of the men decided to leave, one of the remaining players asked Zeke if he wanted to join in. The stakes were small and from what he had observed, the game friendly. Shrugging his acceptance, he moved over to the next table and began to play.

He lost track of time because time didn't matter. All he needed to do was to get through the night. He had positioned his chair so that he could watch the stairs up to the second floor. He knew exactly who had gone upstairs and why. When the game broke up, he knew he couldn't postpone the inevitable any longer. With a nod to the other men, he headed to the room.

Quietly fitting the key into the lock, he eased the door open. The shadowy darkness of the room made it difficult for him to see anything. He closed the door and waited for his eyes to adjust before he moved.

"Zeke?" She murmured the name and he knew that she was far from awake. He smiled.

"Yes," he replied in a low, soothing voice. "Everything's fine. Get some rest."

"I waited for you...I wanted..." Her voice trailed off. She said no more. He figured her to be sound asleep, which was fine with him.

Now that his eyes were adjusting to the dark, the starlight from the window gave him enough light to see. He sat down in the chair and removed his boots and socks. Then he took off his shirt. He'd sleep in his jeans as he had done last night. Much safer that way.

He smelled of cheap liquor and cigarette smoke, although he'd only had a couple of glasses and he hadn't had a cigarette in more than five years.

Contamination by association.

He didn't want that to happen to Angie because of him. She deserved better. There was no way he could take advantage of their situation. She would hate him soon enough, when she found out why he worked for her uncle.

Her relationship to Lorenzo would be another contaminating factor, one that he couldn't protect her from, at least not entirely. However, as long as he kept his objectivity where she was concerned, he would be able to explain her innocence to those in charge and they would have no reason to doubt his word.

All of that would come later. For now, he had to get some sleep.

Zeke silently moved to the bed. With measured movements he stretched out on top of the covers, gratefully acknowledging to himself that, as tired as he was, he would have no trouble sleeping after all.

He closed his eyes and allowed the air to leave his lungs in a peaceful sigh.

Angie stirred beside him, but he continued to lie there without moving, already drifting into restful slumber. Let her think he was drunk. Let her think he was—

His eyes flew open.

Angie had pushed her covers off and was kneeling beside him, placing dainty kisses across his chest. She had neglected to wear anything to bed.

"Not fair," he groaned, his hand resting on her head. Whether he meant to push her away or hold her close, he wasn't sure.

She paused in her soft caresses and looked at him. "You took care of me last night. Now it's my turn." Her fingers found the zipper of his jeans and eased it downward, shoving his jeans and briefs down his legs until they fell off the end of the bed.

Zeke stiffened, knowing that she didn't understand, she couldn't know that—

Reverently she brushed her fingertips across his burgeoning flesh, getting an eager response from the traitorous part of his anatomy.

"Angie, noooo—"

"It's all right, Zeke. Really. I just want to—"

"I know what you want to, but it's not possible. I—"

"But you were prepared. I found this in your bag, so you must have—" She was pulling the item from its foil wrapper.

"Not you, darlin'," he breathed. "I always keep them with me. I—oh, Angie, oh honey, you don't know what that does to me. I can't— I don't have the control to—"

He lost his train of thought. Hell, he was losing his mind. For a young lady with zilch experience she was logical enough to understand design and its application for the aroused male body.

She stroked him, causing his hips to surge upward as though independent of the rest of him. "You're much larger than I thought a man would be."

He heard the quiver in her voice, but before he could think of something to say in reply, she shifted once again, this time stretching out on top of him. He could feel her full, taut breasts pressing against his chest.

The Inquisition could not have come up with a finer torture than what Angie had devised. To make matters much more difficult, she didn't have a clue of the torment in which she had innocently placed him.

"Angie, I—"

Her kiss muffled whatever he had been going to say. Openmouthed, she copied the kiss they had shared on Maria's front porch, her tongue darting to meet his in a playful duel.

Each person has his or her limit and Zeke knew when he reached his...then went tumbling past.

"Angie, honey," he managed to get out before she silenced him once again. He rolled so that she was lying beneath him on the bed. He ran exploring fingers along her body, feeling the taut peaks of her breasts, the quivering of her ribs from her panting breaths, and finally, when he touched her most secret place, he found that she was ready for him.

"So sweet," he whispered, knowing that he was too far gone to stop what had been put into motion tonight. He pulled one of her knees up so that her heel rested along the back of his thigh. "I don't want to hurt you," he breathed, lowering his body imperceptibly closer while he kissed and caressed her, readying her for the next step.

This time it was more than his fingers that found the barrier proclaiming her innocence. Zeke paused, squeezing his eyes shut, knowing that there was no way for him to lessen the pain she was about to feel.

"Zeke? What's wrong?" she murmured. "Am I too—"

"You...are perfect...Princess," he managed to answer between short, shallow breaths. "I don't want to hurt you, I'm so afraid—"

Once again she removed the situation from his control by hooking her heels together and lunging upward, forcing his entry. He heard her gasp and felt her quivering as she clutched him around his shoulders, holding him in a viselike grip.

When he attempted to ease away, she cried out. He held still, his weight resting on his forearms, and placed tender kisses on her upturned face.

"I didn't mean to cry out," she whispered between quick breaths. "I knew there would be some discomfort...I just didn't expect..."

"Don't apologize, Princess. Please, not that." He eased back and she sighed, lifting to him once more.

He let her set the rhythm. This was her seduction. He would let her control it....

Until he could wait no longer. He couldn't hold back, couldn't wait. He needed to—

Zeke took over the pace, afraid he was rushing her but no longer able to—aaahhh, there. The inner ripples were beginning to stir deep inside of her, causing her to stiffen in surprise. They continued to grow and grow, pulling him ever deeper inside until he felt swallowed up in the sensation.

He muffled her cry with his mouth, feeling his own release and knowing that he had never experienced anything remotely like this in his life. The sensations went on and on, as though they were being swept into a huge vortex forcing them deeper and deeper into the black pit of total experience...the place without thoughts, without words, without time.

Infinity.

Six

Zeke heard a soft footfall at the top of the steps. Despite his relaxed state and the fact that he had slept deeply during the night, the tiny sound brought him into abrupt wakefulness.

Angie lay with her head on his chest in an abandoned pose that caused him an unexpected pang to see her trusting vulnerability.

He slipped out of bed without rousing her, had his pants pulled up and zipped before the soft tread paused in front of his door. Reaching into a hidden compartment of his duffel bag, he palmed his pistol and silently moved to the door.

The soft tap on the door was anticlimactic.

"Hey, Zeke. You in there? Time's awasting, man. We gotta get going."

Zeke recognized the voice of Pablo, one of Lorenzo's men. He had no more time than to release his pent up breath before he realized that the knock and voice had awakened Angie. His eyes widened with dismay as he saw her open her eyes, sit up and—

He made a dive and placed his free hand over her mouth.

"Hey, Pablo, I'm awake," he hollered. "Glad you made it. I'll go wake up Angie and see you down stairs in a few minutes."

He waited until the footsteps retreated before removing his hand from Angie's mouth. When she didn't immediately tell him off for grabbing her so unceremoniously, he turned and fully faced her. Her gaze was fastened on his other hand, her eyes wide with shock.

As casually as possible, he returned the pistol to the duffel bag and said, "We overslept this morning, Princess." He sat down and started pulling on his socks and boots. "We should have been up hours ago. Instead, we almost got caught in bed together." He stood up and stomped his feet, then reached for his shirt. "I don't like to think what Lorenzo would do to me if we'd been seen." He concentrated on the buttons. "I'm going downstairs for some coffee and, if I'm lucky, some breakfast. Give me about twenty minutes and come down as though we haven't seen each other since last night. As far as Pablo knows, I tapped on your door on the way downstairs."

When he finally looked at her, his gaze was steady.

"Why do you have a gun?"

Exasperated, he put his hands on his hips. "Did you hear a damn thing I just said?"

"Yes. I just don't understand why you have a gun."

"It's part of my job, Princess." He opened the door. "Twenty minutes, no more."

Angie was left to stare at the dingy door in silence. Mechanically she got out of bed and walked over to the sink. There was no hot water, but it didn't matter. She found some coarse soap and scrubbed her body until it glowed.

Oh, dear God, what had she done? How could she have forgotten everything she had ever been taught? What was it in her personality that impulsively pushed all the limits, only later becoming aware of the consequences?

Why would possessing a gun be part of Zeke's job for her uncle? She didn't understand at the moment, but once she reached home she would insist on some answers.

The flight home certainly helped to get her mind off her questions. Angie hadn't known that Zeke had arranged aerial transportation to rescue them. If so, she would have insisted on something that rolled over the ground.

She hadn't been given a choice. When she had arrived downstairs, carefully following Zeke's instructions, she had met Pablo, once again alarmed at the type of individual working for her uncle. She couldn't imagine why her uncle would need a man who looked more like a wrestler or a bouncer than anything else.

Big and burly, Pablo was certainly not her idea of a pilot, but when, after breakfast, the three of them walked to the helicoptor waiting on the edge of town, Angie realized that was how Pablo had gotten there so fast.

She panicked.

"No, Zeke. Absolutely not. You can go ahead and I'll just wait here. I'll take a bus back to town…or maybe I can rent a car. I'll just— Zeke! Put me down. No! I'm not getting on— I'm not flying agai— Zeeeke!''

She had found herself unceremoniously dumped in one of the seats, her seat belt efficiently fastened around her.

Now Zeke and Pablo chatted away, pointing out areas of interest to each other as they flew much too low to the ground, while she crouched in the small seat behind Pablo.

Once in a while Zeke would look back at her. He'd give her a sympathetic smile, touch her hand or her knee as though making a silent apology.

How could he have done this to her? He knew how frightened she was of flying, particularly after what had happened to them. How could he expect her to go up in the air again when the mere thought… Something flashed from below and she looked out…and kept on looking.

After a while she forgot to be afraid. The two men were obviously unconcerned. She couldn't hear what they were saying because of the noise. She didn't care what they were saying. If they were discussing another crash, she would prefer to be taken unawares.

It wasn't that she feared death. It was the uncertainty of whether she was going to actually die or whether she was going to be subjected to unspeakable and unimaginable pain first.

But if she were to die— Ah, then she could at least appreciate her midnight behavior. Her impulsiveness had led her on a road of discovery that had swept her away into a whole new world of sensation and pleasure.

Yes, she had been foolish. Yes, she might very well live to regret her actions, but for now, all she wanted to do was to relive the night before.

She leaned her head back against the seat and closed her eyes, cleverly distancing herself from the present.

"Angie. Are you all right?"

Zeke's touch reached her at the same time she heard him calling her name.

She opened her eyes and nodded, seeing the silent question in his dark eyes.

He pointed ahead. "That's your uncle's airfield down there. You should be home soon."

She sat forward, trying to see around his broad shoulders and Pablo's bulk. The tin roof of a hangar glinted in the sun. She saw a black limousine parked nearby with a group of men watching their approach.

They looked so tiny, like little toy men with toy cars and airplanes, waiting for a child to pick them up and rearrange them to suit a young mind's fancy.

Their descent was much too fast for Angie. Her stomach seemed to stay in the air. But before she could think about her physical reaction, they were on the ground and her uncle was running toward the helicopter in a crouch, the wind from the blades blowing his suit flat against his body, his tie and hair streaming behind him.

Pablo cut the engine and the blades' whopping sound gradually lessened.

Zeke crawled out, then turned and helped Angie, lifting her by the waist to the ground. As soon as her feet touched, he stepped away and her uncle grabbed her.

"Angela! Thank God, you're safe. I never want to live through such a nightmare again. Nothing in life is worth the scare I've had." He held her for long, silent moments. She could feel the rapid beat of his heart as she lay pressed against his chest.

Eventually he let her go and looked at her. "Come. We need to get you home. You must be exhausted from your ordeal." He turned and slapped Zeke on the back. "You brought her back safely to me. For this, I owe you, my friend."

"Just doing my job, boss," Zeke replied in his low voice. He didn't look at Angie.

They were walking toward the car, Lorenzo and Angie with their arms about each other's waist, when she asked, "Who are all of those men, Tio? You look like you've recruited an army around you."

They reached the limousine and one of the men waiting at the car opened the rear door. Zeke walked around and got into the small seat facing Angie, her uncle and Pablo. Three other men jumped into the front seat.

"Ah, Angie, it's good to have you home. It's been a long time. There's been changes...some good, some not so good." Lorenzo took her hand and patted it. "We'll talk, my angel. Once you're home and settled in, we'll talk."

Angie glanced at Zeke and saw the impassive expression that he had worn so often since she first met him. Was it only a few short days ago? She felt as though she had known him forever, as though he had been a part of her life...and her dreams...since childhood. She knew that look was a shield for his thoughts and feelings. Someday perhaps he would be willing to share them with her.

"So tell me about the family, angel. What has been happening in your life since last spring?"

Obligingly Angie brought her uncle up-to-date on her life as it had existed before she met one Zeke Daniels, who in three short days had managed to turn her world upside down.

"The oil line had been severed, then spliced to come apart once we were airborne," Zeke explained later in the day as he sat across the desk from Lorenzo in his office.

"There's no chance you're mistaken, is there?"

"Nope."

"I'm glad I've sent in a salvage crew to retrieve the plane. I want the evidence."

"Who do you think they were trying to take out?"

"I doubt they cared. They knew the plane belonged to me. It was meant as a warning."

"But if we hadn't lived to tell about it, what sort of warning would that have been?"

"I would have known. I'll put in a call to the owner of the hangar. I want to find out what kind of security the man has working for him. Or it may have been one of his own employees who was willing to be bribed."

Zeke lay in the chair, utterly relaxed. "Everybody has his price, Lorenzo. You know that."

Lorenzo leaned back in his chair. "Of course. I became a success in business because I never accept no for an answer. What I have, I built for myself. I paid my way. I have made others wealthy along the way." He shook his head. "But there are those who are always too greedy. They want more and more. They see me and they want to have it all, all that I have worked for through the years. They think I'm getting to be an old man and that I'll be easy to replace.''

He stared at Zeke. ''They're wrong. They've already discovered this man is much stronger and smarter than they expected.''

''What did you find out about the man you caught trespassing?''

Lorenzo shook his head, disgusted. ''He knows nothing. He was hired to get inside the compound, to find out the layout. The man who paid him offered him an unheard-of amount of money to get in. This character felt like he'd been blessed by a miracle, money raining from the heavens, for what looked to be a simple job.'' The smile Lorenzo gave Zeke held no humor. ''Now he better understands that there is always something expected for payment received.''

''Do you know who's behind the break-in, the damage to the oil line, last month's explosion?''

''I was hoping you'd come up with some of those answers. That's one of the reasons I hired you.''

''Everyone I've spoken to is too scared to talk. I'll say one thing for you, Lorenzo, you make powerful enemies.''

Lorenzo nodded. ''It will take someone with a great deal of power to bring me down. I don't think the man exists.''

Zeke reached for the bottle that sat between them and poured a splash of the imported whiskey over the ice in his glass. When he held the bottle up to Lorenzo, the older man nodded and held out his glass.

"I can't figure you out, Daniels," Lorenzo said, after taking a sip of his drink.

"What's to figure? I'm a simple man, with simple needs."

"On the contrary. You're a very complex man...a walking puzzle. You live by a tough code. You demand a great deal from yourself. You get accused of something that you didn't do and instead of fighting, you walk away."

"So you're still having me checked out, huh?"

"I'm trying to solve the puzzle. I don't like mysteries I can't solve. You showed up at my door at a very opportune time, just when I needed a man of your skills and talents the most."

Zeke propped the heel of his boot on the toe of the other. "You're saying you don't believe in coincidences?"

"You're saying that's all it was?"

"No. I was out of work. There aren't too many openings for a man of—how did you put it?—my skills and talents. Rumor had it that you might be adding men to your staff."

"How long were you out of work?"

Zeke shrugged. "A few months. I had plenty of time to think about how I wanted to handle my situation. I had several choices I could have made." He took a sip of his drink. "I finally decided that I didn't care that much about my reputation. I knew I had handled myself in a professional manner. In the long run, what others thought about me didn't matter. I have to live with myself. I don't have a problem with it."

"You could have fought them...and possibly won."

"Ah. Now there's the big tease. What, exactly would I have won? The opportunity to continue risking my neck for an organization that turned on me at the first hint of wrongdoing? I preferred to move on. I've never found that looking backward gained me much in this world."

As Lorenzo mulled over his comments, Zeke discovered that the philosophy he'd been spouting came more from him than from the persona he had assumed for the sake of the current assignment. If the actual facts of his career were as Lorenzo had been led to believe they were, Zeke would indeed walk away from his career without a backward glance.

The revelation about himself surprised him. But upon further reflection, he discovered what he already knew to be true about himself—he offered loyalty until he discovered his loyalty was misplaced. Then it was withdrawn.

His loyalties were clear in the present instance. He wanted to put the man across from him out of business. He despised everything the man stood for. Either Lorenzo, or someone just like him, had contributed to the death of Charlie, his childhood friend.

Granted, nobody had forced Charlie to try drugs, an experiment that quickly progressed to an addiction. Charlie had changed radically and the broken man Zeke found when he came home from the air force bore little resemblance to the boy he'd grown up with. Charlie had lost his soul chasing that elusive high that would relieve him from his ever-increasing pain. Eventually he had lost his life, as well.

No. Zeke had no use for men like Lorenzo, whose greed sucked the life out of everyone around.

Now that he had gotten to know Angela, Zeke's

anger had grown even colder. How could that innocent young woman have been raised by a man whose
basic code of honor was so distorted by his need for
power?

"So what is between you and Angela?"

If the abrupt end to the companionable silence
hadn't startled Zeke, the question would have. He
stared at Lorenzo, uncertain of what he had heard.
"Pardon?" he asked, straightening in his chair.

"I know my niece quite well, even though I have
managed to discourage her from visiting me for years.
Even without knowing her well, I would imagine she
is easy for most people to read. She wears her
thoughts and her feelings on her face."

"I don't understand what that has to do with me."

Lorenzo took a sip from his glass, watching Zeke
from over its rim. After he set the drink down, he
said, "Angela has been unable to take her eyes off
you since the two of you arrived."

Zeke didn't move a muscle. Nor did he drop his
gaze from Lorenzo's intent stare. "I hadn't noticed."

Lorenzo shrugged. "Perhaps not. She has been dis-
creet, at least." He sighed. "She is a very naive
young woman, I'm afraid. Between her mother's family and me, we have sheltered her too much, perhaps.
We have discussed with her the possibility of marrying, but she wanted to teach school for a while. I
didn't have the heart to discourage her."

"Has she told you she wants to start a school in
the village near here?" Zeke hoped Angie would forgive him for this reference to one of their late-night
conversations.

"Is that what she told you?"

"She mentioned it, yes. She's been eager to come

home to see if it would be possible, so that she could
live here and teach nearby.''

''I wonder why she never mentioned it to me?''

''Perhaps because she wasn't certain you would approve.''

''How did you learn so much about my niece in
just a few days?''

Zeke smiled. ''We were involved in some rather
unusual circumstances together, wouldn't you say?
It's only natural that we would become more than just
acquaintances.''

''Angela is very impressionable.''

''Do you think so? I found her intelligent with a
definite mind of her own.''

''You spent three nights with my niece.''

Once again Zeke was still, waiting for the next
salvo. Lorenzo was operating like a submarine de-
stroyer, randomly dropping depth charges to see what
he might hit. Each shot had been an attempt to startle
Zeke into an admission of some kind. The fact that
they hadn't worked didn't seem to discourage him.

''Yes,'' Zeke agreed.

''And after those three nights together, my niece
can't seem to keep her eyes off you.''

''Do you want to state your point, Lorenzo?''

''I want to know how you feel about Angela.''

Zeke rubbed his nose with his forefinger. ''How I
feel? Hmm. Well. I like Angie. I enjoyed her company. I admire her in many ways.''

''Did you make love to her?''

A direct hit.

Seven

After a prolonged silence that neither man seemed in a hurry to break, Zeke slid back down in his chair and crossed his arms.

In a casual tone that was not reflected in his intent gaze, he finally replied.

"That's none of your business." He never lost eye contact with his adversary.

Lorenzo watched him without changing expression. "I can fire you, you know. I have never tolerated insubordination from anyone."

Zeke didn't flicker an eyelash. "That's up to you."

Lorenzo leaned forward and slapped his hand on his desk. "Dammit, I want to know if you took advantage of my niece!"

"I'm not going to discuss Angela with you. If you have any questions about my behavior while I was with her, you'll have to discuss the matter with her."

He uncrossed his arms and sat up. "Is there anything else? If not, I think I'm going to hit the sack. It's been a long day."

"You'll find that your clothes have been moved."

Zeke frowned. "Where are they?"

"I decided to move you into one of the upstairs bedrooms. I want you closer to the family."

"I thought you wanted me to guard you, Lorenzo. I can do that most effectively when I'm on the ground floor."

"I have others who are doing that now. I placed them there while you were gone. Now that you are back, I prefer that you sleep closer to Angela and me."

Zeke fought for control of his emotions. He would deal with all of this later when he was alone. With a sigh to denote his utter weariness, he asked, "So where am I sleeping now?"

"The second door on the right upstairs. You have a corner room that overlooks the compound. I'll be across the hall in the other corner bedroom. You should be able to hear me should I call."

Zeke stood. "I'll see you in the morning, then." He strode out of the office.

Other than when he was learning the layout of the household, Zeke had not been upstairs. He knew there were six large bedrooms, three on each side of the hallway. He would have expected Lorenzo to put Angela across the hall from him.

The question now was, which of the other four bedrooms was she in? The three bedrooms on each side of the house shared a balcony. If she was on his side of the hallway, that would give him access to her room.

Zeke knew a trap when he saw one. What he didn't understand was why.

Angie woke up early the next morning eager to greet the day. She was home! After tossing the covers aside, she went over to the French doors and opened them, letting in the pale morning light. She walked onto the balcony and peered down at the secluded walled garden below. The only access to the garden was from the formal salon, a room seldom used.

To view the scene from her balcony catapulted her into her childhood. She remembered the days she spent playing there with her imaginary friends—reading to them, playing dolls with them. She laughed from the sheer joy of being at home again and hugged herself.

The sound of a door opening and Zeke's voice caught her attention at the same time. She turned and found him in the doorway of the connected bedroom, leaning his forearm against the doorjamb. His hair was tousled, falling over his forehead. He wore a faded pair of unbuttoned jeans, his chest and feet bare.

"It figures," he muttered, dropping his forehead against his arm.

At least that was what she thought he said. But since the words made no sense, she just smiled and said, "Good morning, Zeke. Isn't it a beautiful morning?"

At her comment he slowly raised his head and, after a brief glance at the bare expanse of leg exposed beneath her short pajamas, looked east to where the sun was only now touching the sky with color.

With his attention seemingly on the sky, Zeke drawled, "You're up early, Princess."

She danced over to him, her eyes sparkling. "I know." She placed her hand lightly on his chest, enjoying the feel of his heated skin against her palm. "I didn't know this was your bedroom."

Leisurely he turned his head until he was staring down at her. "It wasn't. Your uncle moved me in yesterday."

Startled, she asked, "But why?"

"You'll have to ask him."

She studied his face but could read nothing from his expression.

"I don't understand."

"That makes two of us."

"Why would he have you sharing a balcony with me? He's always been so strict about the rules of behavior. He's lectured me over and over about the appearance of things. And now..." She tossed her head. "It makes no sense."

"Unless he's decided that it's already too late to protect you or your reputation. After all, you did spend three nights with me."

"That was no one's fault. Surely he isn't blaming you for—" She seemed to run out of words.

"I don't think *blame* is the word. He may be holding me accountable."

"Well, I shall tell him—" Her eyes widened as he suddenly clamped her hand beneath his, pinning it to his chest. "Zeke, let go of my hand. I need to get dressed and—"

"You should have thought of that sooner, Princess, before you found so much pleasure in rubbing your hand all over my chest." He continued to lean his forearm against the doorjamb while he pulled her with his other arm until she fell against him.

She chuckled, pushing away slightly so that she could see his face. "Zeke," she chided with a hint of breathlessness. "Be careful. Someone may see us."

"Let them," he muttered, hauling her securely against him with both arms and holding her. The woman was flat out driving him insane in those skimpy pajamas, her hair a tumbled mess, her eyes flashing intimate messages while her hand left paths of fire wherever she touched him.

He was a man, dammit, not a machine. He wasn't immune to her charms. On the contrary, their night together had made him ache for her, increasing his desire rather than appeasing it.

As soon as his mouth covered hers, she melted against him like molten lava, her curves fitting to his, her arms snaking around his waist.

This was the reason he hadn't been able to sleep well the night before. He'd known she was sleeping somewhere nearby. He could almost sense her presence. He couldn't seem to get enough of her, even now when he held her snug against him.

With a muffled oath, he swooped her up and hauled her into his room, nudging the door to the balcony closed behind them with his foot. They were in bed in a few quick strides.

Angie was as aroused as he. With trembling fingers she jerked her pajama top over her head, then stuck her thumbs into the waistband of the shorts and slid them off, leaving her bare as she knelt before him. Zeke unzipped his jeans, peeling them off without taking his eyes from her.

When they reached out to each other there was almost an audible sound of combustion. Their hands and mouths were touching and tasting, stroking and caressing, feverishly grasping each other. They fell back onto the bed in a tangle of limbs, seeking relief from this hot desire that had exploded between them.

Whimpering from need, Angie pulled him to her. He lifted her hips and lowered his head, kissing her until she cried out. Then in one surge of male domination he claimed her, filling her while at the same time he covered her mouth with his own.

He kept the pace at fever pitch—never slackening—even when he felt her arch beneath him. Her trembling increased into convulsive spasms that began to squeeze him in a relentless rhythm he couldn't resist. He lost control, filling her with his seed.

His unprotected seed.

The lack of protection only occurred to Zeke long minutes later when he was sprawled out beside her, too limp to move. He'd been too inflamed with his need for her…in his frenzy to claim her he had forgotten to consider any consequences.

He'd totally lost his mind. There was no doubt about that any longer. He was now certifiably insane. How could he have—

She stirred, leaning over him, kissing his nipples with a feathery touch.

He groaned.

Whatever she thought she could stir up at this stage, she was wrong. There was no way his satiated body could respond. He had exhausted himself…totally and completely.

Her kisses trailed downward until she touched him intimately.

Maybe not completely.

How could he be responding, when his arms, his

legs—hell! the entire rest of his anatomy!—seemed to have the muscle power of overcooked spaghetti?

He gave up wondering and closed his eyes, drowning in the pleasurable sensations she evoked.

After she performed a miracle that had Zeke gasping, she moved over his inert body, placing her knees at either side of his waist, and lowered herself until she surrounded and enfolded him in her fiery warmth.

Her movements were delicate and gentle all the while she brushed light kisses across his face and neck. With an enticingly deliberate movement, she came up on her knees, then slowly lowered herself, setting a rocking rhythm that was rapidly building tension throughout his body.

He opened his eyes and stared up at her. She wore a dreamy expression that touched his heart. "Oh, Princess, I'm not believing this," he whispered.

"Just relax and let me love you," she whispered back.

He would have laughed if he'd had the strength. "Relaxing is beyond my capabilities at the moment. What you're doing to me should be outlawed, it feels so good."

"I want to give you pleasure," she murmured. "You have taught me so much. I can never repay you."

He grasped her waist, pulling her down so that her breasts were there in front of his face. He began to tease her with his tongue and mouth, touching and tugging until her breathing became ragged.

Zeke took over the rhythm, guiding her faster against him until she gasped out her release at the same time he felt his. This time she collapsed against him and lay on top of him, unmoving.

He didn't have the energy or the strength to move her.

They fell asleep in that position.

"Good morning, Tio," Angie sang as she came into the breakfast room where Lorenzo and Zeke were eating. She leaned over and kissed her uncle on the cheek. "Isn't this the most beautiful morning?" She pulled out one of the chairs and sat before either man could assist her. "Good morning, Zeke. Did you sleep well?"

Zeke had known he was in big trouble as soon as she came through the door. She glowed, radiating contentment and goodwill, looking adorable. How had this slip of a woman managed to wrap him so securely around her little finger?

And did she have to look quite so well loved this morning? A blind man would have noticed the sheen of sexual satisfaction on her face, and Lorenzo was far from blind.

He met her gaze with an impassive one of his own. "I slept passably well, under the circumstances. And you?"

"What circumstances?" Lorenzo growled, looking up from his meal.

Zeke arched a brow. "Another new bed to adjust to. I haven't slept in the same bed twice in several days."

"Oh." Lorenzo looked back at his breakfast.

Angie caught Zeke's eye and grinned, obviously delighted with herself. He held her gaze without smiling and said, "Lorenzo, I'd like to have a few moments of your time after breakfast, if possible."

The older man nodded without comment.

"I thought I'd go to the village this morning, Tio, if you have no objections. I want to look around, visit with some of the young mothers, talk with them about the possibility of starting a preschool."

Lorenzo carefully replaced his eating utensils beside his plate. "Does that mean you don't intend to return to Madrid?"

Her clear-eyed gaze met his. "Don't you want me here?"

The gauntlet lay on the table. Zeke took a sip from his cup and waited.

"It isn't a case of not wanting you. I'm concerned for your safety. Zeke said you knew the problem with the plane was not an accident. The plane wasn't the first problem with sabotage I've run into. You asked yesterday why I have so many men working for me? Well, I needed to increase the security around here in order to ensure everyone's safety."

Angie had been filling her plate while he talked. When he paused, she looked up and said, "Why are these things happening?"

"Because of my success. Someone is trying to take over. I've had problems at the farms who sell me their wool, the manufacturing plant continues to have delays and inexplicable breakdowns. Several of my shipments into the States have been stopped at the border."

"You think a competitor is doing this?"

"Or someone who is determined to drive me out of business in any way he can."

She glanced at Zeke before looking back at her uncle. "Is that why Zeke works for you?"

"Yes. He's been immensely helpful in setting up some defense strategies."

"I see." She studied her plate thoughtfully, then picked up her fork and began to eat.

After a brief silence, Lorenzo said, "If you still want to go to the village, I'll send one of the men with you. Anyone who knows me knows that you are very dear to me. I don't want to take a chance on someone trying to harm you."

She reached for Lorenzo's hand and squeezed it "Thank you for explaining. The I love you. I don't wish to make anything more difficult for you. This is why you didn't want me to come home, isn't it?"

He nodded. "I had hoped to resolve some of these problems before you came." He smiled at her. "I must admit, however, that I'm very pleased you're here. I have no desire to see you leave, ever again."

Zeke shoved back his chair. "I have a few things I want to check on. I'll meet you in your office in half an hour, if that's all right."

"Fine."

Zeke had to get out of there before he said something. How could a man who obviously loved his niece put her through all of this? Why didn't he just turn himself in and let the authorities handle it? Why would he want to jeopardize her life?

He had been mulling over what he was going to do about the situation since he woke up the second time that morning. Angie had still been asleep, a soft smile shaping her mouth. He'd thought about it during his shower, getting dressed, and during his silent breakfast with Lorenzo.

He had to use his own judgment. He had to decide what he could do that would benefit everyone and still have the desired outcome.

Somehow he had to devise a plan that would protect Angie from what was going to happen to her uncle.

When Zeke walked into Lorenzo's office, the older man nodded. Zeke sat down across the desk from him.

"What's on your mind?" Lorenzo asked.

"I want to know what your game is."

Lorenzo raised his brows. "I'm not following you."

"Why did you choose to put me in the bedroom next to Angie's?"

Lorenzo almost smiled. "How do you know I did?"

"I know. So why are you setting me up?"

Lorenzo picked up a pen on his desk and began to turn it end over end. After a long silence, he said, "I've noticed the interest you've taken in my niece from the beginning. You were fascinated by her picture from the day you first walked into my office."

"Your niece is a beautiful woman. How could I not notice?"

"You need to understand that Angela is the only family I have left. I loved and admired her father. He was my hero. When I lost him and his wife, I vowed to make up their loss to Angela. I never wanted her to go without anything. I've worked years to ensure that she would be financially secure."

Dropping the pen onto the desk, he looked at Zeke. "What I finally came to realize is that Angela needs a strong man who can look after her interests once I'm gone."

Zeke began to see where this conversation was

headed. He felt cold beads of moisture form across his forehead. He was right. He'd been set up.

"I want you to know that I don't intend to stand in the way of a relationship between you and Angela."

"A relationship," Zeke carefuly repeated.

Lorenzo nodded. "Yes. My Angela is a woman now. I have seen the way she looks at you, the way she behaves around you. I know you're attracted to her, as well."

Zeke continued to stare at him without expression, his mind racing with all the implications of Lorenzo's words.

"You want me to marry your niece," he finally stated in a neutral tone.

Lorenzo smiled. "Would that be so bad?"

"You know nothing about me, Lorenzo. Neither does she."

Lorenzo nodded. "Which is exactly why I re-checked your background. You've had an interesting life. You're a tough man, but from everything I've been able to determine, you've been a fair one. You would care for Angela, I believe, and protect her from harm."

"You don't question me about loving her."

Lorenzo shrugged. "Whether you love her at this point or not, you want her. I've seen it in your eyes. You're what she needs. She is what you want. I have reason to think the alliance would work."

"What about her feelings regarding all of this?"

"I'll leave all of that to your discretion. It's up to you to court her. I'm telling you that you will run into no obstacles where I'm concerned."

"On the contrary, you've decided to keep us in close proximity."

"And let nature take its course…yes."

"What makes you think I want marriage from her?"

"I don't. However, rest assured I'll slit your throat if you dishonor her. You have my promise on that."

Zeke studied the older man for a moment. "You missed your calling, boss. You should have been a matchmaker."

"Don't hurt her, Zeke."

"She knows nothing about me, about my background. She would be appalled to know what I've done in the past."

"She doesn't ever need to know. You have a new profession here, taking over my position someday. Men are plotting to take what I am freely offering you."

Zeke stood. "You're placing a great deal of trust in me, Lorenzo."

The older man stood, as well. "Yes."

Zeke was the first to turn away.

Zeke left the house and remained gone all day. He talked with the men who were on guard duty at the gate of the compound. He checked with the men in charge of the guard dogs and the surveillance cameras.

He avoided both Lorenzo and Angie, because he needed time to think. By the time he returned to the house that night, only the men on guard in the house were stirring. Silently Zeke climbed the stairs and entered his room.

After a long, hot shower he pulled on his jeans and

stepped out onto the balcony, breathing in the tranquillity of the night air. There were no sounds in the house or the courtyard. The walled garden looked serene in the starlight. He noted that Angie's doors were closed but made no effort to discover if they were locked.

As much as he had missed her today, as much as he wanted to see her now, he knew that if he saw her, he'd ignore all the reasons why he had to leave her alone and he'd make love to her.

How could this situation have happened to him? Never before in his career had he allowed himself to become emotionally involved…either with the situation or with a person.

However, he had to face the fact that he was deeply involved in this situation and there was no one with whom he could discuss the matter. Frank had been adamant about not breaking his cover for any reason.

He muttered an unprintable word under his breath.

The irony of the situation didn't escape him. Lorenzo was actually grooming him to take his place! If the plane incident hadn't been so dangerous, he might suspect Lorenzo of having planned for them to be marooned together. Had Lorenzo's anger that first night been an act? Had he hoped that Zeke would stay with Angie, anyway, taking advantage of the situation?

The ensuing nights had certainly played right into Lorenzo's hands to further his own personal agenda. What if Lorenzo *knew* Zeke was working for the United States government? What if he were using Angie as the Judas goat to lure Zeke into the trap? If so, the trap should be ready to be sprung at any time.

Was Angie aware of how she was being used, as

well? He thought back over the past few days and knew beyond any doubt that she was as innocent as she appeared, which made what Lorenzo was doing even more reprehensible. Lorenzo was in such a habit of manipulating the people and events around him that he didn't hesitate to sacrifice the only family member he had.

Zeke knew that he had to do something, and soon. He was going to have to risk discovery and get into that office, perhaps bluffing his way out if he were caught.

He couldn't afford to hang around here much longer if he expected to get out alive.

The only question remaining now was Angie. Could he walk away, leaving her to face all the consequences alone? How was she going to be able to cope with knowledge of who and what her uncle really was? Everything she had ever believed in, had ever loved, would be turned upside down, if Zeke was successful.

He felt a strong surge of pain rush through him. He gripped the railing of the balcony and closed his eyes. How could he knowingly cause her such anguish?

However, he'd made a commitment, he'd agreed to this assignment, and a great many lives depended on his carrying out his duties. There had been times in his life when he didn't much like himself or the career he had chosen.

Tonight was one of them.

He had destroyed her innocence. He had also risked getting her pregnant. Was he going to walk away and let her deal with the possible consequences alone?

He'd always been willing to pay for every decision he made. Could he turn his back on her now, knowing

the price would be more than she could face alone?
If she was pregnant and he left her, the disgrace
would destroy her.

But he sure as hell didn't intend to hang around
here and take over Lorenzo's flourishing drug trade!

Zeke wrestled with his demons for several hours
until he decided on the only course of action he could
live with.

Eight

Angie snuggled against Zeke's large, warm body, loving the sensation of being pressed against the muscled surface, enjoying the feel of his warm breath against her cheek—

Her eyes flew open! Zeke was indeed in bed with her. This was no dream. He lay stretched out beside her, propped up on one elbow, watching her.

"Zeke! What are you doing in here? I—"

"What does it look like I'm doing?" he murmured, leaning down and nuzzling beneath her ear.

"I mean, how did you get in here? I remember locking the door."

"Which wasn't very neighborly of you, was it?" He dipped his head and kissed the hollow between her breasts, revealed through her sheer cotton top.

"I didn't want the maid to come in and find you here in the morning."

He straightened, frowning. "Is there a possibility of that?"

"Yes. I wasn't in my room when she came in this morning. I had to make up a tale about where I was." She met his gaze. Her voice wavered slightly as she said, "We almost got caught."

"It certainly sounds that way, doesn't it?" he replied in a mild voice.

She eyed him uncertainly. "Don't you even care?"

"Actually, I do. That's why I'm here. I thought we needed to talk about the matter privately, without interruption." He didn't mention that he'd almost forgotten why he'd picked her lock and entered her room once he saw her lying there on the bed. She slept like a child, bonelessly relaxed, sprawled across the bed.

She touched his cheek. "I know I've been very foolish, allowing my attraction to you to lead me to behave in a way I never would have believed possible." She sighed. "Tio would be devastated if he knew." She dropped her gaze. "I had no idea I could be so weak."

"The thing is, Princess," he began slowly, as though picking his words with care. "There's a good chance that you may be pregnant."

Angie froze. His words had caught her completely off guard. She thought back over the intimate moments they had shared, her eyes widening with realization. "You mean when we—"

"Yes. When I didn't protect you."

She bit her lip, shaken by the fact that she had never considered the possibility. "I never thought about it. I just—"

"Yeah, well, I've thought about it. It's been on my mind all day. I've been trying to work out what to do and I think I've come up with a plan." Once again he paused.

"Well, we can wait to see—"

"Do you honestly think I'm going to be able to keep my hands off you for the next few weeks, Princess? You're damned addictive and I'm permanently hooked. I need a lifetime with you."

She stared at him, uncertain of what he was trying to say. "I don't think I understand, Zeke."

"I want you to marry me."

Her mind blanked out with shock. When she could think again, she managed to say, "You would marry me, even though we've only known each other a few days? I thought I was the impulsive one, but even I wouldn't consider—"

"You do realize, don't you, that your uncle will horsewhip me if he discovers I've been in your bed? Surely you want to spare me that fate." Although the corners of his mouth were slightly curled into a half smile, Zeke's gaze had never been so intent.

She stared at him, bewildered. "You're really serious, aren't you?"

"Yes."

"Do you really want to marry me? I mean, this isn't just a polite gesture on your part?"

The smile he gave her melted her heart. "I want to marry you and to keep you safe more than anything in the world."

Was it possible she was still dreaming? Any moment now she would wake up and discover that she was alone, that Zeke hadn't come into her bedroom, that he hadn't—

"I don't think Tio will approve. We've only known each other a few days. He will insist—"

"Do you trust me, Princess?"

She couldn't resist smoothing her fingers across his cheek. "With my life."

He closed his eyes briefly as though her words caused him pain. Then he said, "I want us to elope... now...tonight. We'll come back in a few days, after he's had time to adjust to the idea. By then our marriage will be an accomplished fact and he'll recognize that there's nothing he can do but accept the matter."

"Tonight! But, it's—" She glanced around the room. "Are you sure we should do this?"

"Absolutely."

She rubbed her forehead, distracted. "My uncle will be furious with me. It will bring back memories of my younger school days when I was always doing something to shock the nuns."

He kissed her before saying, "Honey, I'm guessing the nuns would be pretty shocked with your behavior with me already. Getting married is the best damage control there is at this point."

"But we can't just leave. Tio will wonder what happened, where we are. He'll be worried and upset."

"I thought of that. I've decided to leave him a message in his office. That way we know that he'll be the only one to find it."

"But he keeps his office locked."

"I'm aware of that. I'm also aware there are guards downstairs. However, I'm willing to take the chance if you are. I also know a way to get out of the compound without causing a stir. It's much easier to get out of here than it is to get inside. So why don't you gather a few things while I go downstairs? If I'm not back in half an hour, the safest thing for you to do is to go back to bed and forget we ever had this conversation.''

"The safest thing? You aren't making sense. Leaving my uncle a note isn't dangerous, Zeke.''

Once again he kissed her. "It is when I'm attempting to steal his most prized possession. I'll be back as soon as I can.''

Zeke left her room through the balcony doors, leaving Angie bemused by the sudden turn of events.

Zeke didn't like the odds against him tonight but knew he was out of time. He had to get into Lorenzo's office without being discovered and he had to get Angie to a place of safety.

He didn't want to think about Frank's reaction when he told him that he'd married Lorenzo De la Garza's niece. More than likely he would be looking for a new job, and the current story going around about him would be validated.

Zeke left his room by way of the balcony. He lowered himself over the side and allowed himself to drop to the ground, landing in a crouch. The salon was next-door to Lorenzo's office. He could stay in the salon until the hallway was clear, then hope his skills picking the lock were sufficient to get him inside in the least amount of time possible.

He eased open the outside door to the salon, thankful that no one had thought to check it after he had unlocked it earlier in the evening. Once inside, he slipped through the shadows and cracked open the hallway door.

Two of the men stood by the stairway talking. He waited with trained patience until the conversation had been completed. One of the men headed toward the front of the house, the other toward the back, leaving the hallway empty.

Zeke reached into his pocket for the slivers of metal he needed and eased the door open. He moved without sound to the office and worked the lock, relieved to hear it quietly click in less than a half minute.

He stepped inside, closed and locked the door, and waited for his eyes to adjust before edging toward the desk. He knew Lorenzo kept his records on a personal computer and gave silent thanks he had a working knowledge of the machine.

Using only the light from the screen, Zeke wasted precious moments in an attempt to find the access code. With sudden inspiration he tapped in the name ANGELA and was offered the directory.

There was too much for him to scan. The safest course was to copy as much as possible, choosing the files that looked to be the most promising.

He found the drawer where Lorenzo kept floppy disks and went to work. Every muscle was tense as he listened for any sound from the hallway. So far, everything was quiet.

As soon as he could, Zeke finished copying the files and pocketed the disks. He would leave Lorenzo a note as he promised Angie he would. Leaving the computer screen on for light, he took a sheet of stationery and wrote,

> Lorenzo,
> I decided to follow your advice and marry Angela. Know that I will always take care of her.

Z

Now all he had to do was to get out of there without being spotted.

Several hours later Zeke glanced over at Angie, asleep in the seat beside him in his car. She had slept through most of the night, which was just as well. They would soon be reaching Reynosa, where he intended to stop to get married.

As he guessed, they had had no difficulty leaving the compound. He had hidden her in the back seat once they reached the garage where he kept his car. When he stopped at the gate, he told the men on duty that he was restless and planned to drive into Monterrey to look for a little action. They had laughed at his words and waved him on. Once they were out of sight of the gate, he had pulled over and had Angie join him in the front seat.

He knew she understood that the men would not have been so quick to wave him through if they had known she was with him.

When she asked him where they were going, he explained that he intended to drive to Reynosa. By the time they reached the border city, the government offices should be open and they could get a license. He had taken her hand and laid it on his thigh, where it still rested. Her trust and acceptance had only added to his guilt, but he knew he could live with his guilt easier than he could walk off and leave her to what was coming once he got the information he had to Washington.

"Angie, we're almost there," he said quietly.

She stirred and opened her eyes. In a drowsy voice she said, "I was dreaming about Tio. He's going to be upset that I didn't give him a chance to be at my wedding. He was pleading with me in my dream.''

Zeke reached for her hand. "I still think this is the best way, Princess. Wouldn't you rather him be a little hurt because we ran off to marry, rather than have to face him with the news that you're not married...and pregnant?''

She pressed her hand to her middle and sighed. "I don't wish to hurt him at all. I wonder how many times I have thought that, and said it, after I did something without thinking it through.'' After a moment, she said, "Tio will also be very angry with you, you know. What if he fires you? What will we do?''

He smiled. "I think I'll be able to find a way to support you." He squeezed her hand. "Or maybe I'll put you to work to support me.''

"You're teasing me, but I could, you know.''

He raised her hand to his lips and kissed her knuckles. "I have a hunch you could do anything you set your mind to do.''

She glanced up at him. "I'll take that as a compliment, even though you may not have meant it that way.''

Zeke laughed and replaced her hand on his thigh. He liked feeling her touching him.

He turned onto a main thoroughfare. He used to spend considerable time here in Reynosa with Charlie when they were teenagers. He would find the office issuing licenses and find a judge to marry them. He wanted the marriage legal in case Frank or someone else in the bureaucracy attempted to ignore his attempt to bind Angie to him before all hell broke loose.

Later that morning they crossed the Texas-Mexico

border. Zeke explained to the official at the border that they had just married and showed him the certificate. He pointed out that he was a United States citizen and that Angie would get her papers updated as soon as possible.

Once he was officially across the border into Texas, Zeke felt the tension leave him. The first big hurdle was past. He glanced over at Angie.

"Are you hungry?"

"A little."

He found a restaurant near the airport in McAllen and pulled into the parking lot. As soon as they ordered, he excused himself and headed for the phones. By the time he returned, their order was on the table. He saw the questions in her eyes when he slid into the bench seat across from her, but for the moment ignored them.

"This looks great. I didn't realize how hungry I was." He quickly demolished the food on his plate in silence, finished his coffee and asked, "Are you ready to go?"

She smiled. "Go where?"

"That's a surprise. I've been arranging our honeymoon."

Her eyes widened. "Really?"

"But the only way we can get there is to fly."

"Oh, Zeke!" she wailed.

"I know. But the plane will be large and I'll be right there beside you."

She shook her head. "Couldn't we go someplace closer, so that we could drive?"

"I have to deliver something important before I can be free to enjoy some time with you." He took her hand. "You'll be all right. I promise."

She sighed. "Something tells me I don't have a choice."

He slid out of the bench seat and extended his hand to her. After a moment she took his hand and followed him from the restaurant. "Just because we're married doesn't mean that I'm always going to let you tell me what to do, you know."

He waited to respond to her provocative remark until he got into the car. "I wouldn't dream of always telling you what to do, Princess. Why, I'll treat your every wish as my command from now on."

She watched his profile as he pulled into traffic and followed the street signs to the airport. "My *every* wish?" she asked, intrigued by the idea.

"Weelll," he drawled, "maybe we could negotiate on a few of them."

"I thought so! You're already trying to weasel out of your promise."

He hugged her to him, but waited until he'd found a place in the long-term parking lot and stopped the car before he grabbed her and gave her a leisurely...and very thorough...kiss. They were both flushed when he finally released her.

"Enough of that, woman! You're damned distracting, did you know that?"

They claimed their tickets and found the right gate for the plane that was leaving for Dallas, where they would catch a connecting flight into Washington, D.C. He'd called Frank and told him to meet him at the airport without telling Frank that he would not be alone.

The main thing was that he had gotten the necessary information without blowing his cover, and had gotten himself out of Mexico safely. He'd successfully completed his assignment and as far as he was concerned, he was on his own time once he turned over the disks to Frank.

If Frank was upset, let him fire him. He'd discovered by working with Lorenzo that he had some decidedly marketable skills in the security business. He could always hire himself out as a consultant.

The main thing he had to do was to be there for Angie when she discovered the truth about her uncle.

Zeke spotted Frank in the crowd of people waiting for the passengers to disembark. He wore a pullover shirt and casual slacks, blending in with the people around him. Zeke gave a slight nod when they made eye contact, and waited for the slower passengers ahead of them to get out of his way.

By the time he and Angie were clear he had taken her hand. He stopped in front of his boss, who wore an unprofessionally startled look.

"Hi, Frank! It was great of you to agree to meet us and give us a ride to my place. I told you I had a surprise for you—" Which was a lie. He hadn't told Frank anything but the time of his arrival, when he'd asked him to meet him at the airport. "Here she is. Angie De la Garza and I were married this morning." Before Frank could respond, Zeke continued. "Angie, I want you to meet an old air force buddy of mine, Frank Carpenter. We go back several years together, don't we?"

Frank had his emotions under control, and the smile he gave them both was affable and admiring. "One thing I have to say about you, Zeke, you're a fast worker. I didn't even know you were seeing anyone." He turned to Angie and held out his hand. "I'm pleased to meet you, Mrs. Daniels. I can see that Zeke deserves congratulations.''

Angie's cheeks were pink and her smile radiant. ''I'm very pleased to meet you, Mr. Carpenter,'' she said in her fluent English. ''I must admit that Zeke keeps surprising me. I had no idea where we were going when we left Texas.''

Zeke slipped his arm around her waist and hugged her to him ''I won't let anything happen to you, believe me.'' He kissed her on the tip of her nose, then looked up at Frank, knowing that his boss also got the message.

''The car's this way,'' was Frank's only comment, as he started down the concourse.

The men rode in the front seat while Angie took in the sights from the back seat of Frank's car. Zeke reached over and turned on the radio, setting the sound to come from the back speakers, which he knew would effectively muffle the conversation in the front seat.

''That too loud?'' he asked, glancing over his shoulder. Angie smiled and shook her head, returning her gaze to the sights and sounds beyond the window.

In a barely perceptible tone, Frank muttered, ''Are you out of your mind? De la Garza! Who is she, his daughter?''

''Niece,'' Zeke replied, without looking at Frank.

''Did you abort the assignment?''

''You know me better than that. The information you need is on the disks in the newspaper I just laid at my feet. I'll leave it there when we get out of the car.''

''What in the hell do you think you're doing marrying a member of the family?''

''She doesn't have anything to do with it. She has no idea what's been going on.''

''Does she know who you are?''

''Yes. Just not what I do.''

''Dangerous way to begin a marriage, wouldn't you say?''

''My choices were limited. I did the best I could under the circumstances to protect her.''

''So it isn't a real marriage, then. You're removing her from the scene?''

Zeke was silent. His first reaction had been to deny Frank's statement before he remembered that he hadn't given a thought to anything other than getting her away from a potentially explosive situation. Wearily he ran his hand over his face. ''Something like that, I guess.''

''How do you think she's going to take it when she finds out the truth?''

''I'll deal with that when the time comes. In the meantime, I'm requesting some time off.''

Frank's mouth curved slightly. ''For a honeymoon?''

Zeke cut his eyes around. ''Maybe.''

''Can't say I blame you.'' He glanced into the rearview mirror. ''However, you may have a tiger by the tail once she finds out the truth.''

''Believe me, I've thought about that. I'll just have to deal with her reaction when it comes.''

''Are you going to tell her the truth?''

''Not until he's arrested. I don't want to take the chance she'll warn him.''

''She may never forgive you.''

''That's a risk I'll have to take.''

Frank smiled. ''I'm still in shock. I never pictured

you as a knight rushing to a fair maiden's rescue before. That's quite an image adjustment, let me tell you.''

Zeke turned his head and looked at his superior without expression. ''Go to hell,'' he muttered, before he too watched the traffic and the scenery.

Zeke fished his keys out of his pocket as they walked down the hallway to the apartment he'd rented the year before when he'd been recalled from his European post. ''You'll have to excuse the place. I haven't been here in months. I just hope it's livable.''

Angie felt as though she'd received one shock after another since Zeke had awakened her from a sound sleep last night. She wasn't certain how many more she could handle in one day. ''Why haven't you ever mentioned to me that you had an apartment in Washington?''

He shrugged. ''I guess I never considered the information important enough to bring up. I had to live somewhere once I left my European job. I haven't used it very much, but since I hate staying in hotels, it was worth keeping for whenever I was in town.''

He opened the door and motioned for her to go inside. Instead, she asked, ''Don't you intend to continue working for Tio?''

Zeke placed his hand at the small of her back and guided her into the musty-smelling apartment. He closed the door and edged her over until the door was at her back. He leaned into her, resting his forearms on either side of her head.

Nuzzling her ear, he whispered, ''We've got the rest of our lives to get to know everything about each other, sweetheart. At the moment, I'm kinda distracted.'' He raised his head enough to find her lips with his. He continued to kiss her while he allowed his aroused body to settle firmly against her, more fully explaining his distraction.

Angie went up on her toes and wrapped her arms around his neck. She forgot all of her questions and all of her confusion. She even forgot her guilt about running away with Zeke. She couldn't deny her love for this man and would have followed him willingly wherever he suggested.

He scooped her up in his arms and headed down the hallway. ''I'll show you around later,'' he growled, giving her short, hard kisses until he reached the side of a large bed. ''For the moment I intend to keep you right here.''

Zeke grabbed the bedspread with one hand and jerked it off the bed before he lowered her to the surface. She had become an addiction with him. No matter how many times he made love to her, he could never seem to get enough of her.

He refused to think about the future. Not at this moment, anyway.

He needed this woman now.

His woman.

His wife.

Nine

"**O**h, Tio, Zeke has been showing me around Washington," Angie said into the phone. "He's been a wonderful tour guide since we arrived."

Zeke grimaced at Angie's praise of his abilities, remembering his earlier thoughts on the subject of becoming a professional tour guide. He sat across the room from Angie, watching her speak to her uncle on the phone. He knew that Lorenzo would insist on talking to him in a few minutes and was mentally preparing himself for the verbal assault.

He'd managed to delay the inevitable phone call to her uncle for three days now, but had recognized that morning that he could no longer postpone contacting Lorenzo De la Garza.

He'd been waiting for some word from Frank, hoping that the information he'd gotten to him would be acted upon immediately. But time had run out and

Angie had begun to fret about her uncle, afraid he'd be worried about her, despite the message Zeke had left for him.

"I don't know, Tio," she was saying into the phone. She looked over at Zeke and grinned. "Zeke hasn't said. Here, I'll let you speak with him." Angie handed the cordless phone to Zeke, whispering, "He wants to know when we're coming home."

Zeke took the phone. "Hello, Lorenzo," he drawled, and waited for the explosion.

"Once I got over the initial shock, I realized what you had done, Zeke," Lorenzo said gruffly.

Zeke froze, then murmured, "What do you mean?"

"You wanted to get Angie as far away from what's going on around here as possible. You also knew her reputation would be damaged if she continued to travel alone with you. I understand that. I just wish you hadn't spirited her away in the middle of the night. So although I can appreciate your motives, I resent the manner in which you've carried them out."

"Well, I, uh—"

"In addition, I didn't appreciate the manner you chose to show me the vulnerability of my office security. How did you manage to get inside?"

"It wasn't that difficult, Lorenzo."

"None of the men saw you anywhere near the office. The video cameras didn't pick up anything, either. The only ones who reported seeing you at all were at the gate and they swore you left alone. Were you trying to make me look like some kind of fool, Zeke?"

"Of course not. I—"

Lorenzo gave a loud sigh. "You're good at what

you do, Zeke. Damn good. I should be relieved to
have you on my side, but it concerns me that someone—anyone—was able to breach the security of my
office. What if you had been one of my enemies?''

Zeke met Angie's anxious gaze, then looked away.
Once again guilt gnawed at him. He had no one else
to blame for his present predicament. He also knew
that if he had to relive the past few days, he would
make the same decisions.

But the gnawing at his conscience didn't go away.

''I wanted to let you know that Angie is safe, Lorenzo. She's wanted to call, to explain—''

''I know. She told me. I won't pretend that I'm
pleased at the way you went about things. I would
have wanted to be there, to give her away, to take
part in the ceremony.'' Once again Lorenzo sighed.
''But it's done, now, and there's no reason to continue
to belabor the point. Once we get this mess cleared
up and it's safe to have visitors again, I'll have a
celebration dinner and dance, introduce you to all of
our friends and family.'' Lorenzo's voice lightened.
''At least I've got some good news regarding the attempted break-ins.''

''Let's hear it.''

''I finally got a name—Benito Perez. I'm currently
having him investigated, but I think we've identified
our man.''

''Have you ever heard of him before?''

''Yes. He wanted to buy into one of my compa-
nies…become a partner with me. I told him I worked
alone. He wasn't pleased but I haven't heard anything
further from him.''

''What about the plane? Did you hear who was
behind the cut oil line?''

"I spoke to the owner of the company who owns the hangar. I've used their facilities for years. He was shocked to hear about the accident and is currently having all personnel interrogated. It's possible we can trace something back to Perez." He paused, then reluctantly said, "I'll admit to sleeping better nights knowing that Angela's safe with you. I suppose you did what you felt best. I'm paying you for your judgment calls. I don't suppose I'll always agree with them, especially where my niece is concerned. She sounds happy enough, and I've only got myself to blame in the first place for suggesting you consider marrying her." In a brisk change of voice, he added, "Give me a number where I can reach you. As soon as we trap this guy I'll let you know. In the meantime, take care of my angel for me."

"Yeah, I'll do that," Zeke replied, and slowly hung up the phone. He met Angie's gaze. "He wasn't angry with you, was he?"

She smiled. "No, not really. It was good to talk to him. I apologized for running away with you. He said he'd grown used to my impetuous ways." She moved over to where Zeke sat and slid into his lap. "He didn't sound as though he was eager for us to return."

"No, he didn't."

"I wonder why?"

"I suppose he understood that we wanted some time alone."

She nuzzled his chin. "Well, if we aren't going to starve to death, we're going to have to do some shopping. Your poor cupboard is definitely bare."

Zeke also needed to make a private call to Frank. He glanced at his watch. Hugging her to him, he said, "Why don't you make a list of what we need and I'll

go to the store. I need to get a haircut, as well.''
Placing a kiss on the tip of her nose, he said, ''You'll
probably enjoy having me out from underfoot for a
couple of hours.''

She smiled. ''I could never get tired of being with
you.''

He came to his feet, still holding her. ''Just keep
that thought firmly in mind, Princess, while I show
you what a domesticated animal I've become.'' He
walked into the kitchen and sat her on the counter.
After placing a pad and pencil in her hand, he said,
''Make your list while I go shower.'' He gave her a
slow, seductive kiss, pulling her legs around his waist
and pressing her tightly against him.

''Are you sure you need to leave right away?'' she
whispered, rubbing her breasts against his chest.

He groaned and nibbled at her ear. ''Aren't you
hungry?''

She nodded, her eyes bright, then gave him an imp-
ish grin. ''But not so hungry I can't wait,'' she admitted a little breathlessly when he dipped his head
and nuzzled her breast through her cotton blouse.

Some types of gratification could be postponed,
others couldn't, Zeke decided, hauling Angie into his
arms once again and heading for the bedroom.

He'd call Frank later.

By the time Angie showered and found something
to wear sometime later, Zeke had left. Dreamily she
changed the sheets and gathered up their laundry. For
the first time since the ceremony, Angie realized that
she felt truly married, taking care of domestic chores.
Smiling at the idea, she carried the laundry down the

hallway to the closet where the washer and dryer were installed.

She couldn't plan any meals until Zeke returned, but she could show him her housewifely skills by dusting and polishing the place. With only one bedroom, the apartment was small enough to be thoroughly cleaned in a relatively short while.

Humming with the current hit music being played on his stereo, Angie found the vacuum cleaner in a cluttered closet in the bedroom and lifted it from between a stack of boxes.

The disruption caused another box to slide off the stack and tumble upside down, dumping its contents around her feet. Stifling a muttered curse, Angie knelt and began to scoop up the mess, then paused when she recognized Zeke's picture on one of the documents.

Puzzled, she examined what looked to be a driver's license, but with someone else's name. The address was unknown, as well. She picked up what looked to be a passport. This, too, had a picture of Zeke, but the name and address listed were different.

Angie stared at the documents scattered around her feet with a sense of numbness. She could feel the heavy beat of her heart in her chest as it sluggishly pounded its rhythm. She forced herself to breathe— to inhale, to exhale—to remember the fundamental functions of her body as her mind began to whirl with questions and images.

She remembered the first time she had seen Zeke, waiting at the Mexico City airport. She remembered her reaction to him, even then. He held a fascination for her that was so strong she hadn't questioned the wisdom of believing him, of trusting him.

He worked for her uncle, didn't he? Her uncle would never have hired someone who wasn't trust-worthy. Surely there was a rational explanation for what she had just found.

Was it necessary for Zeke to assume other identi-ties in his job? Quickly she sorted through the various cards and licenses, the passports and visas, trying to make sense out of what she saw.

Was his name really Zeke Daniels?

Did she know the man she was married to?

Angie carefully replaced the scattered pieces of identification in the box, then set the box in the closet. For a moment she stared at the vacuum cleaner as though puzzled by its reason for being there. Then like an automated mannequin she began to clean the apartment, waiting to hear the door open to reveal the man she had married...the stranger she had mar-ried...in hopes his explanation could ease the panicky feeling that had swept over her, threatening to con-sume her.

As soon as Zeke got through to Frank, he asked, "When is the agency going to make their move against De la Garza?"

"I haven't heard, Zeke. Don't tell me you're get-ting bored with the honeymoon?"

"I've told Angie we'd return to Monterrey, but I don't want her down there when they arrest him."

"Have you told her who you are?"

"No!"

"You've really set yourself up on this one, haven't you?"

Zeke scrubbed his palm across his forehead. "I did

what I had to do, Frank. I don't think the man's going to give up easily. I don't want her in danger.''

"You know your marrying De la Garza's niece has hurt your credibility with the DEA, don't you? Now they don't know whether they can trust the information you gave them or not.''

"Dammit, Frank, you know better than that!''

"They don't.''

"Then tell them.''

"You may have to do that yourself.''

"Fine. Name the time and the place and I'll be there.''

There was a pause. "Are you serious?''

"Of course I'm serious!''

"Hold on, I'll see what I can set up.''

Canned music played in his ear while Zeke waited. He'd known none of this was going to be easy. Given the paranoia of the intelligence community, he wasn't particularly surprised at their attitude. Well, he didn't really care what they thought. He'd been turned loose to do what he had to do to get the information needed. He'd gotten the damned information. It wasn't anyone's business that he'd also gotten himself married into the family of a drug kingpin.

Lorenzo was just as concerned about protecting Angie as he was. At least he'd give the man that. Maybe this Benito Perez could be traced to—

"Zeke?''

"I'm here.''

"All right. We've called a meeting here tomorrow at ten. They're bringing over printouts of everything you turned over. They have some questions maybe you can answer.''

"Whatever it takes to get this thing over with. By

the way, Frank, tell them to find out whatever they can on a Benito Perez, who may be behind some of the recent trouble Lorenzo's been having. He may be the link we've been looking for. I figure he's someone in the business wanting to take over the De la Garza shipping routes and contacts.''

''Was his name on any of the information you gave us?''

''I doubt it. I got it today from Lorenzo.''

''You're still in touch with him?''

''Of course. I just married the niece he raised like his own daughter. Hell, Frank! Don't you understand? Angie's all the family he's got left. He's grooming me to take his place once he retires.''

''Have you considered the possibility that you may be in over your head, hotshot?''

Zeke sighed. ''The thought has occurred to me on one or two occasions, yes.''

''I'm not certain whether your decisions have been based on nobility or overactive hormones. Couldn't you have protected the woman without marrying her?''

''Maybe.''

''At least you admit to the possibility.''

''I've never pretended to be perfect, Frank.''

''I've never known you to allow your emotions to get in the way of any of your decisions before, either.''

A woman paused outside the telephone booth and peered inside. Zeke nodded to her and said into the phone, ''Look, Frank, I've got to get off this phone. I'll see you in your office in the morning.''

''Good enough.''

''Thanks for your understanding. I know I've been

acting out of character. I can't really give a logical explanation of my behavior. Wish I could.''

Frank laughed. "Love's never been considered a rational emotion, Zeke. I've always assumed you were immune, that's all.''

Zeke hung up the phone and opened the door to the booth, smiling an apology to the woman waiting. She gave him a dazzling smile, but he never noticed. His mind was too busy repeating Frank's last words...love's never been considered a rational emotion...love's never... *Love!*

He stepped outside of the drugstore and leaned against the brick wall for a moment, his shaking knees too weak to hold his weight without some kind of support.

Love?

What was Frank talking about? What did love have to do with the way he'd been feeling...or acting, for that matter? Whatever his feelings, they had nothing in common with such a sappy, sentimental emotion as love.

Frank had really lost it, hadn't he? The guy didn't know what he was talking about.

Somehow, his conclusion about Frank didn't make his knees feel any stronger. Zeke couldn't understand why he was trembling as though suddenly stricken by a fever, or why he had broken out into a cold sweat.

All right. Exactly what was happening here? He wanted Angie. He understood that. His reaction to her was certainly a very basic one. Not only had he found it impossible to keep his hands off her, he'd discovered a strong need to protect her, as well.

But love?

Impossible.

Now he had to face the fact that he hadn't fully thought out how he planned to tell Angie the truth about her uncle. Nor had he considered how she was going to feel toward him when she discovered his role in her uncle's capture.

He had a hunch she was going to hate him.

What did he intend to do about their relationship once she knew the truth? Did he intend to fight to keep what they had together?

For the first time in his life, Zeke felt helpless to control the outcome of a situation that he had set up. He didn't want to think about a life without Angie. He couldn't imagine not having her there in his arms when he fell asleep at night, or cuddled next to him when he awoke each morning.

With his thoughts and emotions in a turmoil, Zeke managed to find his way back to his car. Forgetting about buying groceries, he headed back to the apartment.

He needed to see her. He felt an overwhelming desire to hold her in order to reassure himself that she was real. She had married him, hadn't she? he reminded himself. She must feel something for him. She would understand why he had…why it was necessary for him to… His thoughts swirled around in his head.

Impatiently weaving his rental car through traffic, Zeke hurried home. He didn't like what he was feeling. He didn't want to feel this vulnerable.

Not with anyone.

Not ever.

He remembered the pain of losing his mother, and later, his best friend. He'd recovered and he'd gone on with his life. He'd also learned that love was too painful to endure when he lost a loved one.

Zeke fought for composure as he locked the car in the underground parking and headed for the elevator that would take him to his apartment. He'd be all right as soon as he saw Angie. Maybe it was time for him to tell her a little about himself, about his background. Maybe he should prepare her for what was going to happen to Lorenzo, to reassure her that he was there for her.

He opened the door of the apartment, only then realizing that he had forgotten to stop for food.

"Angie? Hey, Princess, guess you'd better go with me next time. I forgot all about getting groceries. I got sidetracked and I—" He walked into the living room and saw that she had been cleaning. Everything sparkled. He grinned, the knot in his chest slowly receding.

"Angie?" He walked down the hallway toward the bedroom.

She heard him come in but continued to sit in the rocking chair, which occupied a corner of the bedroom. After she had finished cleaning, Angie had returned to the bedroom and closed the drapes, unwilling to accept the sunshine that poured into the room as though nothing had changed.

Everything had changed. She was lost and adrift in a reality she didn't understand, couldn't begin to comprehend, and had nowhere to turn.

She watched as Zeke paused in the doorway of the bedroom, but she didn't speak. He flipped on the light at the same time he said her name.

"Angie?"

She rocked gently, watching him register surprise,

then concern. Seeing him always had such an impact
on her. He radiated strength...and power...and a cha-
risma that made her quiver.

He crossed the room in long strides. ''Are you all
right? What's wrong?'' He knelt beside her and took
her hand between his.

His hands felt warm and she shivered.

This was Zeke. This was the man who had held
her, who had loved her, who had protected her. This
was the man she loved. Could she pretend that nothing had happened? Was she strong enough to confront
him? Was she strong enough to deal with his answers?

''What happened, honey? You're so pale. Did you
hurt yourself?'' He gave a quick glance around the
bedroom. ''You've been busy, I can see that. You
know you didn't have to do all of the cleaning
alone.'' He took her other hand and held it against
his chest.

Angie pulled her hands away. She couldn't think
when he touched her. And she knew that she had to
think, had to be strong. Taking a deep breath, she
said, ''Tell me who you are.'' Her voice wavered
slightly. She closed her eyes, no longer able to look
at him.

He looked at her blankly. ''What are you talking
about?''

She forced herself to open her eyes but couldn't
look at him. Instead, she studied her hands gripped in
her lap. ''I found the box in your closet, Zeke. The
one with the passports and identifications, with different names and nationalities.'' She finally met his
gaze. ''Each of them has your picture on them.''

Zeke studied her in silence for a few moments before he answered. She couldn't read anything in his expression now. His eyes had gone dark as though a light had been turned off.

"You know who I am, Angie. I haven't lied to you."

"Then why do you have all those phony IDs? Isn't that illegal?"

"They're part of my job. Technically speaking, they are illegal, I suppose."

"What job? Who do you work for...besides my uncle?"

A muscle jumped in his jaw, but he never dropped his gaze. "I work for the government. I worked in Europe for many years and used several of those aliases."

"Why are you working for my uncle?"

"Because he needed someone like me, someone with my background and expertise."

"Does he know you work for your government?"

"No."

"Then you lied to him."

"I didn't tell him the complete truth."

"If I tell him the truth, what will happen?"

He shrugged and looked away.

"It would cause you problems?"

He sighed. "Yeah, you could say that."

"Will you tell me why you went to work for my uncle?"

"I'm afraid I can't. Not at the moment, anyway."

"You're spying on my uncle, aren't you?" Before he could respond, she said, "Why? Why are you and your government spying on him? What do you think he's done?"

"I can't discuss the matter with you, Angie. I wish I could, but I can't."

"You can't tell me why you were in Mexico?"

He shook his head.

"Is Tio supposed to have done something wrong?"

"Even if he has, whatever he's done has nothing to do with you...or with you and me."

She studied him for a long while, trying to make sense out of what he was telling her, wanting desperately to understand. She was frightened. What could Tio have done that would cause the United States government to be interested enough to send Zeke to work for him?

"Why did you marry me?" she finally asked. Angie wasn't at all certain she could face his answer. But she knew that she could no longer pretend that their relationship was what she had originally thought.

"Because I love you, Angie. No other reason." His low voice sounded hoarse.

Oh, how she wanted to believe him! But the doubts had been planted and were rapidly taking root.

She looked around the room. "Why are we in Washington? It isn't because you wanted to spend our honeymoon here, is it?"

"I brought you here because it was the safest place for you to be. Your uncle understands that."

"My uncle's home isn't safe?"

"Have you already forgotten the problems with the plane, the attempted break-ins at the compound? Until we find out who's behind those incidents, then, no, Lorenzo's home isn't safe."

She sighed. "I don't know what to think. My head is spinning. I feel as though I just woke up from a very vivid dream, but one I now know wasn't real at all.''

"Angie, if you don't believe anything else, believe this. I love you. I love you more than I've ever loved anyone in my life."

She eyed him uncertainly. "You've never mentioned your feelings for me before."

"No."

She stared at him for a long, silent moment before slowly nodding. "It was never necessary before, I suppose. But now that I've discovered some of your secrets, you feel it necessary to convince me you love me."

"I haven't lied to you, ever. I won't start now. There are just some things that I can't tell you at this time. But they don't have anything to do with us. If you don't want to believe anything else, believe that I've never lied about my feelings for you."

Her head ached with confused thoughts. She didn't know what to think. She knew what she wanted to believe, of course. Like a child, she wanted to continue to believe in happy ever after.

Angie recognized that she was in over her head. Nothing in her life had prepared her for a situation where she had to trust her own judgment so completely. She had relied heavily on her uncle's guidance. She realized...now...that she had trusted Zeke because her uncle trusted him.

But Zeke had lied to her uncle. Zeke was a man with a mysterious background and a mysterious past whose presence in her life was shrouded in more mystery.

Once again her impulsive nature had betrayed her.

She loved Zeke Daniels. There was no doubt in her mind about her feelings for him.

The question was: did she dare trust him?

Ten

"**I** don't believe you!" Zeke growled, slapping his hand on the top of the desk for emphasis. "I don't care what your so-called experts tell you, I was there, dammit! I know what I saw! Of course this man's running an illegal operation, and the records I turned in should prove that fact!"

Zeke sat at a conference table with five of the men involved in the drug trafficking problems on the Texas-Mexico border. The head of the operation had just summarized their findings with regard to the files belonging to Lorenzo De la Garza.

"All right, Zeke, I can understand your irritation and frustration. All of us were shocked at what turned up on those reports. I'll admit that we thought at first you might have decided to protect him since you married into the family." He paused when he saw the

sudden flash of fire in Zeke's eyes. In a more concili-
iatory tone, he added, "We ran them through cryp-
tology, we did everything possible to make certain
they weren't in some kind of code. What we discovered was that the data is exactly what it looks like—
meticulous business records for De la Garza's operation...and it's all legal." The man leaned back in
his chair, tapping his pencil. "Naturally, we've been
stunned by this evidence, since we've put so much
time into proving his participation in drug trafficking.
What did you see while you were there that makes
you believe we've misinterpreted our findings?"

"His lifestyle, for one thing. The man lives like
royalty. Where else would he be getting that kind of
money, if not from drugs? He's got his own plane,
he has an army of security men around him at all
times, he's got the perfect cover to hide behind—his
factories where he's supposedly manufacturing goods
for export."

"Yes, we know all of that, Zeke. His investments
are definitely paying off for him. What I'm asking is,
did you ever see any drugs? Did you ever see a trans-
action where money and drugs were exchanged?"

"Of course not! The man wasn't going to trust me
to sit in on something that sensitive. He's too smart
for that."

"Didn't you say he used you not only to beef up
his security system but as his personal bodyguard, as
well? Didn't you travel with him?"

"Yes."

"Were there times when he had you stay behind
while he went somewhere alone?"

"No. But I was only there a couple of months."

"Two months is a long time in the drug business. You would have seen something during that time."

"I identified two undercover agents! Don't forget that!"

"But were they on his payroll?"

"They were working for him…yeah."

"Doing what?"

Zeke paused, rubbing his forehead. He had a headache that wouldn't quit. He hadn't gotten much sleep last night, lying there beside Angie, wondering how he was going to break the news to her that her uncle was involved in running drugs. He also dreaded to tell her his part in the operation.

Now he was being told that Lorenzo De la Garza was *not* the head of a drug cartel, that he was exactly what he represented himself to be, a highly successful, very rich businessman who was having trouble with a particularly nasty business rival who was trying to stop him in any way he could.

One of Benito Perez's ploys had been to report Lorenzo De la Garza as a member of a drug running cartel. What was now suspected was that Perez had managed to plant drugs in one of Lorenzo's factory shipments, then Perez tipped off the border patrol to make sure the drugs were discovered. The amounts found were enough to encourage the assignment of an all-out surveillance team. When nothing positive was reported back from those assigned to the case, Zeke had become involved.

He thought about the agents he had identified. "All

right, I see what you mean. One of the agents worked as a yardman, the other one helped in the kitchen.''

"Exactly. They were employees, much like you were. They were paid a wage of sorts, but it wasn't enough to tempt anyone into hiding information.''

Zeke shook his head. "So you're telling me that the large-scale, multidepartmental operation designed to flush this guy out in the open managed to find out that he hasn't done anything wrong?''

"He may be doing all kinds of things that are wrong, Daniels,'' Frank put in. "Just nothing to do with drugs. The man is a financial wizard.''

"His records were impeccable,'' the head of the operation pointed out. "He knows where every peso goes, he knows how and where it comes in. At any given time he has an exact idea where he stands monetarily.''

Zeke dropped his head in his hands. His head was swimming. How could he have been so wrong about a man? How could not just one, but *two* intelligence departments be so wrong about a man?

"Well, he certainly made us all look like fools,'' he murmured.

"Actually, we managed to do that without his help. As far as he knows, the yardman found a better job, the kitchen help had a sick mother.''

"What about me?''

"Good question. How did you leave? Did you give notice or did you walk out?''

"I eloped with his niece. He's expecting us back home once he deals with this Perez character.''

"Then he has no way of knowing that you were

working for us. I doubt that he knows you copied the files. We certainly haven't leaked any of the information. I'll admit to a few red faces in our department over this. We've been after the man for almost three years. Three years! This type of news is exactly what we don't want getting out to the press corps—how we're spending the taxpayer's money!''

Another one of the men spoke up. ''But we also follow up every lead we're given and the situation looked suspicious to us. Of course it was supposed to. We were shown just enough to whet our appetite, thinking we were on to something.''

''It looks like the joke's on me, gentlemen,'' Zeke said slowly, leaning back in his chair. ''Mr. Lorenzo De la Garza has plans to groom me to take over his operation when he retires. I thought he meant the drug trade. I can't believe I so completely misread a situation.''

''Don't be too hard on yourself, Zeke,'' Frank offered after a moment. ''We're trained to look for ulterior motives, for cover-ups, for illicit practices.''

''Even when none exist!'' Zeke replied. He still had to look at all the implications where he was concerned. What was he supposed to do now?

He could go back to Mexico. He could quit this job and work for Lorenzo for real. He could go back to Angie and explain that—

Explain that he had been gathering evidence to put her uncle behind bars only to discover there wasn't any evidence to be found?

Not likely.

''Zeke?''

He looked at Frank. "You did a hell of a job for us. I believe your explanations today have given us a clearer picture of the situation. I think we'll let this terminate your part of the operation. If you decide to take Lorenzo's offer, I'll certainly understand. After all, you're part of his family now. Whatever you decide, let me know, all right?"

Zeke pushed his chair back from the table and stood. "I can't say I'm sorry about the outcome of the investigation, gentlemen, given my circumstances. Angie would have been devastated with news of her uncle's involvement in illegal shipments of any kind."

Frank stuck out his hand. "At least now we have a new lead. I'll see what happens when we place Benito Perez under a magnifying glass."

Zeke shook Frank's hand, nodded to the other men and left the room. He'd go back to Angie and tell her what had been happening. He had a hunch that Perez would soon have his hands full with other problems and wouldn't have the time or resources to continue to harass Lorenzo.

Zeke felt as though a huge weight had been lifted off his shoulders. He could make whatever explanations he had to, then get on with his new life. If necessary he would spend the rest of his life convincing Angie that he loved her.

He was looking forward to that particular assignment.

"Angie?" he called as soon as he opened the door to the apartment.

There was no answer. He strode down the hallway. "Angie, honey, where are you?"

The bedroom was empty. So was the dresser where she had placed a few of her possessions. A sudden pain caught him in the region of his heart when he noticed that the only item on the dresser was an envelope with his name written on it. A sense of foreboding made him hesitate before he picked up the envelope and opened it. Folded sheets of paper lay inside. Fumbling them open, he read:

"Zeke, I've taken the coward's way out, I know, but my feelings for you are too strong to be able to tell you in person that I have decided to leave.

I don't know why you were working for Tio, but I feel you and your government were hoping to find him doing something wrong. I believe that you used my feelings for you for your own purposes, so that you would have a bargaining tool against my uncle.

For everyone's sake I've decided to return to Monterrey. I don't want to be a part of whatever you are involved in. I love my uncle too much to ever allow my impulsive decisions to hurt him.

I hope you will be able to forgive me someday. If you wish to have our marriage annulled, I will agree to whatever necessary. I'll wait to hear from you.

Angela

Zeke sank onto the side of the bed and stared at the feminine handwriting. A part of his mind refused to take in the contents of the letter, focusing on the neat penmanship instead. He'd never seen her writing before. There was so much he didn't know about her.

She loved her uncle. That much he knew. She would never forgive Zeke for what he had attempted to do. Somewhere deep inside he had known that, as well.

What did he intend to do now? Ignoring his feelings for the moment, he knew that he had originally whisked her away from Mexico in an attempt to protect her. She no longer needed his protection.

She no longer needed to be married to him.

He could go back and attempt to explain, or he could accept her decision to get out of his life. He knew what he wanted to do, but for the first time in his life, Zeke discovered he didn't have the courage to face the possible outcome. His feelings for her were too strong to face her when she told him she no longer wanted to be a part of his life.

Zeke stretched out across the bed and closed his eyes. He concentrated on blanking out the memories. He needed every ounce of energy he could summon to help him to forget.

How long would it take for him to recover from the self-inflicted wound of loving Angela De la Garza Daniels?

"Would you care for something to drink, Ms. De la Garza?" the flight attendant asked Angie, drawing her out of her reverie.

Angie glanced up from the magazine she'd been

mindlessly studying and attempted to smile at the friendly woman who was being so solicitous to her first-class passengers.

"Thank you, no."

After the woman moved away, Angie dropped the magazine to her lap and stared out the window of the plane. Now that she was on her way to Mexico, there was no turning back. She had to come to grips with what she had done. Tio would want some kind of explanation for her inexplicable behavior. She had so little excuse for her impulsiveness this time. What could she say?

The one thing she knew for certain was that somehow she was going to have to stop running and face the consequences of the decisions she had made in the past few weeks.

Although Tio had strongly resisted the idea of her coming to Mexico at this time, she had come anyway, determined to share with him her dreams of starting a school in the village, of making her home permanently in Mexico. She'd never gotten around to telling him about all her detailed plans. Instead, she'd allowed her instant attraction to Zeke to distract her from her goal. Oblivious to the inherent dangers of becoming intimate with a man she barely knew, she had thrown herself headlong into a relationship.

She had trusted Zeke because she trusted Tio's judgment. What she hadn't taken into consideration was that Tio's trust in the man had to do with his profession, not as a prospective member of the family.

She'd been such a fool...immature, impossibly naive, and irresponsible.

She recognized that at the moment she not only was running from Zeke, she was running from herself, which was certainly an exercise in futility. She sighed, rubbing her hand across her forehead where a throbbing ache had found a seemingly permanent home.

There was no one to save her this time from her impulsive choices. Neither man in her life could rescue her. She had placed herself in a situation that needed to be looked at with maturity, a trait she feared was truly lacking in her makeup.

Fact: she was now married to a man who worked for a foreign government while ostensibly working for her uncle.

Fact: he would not tell her why, an ominous lack of trust.

Fact: she had walked out on a week-old marriage because she didn't know how to handle being a wife.

The question she had to face at this time was what did she do now? Should she warn her uncle of Zeke's dual occupation? If she did, would she be placing Zeke in a possibly dangerous situation? Loyalty to one man could be disloyalty to the other. Did she owe Zeke her loyalty, regardless of their legal tie? He had lied by omitting to tell her some important information about himself, information that might harm Tio.

She closed her eyes, wishing for the wisdom of Solomon to know what to do now. How could she consider staying married to a man who lived in another country when all she could dream about these past few years was to get back home to Mexico? She'd easily responded to Zeke's suggestion to marry when she thought that he would continue to work for Tio there in Mexico. It was another thing entirely to think about living in Washington, D.C., while her husband traveled, leaving her alone.

What she had finally admitted to herself earlier in the day was that she wasn't ready for marriage. Unfortunately for everyone concerned, she had left the discovery of that particular insight a little late. Acknowledging this latest piece of awareness had, if possible, dropped her self-esteem another notch down on her personal evaluation scale...causing her to teeter dangerously close to self-loathing.

So where did she go from here, besides flying home to throw herself into Tio's arms? She'd messed up in a really big way, with no idea what to do next.

When the plane reached Dallas, Angie had a two-hour layover. She called her uncle to tell him she was on her way home and to ask him to meet her plane.

"Is Zeke with you?"

"No, Tio. I'm alone."

"But why? Isn't it customary for a couple to honeymoon together?"

"I've left him, Tio. I should never have run off with him like this." She bit her bottom lip, hard, to gain some control over her emotions.

"What did he do to you?" Lorenzo demanded to know.

"It's more like what I did to him. I trapped him into marrying me, then didn't have the courage to live with my actions."

"What do you mean, you trapped him? What's going on with you two?"

"I'll explain everything when I get home, Tio. I promise. I hadn't realized until these past few days how very childish I've been, wanting whatever attracted me without regard to whether it was good for me or not...or if I could handle the consequences. I've discovered that I've made a lot of mistakes recently. Now I've got to face each one of them and do what I can to find a solution."

"I don't understand what you're talking about, but we'll discuss it further when you arrive."

"Yes, Tio. Thank you for being there for me." She hung up before her voice could break.

In the following weeks Angie spent most of her time alone. She took long walks, she visited the village and talked with the mothers, she discussed some of her ideas about a preschool with her uncle.

She made no attempt to contact Zeke. Not that she didn't want to talk with him...to hear his voice again. Not that she didn't miss him with every aching breath she drew. No, she didn't call because she didn't know what to say to him.

She had hoped that he would contact her, that he would in some way open the line of communication between them so that she could attempt an explanation of some of the things she had discovered about herself.

Regardless of her confusion, she knew with a deep certainty that she loved Zeke with every fiber of her being. When he didn't call or return to Mexico, she knew that she had blown any chance she might have had to apologize to him for her behavior.

Angie lost track of the many letters she had written to him, then had torn up. How could she begin to excuse her inexcusable behavior?

She tried to imagine what he was doing now, wondering if he was still in Washington or whether he had returned overseas to work once again.

It was time to pick up the various pieces of her life and get on with what she had to do to survive the emotional backlash of her impulsive behavior.

Zeke rolled over with a groan, burying his head under his pillow to muffle the steady pounding. Why didn't whoever was trying to beat down his door go away?

He'd lost track of time since Angie had left. Days and nights had run meaninglessly together. He'd managed to go to the store and buy some food and several bottles of his favorite brand of bourbon. The bourbon was for medicinal purposes…to help him create amnesia.

Unfortunately the damn stuff wasn't doing the job.

He'd unplugged the phone two…maybe three… days ago. He didn't want to talk to anybody. He didn't want to see anybody. He just wished the jerk hammering on his door would give up and go somewhere else.

The steady pounding continued, despite the muffling effect of the pillow.

"All right, all right!" he finally muttered, throwing the pillow across the room and rising. His head kept a pounding counterpart to the noise on the front door. He fumbled for his jeans and drew them up to his waist. They hung loosely, reminding him that he'd been skipping a few meals lately.

The room was dark, which didn't mean much since he'd kept the drapes pulled. He had no idea what day it was, or what time it was. He didn't much care.

Rather than turn on a light, he felt his way along the hallway until he reached the front door.

He attempted to peer through the security peephole but couldn't focus. He finally gave it up. "Who is it?" he demanded gruffly through the door.

"Lorenzo."

Zeke blinked in disbelief. Lorenzo? He fumbled with the lock and jerked the door open in disbelief. His former employer stood before him, nattily dressed as always, looking as though he was prepared to camp in the hallway if necessary.

"Are you the one who's been making all that racket?" His puzzlement slightly softened his distinctly hostile tone. But not by much.

"May I come in?" Lorenzo asked politely.

"Why?" was the bald response.

Lorenzo's mouth twitched slightly. "Because I prefer talking to you somewhere other than the hallway—" he glanced around him "—private though it may seem at the moment."

Zeke ran his hand through his hair, shook his head in an attempt to clear it, then shrugged and stepped away from the door. "Come in, if you want," he said, turning away. "I'll be back in a minute."

It took longer than a minute for him to shower and shave, but he needed the time to adjust to his unexpected company, to get awake, and to prepare himself to face whatever Lorenzo had felt was important enough to come to Washington to tell him.

He looked at the bloodshot eyes of the man in the mirror and shook his head in disgust. He looked like hell. He hadn't shaved in days and winced as he nicked himself, wondering if he'd forgotten how to shave. He reminded himself that there was no need to hurry. Obviously Lorenzo didn't intend to go anywhere until he'd said his piece.

Zeke grabbed a towel and gingerly patted his face dry. He combed his wet hair, noticing that he needed a haircut. Then he went into the bedroom and found a clean shirt hanging in the closet. The shirt and a clean pair of jeans made him feel almost human again.

Without bothering to search for socks or shoes he headed toward the living room, pausing in the doorway. Lorenzo stood at the window looking out. Without turning around, he said, "Nice view of the city."

Zeke glanced out the window, finally registering the blackness outside. He went into the kitchen area that was separated from the living room by a bar. "You want some coffee?" he asked, reaching for the canister.

Lorenzo turned and nodded. "Yes, thank you."

"When did you get in?"

"Yesterday. I've been trying to reach you for several days now, but there was no answer." He glanced around the room and saw the phone sitting on a side table, unplugged. "I'm beginning to understand why."

Zeke made no comment. He measured coffee and water as though no one else were around.

"You look like hell, Zeke," Lorenzo finally said.

Zeke glanced up, his gaze meeting Lorenzo's briefly before he looked away. He reached for a couple of coffee mugs, filled and carried them into the living room. After offering one to Lorenzo, he sat down in the large overstuffed chair.

"So how did you find me?" he finally asked.

Lorenzo sat down on the sofa across from him and leaned back with a sigh. "It wasn't easy. I had to go over your résumé and call some of the numbers listed. It took me two days until I was finally connected to Frank Carpenter."

Zeke had been staring at his coffee during Lorenzo's explanation, but glanced up in surprise at the mention of Frank's name. He straightened in the chair. "Frank told you where I lived?"

Lorenzo smiled. "Is it supposed to be a secret?"

Not a secret, exactly, but Frank was notoriously closemouthed about things. He strictly adhered to the "need to know" policy in the business. "I'm just surprised."

"I went to his office this morning in hopes of getting some clarity on the situation."

"What situation?"

"On your showing up to work for me, then not returning."

Zeke relaxed into his chair once more and drawled, "I hope he gave you what you were looking for."

He was taken by surprise once again when Lorenzo nodded. "He helped me to see the big picture. Actually, he was a great deal of help. He gave me enough solid evidence on Benito Perez to turn him over to authorities when I return home. He said it was the least he could do since I had paid the salary for the man who obtained the information. I understand he was part of my kitchen help." Lorenzo's smile was filled with self-mockery. "I owe your government for their help in getting that particular matter resolved."

"Frank was a regular chatterbox, wasn't he?" Zeke muttered, shaking his head.

"Under the circumstances, he felt your organization owed me more than an apology for their infiltrating my operation. I'll admit that being able to rid myself of Perez goes a long way to placate my anger at the loss of my privacy."

"I'm sure Frank appreciated your viewing the matter in such a positive light." Zeke took another sip from his coffee, slowly feeling the caffeine work its magic in his body.

"I'm a businessman, Zeke. I don't have to like a situation to understand why it was necessary. I had no idea I was under suspicion for distributing drugs. When you first appeared, my only concern was that you weren't planted there by my adversary." He paused to drink from his cup before continuing. "Once I discovered your background, I knew you wouldn't have been recruited to sabotage my business. It never occurred to me that I was your target."

The coffee helped to clear Zeke's head. He went back to the kitchen and returned with the carafe, refilling both cups.

Once he sat down again, Lorenzo said, "You were

a great help to me, Zeke. I want you to know that. Regardless of the reason you hired out to me, I owe you a debt of gratitude...not only for the way you set up the new security system, but also the way you took care of Angela.''

Zeke flinched at the mention of the name he had known would eventually become part of their conversation. ''Oh, I took care of her, all right,'' he muttered into his cup before draining half its contents.

Lorenzo sighed. ''What's between you and Angela is none of my business, I know, but when two people I care about are so desperately unhappy, I feel it imperative to do whatever I can to help.''

Zeke eyed the man across from him. ''Are you implying I'm desperately unhappy about something?'' His gruff voice once again had an edge of hostility.

''I've seen you in better shape than this,'' Lorenzo replied.

''I'm on my own time now, doing what I want to do.''

''Which is?''

Zeke shrugged. ''Resting between assignments.''

''Ah.'' Lorenzo set his cup down and made a steeple with his fingers. ''Then you don't intend to return to Monterrey to learn my business?''

Zeke stared at him in disbelief. ''You mean you still want me to work with you?''

''Yes.''

Zeke couldn't think of anything to say about this totally unexpected development. After a moment he shook his head abruptly, his laugh sounding harsh and unamused. "Right. I can just see how that would work."

"Why wouldn't it?"

His irritation at his need to explain was echoed in his voice. "I have no intention of going anywhere near Angie."

"Why?"

Zeke scowled at the other man's obtuseness. "Why?" he repeated, his voice rising. "In case she hasn't mentioned it to you, she wants no part of me or our hasty marriage. She's convinced I was just using her to get to you."

"Were you?" Lorenzo asked mildly.

"Hell, no! I didn't *need* to use her for anything. I was already set up with you before she ever showed up." Unable to sit still, Zeke sprang from his chair and began to pace. "What was going on with us had nothing to do with the job I was hired to do, either for you or the government!"

"Did you ever explain that to her?" Lorenzo asked in the same mild manner.

"Ha! She never gave me a chance! She jumped to all kinds of conclusions—" he turned and glared at Lorenzo "—most of which were wrong, I might add. Just because I couldn't tell her the truth about why I was there, she decided she couldn't trust me." He stalked over to the bar and poured himself a double shot of bourbon. "Which is fine with me!" He lifted the glass to his mouth.

"I can see that," Lorenzo quietly replied. "Is that why you've crawled into that bottle, because you don't care that your new wife doesn't trust you?"

Zeke lowered the glass and glared at Lorenzo. "I never asked her to trust me."

"Maybe you should have."

"Maybe I should have done a lot of things that I didn't do." He glanced distastefully at the full glass he held in his hand and slammed it down, spinning away from the bar and going to stand in front of the window. "I sure as hell know I *did* a lot of things that I shouldn't have. But you don't have to worry, I'm paying for every damn one of them!"

"I'm really surprised at you, Zeke. You never struck me as the kind of man to sit around and sulk."

Zeke stiffened, feeling the steadily building rage within threatening to break through. Sulk? The man had the audacity to accuse him of some infantile attitude when he— Slowly he turned to look at Lorenzo, who was comfortably leaning back on the sofa, watching him.

"Is that what you think?" Zeke managed to say between his clenched teeth.

"What I think is that you have the opportunity of a lifetime to come in and learn my business with the idea that you will take over when I retire, and that you would prefer to throw that opportunity away rather than face one rather petite individual and tell her the truth about yourself and the job you were hired to do."

"Why should I waste my time? The conclusion she jumped to, while not really right, isn't nearly as bad as the fact that I was actively gathering evidence to put her beloved uncle behind bars. I don't consider my unwillingness to beat a dead horse the same thing as sulking.''

''I see. It's lack of courage, then?''

''You know, Lorenzo, you're really beginning to irritate me,'' Zeke replied in a menacing understatement of his mood.

Lorenzo's grin was filled with humor. ''God, I hope so! It beats that whipped-dog look you wore when I first laid eyes on you. What's wrong with feeling some honest anger?''

Zeke couldn't believe what he was hearing. ''You mean you've been deliberately provoking me?''

''Something like that. More like pulling the tiger's tail in an effort to wake you up.''

''I'm awake, you son of a—'' Zeke threw up his hands and turned away.

''Angie's dealing with her own pain, you know.''

''Good for Angie,'' Zeke threw over his shoulder, looking at the lights of D.C.

''What happened between the two of you happened very quickly. That doesn't mean that it was any less real than a long-term courtship. I'm doubly impressed that you removed her from danger, even more so when I realize you thought some of the danger might be generated by me.''

''Oh, yeah. I just barged right in, in my shiny savior suit, and carried her off on my trusty steed.''

''You did what you thought best in a dangerous situation.''

''Good for me. Sainthood is the logical next step, wouldn't you say?''

Lorenzo laughed. "Somehow I don't think we have to worry about that just yet."

Without turning around, Zeke muttered, "I'm real glad you find me so damned amusing."

Silence settled in the room and for several minutes Lorenzo found no reason to interrupt it. Eventually he said, "You've never been in love before, have you?"

"Who says I'm in love?" Zeke said to the window.

"It's a scary place to be. I for one have always run whenever I found myself in danger of falling in love. I have a hunch you would have run, as well, if you hadn't been committed to doing your job. As I see it, you have a couple of options. You can use Angie's leaving you as an excuse to not have to deal with these new and very confusing feelings you're experiencing, or you can face up to them, deal with them, and do whatever you can to make your relationship with her work."

Zeke didn't say anything.

"So." Lorenzo stood. "I have done what I came to Washington to do. My good judgment in hiring you has been confirmed. My offer to keep you on the payroll has been extended. Whatever you decide from here is up to you."

Zeke didn't turn around.

"I can let myself out," Lorenzo added, heading toward the door. He opened the door and looked at the man standing with his back to the room. "Thanks for the coffee…and good luck, whatever you decide." Quietly he closed the door behind him.

Zeke continued to stare out the window, relieved to be alone once again.

Lorenzo might be a wizard in the business world, but he knew nothing about relationships. Oh, he was good at dishing out advice, but he'd never bothered to commit himself to a woman.

Zeke's mistake was in marrying Angie in the first place. Why had he been so quixotic? There had been no reason to—

Wait a minute. Hadn't he argued the point that she could be pregnant? Hadn't he wanted to protect her in case their lovemaking had—

How could he have forgotten? Would she tell him if she was pregnant? Maybe she wouldn't want to be around the father of her child, even if she were pregnant.

He could call and talk with her. He could ask her point-blank if she was going to have his child. Lorenzo couldn't be more wrong in his observations. He wasn't sulking and he certainly wasn't a coward.

He just couldn't remember a time in his life when he'd felt so much pain.

Eleven

He found his car in the long-term parking lot at the McAllen airport. It would probably cost him a fortune to pay the charges, but there was no reason to abandon the car he'd bought when he first returned to Texas several months ago.

Zeke had spent several miserable days in his apartment in an effort to forget or ignore Lorenzo's comments, but in the end he knew that Lorenzo was right.

He was a coward.

From the time he'd first met Angie, he'd had difficulty keeping his hands off her. Now that he knew exactly how she felt in his arms, he was afraid that not even with his renowned self-control could he handle being in her presence without grabbing her and insisting that she forgive him.

He hated to admit that he'd been hiding in his

apartment like some animal in his lair, licking his wounds. Whether he liked the idea or not, he knew that he had to face Angie and tell her exactly what he had done and why.

He'd rather face the KGB any day.

He crossed into Mexico a little after one o'clock and headed south. Despite the danger inherent in the many assignments he'd covered over the years, he had never experienced such a gut-level dread. He hated what he was feeling because he felt so helpless. His future was all wrapped up in the hands of the woman he'd been unable to resist from the time he'd first seen a photograph of her.

He resented her control over his life, but his resentment couldn't take away the love he felt for her.

By the time he reached Lorenzo's compound, he felt grim. A brief glance into the car mirror revealed that he looked just like he felt. The guard at the gate grinned and waved him inside. Once he parked the car in front of the house, his jaw was clenched and his muscles taut.

He stood by the car and stretched, deciding not to remove his aviator sunglasses. His eyes still looked like road maps with their multitude of red lines. Zeke took a deep breath and walked to the front door. It opened after his first rap.

"H'lo, Freddie," he said to the man who had opened the door. "Good to see you again."

"Zeke! Hey, welcome back. It's great to see you, man. We've missed you around here."

Zeke nodded. "I had some business to take care of. You know how it is."

"Sure, sure. Just glad you're back. Lorenzo's in his office."

"Oh. Well, uh—thanks."

He supposed he needed to tell Lorenzo that he was back. He started down the hallway and was even with the salon doorway when he saw movement inside. He glanced into the room and froze. Angie was arranging flowers at one of the tables, flowers she'd obviously just brought inside from the courtyard, since the French doors stood open.

He drank in the sight of her, his eyes darting quickly to trace her profile from her head to her feet. She looked thinner than he'd ever seen her...and pale. His breath caught in his throat. Was she ill?

Still hovering in the doorway, he said, "Hello, Angie," in a quiet voice.

She spun around with a muffled cry, knocking some of the flowers to the floor.

"Zeke!"

Now that she was facing him, he could see the dark smudges beneath her eyes. He walked into the room, stopping a few feet from her. "How have you been?"

She rested her hand on her chest. He could see a tremor in her fingers. "I didn't know you were coming," was all she said in reply.

"Didn't you? I figure we have some things to discuss."

Her eyes widened slightly, and he realized that his tone sounded menacing. He glanced around. "Could we sit down somewhere?" *Before you fall down,* he wanted to add. This close he could see that she was shaking.

She edged over to one of the nearby chairs and sat. He pulled another one near so that they sat facing each other. "Are you afraid of me?" he demanded.

Angie looked surprised. "Of course not. I've never been afraid of you."

"So why are you shaking in your boots like the bogeyman just walked into the room?"

She dropped her head, but he saw the slight tilt of her lips and the slight relaxing of her shoulders. "You surprised me, that's all. Why didn't you tell me you were coming?"

He thought about that for a moment, then gave a gusty sigh. "All right. I promised that I would tell you everything. That I wouldn't lie about anything, okay? The truth is I was afraid if I told you I was coming, you wouldn't be here when I arrived."

She looked taken back. "Oh."

He ran his hand through his hair, trying to remember what he had planned to tell her, trying to remember how he had planned to tell her.

His first words were, "Are you all right? You've lost weight."

She clasped her hands in front of her, resting them on her knees. "I'm all right. I just haven't been eating much."

"Do you know if—I mean, has it been long enough to know whether you are—uh—"

She rescued him by answering his unspoken concern. "I don't know, actually. I suppose there is that possibility, but everything in my life's been so chaotic...and I've been so upset that it could just be nerves."

"Aren't there tests you could take?"

"I suppose. I guess I wasn't ready to find out, one way or the other."

"Oh." Well, that certainly didn't tell him much. "Did Lorenzo tell you he came to see me?" he finally asked.

She glanced up from where she had been intently studying her clasped hands. "Yes."

Angie was certainly being a fount of information today. He reached over and took her hands and held them. They felt as though she'd had them submersed in a mountain stream. He stroked them, willing her not to withdraw them. She raised her head and met his gaze.

"I, uh, need to explain what was going on when we met. I finally got clearance to tell you."

"Clearance?"

"Yeah."

"From your government?"

"That's right."

She tugged her hands free and returned them to their nesting place in her lap.

"Dammit, Angie, will you at least give me a chance to explain?" He came to his feet in a lunge and strode over to the French doors. It had been a stupid idea to think he could get her to listen or to understand.

As though responding to his thoughts, she said, "I'm listening, Zeke."

He spun around and faced her. She looked more composed somehow, and her cheeks were tinted with becoming color. Why did she have to be so damned beautiful? He hated feeling so vulnerable, absolutely hated it!

Taking a deep breath, he slowly exhaled and forced himself to sit down once again. "All right. I can see where you felt that I'd lied to you, but I haven't. I really haven't. Everything I told you about myself and my life was true. The work in Europe was for the government. I did a great deal of covert stuff for years, but with all the changes over there I was re- called to Washington. Then I was loaned to another agency to work down here in an attempt to stop the flow of drug trafficking along the border."

"You thought Tio was involved in drugs."

He heard the certainty in her voice and asked, "Did he tell you that?"

She nodded.

"Then you understand why I was working for him?"

"He told me what he'd found out while he was in Washington. He's grateful that you and your govern- ment helped him to deal with the threats on his life and his property." She lifted her chin and faced him. "He reminded me that you saved my life with your flying skills. I already knew that."

Zeke watched her warily. "Then you already know everything I've come here to say. Does any of this make a difference to you? I mean, do you still want to end our marriage?"

She stared at him for an endless time, searching his face, seeing the pain there. "I never wanted our mar- riage to end, Zeke."

"But you walked out."

"I know. I don't think I can find the words to explain. I was hurt…and confused…and unprepared to face the reality of our situation." She shook her head, impatient with her inability to find the necessary words that would help her. Restless, she stood and walked over to the window. "I've been such a child, in so many ways," she said without looking at him. "I've led such a sheltered life that I've never been emotionally involved with anyone before. I was totally unprepared to handle my strong reaction to you when we met." She turned and faced him. "Everything happened so quickly between us. I was caught up in something so new and so wonderful that I never thought about where it was all heading." Angie walked back to where he sat and sank down into her chair once more. "I realize that you married me because you wanted to protect me. What I didn't realize at the time was that I needed protection from myself most of all."

"Don't you think you're being a little hard on yourself?"

"Am I?"

"Yeah, I think so. I mean, if we could all function as nonfeeling intellectuals, using only logic and reason, we'd probably grow pointed ears and hail Vulcan as our home planet." He reached over and took her hand. "What have you done that you feel is so bad?"

She forced herself to meet his gaze. "Walking out on you certainly wasn't the most mature move I've ever made."

"I don't know about mature. It certainly created a

great deal of pain and from what I can tell, the pain wasn't all on my side.''

"That's my point. I was so wrapped up in my own feelings that I didn't give a thought to how you'd react when you came home and found me gone.''

Zeke looked away. "Something tells me Lorenzo had a few tales to relate about me when he got home."

"He said I hurt you badly."

Zeke shrugged without answering.

"You are the very last person I would want to hurt, Zeke. I knew I wouldn't be able to talk, even if I attempted to call you. I knew that as soon as I heard your voice I would break down. After that I tried to write and tell you what was in my heart, but it was hopeless."

"I'm here now, Princess. Can you tell me what you want to do about us?"

"When do you have to go back?"

"I don't. I've resigned the Washington job. Lorenzo offered me a place in his organization while he was there. I'm seriously considering it."

"But you haven't made a final decision."

He shook his head. "No. I couldn't continue to live here and see you on a daily basis if I didn't know I would go to sleep every night with you in my arms."

"You're very forgiving."

"No. Just realistic. I agree that you and I got too involved too quickly. I willingly accept the blame for that because I'm old enough…and experienced enough…to know better. Once we'd been together, I couldn't keep my hands off you. The best damage control, under those particular circumstances, was to marry you.'' He gave her an endearingly lopsided smile. ''Nothing's really changed, you know. I'm having trouble sitting here right now when all I want to do is to haul you upstairs and love the daylights out of you.''

''As though nothing's wrong between us?''

''Well, the way I figure it is, if we love each other enough, we've got the rest of our lives together to work out all the details. I'm sure this won't be the only time we get crossways with each other. All I'm asking is that you don't walk away from the problem. Is that too much to ask?''

Angie slid to her knees beside his chair. ''Oh, Zeke, I love you so much!'' She put her arms around him. With little effort he pulled her onto his lap. They sat there holding each other, each regretting the pain inflicted on the other, each silently vowing to make up for their past actions.

''Well, it looks as though you two have made up,'' Lorenzo said, striding into the room. ''I just got word that you arrived, Daniels. Are you ready to go to work, or are you just visiting?''

Before Zeke could answer, Angie said, ''He's here to stay, Tio. But don't plan to put him to work immediately.'' She smiled into Zeke's eyes. ''I have some plans of my own for the next few days that will occupy most of his time.''

Zeke glanced up at Lorenzo's startled expression, then down to his wife, whose saucy response was accompanied by a beautiful blush.

''Looks like I've found myself a new boss,'' Zeke

said with a grin, hugging her even tighter. "I'll do my best to make you both happy, no matter how long it takes!"

Lorenzo laughed, shook his head and walked out of the room, saying, "You've definitely got your job cut out for you."

Zeke glanced down at Angie and grinned. "Maybe so, but I sure do like all of the fringe benefits."

He picked her up and started for the stairs.

Epilogue

Zeke picked up the phone on the first ring and heard a voice from his past…from another lifetime…greet him.

"Frank! You ol' son of a gun. How've you been?"

"Working to keep myself alive. I hadn't talked with you in some time. Thought I'd give you a call to see if you were bored with the business world, yet."

Zeke laughed. "Believe me, my old life was tame compared to what goes on at some of these board meetings. I've wondered at times if I was going to get out in one piece."

"And you love it, right?"

"Yeah, I guess I've always been a sucker for a challenge."

"How's Angela?"

"She's doing very well these days, considering."

"Considering what?"

"Well, she's expecting...again."

"My God, Zeke, it's a wonder you have *time* for business. What do the girls and Ty think about the new addition?"

"We haven't told them, yet. We still have a few months to break the news."

"But four kids in five years, Zeke!"

"I know, Frank. I know. I, uh, well, we didn't exactly plan it this way, we just seem to—what I mean is, we, uh—"

"Hey, man, you don't have to explain to me. I get the picture." His amusement was obvious, which wasn't surprising. Zeke still had trouble seeing himself as a family man, but he was certainly enjoying every aspect of family life.

Frank's voice sobered when he continued. "I wanted to pass on an official acknowledgment and appreciation for what you've been doing. You've passed on some very useful information over the years that's been very helpful to us. We just picked off a well-established ring down there this week."

"I read about the bust in the paper. I'm pleased I could help you."

"You know, Zeke, a couple of times you've made the local agents look like amateurs. You've managed to obtain information they've been after for years."

"We have developed a helluva network here, Frank. We sort through all kinds of information on a daily basis. It helps us stay in business. If some of it can help you, it doesn't cost me anything to pass it on.''

"I was told to give you an official word of thanks and offer whatever payment you needed.''

"I don't need or want payment. I've told you that more than once.''

"I know. Just doing what I'm told.''

"Good enough, Frank. Glad you called.''

"If you ever get up this way, I'd enjoy visiting with you.''

"I'm surprised you're still around,'' Zeke replied, grinning. "I figured the whole complex would have been sold by now.''

"Don't I wish! I wouldn't mind retiring, myself. Well, hang in there. Give my regards to Angie.''

"I'll do that, Frank.''

Zeke hung up the phone and turned his chair so that he was looking out the large picture window into the courtyard. He spent a lot of his office time enjoying the garden and watching his family, who spent many of their afternoons there.

After the scare with Lorenzo's heart, he'd turned everything over to Zeke. He'd insisted that all he wanted to do was to stay home and be entertained by the children.

Watching him now, Zeke could well believe him. Linda and Connie sat in their tiny chairs at his feet while he read to them. Tyler sat on his lap, nodding off to sleep. Angie was nearby, mending one of the children's shirts, listening and smiling at Lorenzo's dramatic interpretation of a well-known children's classic.

Zeke waited until Angie glanced up. He waved, catching her eye, and motioned for her to come inside. After placing the mending next to her chair, she got up and headed toward the door of the salon. By the time she reached the hallway, he was waiting for her.

"What is it? Is something wrong?"

He shook his head and, taking her by the hand, led her upstairs.

"Zeke? Where are we going?"

"I thought we needed to rest. Lorenzo has the children enthralled. They'll be just fine."

"Oh, but I—"

"Oh, but you have to make sure I don't have nightmares. I sleep much better with my arms around you."

"You're so silly." She shook her head in mock despair.

As soon as they reached their room, he insisted she get comfortable. His idea of her comfort was to carefully take off every piece of her clothing, despite her attempt to slap his hands away.

"I like to look at you, okay? I love to see the baby. Relax, will you? I'm not going to molest you."

"That will be a first."

"You've got a smart mouth, woman. Anyone ever tell you that?"

She smiled, and allowed him to lead her to the bed. She stretched out on the bed and he curled around her. "I learned everything I know from you," she admitted, sighing as he began to rub her back in the exact place it ached.

"You've taught me more."

"Oh, sure I have."

"You have. It scares me to think that we might not have ended up together."

"I'm just glad you were sent down here to work for Tio. Otherwise we would never have met."

"And that would have been the greatest tragedy of all," he murmured, holding her close to him and stroking the curve of her body that sheltered another new life.

Frank's call had reminded him of his old way of life. He had heard the envy in Frank's voice. He didn't blame him. He wouldn't give up what he had now for any other lifestyle.

Life was good. Love was a gift he'd never thought to have. It had changed him, forced him to grow and to accept his vulnerability.

The rewards had been worth it. Tucking Angie closer against him, he fell asleep with a smile on his face.

*　*　*　*　*

Uncover the truth behind

CODE NAME: DANGER

in **Merline Lovelace's** thrilling duo

DANGEROUS TO HOLD

When tricky situations need a cool head, quick wits and a touch of ruthlessness, Adam Ridgeway, director of the top secret OMEGA agency, sends in his team. Lately, though, his agents have had romantic troubles of their own....

NIGHT OF THE JAGUAR
&
THE COWBOY AND THE COSSACK

And don't miss
HOT AS ICE (IM #1129, 2/02)
which features the newest OMEGA adventure!

DANGEROUS TO HOLD is available this February
at your local retail outlet!

Look for ***DANGEROUS TO KNOW,*** the second set of
stories in this collection, in July 2002.

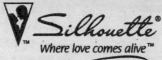

Where love comes alive™

DYNASTIES:
THE
CONNELLYS

A brand-new Desire® miniseries about the Connellys of Chicago, a wealthy, powerful American family tied by blood to the royal family of the island kingdom of Altaria

Filled with scandal, mystery and romance, *Dynasties: The Connellys* will keep you enthralled in 12 wonderful new stories by your favorite authors, including Leanne Banks, Kathie DeNosky, Caroline Cross, Maureen Child, Kate Little, Metsy Hingle, Kathryn Jensen, Kristi Gold, Cindy Gerard, Katherine Garbera, Eileen Wilks and Sheri WhiteFeather.

Don't miss
this exciting program,
beginning in January 2002 with:

TALL, DARK & ROYAL
by Leanne Banks
(SD #1412)

*Available at your
favorite retail outlet.*

Where love comes alive™

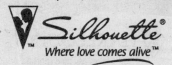